I0604914

The Desolation of Mitra

Michael Taylor

The Desolation of Mirra

Michael Taylor

For my wonderful children. Every single day you make me proud.

Prologue

Millennia ago, in a far-off corner of our universe, an argument rages...

"Our sun is dying!" The speaker jumps to his feet and slams a fist on the table so hard a crack appears in its burnished, centuries-old stone surface. "Our sun dies yet you wring your hands and huddle together in your *little* council, pretending to seek solutions!" Anarkus is panting and his sharp, cruel eyes sweep round the table, dripping with contempt. A few of those gathered meet his gaze; most do not.

"And you!" Anarkus points a long finger toward the wizard at the head of the table. "You, Laiis, are worst of all. Call yourself a leader? For centuries we've searched the furthest reaches of the universe for a new home, without result. Yet you just sit and hope for a miracle. You're pathetic!"

"Enough of your whining." Laiis's voice deliberately reveals only a tired boredom and Anarkus flushes with anger. "How many times will we have this debate? We must protect all races, not just our own!"

It is the difficulty they face, for many races live within their galaxy, some friendly, others not. But because each occupy their own planet, all exist in relative peace. Finding a single planet, close enough to a star where they, the wizards and witches, can live and prosper would have been a simple enough task. But to find a galaxy with enough planets to house all races has proved a problem for thousands of years, since the search began.

"Let them all die, I say!" Anarkus sneers. "What purpose do they serve anyway?"

Some of those who have so far not spoken look up sharply, but most look quickly away again and none dare offer a challenge. Anarkus has a power to intimidate and most avoid him where possible; it is a power he enjoys.

"Ah, none dare speak." He smiles contemptuously. "Well, let me ask you this. Why do you listen to our *exalted* leader? If I were in his place, we would have found our new haven long ago and be reaping the benefits!"

"Do you offer a challenge, Anarkus?" Laiis smiles inwardly, knowing he does not. Challenging a council leader is sedition, punishable by death, and the veiled threat is met with silence as he rises to his feet.

High in their mountain fortress, the council room has only three walls, mostly lined with shelves containing the ancient histories of the two races. The fourth side is open to the sky with a large, semi-circular balcony jutting out from the mountainside, the long drop to the sea below protected only by a low stone balustrade.

It is to this that Laiis now walks, slowly, lost in thought. That Anarkus seeks ultimate power has long been evident, at least to him and Portia.

But most of the other younger and more inexperienced members don't realize he'll stop at nothing to achieve his aims, he muses. Feeling the eyes of the eleven other members of the witch and wizard council boring into his back, he seeks an excuse for his wandering that won't suggest indecision. For Laiis is tired. His nine-thousand-year term as leader is almost done; a mere three centuries remain.

If only our sun could last a little longer so I don't have to face this final challenge. He thrusts the thought aside, recognizing it as weakness.

All are welcome at any time to enter this room and observe the universe through the star-scope. Laiis puts an eye to it and instantly his vision is filled with a vast, colorful vista almost painful in its brightness. Far-off galaxies, invisible to the naked eye, leap into life, a swirling riot of reds, oranges and yellows, blues, purples and greens. Meteors streak across the blackness, millions of kilometers distant, and an asteroid suddenly fills his vision, making him jump back, startled and certain it will collide. It is, of course, far away and he feels foolish, hoping no one has noticed.

Focusing the scope once more, he turns to where their sun lies, so faint now in its death throes that he can do so without fear of blindness.

"There is a darkness within you, Anarkus,"—he turns from the scope—"which bodes ill for your continued membership of this council." But it's an idle threat and Laiis sighs. To remove someone with such an impeccable pedigree would be nigh impossible.

It might be possible if only some of them displayed a little backbone, he ruminates, his old frustration welling up.

"Let me remind you of our duty and the oaths we have sworn. We wizards and witches are the pre-eminent races in this universe, sworn to protect all others whether they be good or evil. Yes, Anarkus!" Laiis sees the wizard bursting to interrupt. "Even the demons!"

"Laiis," a voice speaks for the first time, shakily and sounding surprised at its own temerity. "How long do we have before our sun fades at last?"

He smiles at the young witch, acknowledging the courage it has taken to ask the question. Rosalind is the newest addition to the council, admitted upon her mother's death only a few months past.

"Ah, Rosalind, welcome to our council and my thanks for speaking up." The ironic tone is not lost on those who have so far remained silent. "You wisely go to the heart of the matter."

Rosalind blushes, embarrassed to have all eyes turned on her, particularly Anarkus who fixes her with a speculative gaze. He might intimidate some, but he *terrifies* her.

"Who can say? It is difficult to judge accurately. For our own planet, a few centuries perhaps? But some of the outlying planets have already gone cold." Laiis hesitates at the news he must now impart. "Yesterday I had word that the last of the Dweeble race perished." He pauses to allow expressions of regret to be heard. There are tears in the eyes of some, including Rosalind. Only Anarkus is unmoved. No, not entirely; Laiis is certain he sees a glimmer of satisfaction in his expression. "As for others, the goblins and the demons for example, most are closer to the sun and can survive a while yet. Another millennia perhaps, no more."

"And we should abandon them! Particularly the demons!" Anarkus interrupts. "They have long been a thorn in our side and their numbers multiply. We have the chance to wipe them out, leave their threat behind. We court disaster if we do not!"

"Yes," Laiis agrees, looking around his council, "Anarkus is correct. We *do* court disaster if we take them with us."

If Anarkus is surprised at the acknowledgment, he doesn't show it. But a smile of satisfaction touches his lips.

"But just as we show friendship to those who do *not* threaten us, so we must show mercy to those who do," Laiis continues. "I would remind you all we are not murderers. We do not use our power for evil; it is a path that leads only to darkness." He draws himself to his full height, reminding those gathered of his absolute authority. "Whatever the consequences for the future, the demons and all other races come with us. And if we cannot find a home for us all, then we will perish together. On this there will be no vote. My word is law."

Laiis raises an eyebrow at Anarkus, inviting him to challenge. But Anarkus is not stupid and merely smiles to mask the hatred he feels. "So be it." He nods. "As you say, your word is law, but let me say this. It will be a joyous day indeed when your term ends, as it will soon, and we have a new leader!"

"Which will be me." The witch who now stands has a calm, regal bearing. She exudes authority without consciously trying and even Anarkus hesitates to cause offense. Portia threatens him in a way that Laiis somehow does not, for she has power greater than most of the others in the council combined. "I do wonder, Anarkus, where this anger inside you comes from. Even as a child you were the same. I'm just thankful your father didn't live long enough to see the man you have become."

There are a few sniggers, quickly smothered as Anarkus's gaze rakes them once more.

As for Portia, she doesn't attempt to hide her own smile. "If you had bothered to attend the last few meetings, you would know—"

"What is the point!" Anarkus interrupts. "Why should I *bother* when all you all do is rehash the same old arguments time and again?"

"*If,*" Portia smoothly takes control once more, "you had been here, you would know there has been a breakthrough. Our searchers may finally have found the answer to our plight." She nods to Rosalind, who has been working closely with the scientists.

"Thank you." The young witch looks around at the expectant faces. "There is a small galaxy," she begins. "A spiral galaxy…"

"Where?" The question is barked harshly, as if doubting her words.

Rosalind is startled. "It is far away, Anarkus."

"Where? How far!" His tone is bullying.

"Oh, stop it, Anarkus," snaps Portia. "Leave the girl alone and keep silent! Continue." She smiles kindly at Rosalind.

"This spiral galaxy," Rosalind resumes. "On one of its arms lies a small solar system of fifteen, perhaps sixteen, planets. That is more than adequate for our needs. It has its own star; a strong one, barely halfway through its life." There are nods of approval at this.

"Adequate?" It is another council member, silent so far, who speaks. "These planets can hold life?"

"Yes," Rosalind confirms. "Not all of them; some are gas planets. But five or six at least."

There are more murmurs and some of those gathered break into smiles.

"There is something more." The murmurs stop and anxiety

permeates the room. "One of the planets actually has lifeforms..."

She pauses and Laiis interjects. "Well, that is no problem. You say there are enough planets—"

"Some of the lifeforms are the same as we are!" Rosalind's anxiety causes her to interrupt the leader and she cringes inwardly. "But most do not have our power; a few only."

There is a stunned silence, eventually broken by Anarkus. "That's impossible! She's lying. This whole thing is nonsense!"

"Anarkus, be quiet!" Portia is furious. "If you interrupt again you will be removed!"

Rosalind, despite her fear of him, regards Anarkus defiantly. "It's true. They call themselves humans and I am assured by the scientist that they are just like us, even down to their DNA. Excepting the witch or wizard gene, obviously."

Humans. The word is unfamiliar to them but saying it aloud lends credibility to her words.

"There is one other thing." She hesitates, for this is news she has dreaded telling.

Laiis sighs. *What now?* He wonders.

"Here, our planets are close, meaning we can monitor the other races easily and keep them under control."

"Yes?" says Portia, sensing trouble.

"Well, the planets in this new solar system are not. They are many millions of kilometers apart."

"Meaning it would be difficult to maintain control. Particularly of the demons." Laiis sees the problem at once.

"Yes. The scientists believe it will be impossible."

"I told you it was too good to be true! Look at you all, salivating at your *salvation!*" Anarkus laughs contemptuously. He can control himself no longer and his anger erupts. "This is a fool's errand. She"—he points at Rosalind—"is a liar!"

"Enough! You have been warned!" Portia's hand twitches instinctively toward the wand at her belt. She opens her mouth to call for the guards. Then, without conscious thought, Anarkus's wand is in his hand, leveled at her. An instant later eleven other wands are pointing at him.

"Put it down," Portia warns, but he ignores her. "Anarkus, put it *down!*"

"What? And have you blast me where I stand?" he mocks, backing away toward the balustrade. "We both know I won't leave this room alive if I do."

"Anarkus." She speaks as if scolding an errant child. "It is no secret I do not like you." Her look is pure ice. "But I do not seek your death. *That* choice is yours."

There is a long, unbearably tense pause and the silence can be tasted. Then Anarkus makes up his mind. His wand sends a barrage of fire sweeping across the room. Portia evades it easily but three of the council are slower. In an instant, two younger wizards and a witch who has served faithfully for a thousand years lie dead.

And then it is chaos as the room becomes a cauldron of noise and light and the acrid smell of wand fire. Bolts of searing hot light are exchanged and within seconds the ancient, tinder-dry paper of their histories is ablaze and thick, black smoke fills the room.

Anarkus jumps onto the balustrade and performs an intricate but graceful dance, twisting and turning to avoid or block the bolts of ardent fire flung at him by the entire council, returning fire when he can.

Peace has reigned on the planet for so long that most of the council are inexperienced at fighting. But Anarkus ignores them, concentrating most of his fire on Laiis and Portia; partly to stay alive and partly because it is their deaths he seeks above all others.

Faintly, banging on the door can be heard and Portia recognizes it as the guards trying to gain entry. She remembers that Anarkus had been the last to enter the room. *He put a spell on the door!* she realizes. *He planned this!* She considers lifting the spell but does not, knowing it would mean death for the guards.

The smoke is now so thick it's impossible to see, and suddenly Laiis ceases firing. He creates a shield that encompasses the entire room, and try as he might, Anarkus cannot penetrate it. Gradually, the fighting stops.

"Lay down your wand," orders Laiis.

Anarkus laughs, a deep belly laugh containing not a whit of humor. "No."

"We will *all* lay down our wands." Portia shakes her head vigorously but Laiis ignores her.

"And then?"

"And then we will talk. All of you, put them down."

Slowly they obey. Laiis nullifies the shield and puts down his own wand, nodding at Anarkus, who does likewise. But only Portia has noticed that in the confusion Rosalind has hidden behind one of the pillars at the edge of the room. And that she still holds her wand.

"So, Laiis," he says mockingly, "what now?"

"Now, we talk." He steps forward, and as he does so, Anarkus stoops quickly and takes back his wand, sending a lightning bolt that tears Laiis's chest apart in an explosion of blood and tissue.

Her utter shock slows Portia's reflexes and before she can react, Anarkus has his wand leveled at her head.

"Don't," he advises calmly.

"You cannot escape. Even if you get past us, which you *won't*, there are a dozen guards outside."

"Yes, I know," he says mockingly. "Quite the predicament." But despite his bravado, Anarkus is desperate. He knows she speaks the truth and he glances behind him into the void, searching for a way out. His spirits soar as he sees a small outcrop of rock a few meters below.

But as he is distracted, Rosalind steps from the shadows and sends a bolt of fire raging toward him, fuelled with her anger at Laiis's murder. Only Anarkus's catlike reflexes save him. He sees it at the last second and turns his head. The bolt glances across his forehead, leaving a long, ugly burn.

Stunned, he stares momentarily at the witch. "I will remember you!" he snarls, then sick and dizzy, he almost collapses, but flings himself backwards, reaching desperately for the outcrop, gripping it with the tips of his fingers and preventing his fall. But he has been deceived; the rock is not solid, merely slate which crumbles beneath his hands and suddenly he is holding air.

Portia runs to the balustrade in time to see Anarkus, already a tiny speck in the distance, plunging toward the ocean far below. As the others reach her side, they see him spread-eagled on the rocks, limbs bent at unnatural angles as the sea washes gently over and envelops him in its embrace.

*　　　　*　　　　*　　　　*

For the next twenty years, scientists wrestle with the problem of the far-distant planets until, one day, they approach the council with their solution.

"Dimensions."

"Pardon?"

The scientists flush, embarrassed and nervous. This leader is less approachable than the last. Less likely to accept failure. Or excuses.

"Forgive us," they falter, and Portia sighs. *I've tried to be less impatient, truly I have.*

"Please," she says reassuringly. "Explain what you mean."

And so they reveal how it should be possible to take some of the inhabitable planets described by Rosalind and hide them as dimensions, in a different time and place, in the human world. In each dimension would be housed the different races; goblins, demons etc, as well as the witches and wizards themselves.

"The idea has merit," Portia concedes at last. "But for our two races to live apart? We are a council of witches *and* wizards."

"But the human world is a green and pleasant one, with much abundance," counter the scientists. "Much nicer than this one. It is our thought that only the council will live on one of the outlying planets, better to keep an eye on everything."

"It even has its own satellite which might be suitable," ventures another. "It's *very* close to the mortal world."

"Mortal?" Portia enquires. "I thought they were called humans?"

"They are," he says, "but they are not long-lived as are we. Their lives are very short. So we call them mortals."

"I see," replies Portia, impatient at what seems to her an irrelevance.

"The plan is a sound one. Are we all agreed?"

"To concoct a spell of this magnitude will take decades," objects one of the council.

"Then," observes one of the scientists, braver than the rest, "you'd better get started."

*   *   *   *

As word spreads, so the disagreements on whether other races, particularly the demons, should be allowed to travel too, spring to the surface once more. The demons themselves, seeking to make the most of the disorder and led by Kanzser, their king, wage a war which lasts fifty years.

When they are suppressed at last, there are a thousand spells to be worked out and cast, some simple but others mind-bogglingly intricate. Add to that the tens of thousands of other details necessitated by a project of this size and it is a hundred years, from the first discovery of the spiral galaxy before preparations are complete.

The wizard race, uncomfortable at leaving the council unprotected, elect to remain with them. The witches choose to inhabit their own dimension on the mortal world.

Then one day they are ready. Almost. There is one last detail which has long worried Portia. She will not allow the plan to proceed until it is solved and she calls the scientists for a final time.

She comes straight to the point. "By using the human planet in this way—"

"Mortal," she is corrected. "They are mortals."

"*Mortal* then." She grinds her teeth, striving for patience. "By using their planet in this way, we make them vulnerable. Should any, the demons for example, escape their dimension…"

"Impossible," they object. "That will not—"

"Nevertheless." Her tone allows no argument. "You will take one last planet and form another, final dimension; a barrier between the dimensions already created and the *mortal* world. A kind of… sanctuary." She smiles, pleased at the name. "Yes, I like that. It will be called the Sanctuary. Its purpose will be to protect the human race,"—she glares at the scientists—"from *any* evil which threatens it."

There are mutterings of approval and one of the council, a wizard, speaks up. "It will need a leader."

"Yes," agrees Portia, amused. She has long known Thaddeus aches to be a part of the new adventure. "Are you volunteering?"

"It will be my honor." He grins, happy to get his wish.

"You will need allies," she advises. "You may choose who you will take with you. Not from this council, of course. It will be hard enough to replace you."

"And my wife and son?"

"Naturally, Thaddeus, that goes without saying. I believe that your son is by the door, trying to push past my guards and intrude on this council."

"It is." Thaddeus tries and fails to look contrite. "May I invite him in?"

The child comes hurtling into the room, only just in time remembering that he should perhaps show some decorum in this hallowed place. He is seven years old and already tall for his age.

"What is your name, child?" Portia asks gravely, although her eyes sparkle with amusement.

"Cornelius." The boy is overawed but not intimidated to meet the witch and wizard council leader. "My name is Cornelius and I will be a great wizard one day. Just like my father."

Portia laughs; she already likes this precocious child. "I'm sure you will," she agrees, little knowing how prophetic the boy's words will be.

And with that, the exodus to new worlds and to a new life begins.

PART ONE

Chapter 1

As the realm of the Demon King crumbled into dust, the Dark Wizard, Logan, stepped through the doorway from the cavern that had almost become his tomb and into the land of the Necromancer. He looked with distaste at the sparse, arid landscape, which stretched far in every direction. This would not be the last time he'd wish himself back in his own world, his own time. Back in London, his home.

When he'd left the Demon King dying before him, Logan had been tempted to leave that foul place the same way he'd entered, through the cave and past the village of his and Morgan's birth. But he'd had no choice but to take this path, for as far as he knew it was the only way he could reach the land of the goblins.

His earlier jubilation quickly turned to anger and resentment as he set out, for he knew a long journey lay ahead. But cross it he must. With the anger, his humiliation rose as he thought of that damned dog and the so-called wizard who called himself by that ridiculous name; Landlord, or something.

I should have killed him when I had the chance!

He didn't want to dwell on how the Landlord had been *lucky* enough to escape and, in his arrogance, Logan dismissed him scornfully and spent a few moments dreaming about his day of reckoning. Then, sighing heavily, he set off down the hill.

*   *   *   *

After the defeat of the Demon King's army, the Landlord had not stayed around to celebrate. He'd not been involved in the victory after all, having carelessly allowed himself to be captured by the Dark Wizard. The Landlord couldn't have explained why this had happened, except that the reasons were complex and inextricably linked to his past. And he couldn't quite fathom why, all at once, he felt so guilty, so uncertain about his purpose; why he let himself remain alive on this earth.

As soon as he could, he'd slipped away from the Sanctuary and returned to his beloved Wales. But he knew the time had come to face those things that troubled him deeply, but which had remained hidden for centuries in his unwillingness to delve so deeply into his soul. So, he'd journeyed deep into the mountains and there he'd thought back over his long life. For nearly six months he and his dog, Oscar, encountered not another living soul until at last, he felt cleansed and ready to return home.

Now he stood on the narrow chalk road that traversed the rim of the valley and gazed with indecision at the thatched roofs of the village below. The Landlord badly wanted to go down and see his friends, for he'd had no news for a long time. He knew that Ffranc would have learned of his disappearance and seen the destruction wrought on his home. The old man would be worried, as would his granddaughter, Catrin.

His mouth tightened when he thought of the beautiful, gentle child and the harm that had been done to her by Logan; yet another crime for which he was accountable.

More than a year had passed since Logan had tried and failed to gain entry to the Demon King's lair, and in his anger, he had taken his failure out on the village's inhabitants.

The Landlord looked across to the mountain that rose steeply on the other side of the valley and his eyes were drawn, unwillingly, to the small cave two-thirds of the way up. He had never stepped inside but he, like everyone else hereabouts, knew what went on in that cursed place.

Oh yes! The Landlord knew all about demons and was thankful that from his position he couldn't see further round the mountain to the copse of trees, where the blood moon had been created so long ago.

He shook his head to banish unwelcome memories and his mind returned to the girl. Catrin had been brave enough – *brave but foolish,* he mused sorrowfully – to stand up to Logan, and in return he had robbed her of the power of speech. Since that day, she had not spoken, and because of the vagaries of wizardry, one of its many idiosyncrasies being that it forbade one wizard altering the spell of another, except to save a life, the Landlord had been prevented from lifting the spell.

Suddenly dejected, he sighed and turned away. He whistled to Oscar and trudged along the road toward home.

Chapter 2

Most lands, even the driest and most deserted, have some redeeming features. A rock formation that soars majestically to the sky perhaps, or a delicate flower thriving against all odds. Such is the wonder of nature that even the most forbidding of landscapes is a thing of wondrous beauty. But this land held neither beauty nor living thing; it was entirely empty. This was the land of the Necromancer, poisoned by the evil with which the creature had corrupted all.

Nobody ever passed through that land, or that of the witches beyond, which Logan must also cross. It was for this reason the goblins had chosen to make their own home beyond even those, for they were a secretive race who didn't tolerate outsiders. Again, Logan cursed the Landlord, whose actions had forced him to enter this desolate landscape, even though he knew that, with the diminishing of the Necromancer so long ago, he was in no real peril.

These worlds, or dimensions, hidden eons past by the old wizards and witches, were not large, for they had taken such immense power as to test even them. To the north, whence he had come, was the now extinct realm of the demons, while to the south lay the land of the witches, and after that, the goblins. To the west lay the Chasm of Nothingness, a dark, dead place untouched by the ancient councils, where neither light nor living thing existed, and beyond it, the golden contrast of Aeryn's world.

Lastly, to the east, close by and always in sight, an impossibly high and sheer cliff face that reached seemingly never-ending into the distance. This towering wall of rock perhaps held the deepest purpose of all, for it held a secret doorway of which Logan was, as yet, ignorant.

It would take many days to reach his goal, and at first he strode rapidly, eager to reach the other side, and his long legs ate up the kilometers. But as noon approached and the hot, merciless sun beat relentlessly down, tiredness began to creep in and his pace slowed to a walk. It was then he became aware of the first pangs of hunger and he cursed himself for not having had the foresight to bring food. He'd been so excited to wreak his vengeance on the demons that he'd given no thought to what would happen after, beyond his need to find a wand.

As the afternoon wore on, he pushed the need for food aside and continued grimly, almost shuffling now until at last, as darkness came, he collapsed to the ground and slept the sleep of the dead.

The next morning, despite his exhaustion, he was awake early as the rock-hard earth penetrated his consciousness. Struggling to his feet, he groaned at the screaming protest of every muscle. Shivering in the cool morning air, he concentrated on putting one foot forward, then another, until gradually his limbs eased and he made good time, although with none of the eager swiftness of the day before. And so it went on, every day harder than the previous, until he traveled only a few kilometers each day.

For the first time, he doubted he would reach his goal and with it came despair and the first thoughts of giving up. Then Logan thought of his brother, safe inside his sanctuary. Morgan, the favored one. *How I hate him!*

And it was this hatred that galvanized him to find new strength and determination and, for the first time in days, there was a spring in his step and he knew with certainty that he would succeed.

*   *   *   *

The prospect of spending the night in the cold ruins of the inn, or railway station depending on which century you were in, held no attraction for the Landlord and it was with a heavy heart and slow tread that he began the short trek home. Tomorrow he must begin its repair, and reform the link between this world and the Sanctuary.

As he walked, he looked down at the houses, each with the light from their fires streaming through the windows and landing, like golden pools onto the ground outside. He sighed longingly, and at that moment he thought he'd never seen anything quite so welcoming. He looked at Oscar, who trotted silently beside him, tail tucked firmly between his legs.

"What d'ya think, boy?" The Landlord stopped suddenly. "Think the repairs can wait for a while?"

The little dog's ears pricked up and he barked hopefully, his body quivering and his tail wagging furiously.

The Landlord kept him in suspense for a few seconds more, then grinned. "Go on then, let's go!"

Oscar was already running full speed down the slope and the Landlord felt his spirits lift for the first time that day as he followed. It was Catrin the dog found first, and he flung himself into her arms and began licking her face.

"Oscar!" she cried in delight, laughing and trying to avoid his tongue. "What are you doing here? Where's the Landlord?" But just then she saw him, long legs striding up the main street of the village, and she let Oscar down and ran to meet him. "Landlord, where've you been? We haven't seen you in ages!"

He didn't reply but simply stared at her in amazement. *What? How? She can speak again,* he thought stupidly, before his brain caught up. *Of course! The spell ended when I broke Logan's wand!* He caught her in his arms and swung her around, laughing and shouting gleefully. "You can speak! You can speak!"

"Put me down!" she shrieked, laughing. "I'm not twelve anymore!"

He stopped spinning and let her go, feeling slightly dizzy. "But it's marvelous news! And wait, I have my own news; where's your grandfather?" Soon he was seated in the main square of the village, a foaming pot of beer in each hand. "My friends," he began, pausing to take a long, welcome drink, "I bring good tidings. The demon army has been defeated."

There was silence and the Landlord was momentarily disappointed. But then he laughed ruefully. *Of course, they know already; it is many months since the battle.*

But then someone cried out, "We should celebrate!" and after a short pause, "Again!" The Landlord laughed; this was Wales and these people needed no encouragement to start a party. Cheers rang out into the night sky and people hugged the person next to them, some of the more adventurous sneaking a kiss from those they'd been admiring. Someone fetched more beer while another took up a fiddle and began playing. Soon, music filled the air and the dancing commenced in earnest.

Children's bedtimes were forgotten and they danced and sang along with the rest, and even though the very young ones didn't quite understand the reason for the celebration, they didn't care. And as the night wore on, petty feuds were forgotten, some mended. Young lovers snuck away to be alone and some of the older, more staid members of the village let their inhibitions slip a little, at least for one night.

Ffranc watched, contented as the villagers, his friends, became louder and louder as the beer and wine flowed. *They deserve it*, he thought, *they've had it hard the last few years.* His eyes moved to where Catrin danced with Grufydd, her head thrown back, laughing, eyes shining. Ffranc was glad she'd finally accepted the boy; they'd been sweethearts from childhood, but when the Dark Wizard had robbed her of speech, she'd felt worthless and had pushed the boy away. Ffranc's lips tightened at the memory and anger threatened to sour his mood.

"Relax, my friend," the Landlord said, accurately interpreting the cause of his distress. "Logan can hurt her no more."

Ffranc nodded. "I know, but it could all have been very different."

"Well, thanks to the Sanctuary, it is not. And to Aeryn too," he added.

Ffranc nodded again but did not answer. There was deep disquiet within the Landlord's eyes and he wondered at its cause. Ffranc studied him surreptitiously for a while, trying to work it out until, all at once, he had it. "He escaped, didn't he? The Demon King, he's not dead."

The Landlord had long ago ceased to feel surprise at the shrewdness of his friend. Ffranc was far from stupid, indeed he possessed a little wizard blood himself, although it had become watered down across many generations.

"He lives," he admitted, knowing denial was futile, "but his army is gone."

"But he will come again, not yet perhaps, but one day, when he has rebuilt his army."

The Landlord stared silently into the flames for a long time until finally he looked up and grinned. "No point in inviting trouble, Ffranc, you should know that. We can only wait and see what fate decrees."

The party continued late into the night, but the Landlord declined Ffranc's invitation to stay until dawn. He arrived back at the old railway station shortly after midnight and, despite his despair at the ruin of his home, slept more soundly than he had in a long time. He awoke feeling refreshed and ready to face the challenge ahead, but even he balked a little when he realized the magnitude of the task before him in the cold light of the morning.

It was a scene of chaos; furniture was smashed into firewood, broken bottles crunched underfoot, and cups and plates lay broken and strewn throughout. Doors hung from their hinges, chandeliers hung crookedly, dancing in the breeze like jigging marionettes, flickering as their exposed wires sparked dangerously. Above, several large holes in the roof let in the rain and scores of pigeons who lined the rafters, sheltering from the biting Welsh winds. Their guano coated the floor, making it slippery and treacherous and adding to the general miasma of decay.

Have to get the builders in for that, he thought distractedly, as a large glob of pigeon poo narrowly missed his shoulder.

The Landlord stood for a long time staring, unwilling or unable to comprehend what he witnessed. Unbidden, tears filled his eyes, although whether they were tears of sadness or anger, he could not have said. Mastering himself, he sighed heavily as he assembled mops, brushes and other accoutrements, and filled a bucket with hot water.

"Well, I suppose I may as well get started," he complained to Oscar without enthusiasm. The dog didn't reply and the Landlord stared at him intently. "Did you just roll your eyes at me?"

Oscar barked sharply, twice, and looked up deliberately at a small cupboard fixed to the wall behind the bar.

"Nope, I'm not going to use it to clean this place up; t'would be disrespectful. As for the repairs to the roof and walls,"—he shrugged—"I suppose we can get someone from the village to have a look." He adopted a nonchalant attitude and took up a sweeping brush, ready to begin. "Anyway, honest hard work never hurt." But then a terrible thought struck him. He dropped the brush and went to the cupboard, inspecting it minutely, searching for any signs of tampering. "Oscar," he said slowly, hardly daring to breathe, "would you fetch the key?"

The dog scampered out onto the old station platform to a long row of lichen covered pots in which weeds now grew in place of the flowers they had once proudly contained. Oscar cocked his leg at the first and allowed himself briefly to bask in memories of happier times. Then he scampered to the eighth one along and nudged it gently aside. Underneath, where it had lain hidden for centuries, was a small silver key.

But if he'd wanted to see inside, he would've just smashed it, wouldn't he? the Landlord thought as he waited.

"C'mon, Oscar," he muttered, "c'mon."

On cue, the dog came running, full pelt into the room, and tossed the key into the air a mere second before he crashed into a pile of debris, scattering it everywhere. The Landlord caught the key deftly and took a deep breath before unlocking the cupboard. He glanced at Oscar, but the dog was staring intently as if he too were saying a silent prayer. Seconds later, both man and dog heaved a sigh of relief as there it lay, undisturbed as it had for so long.

The last time the Landlord had used his wand had been to forge the link between his adopted homeland of Wales and the Sanctuary. He had done so, albeit reluctantly, at the request of Morgan, with his new-fangled ideas.

Countless years before Morgan was born, the Landlord had sworn a vow never to take up his wand again. It was a measure of the regard in which he held his friend that he had not only forged the link but had agreed to maintain it. But the wand had remained untouched since then, waiting patiently until it was needed again.

Now, as if in anticipation of being handled once more, it expelled sparks of blue static. The Landlord picked it up and the wand nestled immediately into his palm, its purple translucence glowing softly, and the tiny silver stars with which it was inset shone brightly, almost painful to the eye. Despite the centuries since he had last held it, he marveled at how familiar it felt.

He smiled and wondered why he had been so worried; the Dark Wizard would never have had the strength or skill to manage a wand like this. Anyway, it would never allow itself to fall into the wrong hands. Reverently, he said a silent thank you as he replaced the wand and locked the door.

He picked up the sweeping brush and began shifting debris into a large pile in the center of the room. *Perhaps I should just pay someone from the village to do it all,* he thought as the magnitude of his task began to dawn. *Old Mrs. Thomas and her daughters would love to tackle this, and I can get Grufydd to mend the roof at the same time.* The more he thought about the idea, the more he liked it. *And Dai the blacksmith is a dab hand at wall building.* Mind made up, he threw the brush to one side with a happy grin.

He was about to whistle Oscar, who was sunning himself on the platform outside, when the ground beneath him shifted and he was sent sprawling. Oscar gave a loud yelp and disappeared into the fields beyond.

What just happened? he wondered, as he sat there, once more surrounded by debris, the work of the past hour undone. *An earthquake? Here?* The Landlord forced his mind into stillness as he reached deep within his senses. He remained, unmoving, as the sun passed the midday point and moved halfway to the horizon.

At last, he took a deep breath and opened his eyes, surprised to find the day nearly gone. Oscar had crawled into his lap and was sleeping, soft snores escaping his nose. He reached down and ruffled the dog's ears fondly. Oscar awoke and licked his hand, then settled back to sleep.

"So, Kanzser is dead at last," he murmured. "But how? And who?"

Logan. The answer entered his head immediately. The Landlord wasn't sure how he knew the Dark Wizard was responsible but somehow it made perfect sense. What was less certain was how on earth he'd managed it.

I should go to the village and tell Ffranc at once. He moved Oscar gently to one side and stood; the dog didn't stir. *No, Ffranc will have worked it out already.* Another thought occurred to him: *And they'll already be preparing another party.* He sighed as he realized the chances of persuading anyone to help with the mess had just disappeared, for the next few days at least.

He sighed again, more heavily this time, picked up the brush again and began to fashion order from the chaos.

Chapter 3

With his newfound determination, it was only another day before Logan sensed a change in the air. *Warmer, most definitely,* he thought, *and something else.* He tried to work out what it was and all at once he had it. *The air,* he realized, *it's sweeter.*

He'd noticed it the second he'd left the demon world, a strong smell of decay that permeated the atmosphere. But, as always happens, he'd become accustomed to it until soon he didn't notice it at all. Now it was certainly changing, fading away to be replaced by a much more pleasant aroma.

Then quite suddenly it was as if he had crossed a line, which indeed he had. The scenery changed from stark, bleak harshness to a lush green carpet dotted all over with wildflowers of every kind, and he knew he had passed into the land of the witches. It was a place of incalculable beauty, for the witches were creatures of grace and intellect; *were,* because now their numbers were few, diminished by time and war. For this reason that their border was no longer maintained and Logan was able to walk across it unharmed.

Not for nothing did he endure this perilous trek, for if one requires something badly enough, it makes sense to go to the best. But now, as he stood at the border of the witches' world and surveyed the scene before him, the danger he faced was palpable.

A perilous place indeed, he thought, *but at least I will find food.* And so it proved, for everywhere were trees and bushes bearing all the fruits he could desire. Logan fell upon them hungrily, his caution momentarily forgotten. He barely had time to cram his mouth with one fruit before running to the next, juice plastering his face, running down his neck and splashing his clothes.

Eventually, sated at last, he sat and enjoyed the feel of the sun, hot still but no longer brutal. Presently he slept, only to be half-awakened again by a sound that nagged persistently.

"Water," he murmured, still more asleep than awake. "Sounds like water." Eventually, it would no longer be ignored, and Logan hauled himself to his feet. Turning toward the noise, which seemed suddenly loud to his ears, he saw where the landscape rose into a small but sheer promontory, so close he wondered how he'd not noticed it before. And at its top, a small but powerful stream arced gracefully over the edge like glittering silver ribbons, plummeting into a large pool of frothing turbulence before meandering its way down the slope.

All at once he was aware of the stickiness of his face, the dirt under his fingernails and the aroma of stale sweat from his body. He hurried to the edge of the pool and, scrambling onto a nearby rock, stood for a moment to enjoy the spray stinging his face before executing a perfect dive.

*   *   *   *

The Landlord wandered around the ancient inn, or railway station as it had more recently become, and marveled at the changes a few days had wrought. The helpers employed from the village had worked wonders and the place was clean and habitable once more. Even the holes in the roof and walls had been repaired by the skillful hands of Dai the blacksmith and his helper, Grufydd.

He hauled open the heavy back door and with one step was in Seventeenth Century Wales. Spotting a rabbit, Oscar chased it joyfully up the steps and onto the path, which led to the village where the twins, Morgan and Logan, had been born, and where Ffranc and his granddaughter Catrin now lived. And where, nearby, the cave entrance to the demon lair could be found.

Smiling, the Landlord didn't bother to call him back. He knew the rabbit was unlikely to be caught and that the dog wouldn't harm it in any case. Oscar would most likely run on to the village and seek out Catrin, who would lavish all her attention on him.

Leaving the door open for the dog's return, he walked to the front of the building and back into the present day. He surveyed the railway track, or rather, where the track had been before his home was destroyed by Logan and its magic lost.

Temporarily lost, he thought as a rare wave of anger swept through him. His treatment at Logan's hands had been brutal, and he knew it had been his intention to kill him. *Eventually,* he thought, *if he could ever have mustered the courage.* The Landlord thrust away his thoughts and looked beyond the line of the track to a point where a slight shimmering distorted the air, a meter or so above the ground. Still he hesitated, for what he contemplated doing next was difficult to think of.

And there has been so much pain, so much heartache already... He jumped slightly as Oscar, who had given up his chase, came bounding up, still barking excitedly.

Get a grip, he told himself, and jumped nimbly from the station platform, but when he reached the small, shimmering patch he hesitated, then gathered Oscar into his arms. After a brief look around to ensure nobody was watching, not that there could be anyone to see, he stepped into it.

Now, some portals are instantaneous and some are not. Think of the one from the mortal world to the Sanctuary; to pass through it takes as long as it does to get from the circular room and along the passage-between-the-worlds. But to get from the realm of the Demon King to that of the Necromancer is a single step, a matter of seconds, while the portal linking Wales to the Sanctuary is, or *was,* a train ride of several hours.

And the portal at which the Landlord now stood? Well it was many ages since he had vowed never to use it again and had sealed it, so he thought, forever. But now he found the incantation came to his mind as readily as if he'd spoken it only yesterday. He acted swiftly before he could change his mind and stepped into the portal and, almost instantaneously, into the world of the witches.

Chapter 4

Safe from prying eyes, the Landlord surveyed the land before him, a land once so familiar. That the portal lay hidden behind the waterfall was no accident, for there had been a time when he was unwelcomed in this land and had been forced to enter in secret. *So long ago,* he pondered as he stared through the roaring torrent at the pool beyond, where he and Mitra had spent so many happy hours.

So long ago…

"Cornelius!" Mitra broke the surface of the water, spluttering and laughing at the same time. Wiping her eyes briefly, she again screwed them tight and shook her head from side to side, sending her long black hair flying in all directions like skewers of liquid anthracite. Thousands of tiny droplets caught the sun and enveloped her in countless rainbows. Watching her, Cornelius thought he had never seen anything so beautiful.

Interpreting his look, she blushed and, to forestall the compliment she could see forming on his lips, she launched forward and ducked him under the water.

In turn, he swam quickly back to the top and tried to reach her, but she evaded him easily and, being the stronger swimmer, did not allow him to catch her until they had reached the far side of the pool and the shade of the overhanging trees. There they moved into each other's embrace; Cornelius tilted her chin gently upwards and they kissed, long and languorously.

They were happy to snatch these few rare, forbidden moments, yet they were never enough, and this became the source of their only disagreement. Although friendship between the two races was encouraged, romantic liaisons between wizards and witches were forbidden. It had always been so, and the reason was as obvious as it was practical; the inhabitants of each race held too much power. As such, all feared the power the progeny of such a liaison might hold, and if this should be turned towards evil, well, all knew that the Demon King himself had resulted from such a disastrous coupling. And so there was only one punishment sufficient to deter those who might be tempted, yet Mitra would have taken the risk had Cornelius not stood firm. Therefore they both had to be content with the meager time they had.

Time. So little time...

The Landlord's mind returned to the present and, for some reason, he recalled how he'd once tried, without success, to explain to Catrin his concept of time. Because they have much less need for sleep than mortals, many witches and wizards, especially those in rural parts, measure time by the moon as much as by the sun. They know no names as such for days, weeks or months, having no use at all for deities, gods or prophets. The days before and after the full moon are times of great industry, where they may have little or no sleep at all, and this is why the arrival of the new moon, when the earth is at its darkest, is welcomed by many. The night of the new moon and the day that follows are known, in the witches' tongue, as Cueris Axxilara, literally, *when I can banish all my cares.*

Only on each Cueris Axxilara, knowing it offered a modicum of safety, with all witches at rest within their homes, would Cornelius allow Mitra and he to meet. From sunset on the night of the new moon until sunrise the day after next was all the time they had together in each lunar cycle. And on this, they differed vehemently...

"We could have longer!" Mitra would plead, but Cornelius, who longed to agree, would shake his head sorrowfully but stubbornly. At the end of their allotted time, he would stand, hold her close for a moment, then leave, closing the portal behind him so she could not follow. Then Mitra would stamp her feet and curse the intransigence of wizards, before returning cautiously to her home. Once inside, she would smile and touch her bruised and swollen lips, already thinking of when she would see him again.

They might have continued like this for who knows how long? But deep down, both knew it could not last, that something must change. These moments snatched secretly as if they were criminals, they were not enough. Could never be enough! Better they be caught and die if they could not be together as lovers should. Both thought it, said it and perhaps they even believed it. Until, that is, it really happened.

It was the old witch, Racine, who noticed the difference in Mitra, how as each new moon approached, she became increasingly distracted, then excited until she could hardly contain it. And then, after the Cueris Axxilara, *the girl's utter melancholy until gradually, as the days passed, her agitation began to grow again. Racine said nothing but watched closely. Said nothing, until she was certain.*

A noise interrupted the Landlord's reverie and he returned to the present. But he could not prevent himself from recalling the secrecy of those distant times, where each noise might signal discovery, and his stomach clenched involuntarily. But it was only a toad, hopping from leaf to leaf, and he smiled wryly at the belief of some mortals that toads were witches in disguise.

Even now, in this so-called modern age! He almost laughed, but then, inevitably whenever mortals entered his mind these days, his thoughts turned to Cissy and Penelope. *I wonder what they're doing right now...*

While the Landlord idled in the land of the witches with, unknown to him, the Dark Wizard growing ever closer, and while Franc and Catrin celebrated the demise of the Demon King, while life in the Sanctuary continued, and the goblins were soon to receive an unwelcome visitor, while all this and more was happening throughout the dimensions created by the ancient witches and wizards, none suspected they were being watched, with great interest, from far away.

Or, perhaps from not so far away; who can say with certainty, for the distance between dimensions cannot be measured in the usual way. It could be as infinite as... well infinity, or no further than the width of the neutron within an atom. But someone, somewhere, was most definitely watching...

*　　　　*　　　　*　　　　*

Anarkus barely survived the fall from the balcony of the council chamber. Only his power and supreme command of the elements saved him from obliteration on the rocks far below, but even so, his injuries were terrible. These, and the price exacted for using such powerful magic, diminished him greatly, and for many years he was forced to wander the wilderness, able to perform only the most rudimentary magic.

If the killing of Laiis gave some satisfaction, his failure to murder the entire council and take control gnawed at him constantly, feeding the fire within that burned for revenge.

With infinitesimal slowness, Anarkus's strength returned, and with it his magic. But when he should have focused on defeating the council, he reveled in his fast-returning power. He delighted in causing acts of desecration, dreaming up ever more inventive ways to torture, murder and destroy, so that far and wide, his name became synonymous with terror.

Inevitably, rumors of his evil-doing reached the ears of the council. But as their sun flickered in its death throes, they were caught in the final, urgent preparations for escape. It was easy now to say they should have found time to deal with the threat of Anarkus's increasing power, but they did not. It was an omission that would not be without consequences.

And so the migration was completed. Planets disappeared from the skies around the mortal planet as the powerful witch and wizard council used them to create dimensions in which were placed goblins, witches, demons and others. Then, from the planet they had chosen for themselves, they waited and watched with interest the development of the mortal race.

Disappointed that the mortals were so primitive, Anarkus also watched from one of the remaining planets, one the witch and wizard council had not thought worthy of consideration. It was more distant than the others they'd left in the sky, freezing and bleak. It suited Anarkus perfectly, for here he could remain, unnoticed, biding his time.

As centuries passed, the achievements of the mortal race left him cold with boredom, but their ever more inventive ways of killing each other did not. He was entertained by the death and destruction of the First World War and laughed aloud, clapping his hands in appreciation, when they dropped their atom bombs at the end of the second.

He was thoughtful after the creation of the blood moon. Cornelius had been a mere boy when they'd last met but now, clearly he was a wizard of exceptional power. *A pity the witches didn't kill him when they had the chance,* he'd thought, sensing trouble ahead.

He watched, fascinated, as the Demon King manipulated the boy Logan and with interest as the feud between him and his brother blossomed. He silently applauded when Logan murdered their father and cursed when Morgan became leader of the Sanctuary, an institution he detested.

And now, at last, he was getting bored. He looked around with distaste at his cold, empty world. *I like these mortals,* he thought, *they've become much more interesting...*

Chapter 5

Racine couldn't have said exactly why she hated Mitra so much. Perhaps it was the delicate exquisiteness of her features, or the kindness and love that emanated from her, a gift that made her well-liked by all in the village and one that Racine didn't share.

Even the birds, robins and kingfishers, finches and nightingales, the small animals, rabbits and hedgehogs, otters and badgers, foxes and squirrels, they all loved her, for it was she more than any other who kept them alive during the bitter, harsh winters that often descended upon the land.

Racine had always been disliked, for she had only the ability to push people away and not to draw them close. She'd been pretty once, but hers was a cold, distant beauty that attracted and repelled all who knew her. Now she was old and embittered, all vestiges of that beauty faded long ago, and her capacity to cause harm and discord magnified tenfold with each year that passed.

As she followed Mitra past the outskirts of the village and into the darkness of the countryside, she was determined to discover at last whatever secret the girl was hiding.

The night was cold and Racine shivered despite the extra cloaks she had thought to wear. The effort of keeping hidden, frequently ducking out of sight as Mitra paused to gaze around at her surroundings and the way the dampness of the night seemed to penetrate her bones, all were taking their toll. This was the night of the new moon and she felt her tiredness even more acutely than usual.

Why is she so secretive? What is she up to? Racine didn't think she could go much further and was about to give up the pursuit when Mitra stopped, having seemingly reached her destination.

Why here? And with such stealth? Racine was puzzled, for there were many pools and lakes, rivers or streams much closer to the village. And why would anyone swim at night, especially in this cold?

Except that Mitra wasn't swimming. Instead she stood, gazing intently at the waterfall as if the streaming torrent held some kind of mystery, as yet unrevealed. Even from where she hid, Racine could see that the girl's body was stiff with anxiety as she stood, unmoving, waiting.

Then, suddenly the tension vanished and a look of joy transformed Mitra's features as a figure emerged from behind the curtain of water and Mitra, with cries of excitement, ran toward it. Racine rubbed her eyes shortsightedly as she tried to determine who it might be, then her mouth dropped in utter shock. Rage overcame her, so much so that she nearly stood and screamed at Mitra for her betrayal, for the man who now gathered her into his arms and kissed her frantically while she laughed and cried with absolute happiness was a wizard.

Not that wizards were unwelcome in this land, for there had

always existed harmony between the two kinds, but this one... Oh this one was most definitely banished! Racine rubbed her hands together with glee, her anger forgotten. Mitra had just signed her own death warrant. *And when the other witches find out there will be no saving either of them!* For this was the wizard Cornelius who had fought against the Necromancer. Cornelius who had persuaded the witches to join in the fight. Cornelius who was responsible for the deaths of so many of her kindred.

The following weeks passed interminably for Racine, and she often had to fight the impulse to denounce Mitra there and then. But at last, it was the night of the new moon once more. As dawn broke the next morning, Racine stepped quietly into the dwelling of the elder witch and shook her awake. At first Agnes could make no sense of what she was being told but finally comprehension dawned and within minutes she had gathered six of her most trusted brethren. Together, led by Racine, they quietly left the village.

Racine felt none of the tiredness she had the last time she'd made this journey. Instead, there was only a mounting sense of excitement as they approached the waterfall and concealed themselves. Then, as they crouched, hidden, she simply pointed. Even until the last moment, Agnes had hoped Racine was somehow mistaken or deluded, but now, with tears of sadness welling in her eyes, she motioned to her companions and they stood, wands raised, and approached the unsuspecting lovers.

*　　　　*　　　　*　　　　*

If his wand had been close by he could have compelled it to come to him. But the witches were wise and they knew this. Agnes had hidden the wand, buried deep into the earth, far outside the village. She had acted alone so that none but she knew where it lay.

Agnes had questioned the old witch, desperate to find another solution, some mitigating evidence, an answer that might prevent the pronouncing of the sentence for Mitra's crime. The sentence of death.

"What grievance do you have against her, Racine?" she asked. "What has made you so hollow and empty inside, so eager to wish harm for others? Mitra in particular can have done nothing to make you bear her ill!"

And the mocking reply, "Save your words, Agnes, for they mean nothing. You, me, everyone knows there is only one outcome to this. The girl must die! Pointless to bother with a trial at all really!"

The light of malice in the old witches eyes told Agnes it was pointless to argue further and she could only vow that, despite any influence Racine might try to have on the other witches, the trial would be impartial and without prejudice. But her words were empty and Agnes knew she spoke in vain. Mitra would indeed receive a fair trial, but there could be only one outcome. The evidence of her crime was clear: it lay chained within the strongest cell the witches could build.

Mitra was kept guarded within her home, allowed to speak to no one. She was not even permitted outdoors lest she somehow reach her wizard lover and they contrive some means of escape.

When it came time for Agnes to question the girl, Mitra would say nothing except to plead for Cornelius's life. Her own, she knew, was forfeit; to this she was resigned and made no plea. Even Agnes's entreaties that she agree to give him up, to see him no more in the hope of a lenient verdict, carried no weight and were rebuffed. Agnes could only reassure her that the wizard would be released after. At this point, she'd been so overcome with tears that it was Mitra who turned from comforted to comforter. Although Agnes was the 'elder' witch, meaning she led the village, she was in fact still quite young, only ten or so years older than Mitra. She'd never experienced anything so difficult and felt her heart must break.

The problem of what to do with the wizard was a thorny one too, and some called for his execution also. Most would regret the girl's death and didn't see why he shouldn't pay the ultimate penalty too.

We wouldn't dare! Agnes shivered, for she saw what others clearly could not, that to kill the wizard would likely provoke a war from which neither side might recover.

So it was that preparations began for Mitra's execution, with Agnes finding delays wherever she could, in the hope of finding some miraculous solution, and Racine chafing to see an end to it, whispering mistrust and hate wherever she could.

One night, a few days after the capture, while Mitra slept and her two guards dozed lightly by the fire, a tiny wren hopped on to a windowsill of the cottage. Seeing all was silent within, it squeezed through a tiny space where the guards had neglected to close the window securely. It flew over to Mitra, hopped onto her pillow, and pecked her nose sharply. She awoke, startled, but had the presence of mind not to cry out. Within seconds the wren was chirping softly, its voice inaudible to any but the girl.

"Do not despair," it said, "there is a plan. We will set the wizard free! He will come for you!"

It was true that when Agnes concealed the wizard's wand she was alone, for she could not risk the other witches finding it. Mitra had many friends and some might think to rescue her, thus putting themselves in danger. Agnes would not put temptation in their way.

But she disregarded those that *were* present and many eyes watched from far up in the trees or concealed deep within the undergrowth. Now, even as the wren spoke softly into the ear of Mitra, its friends had summoned some of the animals of the forest, seeking their aid. They were there in number, for all wanted to be involved in helping the young witch, of whom they were so fond.

There had even been disagreement between some of the foxes and badgers as to who should have the honor of digging up the wand. It had become quite heated at one point until some of the birds had chirruped angrily at the noise they were making. In the end, a venerable old badger had prevailed, his argument being that he was the oldest creature in the forest and therefore the wisest.

It didn't take long to dig deep down until the wand was revealed and there was a collective sigh of relief. Eagerly, the badger reached out to retrieve it then stopped, puzzled as an invisible barrier prevented him taking hold. Time and time again he tried, without success. Others took his place but had no more luck until, at last, the awful truth dawned.

"A spell has been placed," said the badger in a low-pitched growl.

"That must be it!" barked several of the foxes.

"What will we do?" squeaked a small group of field mice, out on their nocturnal jaunts and eager to join the escapade. There was a general hubbub of suppressed chatter as they shared opinions on how best to get hold of the wand.

"Looking for something?" The words were loud in the quiet of the night and all present jumped guiltily. Agnes's footfalls had been so soft they had not alerted even their acute senses. "You cannot get past the spells I have placed to guard the wand. Oh, the wand itself will break them eventually but by then it will be too late." There was a wealth of sadness in her words at the realization that, by concealing the wand, she herself was ensuring Mitra's sentence would be carried out.

It is the law! a voice screamed at her from within, *it is not my fault!* And another voice answered, *but it is wrong!*

Her words provoked an angry outcry, all thoughts of concealment forgotten, but Agnes ignored them as she stared at the wand and thinking, battling with her conscience. Several more minutes passed before the animals began to nudge one another into silence and the birds ceased their outraged chattering.

Agnes was no longer looking at them but stood, eyes tight closed, strange sounds coming from her lips. Suddenly, all belatedly remembered the need for stealth and the forest became silent again but for her chanting. They realized that something strange but important was happening.

The chanting seemed to last forever and some of the younger animals were getting restless, when suddenly it ceased. Then there was a suppressed cheer of relief as the wizard's wand appeared at the top of the hole and floated up into Agnes's hands. She herself gave a small smile of satisfaction.

Now who are the best climbers here? she mused, before summoning a small red squirrel who perched on a nearby branch. "Are you brave enough for an adventure?" she asked quietly and the squirrel nodded. Agnes handed her the wand and asked, "You know what to do with this?" The squirrel nodded again and this time her eyes shone with pride.

"It must not be suspected that I have helped the girl, or the wizard." As she addressed the throng, she shivered inwardly at the thought that *she* would face execution if the truth were discovered. "Wait one hour then take it to the wizard. He will know what to do." She traced an arc across the sky to indicate how far the moon must travel for an hour to pass, and then she was gone.

From then, the plan went without a hitch. The squirrel performed its task beautifully and within seconds Cornelius was free. Within minutes, Mitra also. Stealthily, they crept from the village and returned to the waterfall. Mitra was giddy with relief and glee as she thought of the look on Racine's face when the village awoke to find her gone. Cornelius had told her that Agnes was responsible for their deliverance and there was a tinge of regret that Mitra would never be able to thank her.

They reached the waterfall and, while Cornelius opened the portal, she gave a last, regretful look down the valley to the distant forest, beyond which lay hidden the village of her birth.

Then she took Cornelius by the hand and they stepped into the portal together.

And so began a new life for them both; a life of blissful happiness where they laughed together.

Oh, how they laughed! And loved. Oh, how they loved! And if Mitra ever missed her own kind, her old way of life, never by word or gesture did she make it known.

Still, they could not be together always, for the world and time in which Cornelius lived was an unenlightened one, where mortals viewed any but their own kind with deep mistrust. Cornelius had lived there for many years of course and was at least tolerated across the land and well-liked by most.

But for Mitra it was different; she was unknown, but powerful. And somehow, witches had always been regarded with more suspicion than wizards. To openly consort with each other was asking for trouble, both knew this instinctively.

Mitra set up house in a village not too far away where, although shunned at first, she gradually won over the inhabitants with her gentle kindness and her healing powers. And who would question if she sometimes disappeared for days at a time? She was a witch after all, and everyone knew you should never meddle in the ways of witches.

So it continued, until the years became decades and somehow it became less of a burden that they still lived apart; they spent most of their days and nights together anyway. The decades became centuries, and when a new menace evolved, and the nearby village was forced to dwell in the shadow of the Demon King, Cornelius became their protector on the occasions, not infrequent, when Kanzser sent his demons out to pillage and kill.

Mitra had become loved by those in her adopted home, was accepted as their unofficial leader and, as with Cornelius, their protector.

Time passed quickly, in the way that time does and might have continued to do so, until that fateful night when everything changed.

The night that Cornelius captured a demon.

Chapter 6

Despite the anomaly in time and dimension, Morgan sensed the re-establishing of the link to the witches' realm and smiled. He wasn't surprised the Landlord had decided to visit there; he had sensed a change in his friend after the defeat of the demons. *I think he needs to be alone with his memories; closer to Mitra perhaps,* he mused.

Morgan still felt guilt at leaving the Sanctuary, but this was tempered by his own happiness and the knowledge that it was in good hands; that Cissy would prove to be a strong leader. *It's the right time,* he told himself. *The Sanctuary is ready for new blood and there are enough of the old guard, Molly, Wallace...*

His musings were interrupted by the door crashing open as an irate figure burst in.

"Morgan, I can't decide whether to invite the Viangg tribe. Daraproud is really testing my patience on this!"

"I know she is, Aeryn, but they are our traditional enemies, I'm not sure it's a good idea..."

"But Daraproud *wants* them here," Aeryn insisted. "If she's mentioned it once, she's done so a thousand times! I'll be glad when this damned wedding is over and the two of them can stop pestering me!"

"Actually, it's Alessandro who wants them here; some foolish notion about promoting peace across the realm, even though we all know the Vianggs to be incapable of it."

"Alessandro!" she exclaimed. "That boy? He really should stick to being a cook; it's what he does best."

Morgan winced at the thought of telling Alessandro he was a mere cook, but he smiled at her flushed cheeks and the strands of hair that had fallen forward over her face. "Well, perhaps we should just let them get on with it; it's their wedding after all." He looked at her quizzically. "I don't suppose we could just, well, you know, disappear somewhere until after it's all over?"

Aeryn grinned. "That's tempting, I must admit." She cocked her head to one side and put a long, delicate finger to her chin, as if considering. Then they looked at each other, shook their heads and said, in perfect unison, "Nah!"

They walked out to the balcony and stood for a while, enjoying the wonderful vista before them. But all at once Morgan felt a sharp pang of anxiety in the pit of his stomach. Surprised and without knowing what it meant, he found his eyes were drawn to the faint, almost indiscernible haze that was ever present to the west.

"What's wrong?" Concern showed in Aeryn's eyes. "Has something happened?"

He shook his head, still distracted. "I don't know," he admitted, "a disturbance; something not quite right." He looked at her. "I... I have to go out." And with that he left abruptly, leaving her staring after him in astonishment. A few minutes later, she heard him call for his horse and almost immediately gallop at full speed through the castle gate.

Morgan knew the legends, of course, for they'd been handed down across the ages, and when he'd quizzed the Landlord about it, his friend had reluctantly revealed his part in the demise of the Necromancer.

The ability to open gaps, to exploit flaws in the councils' creation, was first noticed by the witches – it has already been said that they were a race of intellect – and it was to have consequences none could have foreseen, for it allowed races to unite against a common enemy.

It was the old goblin queen, Kamontip's own ancestor, who became increasingly worried about the growing influence of the Necromancer and decided something must be done. She would fight this menace, for she held the Queen's Wand, a thing of beauty and power. But not the other goblins; they were not warriors and, in the ordinary way of things, would not fight. Of course, this was not the ordinary way of things, but still, such a wholesale slaughter of the goblin race – for slaughter it would have been – was not to be considered.

But the witches, oh, they *were* a war-like race and their numbers were great. Allied with the power of the Queen's Wand, surely they would prevail. But no, the witches refused to fight, not while the goblins lay dormant. *Why should our kind die while yours hide in their homes like cowards?* came their angry response.

Discouraged but not despondent, the goblin queen went to the great wizard Cornelius and spent many days trying to persuade him.

It was no easy task, for all knew of his abhorrence for killing. But he recognized the threat and that now was the time to end it, so he went to the witches and argued, threatened, and eventually shamed them. Thus it was that together, wizard, witch and goblin queen marched through the gaps in the dimensions and into the land of the Necromancer.

Even with such combined power they were close, so very close, to failure! Many witches died, their race decimated forever; the goblin queen fell also, and it was only when, at the absolute limit of even his great strength, Cornelius struck the final, despairing blow, that the battle was won. Sadly, he had looked round at the scores of dead and dying witches, many of whom were friends, and he knew that the world, dimension, *universe* even, would never again hold the same sense of wonder and joy for him. Gathering up the remaining witches, only a score or so now, he retrieved the Queen's Wand, returned to the goblin world and presented it to the new queen, before retreating, hurt and grieving, to his own land.

And so the Necromancer, despite his awesome power, had been defeated, never to be seen again... almost. Almost, because carelessly, as the wizard Cornelius might reluctantly admit – but only after drinking rather too much of the strong Welsh ale he liked so much (probably because he'd invented it) – a tiny seed had been allowed to escape. Oh! Smaller than a speck of dust! But a seed nonetheless, and it was this that lay dormant, waiting through the ages until it could return to reclaim its land and wreak revenge on its tormentors. And return it did, and so recently that it should strike terror into all who read these pages, but ultimately it was the Necromancer's lack of patience and his supreme arrogance that was his undoing.

He returned too soon! He was still too weak!

And so came the greatest task the Sanctuary had yet faced. Or rather, which Morgan had faced, for he would let nobody accompany him, lest they all perish and the Sanctuary be left defenseless. Molly would still tell the tale of how she'd watched her friend close the door behind him on that fateful day long ago, how she'd not known for sure but had doubted he would ever return.

And thus began an epic battle between the two, between good and evil, if you will. For two days the struggle went on, the advantage changing hands a score or more times. Weak though he was, the Necromancer was still formidable, but so was Morgan. The wizard discovered new heights to his power and became truly magnificent. On and on he went, wand in one hand, sword in the other, and at last the Necromancer's supreme confidence began to fail, his arrogance turning to fear.

As Morgan's wand rebuffed the Necromancer's curses and spells, his sword searched desperately for the opening that might end this menace. Time and time again he almost had it, only to narrowly avoid being disemboweled by the vicious claws of his foe. But eventually, there it was, the one chance! Fast as lightning, he darted forward and plunged his sword into the heart of the Necromancer, then just as quickly sprang back as, all strength deserting it, the creature sank to its knees then pitched forward, its body – although not its spirit, which was only diminished – quite dead.

But Morgan's strength was spent and he collapsed, almost instantly fading into unconsciousness while the acidic liquid of the Necromancer's rotting body threatened to engulf him. And it was left to Molly, truest of friends who had agonized over her promise not to follow, to save him. For two days she kept that promise, but all the while her instincts screamed at her to break it. When she eventually did, it was just in time to find Morgan, moments from being engulfed in acid, gather him into her arms and bear him back to the Sanctuary.

Afterward, it was something they never spoke of, even after so many centuries, for words were not necessary and some memories were best left alone...

Why am I thinking of it now? Morgan wondered. *I haven't thought of that vile creature in decades.* He peered intently across the Chasm of Nothingness, trying to make out the arid landscape beyond it, knowing as he did that it was fruitless, that nothing could penetrate the thick miasma of fog, said by the superstitious to be made from the souls of the damned.

Only days before, he had stood on this spot and rejoiced as he sensed the demise of the Demon King, although the means had remained hidden. *I must speak to the Landlord about it. If anyone knows, it will be him,* he'd thought then. Now though, something or someone was abroad in the land of the Necromancer; he knew that much for sure, just as he sensed that whoever it was had no business being there. *Perhaps it is linked to the death of the Demon King,* he guessed, but who could say? The swirling gray cloud into which he peered cloaked not only his sight, but much of his wizard sense, as effectively as a curtain blocked the light.

Frustrated, Morgan turned away and walked his horse slowly home, knowing as he did so that troubled times lay ahead.

Chapter 7

To think of the past and lose himself in his memories of Mitra was painful but strangely cathartic, and the Landlord was in no way ready to put those memories aside. So he cursed softly in irritation when faint whistling brought him back to the present. But irritation quickly turned to caution and he stepped deeper into the shadows behind the waterfall. It was possible the witches' feelings towards him had mellowed after all this time, but somehow he doubted it.

Cautiously, he peered around the edge of the cascading torrent and glanced around, but nobody could be seen. It occurred to him that the sensible thing would be to simply step back into the portal rather than risk detection, but his curiosity won and he stayed where he was, waiting.

Gradually the sound became louder and he risked another peep. This time he could see someone, still indistinct but getting larger by the second. *Who can it be?* he wondered, but some instinct told him that whoever it was, it was no witch.

As he watched through the water, the approaching figure seemed familiar somehow, but it was impossible to be sure through the distortion of the waterfall. Then the intruder jumped, fully clothed, into the water and the Landlord suddenly felt vaguely ridiculous standing there, doing nothing. He stepped forward until only his nose and eyes protruded through the cascade and what he saw nearly made him cry out in disbelief. He jumped back so violently that he slipped on the wet stones and banged his head, at the same time, making an awful lot of noise. Luckily the thundering torrent hid any sounds and he remained undetected. The Landlord got to his knees and once more stared through the curtain of water, trying to make sense of what he saw.

Logan! What is he doing here? How? Why? But it didn't take much thought to realize the Dark Wizard must have traveled through the land of the Necromancer to get here. *But how did he get here from the demon lair? I know of no portal that would allow it. And what is his purpose?*

But with the Landlord's quick intellect, the answer, to the second question at least, came easily. *Of course! The goblins! Logan needs a wand!*

He watched impassively, remaining utterly still and silent as Logan splashed around, clearly oblivious to the presence of another.

But perhaps some instinct warned him, for all at once he was struck by a feeling of furtiveness and Logan crouched in the shallows, looking warily around. He was suddenly acutely aware of his lack of caution and he shuddered at the thought of what the witches might do should he be caught. They had no love for him, that was certain, and without a wand, he was vulnerable.

He spat with disgust. *Probably kill me and deliver the body to my sainted brother.* The thought of Morgan winning yet again was almost worse than being dead. He pulled himself quickly from the pool and, water streaming from his clothes, made his way up the hill, this time with the utmost care. He walked quickly and cautiously for the next few hours, clothes steaming and drying in the hot sunshine, ever watchful for danger.

With equal caution, the Landlord stepped out from the waterfall and followed. At first he felt enormous satisfaction at having Logan so entirely at his mercy, for it would have been simple to return through the portal, retrieve his wand and send a lightning bolt into his back, extinguishing him forever. And there were many who would say Logan had deserved it; not least the Landlord himself.

But that would have been the work of a coward and a coward he was not. Nor was he a murderer. The Landlord allowed himself a moment to shy away from his memories, from that tiny, niggling voice in his head that insisted, *Yes, you are.*

Soon his amusement palled, for this was a petty revenge when one considered all the trouble and heartache Logan had caused. Not for the first time, he rued that Morgan had not killed his brother years ago; nobody would have blamed him, for he'd had good reason, not least the murder of their father when they'd been only boys.

The Landlord thought with regret about the events of centuries ago. He'd liked the twins' father and not for the first time he wondered if he himself could have done more to prevent his murder. But Owain had been stubborn, naïve in his blind refusal to accept that Logan was being coerced by the Demon King, in his refusal to believe his son would so blatantly defy him and enter a world he knew was forbidden to all.

Even Morgan had known about his brother's clandestine visits and had tried to convince his father, eliciting a rare anger from Owain. This was brought about, at least in part, the Landlord knew, by his guilt at the favoritism he could not help showing toward Morgan, the elder son by mere minutes. But those minutes meant that he would inherit all while Logan would not. And anyway, there was something in Morgan's make-up that made others like and look up to him. Logan possessed few of those qualities and nor had he inherited his brother's strength of body and mind. Thus he resorted to other, darker means to try and succeed, which did not go unnoticed, so he was shunned by the village's inhabitants.

The Landlord sighed. *No, he wasn't an easy boy to like, sure enough,* he thought, *but you, Owain, must share some of the blame for how he turned out. If only you hadn't been so blind, so naive!*

That Morgan had inherited some of his father's naïveté had also long been clear to the Landlord. It would have been better for all concerned if Logan had died long ago! But, he was forced to concede, perhaps the qualities that had prevented Morgan from doing away with his brother were the very ones which had helped him protect the mortal world for so long.

And who am I to criticize anyway, he mused, *with my own crimes unanswered, unpunished for so long?* Once more he thought of Mitra, and again the guilt threatened to crush him. Suddenly he felt a longing to hide away from the doings of wizards and mortals once more, to return to his home and stay there.

But what of the Sanctuary? a quiet voice in his mind insisted.

Morgan is gone; the girl may need your help.

"She has Molly to guide her, and Wallace," he answered aloud. "And she has Luke. And I should re-establish the link to the Sanctuary."

She needs your advice, and she needs to know that you and Morgan have not abandoned her, answered the voice inside his head. *And you know well that the link can wait.*

Chapter 8

Penelope was being buried alive. Resigned to her fate, the girl, who had just turned ten years old, lay back in the shallow trench that had been dug for her and closed her eyes. The hot midday sun beat down on her prostrate form and caused beads of sweat to break out across her forehead. She allowed herself to think back over the momentous events that had so completely altered her young life.

Almost a year had passed since she'd been caught up in the Dark Wizard's attack on the

Sanctuary and found clinging to the body of her mother. Not knowing what else to do, Molly had taken her into the Sanctuary and there the girl had encountered a magical world filled with curious and fascinating people.

Then Morgan and his companions had battled the Demon King and his army. For a long time, it had seemed they must lose, even when Cissy had been revealed to possess enormous power. It wasn't until Queen Aeryn had appeared from her own world that things had finally swung in their favor, and Penelope was immensely proud of the part she'd had in making that happen.

As Cissy covered her with sand, careful to avoid the girl's face, Penelope dozed, and a smile stole over her face as she thought about the friends she'd made. Morgan and Molly, of course. Morgan, the most powerful of wizards, a bit strict at times but very kind underneath, and Molly, dear, fat, irritable Molly who the demons had so badly underestimated, much to their cost. Cissy and Luke, mortals like herself but very much a part of the Sanctuary, although Penelope still didn't quite understand where Cissy had suddenly got all that power from. Wallace, who didn't say much but of whom she was as fond as the rest of them, and Peter, Luke's father, who'd so nearly been killed in that same attack by the Dark Wizard.

Then there was Alessandro, the crazy Italian chef who was in love with Aeryn's sister Daraproud, and the cook Hans who'd spotted her sneaking from the Sanctuary when she made the spell that took her to Aeryn's world.

Penelope was fast asleep now and didn't even notice she was almost completely buried as she dreamed on...

... so many! Aeryn herself, and her son, Dominic. Grufydd, who'd returned with Molly from seventeenth-century Wales when she'd gone to find the blood thorn. And the Landlord and Oscar, oh, and the faeries! So many...

*   *   *   *

Kamontip, the goblin queen, was annoyed. She had long ago predicted when the Demon King would die, for all knew that goblins had the gift of prescience, and Kamontip had known, almost to the day, when his demise would come. What she *didn't* know was the manner of his death. She suspected though that it had something to do with the wizard who even now traveled through the land of the witches and who, very soon, would trespass on her own land.

And this was the source of her annoyance, for goblins were a secretive race who disliked the intrusion of strangers and did not welcome them easily. Still, if he was indeed the cause of the Demon King's death, it would be interesting to find out how the wizard had achieved it and perhaps he would, after all, deserve her gratitude. That Kanzser no longer lived could only be a cause for celebration.

The goblins had been tasked, eons past, with the making of wands, by the council of the witches and wizards, and they had become famed across many worlds for their skill. Sure, others could make them, but all knew those to be inferior copies, lacking the craftsmanship and power of a goblin wand. Kamontip suspected this was why the wizard was about to intrude on her and she sighed in vexation.

She was tall for a goblin – all goblin queens were – and her figure was lithe and slim. Her features were pleasing to the eye; what mortals might describe as oriental. In the mortal world, of course, goblins were described as ugly, with big noses and large, pointed ears, but this was a stereotype; they were not like this at all. Nor were they evil, as they were usually portrayed. Mischievous yes, but evil, no.

She smiled grimly. *We have outlived the Necromancer, now the demons, and we will outlast the race of men, and this fool, wizard though he may be, is still mortal.* Nevertheless, her curiosity was even greater than her annoyance as she gave the order for a door to be created between the two worlds, her own and that of the witches, to allow the wizard entry.

Chapter 9

Once a numerous race, the witches' numbers had been greatly diminished during the battle with the Necromancer and, nowadays, nearly all witches were to be found in their villages, far to the west. And so, despite his fears and the caution he now observed, Logan encountered nobody in the few days it took to cross their land.

Truthfully, if not for the constant need to be on his guard, he might have enjoyed the journey, for this truly was a land of beauty. A panorama of gently rolling hills engulfed him, sweeping to the far horizons like a painting of green, yellow and brown pastels, merging hazily at last, as if the artist had smudged them with an expert thumb.

In the distance, streams meandered between the hills like threads of quicksilver that shimmered in the heat of the sun, and forests clothed them in sumptuous gowns of larch, pine and beech. There was an abundance of wildlife all around; birds soared above or chattered in the trees while rabbits gamboled in play, the white tufts of their tails disappearing underground at the vibration of his footsteps. He saw herds of deer, the bucks with their majestic antlers in one small group followed by the does and their offspring. A tiny fawn, perhaps more curious than the rest, wandered towards him before being swiftly nudged back into the herd by an anxious mother.

Such was the abundance of wildflowers that butterflies fluttered constantly, their soft gossamer brushing his face, and the loud humming of bees was a constant musical accompaniment. At night, eyes shone in the light from his campfire, regarding him warily; foxes, perhaps, or badgers, he guessed.

On the third day, he encountered a herd of wild palomino ponies, their manes streaming in the wind as they frolicked and played together, ecstatic with the joy of being alive and free. As he sat and watched, Logan felt a rare contentment steal over him, and at first he failed to recognize it. *Is this what it feels like to be happy?* The thought entered, unbidden, into his mind and he wondered at it, before discarding it with his usual cynicism. Yet he couldn't help feeling disappointed that the little horses kept a wary distance, perhaps sensing the evil within him, and ignored his proffered hand with its gift of apples taken from a nearby tree.

A wave of self-pity at their rejection arose and he thrust it swiftly away, replacing it with anger. As he jumped to his feet, the palominos nickered high-pitched warnings and scattered, their hooves drumming and becoming ever fainter.

From then on his surroundings held no interest to Logan and he marched grimly on, head down as if to deny his weakness in appreciating the beauty with which he'd been gifted and the brief happiness it had wrought. As night fell, the sun's heat was replaced by a cold, biting wind, and it was with relief that he spied a thick forest in the distance. There at least he would find shelter.

But the moment he entered he felt a sense of menace and, not for the first time, cursed his lack of a wand and the man who had taken it. He was tempted to retrace his steps and find a way around this accursed place, but the forest had stretched out of sight in all directions. He suspected he'd reached the border of the witches' land and that the forest formed some kind of protection; that there was *no* way around it.

The trees grew denser until he was forced to grope his way forward, arms stretched in the utter blackness. Branches whipped painfully across his face and body, whether he'd touched them or not, and sunken roots rose to trip him and bar his way. Soon he could go no further as the trees closed in, encircling him like sentinels through which there was no path. Already exhausted, he collapsed to the ground in despair.

Not daring to light a fire for fear of what it might reveal, he huddled miserably against a tree and imagined that eyes watched him from every direction. Each sound was magnified and he flinched repeatedly; the wind through the leaves whispered dire threats.

Nevertheless, he eventually fell into a fitful sleep, broken a few hours later by the cacophony of the dawn chorus. By the meager light of the morning, Logan saw the trees had thinned and his way was no longer barred. Hurriedly, he got to his feet and now made faster progress than at any time since he'd entered the forest. The breeze, malignant the night before, spoke its amusement, as if the forest had enjoyed the fright it had given him. But Logan no longer cared, for he could see daylight in the distance and knew his ordeal was nearly over.

All at once he saw a figure, the first he'd seen since leaving the demon world, and he slowed, cautious once more. But the witch neither spoke nor threatened, merely nodded with a sardonic smile before turning and blending into the forest's darkness. Then, suddenly Logan was out of the trees at last and he gazed around, relieved.

Far away on the horizon, he could see where the rolling hills of one dimension ended abruptly, replaced by soaring, jagged mountains of another. The terrain around him was sparser and rockier, with none of the fruitfulness of the witches' land, but Logan thrust his way eagerly into the goblin domain, towards where, in the next valley, he could see smoke drifting into the air. Presently, the aroma of woodsmoke invaded his nostrils and, reaching the lip of the valley at last, he looked down at the town spread before him.

No matter in which dimension or period of time it exists, a goblin town never really varies much in size or style and such was the one in which Logan found himself. It was quite big, but not huge; busy but not overcrowded. But while most towns have some pretty parts, some ugly, goblin towns do not.

They are all, quite simply, beautiful.

Its houses, whilst subtly varied in design, all followed a theme; tall and narrow with many windows to allow the sun, which always shines during the day in the goblin world, to fill them with light and warmth.

They were made from tiny bricks of pastel colored stone – yellow and ochre, cream and brown – quarried from the hills and mountains both near and far. The walls of these buildings were solidly built by craftsmen but hardly ever uniform or precise, more often being not quite straight and set at odd angles. This was entirely dependent on how much sleep the goblin in question had had the night before or, more usually, how much beer he or she had consumed – beer drinking being a national pastime. But the effect, which was one of subtle imperfection, provided a charm that juxtaposed beautifully with the absolute perfection of their roads.

Most were made from the same many-colored bricks, this time arranged with precision and covered for protection with a thick, shiny coating, much like a potter's glaze. And the reason for this perfection was that their creation involved a liberal use of magic and a lucky accident from way back in the mists of time.

No one really knew why, but legend told that once, long ago, in an unknown place or time, a goblin had enchanted the roads of his or her town so they could be moved around at will, resulting in nobody knowing where they were and everyone losing their way.

Annoying as this undoubtedly was, it was soon realized it was also a superb defense against any who entered the town intent on causing harm. Unwanted strangers could simply be made to wander for an eternity, or at least until, in desperation, they were glad to escape.

It was for this reason that the streets of all goblin towns tended to be laid out rather chaotically without any observable pattern, although nowadays, in these more peaceful times, it was only the main street, reaching from one end to the other, which tended to be enchanted.

This one was paved with slabs of golden-yellow stone of all different shapes and sizes; squares, circles, octagons and the like, but which somehow all fitted together perfectly. They were so closely set that the gaps in between measured a mere hair's breadth, almost invisible to travelers, but when viewed from above the pattern could be seen as a perfect spiderweb. Clearly its creators had a sense of humor, intending to warn travelers not to tarry, lest they become ensnared.

And for the unwary or unwelcome, it was *filled* with snares. Sometimes it was so short that you came to the end almost immediately, before you'd even begun, with no further to go. Or it could grow so long that one might walk for an eternity and never reach the end. And the creators' favorite, particularly when discouraging someone they really disliked, the road became circular, causing the intruder to go endlessly around and around until the circle diminished and they found themselves literally spinning on the spot.

It was onto this perilous road that Logan now stepped, watched by scores of unseen eyes. Mercifully, he didn't have to walk far when, as dusk fell, he was met by a group of figures who stepped into his path, wands raised and shining brightly so that he was momentarily blinded. Without speaking, they turned and set off down the road with the implicit invitation – or instruction – that he should follow.

For the next hour they walked, and the next. Gradually, Logan noticed the houses that lined the sides of the road becoming more numerous and surmised they were reaching the central, more populated part of the town. But still the small group of goblins continued, much to Logan's chagrin, as he was becoming tired and footsore. His annoyance would have been far greater had he known they'd passed their intended destination at least three times already and the goblins, mischievous as ever, were simply toying with him.

Finally, as he was losing patience and about to demand where they were taking him, they stopped abruptly then melted into the darkness as a taller figure appeared before him, wand held high, bathing the road in a golden sphere of light.

"Welcome, Dark Wizard," said Kamontip, queen of the goblins.

Chapter 10

Cissy smiled at Penelope, relieved she didn't appear scarred by her recent experiences.

"You're very good with her." The old lady, seated in a nearby deckchair, looked up from her book and smiled at Cissy. "She's very lucky to have a big sister like you."

Cissy smiled politely but didn't bother to correct the mistake. She'd been watching the sleeping child, thinking of all she'd been through – what they'd all been through. *We only just made it,* she mused, a strange melancholy descending on her, *and that was with Morgan as leader and with Aeryn's help.*

She glanced again at the old woman who'd returned to her book. *If you only knew the truth,* she thought wryly, but then acknowledged, *I suppose Pen has become more like my younger sister.* She lay back on the sand and closed her eyes, enjoying the feel of the sun warming her. But her thoughts were troubled. *I'm supposed to be in charge now; how am I gonna manage that?*

"I wish the Landlord had stuck around," she muttered, not realizing she had spoken aloud.

"Pardon, dear?" The woman looked up again. "I didn't quite catch that." Her brow furrowed with concern as she saw the worry on Cissy's face. "Are you in some kind of trouble?"

Yeah, a whole heap of trouble, she thought. Aloud she said, "It's okay, honestly. Just one or two worries I suppose; nothing serious."

"What in this world can a lovely young girl like yourself have to worry about?"

What indeed? thought Cissy. *It's not this world that's the problem.* She opened her eyes and smiled again at the old woman. "Oh, nothing much really," she lied, "nothing I can't sort out." Cissy crossed her fingers tightly for luck as she said it.

"Well I'm sure you will, dear. And you do a fabulous job of looking after your sister."

At that moment, Penelope awoke and announced, "I'm getting hungry."

Relieved at the interruption, which spared her from telling more lies, Cissy stood and began gathering their things. Then they said their goodbyes and trudged through the sand, up the path to the cottage.

Penelope spotted him first; a tall figure leaning against the door of their holiday rental.

"Landlord!" She ran at full speed and threw herself into his arms.

"That's a ridiculous name,"—he grinned as he swung her around, making her squeal with delight—"and it seems to have caught on. Landlord is my *occupation;* well, sort of. It's not my name."

"So, what is your name then? I never did find out; Morgan wouldn't tell me."

"That's because he knows the value of privacy, particularly from nosy little girls," he deadpanned. "Even Cissy doesn't know."

She was about to protest, when he winked, his face cracking into a smile, and she burst out laughing. "Don't be horrible!" And she whispered, so Cissy wouldn't hear, "Tell me! Please do. Then I'll have a secret!"

"It's Cornelius." He smiled, whispering back, "My real name is Cornelius. Now, would you do me a favor? There's a big pile of firewood round the back that needs fetching and putting by the fireplace. Could you?"

Penelope rolled her eyes. She knew very well when grown-ups wanted rid of her so they could talk. But she went willingly enough, followed closely by Oscar, who was eager to check out the rabbit situation around here.

"Cornelius, eh?" Cissy teased. "Why've you kept it a secret? It's a nice name."

"It's never been a secret, Cissy, just more a denial of what I used to be. And to help keep the memories at bay. The thing is, Logan is on his way, as we speak, to the land of the goblins. He is desperate to replace the wand I took from him. I suspect that Kamontip, the goblin queen, will limit his power; she is far from stupid." He paused. "But Logan is not stupid either, despite what Morgan may like to think and whatever he may have told you."

Cissy made a gesture of denial, but he waved it away, impatient.

"It doesn't matter, but the Demon King is dead." He stopped as she looked at him in surprise. "Oh yes, the combined might of the Sanctuary, including yourself, could not defeat him yet I suspect Logan did. How, I am not entirely certain, but I believe he not only found a way to do so but then managed to escape the demon realm."

She shrugged dismissively.

"Cissy, you cannot, must not, underestimate him!"

"But I don't understand; surely she won't just make him another wand, just like that?"

"She may not have a choice. Even without his wand, Logan still has the power to do real harm, and his plotting and his machinations never cease. Perhaps he will make some kind of deal, threaten the goblins, in order to get a wand." He sighed heavily, for he was tired of the entire business. "But who knows? The goblins are nothing if not devious and certainly the goblin queen will do all she can to thwart him in his quest to regain the power he craves."

He stopped talking and Cissy was silent for a while until she asked, tentatively, "So what should I do, Landlord? How I wish—"

"Cornelius," he reminded her gently, "my real name is Cornelius."

She nodded. "So, *Cornelius,* what should I do next? How I wish Morgan was still leader of the Sanctuary; how can I even begin to fill his shoes?"

"You will fill them," he said, and there was such certainly in his voice that when she looked up into his eyes and saw the endless kindness within, she believed him, utterly. "And don't forget your own power, Cissy, it is not insignificant, you know. And you have Luke to fight beside you; Molly and Wallace to guide you."

Penelope was sick of waiting around while the grown-ups had their secret chats. First, Cissy had been in the lounge with the Landlord while she, Penelope, was asked to sit in the kitchen with strict instructions not to interrupt.

Now, Penelope was not averse to listening at doors. *Which is a good thing,* she thought self-righteously, *or else I wouldn't have gotten the information when Molly and Morgan talked about the blood moon.* But this time, no matter how much she strained to hear, she could only make out the faint murmur of voices. She was not to know that Cissy, suspecting the girl would be trying to listen, had placed a cone of silence around herself and the Landlord.

The lounge door opened at last and Penelope only just had time to grab a magazine from the table and pretend to read – but she accidentally held it upside down. The Landlord winked at her but didn't speak as he put on his long, black coat and went outside to find Oscar, who had still not returned from chasing rabbits.

"So, what was all that about?" Penelope began immediately. "I know it was about me!"

"Actually, it wasn't. Well, only a little," Cissy admitted. "Mostly he was giving me advice for when I'm back at the Sanctuary, and he also advised I don't leave it too long before I return."

"Before *we* return," Penelope corrected.

"Well," Cissy hesitated, "I need to talk to you about that. The Landlord thinks..."

"I don't care what he thinks, it's nothing to do with him, he's just a stupid old wizard!"

"That's enough, Pen!" Cissy cut in sharply. "Show some respect!" She turned away and busied herself moving crockery from the drainer to give herself time to calm down. Eventually she turned and saw the girl was still standing there forlornly, lips trembling. "Anyway, you're right, it is nothing to do with the Landlord. My parents adopted you and it's up to them. I hope you don't think they're stupid too!"

"I'm sorry!" Penelope exclaimed and ran to take hold of Cissy's hand. "Of course I don't think that, or the Landlord either. I know I shouldn't have said that. I didn't mean it, Cissy, honest, I didn't. I love the Landlord, I really, really do!" Her tears were flowing now, and she was becoming hysterical.

Alarmed, Cissy quickly drew her close and stroked her hair.

"Hush, Penelope. Hush now, it's ok." She could feel the girl sobbing against her chest and she bit her lip guiltily, knowing she'd been too sharp. Penelope had played such an important part during the demon war that it was easy to forget she was still only ten years old.

Gradually she became calmer and pulled away from Cissy's embrace, wiping her eyes and nose on her sleeve.

"I was going to say," said Cissy gently, "that the Landlord thinks you *should* come back with me to the Sanctuary."

"He said that?" She smiled tremulously. "Really?"

"Yes. And so do I." She gazed out the window for a moment, deep in troubled thoughts. "But I still wish Morgan was there."

Later that evening, Penelope got the Landlord to herself at last and had spent the last half hour bringing him up to date with events.

"Then the moon turned red and the demons toppled over, dead. Aeryn, that's the queen who came through the rip in the sky and turned out to be Morgan's long-lost love,"—she paused for breath, but only a quick one for she had a lot to say—"she's the one who made it happen, the moon going red I mean, but it was me who reminded her it would kill the demons and win us the war. Even Morgan didn't know!"

The pride in the girl's voice was evident and the Landlord smiled to himself as he closed his eyes, content to let her prattling wash over him. Presently, he dozed and only occasionally did her words filter through.

"... the book from the library in the Sanctuary said the blood moon is a curse set by a powerful wizard many years ago..."

Have three thousand years really passed since then? he thought. *Where did all that time go?*

The girl's voice gradually mingled with the noise of the seagulls outside and the crashing of the waves on the nearby shore.

Mention of the blood moon had awakened memories; unwelcome memories he would like to submerge forever. He could still recall the look of horror and disgust on Mitra's face as he cut the demon's throat. Oh, it had been necessary; even after all this time he still believed that. But there had been consequences that he'd not foreseen.

If only one could alter the past...

Chapter 11

Mitra. Witch.

Yet to call her a mere witch was to vastly underestimate her talents. Perhaps the first of the truly great witches to have possessed unimaginable knowledge and power.

Power that surpassed even mine, the Landlord was forced to admit as an image of her formed in his mind. *And she was good,* he mused, *good and kind, generous and fair. Never once did she abuse her power or use it to cause harm.*

Now, as he looked back across the centuries, her image was so strong it was as if she stood before him, and he was filled with longing to see her again.

And beautiful! Even so long after her death, the Landlord felt his heart beat faster when he thought of it...

What was it about Mitra that first attracted me? That day we met, the day she tried to take a shortcut through the bramble hedge. Always so impatient, trying to save time, instead of walking the long way around! Her hair, long and russet-red, the color of autumn leaves. The wind so strong that her half-hearted attempts to secure it with pins had been quickly undone and it became caught, impossibly entangled in the brambles.

It was her cries he heard first. Or rather the curses she uttered as she tried to free herself, so at odds with the vision of beauty that awaited him as he followed the sounds and clawed his way through the hedge to reach her. And when at last he saw her he stood, transfixed, unable to move or speak until she cleared her throat slightly, the sound itself mocking and full of irony. It was then that he noticed her eyes, green and sparkling with amusement, fully aware of and enjoying the effect she had upon him.

It took an hour to free her and by the time that hour had passed, I was already lost. Completely, utterly in love. The thought of not seeing her again felt like a dagger in my heart.

Free at last, she'd thanked him, gratefully. Yet while she picked the leaves and thorns from her hair, she'd asked him no questions; not even his name. And, it only occurred to him later, she'd been very adept at avoiding answering his. And then he had no more excuses to try and keep her longer.

'I'll not ask you to walk me home,' she'd told him, trying but not succeeding in keeping the laughter from her voice. 'But I should be safe; I'll not be clambering through any more thorn bushes.' The mischief in her grin, which displayed small, perfectly white teeth, had set his heart racing again. 'Anyway, my brethren might ask questions.' Her eyes narrowed speculatively. 'Like what is a wizard doing snooping around where he's not supposed to be?' With that, she'd skipped gaily away, so quickly he barely had time to gather his wits.

'Will I see you again?'

'Doubt it! The other witches really don't take kindly to strangers! And anyway, you'd never find my house!'

Even as a crushing weight of disappointment descended upon him, he heard her again, her voice faint now. 'It's very hard to find, being the one right at the top of the village, near the windmill. The one with the bright green door!'

He'd laughed then with delight and waited, determined to watch her until she could no longer be seen. Then a thought had occurred. 'You still didn't tell me your name!' And the reply, so faint now as to be almost inaudible, 'Mitra!'

"What are you thinking about?" Penelope's voice cut into his thoughts and jerked him back to the present.

"Oh, nothing." He smiled at the child.

"You were daydreaming," she pointed out, "and smiling." She looked into his kindly face, noticing for the first time how it appeared both young yet incredibly old at the same time. "It didn't look like nothing to me."

"A friend, from long ago." He laughed, amused at her curiosity. "A witch I once knew."

"A witch?" she exclaimed. "Like Molly?"

"Yes," he agreed. "Like Molly but infinitely more powerful."

The girl took a moment to digest this. "More like Siwaraksa then?" Penelope had learned of the famous old witch from Morgan, who had known her well. Fascinated by the stories he'd had to tell, she'd scoured the ancient library of the Sanctuary to find more. The girl had come to love its smell of old wood and beeswax and the hundreds of books that lined the shelves, some of them many centuries old. It was during her searches that she'd found ancient lore that had helped to cure Luke's father, Peter. It was also how she'd found the spell she'd used to reach Queen Aeryn's world.

"Yes," he replied, "like Siwaraksa, but more powerful than her as well."

But not powerful enough in the end, he added silently to himself. "Mitra was a distant ancestor of hers actually."

"Mitra? That's a nice name; sort of, I don't know... kind somehow." Then another thought struck her. "Hold on, you said you were friends? How, if it was so long ago?"

He grinned at her directness and said laconically, "I'm a tad older than I look, Penelope."

"So, is your friend still alive as well?"

The grin vanished. "No," he replied and lapsed into silence, no longer looking at the girl.

"I'm sorry," she stammered, mortified.

The Landlord forced down the tide of guilt, which always threatened to engulf him whenever he thought of Mitra's death.

Will I always blame myself? he wondered, as he had done many times over the centuries. And always the same answer creeping into the back of his mind, *but you are to blame, aren't you?*

Sensing his mood, Oscar jumped into his lap and began licking his face so that the Landlord was forced to laugh. He looked at Penelope's forlorn expression and felt a little ashamed.

"Don't worry, Penelope, it was a long time ago," he said gently, and was rewarded with a tremulous, slightly tearful smile. He ruffled the dog's ears and Oscar cocked his head to one side in enjoyment. "Want to go outside, boy?" And before he could say anything else,

Oscar began charging round the room, barking shrilly. "Would you like to take him?" the Landlord shouted above the noise.

"Can I?" she yelled back, a broad smile now creasing her face.

He nodded, amused at the transformation. Despair turning to joy in a matter of seconds; such are the emotions of children. When the door finally closed, he listened as the sounds of excited chatter and barking faded into the distance. When they were no more, he picked up the iron poker from the side of the fireplace and stoked the fire, adding more coal. He returned to his armchair and watched as the flames burned slowly through. Soon it was blazing once more and the room, which had started to feel a little cold, became warmer. The Landlord closed his eyes and before long he had returned to the distant past...

Chapter 12

"I want a wand." The moment he spoke, Logan realized how rude it sounded and he added somewhat lamely, "please." Not that he would usually have cared; the feelings of others mattered to him not at all. But something about this creature disturbed him, even intimidated him. Perhaps it was her beauty or those serene, gray-green eyes that seemed to look right into him, to know his every thought.

Or maybe it was the sense of confidence she exuded; Logan had the sense this was someone he might struggle to get the better of. But most of all he suspected it might just be the slight air of mockery in the way she spoke, as if she didn't take anything, or anyone, too seriously; him in particular. If the arrogance of his demand had offended her, Logan was unaware of it for the expression in her eyes altered not one iota and nor did the smile on her lips change.

"A wand?" she asked sweetly. "Why, did you lose yours?"

Logan flushed with embarrassment. *She is mocking me,* he thought sourly, *I know she is!* But he also knew he couldn't afford to offend the goblin queen. *I need this wand!* He was also uncomfortably aware that he was far from home in a totally unfamiliar country. No, not a country, a *world*.

Nonetheless he was sorely tempted to retort that it been stolen; they were only goblins after all. This creature might dress herself up as a queen, but she was still inferior by far to himself; a mortal and a wizard. *A goblin could never be equal to a wizard,* Logan laughed inwardly, thus proving that the prejudice toward those who were simply different could never be wholly eradicated, no matter in what world or dimension it was found. For once, common sense prevailed, and he remained silent. But Kamontip had noticed his reaction, just as she had accurately interpreted some of his thoughts.

"Is there a problem, Logan?" Her enquiry was polite, measured. "I *may* call you Logan, mayn't I?" She didn't wait for a reply but snapped her fingers as if something had just occurred to her. "But perhaps you are wondering how you will return to your homeland,"—she paused for a second and now the smile left her face—"without a wand?"

"Oh, of... of course you may," he stammered slightly, wrong-footed. Logan preferred argument and conflict; he didn't understand this niceness. But then the full impact of her words struck him, and he paled. He had never once considered how he might return home should he not get a wand; that possibility had simply never occurred to him. Realizing that this might not be so simple after all, Logan shifted uncomfortably from foot to foot. Without a wand he would be trapped! "Well, I'm hoping,"—he shrugged, a display of nonchalance that fooled nobody—"that you will help me with that." He hesitated then, unsure of the correct manner of address towards this so-called goblin queen. "Your Majesty."

The goblin queen's laughter rang out strident and clear like bells on a cold winter's morning. None too hurriedly, she covered her mouth to stifle it, her eyes still shining with mirth. "I'm sorry," she said, seeing his mouth tighten and his forehead crease into a frown, "I truly am."

She motioned those around to still their own laughter and waited until only a few sniggers and smirks remained.

Kamontip took him by the arm and led him away, realizing to her surprise that she didn't enjoy seeing him embarrassed in this way. Waiting until they were alone, she continued, "It's just that, although I am queen and am respected as such, we hold little value on ceremony here." Kamontip noticed they were being followed, none too discreetly, by half a dozen of the bolder goblin children and she shooed them away. "You may call me Kamontip." She smiled, inviting him to sit. "We all have only one name, not several, as is the mortal way." There was a note of scorn in her voice when she said *mortal,* but she saw he hadn't noticed and was listening avidly.

"We have no use for hierarchy; my title is a relic of a centuries-old tradition, though I do have the final say in matters of dispute, although these are rare. Nobody here is poor, just as no one is rich; we have none of your metal coins, we hold no patience with mortal ways at all, with their petty arguments and wars." Kamontip paused, suddenly embarrassed; it was unlike her to let her tongue run away with her like this.

Logan had been about to protest that while he was *technically* a mortal in the sense that he was human, it was unfair to compare him, a powerful wizard, with the rabble that inhabited the mortal world. But now he noticed the blush which infused the goblin queen's cheeks and wondered...

She in turn scrutinized him and tried to analyze why he disturbed her so much. *Handsome, certainly, and with a certain charisma, no doubt.* Kamontip had been prepared to welcome a fool into her land. *Well, a fool he might be, but he is also a dangerous one. I should not underestimate him.*

In some ways she recognized a kindred spirit. *I like this man's capacity for mischief.* She sighed. *But not, unfortunately, his capacity for evil.*

She could tell how damaged he must be, astute enough to see it, and wondered what had happened to him. Kamontip sighed again; she would have liked to help him but there was no way she could give him the power he craved.

Belatedly, she realized he was staring at her just as she was him, his dark, handsome eyes seeming to read her every thought. She had intended to keep this interloper waiting a fortnight, just for the pleasure of watching him squirm with impatience. Now, angry with herself at her earlier reaction to him, she found herself saying, "You will have your wand," and then, curtly, "but it will take a month."

"A month!" He sprang to his feet in anger. "It can't possibly take…" Logan bit off the words and sank slowly back into his seat. "I thank you." He bowed deeply. "You are most generous."

Kamontip inclined her head graciously. "And you are most welcome. And please be assured,"—she crossed the fingers of both hands behind her back—"that your wand will be the best." She felt the collective wince of those behind who'd disobeyed her order to back off. "The very best it is possible for our master goblin to make."

"Thank you," he acknowledged, meaning it this time, impressed by her promise.

"It is the least I can do; the wand must be fitting for a wizard of your talents." *That's true at least,* she thought gleefully. *Let it never be said that the goblins do not treat strangers in the manner they deserve.* She looked into his eyes, all the while thinking of the instructions she had already given her wand master:

"Tell me, wise one, who is your least apt pupil?"

"The *least* apt?" The question had caught him by surprise. "Why, it is Pyx, my lady." The old goblin still clung to the old traditions, had never got used to addressing his queen by her given name.

"He shows no improvement?"

"None at all, my lady." His sigh was as eloquent as his words. "I despair of him ever making a wand worthy of the name." Then, fearing he'd been too harsh and not wanting the young goblin to be in trouble, added hastily, "But he's a good lad, it's just that, well, perhaps his talents lie elsewhere."

"Yes," Kamontip replied, "I'm sure you are right, but not yet. No, most certainly not yet." She refilled his cup and grinned. "Wise one, I want you to have Pyx make a wand for out visitor, the wizard."

He spluttered his wine then hastened to try and wipe where a drop had stained her sleeve. "But it will be of no use to him; the wizard will be so angry!"

"That's entirely the point." She laid a smooth hand atop his wizened one. "But here's the thing, do not allow Pyx to put the magic into the wand; I alone will do that." Her voice held a warning note as she stood abruptly and kissed the old goblin on the cheek. "He and no other, remember!" She threw back over her shoulder as she left, "I'm sure Pyx will make the perfect wand for our guest!"

And slowly, the wise old goblin began to chuckle.

It took only a week, for it was indeed of poor quality, and just a further week to insert the magic, for there was hardly any to *be* inserted. Pyx was even worse than she had suspected, and she'd been forced to polish it up a bit to not raise the Dark Wizard's suspicions.

Still, she thought, *it does look quite presentable on its bed of green velvet.* She glanced at Logan. *And the wizard seems pleased enough.*

"Thank you, it's beautiful." *Not really,* he thought, *perhaps these goblins aren't as good as they think they are.* He reached for the case. "Do you mind if I try it?"

"Oh no." She snapped the lid hurriedly shut. "Please don't." She smiled coyly. "I'd be embarrassed."

Chapter 13

Their friendship had never been quite the same after the killing of the demon, the act which had enabled him to create the blood moon. Oh, she'd seen the necessity of it, he knew, but her innate goodness would not allow her to reconcile herself to the act. Even though that creature had been foul and disgusting, she could not find it in her heart to justify the demon's murder.

Yet Mitra had never once criticized him openly. In fact, she never again mentioned the incident. Not by word or tone of voice did she betray the fact that something had changed between them, but the reserve they felt in each other's company grew until it became a barrier. Gone was the carefree laughter, the teasing and the banter, the closeness of spirit only true friends can achieve.

Then Mitra began to find excuses and reasons to avoid him, at first only for a day or so, but before long a week or more might pass without them meeting. Only when several weeks passed and he hadn't seen her did he finally decide to sort things out between them. Swallowing his pride and gathering his courage, he made the short trip across the valley to her home. The door to the cottage was unlocked as always but when he went inside it was instantly clear that no one had been there for quite some time. It was winter and the place was freezing; obviously no fire had been lit recently. But somehow, the most worrying thing was the dust that coated every single surface, gray and thick. He knew Mitra would never have let the place get in such a state.

Alarmed, he made enquiries in the village, but no one could tell him anything of use. Mitra was popular and some tried to give helpful suggestions; she was visiting relatives, perhaps, or maybe she'd gone on holiday. Some were of the opinion that, being a witch, she was off somewhere doing some secret, witchy thing. Cornelius, while grateful for their efforts, dismissed them impatiently. Mitra had no relatives and the idea of her going on holiday was ridiculous. As for some kind of secret mission, she would have told him about it; wouldn't she? Not long ago he would have been certain, yet now doubts crowded his mind. But really, the idea seemed ludicrous.

He searched far and wide over the next few weeks but found no trace, and at last he was forced to admit defeat. He spent another week walking around in a kind of daze, living and working without conscious thought and spending hours gazing across the valley, hoping she would appear.

It was while doing so one day that he watched the sun set and night steal across the land. He was about to give up when the moon rose over the horizon. But it was not the white, crystalline glow that usually lit the countryside; this was the blood moon, crimson and magnificent yet somehow eerie and slightly sinister.

Cornelius jumped up, smiting his forehead with a clenched fist.

"Stupid! Stupid!" He would find Mitra at the place he'd created the blood moon. He'd not bothered to look there, convinced it was the last

place she'd want to go. But now it seemed so very obvious.

"Idiot!" He banged his forehead again. It took him some time to reach the place, for the night was cloudy and the shadows dark. At first, he could see nothing but the black outlines of the trees above him, those same trees where he had killed the demon. But as he made his way up the slope, he thought he could see something else, a figure perhaps. He peered intently into the darkness and just then the moon appeared from behind the clouds, bathing the hillside in red satin, and there she was, standing, silently watching.

"Mitra," he breathed, "at last." He started forward eagerly but as he grew closer, he stopped again, uncertain; her very stillness was disquieting. "Mitra?" There was something different about her, something strange in the way she stood, as if she were guarding herself against his approach.

"Welcome, Cornelius, so nice of you to come at last." Her voice was high pinched and unnatural. "Too late, of course, much too late to help your friend." The word friend dripped with sarcasm and was uttered with such vitriol he flinched, and now, as he saw her clearly for the first time, the shock made him sink to his knees.

Her arms and legs were covered with deep, vivid scratches and her face was gaunt and dirty, plastered with mud and grime. Her hair was a wild, tangled mess that hung lank across her face. But it was her clothes that shocked him the most, torn and ruined, hanging from her body in strips of cloth so that one breast was exposed. And now he saw that she was thin; stick thin as if she'd not eaten for a long time. It was then that his heart began to break.

"Mitra!" In his anguish he rushed forward to take her in his arms.

"Don't touch me!" she screamed, and now she did look at him, eyes

blazing with fire and filled with hatred.

Cornelius froze and dared not go closer for fear of exciting her further. Instead, he held out a hesitant, imploring hand and the fire left her eyes.

"Cornelius?" Her voice was soft now. "Where were you when I needed you? Why didn't you help me?"

He was stung by the accusation and he didn't understand it. "Tell me, please, you have to tell me what happened."

"Why didn't you help me?" She began to pull at her hair, ripping out huge clumps, and the sound of tearing flesh sickened him, but still he dared not go to her, not even when she began gouging her face, raking it with long, dirty fingernails.

"Mitra!"

"Don't touch me!" Her scream pierced the night air. "You want to kill me!" She collapsed and began hammering her fists on the ground.

"Please, Mitra, let me help!" Cornelius was beside himself with despair, but her eyes were wild again.

"Get away from me, demon!" Froth streamed from her mouth. "Run for your life!" Mitra cackled and stared right at him, yet through him and beyond, unseeing, unheeding.

Now he did go to her, unable to stand it any longer, but she scrambled to her feet and raised her hands, claw like, as if ready to attack should he come any closer.

"Necromancer beware! No longer will I submit to the desolation of my body and my mind!" She clawed at her throat as if trying to rip out the unclean words.

And Cornelius sank to his knees and wept for the woman he loved so deeply. Wept as he realized, at last, that Mitra was insane.

Chapter 14

"It's not right, that's all I'm saying," Molly grumbled, adding for the tenth time that morning, "It's just very bleedin' inconsiderate." They were sitting in the lounge and she was bored with the unnatural quiet that pervaded the Sanctuary.

Morgan, who she missed terribly, had left to be with Aeryn. Cissy had taken leadership of the Sanctuary, but she and Penelope were on holiday in Cornwall. Even Luke was missing, spending time with his family, particularly his father. Peter had long been a prisoner of the Dark Wizard and he and Luke had met for the first time only recently.

"Oh, for goodness' sake," Wallace complained, but without heat, "can't you stop? Surely you don't begrudge those children a holiday. They have been through rather a lot, you know."

"Yeah, and haven't we all," she replied uncharitably, "haven't we bleedin' all." Molly glanced at the old grandfather clock, which showed ten past eleven and decided to sulk for a while before lunch. She turned her back on her friend and lapsed into silence.

Wallace smiled, amused at the tense, rigid shoulders that dared him to speak. Instead, he remained silent and returned to the old sword he'd found at the back of an old cupboard and had been restoring.

It was similar in style, though smaller and not so heavy, to the English broadsword used by mortals in the time they called the middle ages. But this sword, he knew, was much older than any that had ever been held by mortal hands, for as soon as he touched it, he sensed a faint magical quality, proven by the runes etched into the metal blade. He knew they were ancient but beyond that he could not say. Morgan perhaps could have read them but Wallace did not have this skill.

After a week of loving attention, it looked almost new. The gold and silver wire that gave the handle its grip was nearly all gone; worn away so that only a few strands remained. Wallace had carefully replaced each one and added, on Molly's insistence, alternate colored strands of copper wire which, according to her, would add something she referred to as *style*.

Wallace shook his head in bemusement; he had no concept of what that meant. But the sword was handsome, he supposed, and as he polished away the last few speckles of rust, he felt proud of his achievement.

Luke will like it, he thought, pleased. It had been Molly's idea to give it to the boy after Wallace confessed his worry that his current sword would not last another battle, should one occur. Truthfully, he had been relieved it hadn't broken during the recent war with the Demon King. Luke had thrown himself into the fighting without hesitation and although the sword was a good one it had not been built for such use against demon metal.

With a satisfied smile, Wallace stood and held the sword before him, pretending to scrutinize it but in fact squinting to check out whether Molly showed any sign of relenting. "There, it's finished at last."

But Molly, who was determined to sulk a little longer, ignored him, and although she no longer had her back turned, she found the book she held in her hands thoroughly engrossing.

Wallace angled the now gleaming blade so that it caught the light and shone into the corner of Molly's eye. With a tssk of irritation, she shifted her position; Wallace promptly did it again.

"What the bleedin'..." But when he winked, it was a gesture so unlike him, so out of character, she couldn't help but laugh.

"It *is* beautiful," she admitted. "May I?"

Wallace handed her the sword, amused to see how small it looked in her huge hands, but he quickly became alarmed when she began to swing it above her head. It was a truly fearsome sight and he had to move quickly to grab her wrist and retrieve the weapon.

"I'll take that, if you don't mind." He grinned a little shakily. "Why don't you stick to using your wand; less dangerous."

She nodded, panting a little, but didn't reply. Instead she crossed the large room to the door that was set into the far wall, but incongruously nearly a third of the way between floor and ceiling so that she had to stretch to reach the handle.

"Why Morgan couldn't have put steps here to make it easier I'll never bleedin' know," she grumbled as the door swung inward and she peeped out into the passage-between-the-worlds. It was deserted. *As always, these days,* she thought morosely.

"You miss him, don't you?" Wallace had come to stand beside her.

"Morgan, I mean."

"Yeah, I do," Molly said, abruptly, "but there's nothing to be done about it. And anyway, he deserves his chance at happiness."

Wallace nodded and sat on the large sofa nearby. He was silent for a while before he spoke up suddenly. "I miss him too; and the others. Cissy and Luke, young Penelope. Even those damned faeries."

Molly looked at him in surprise; it was most unlike him to open up with his feelings like this. "You miss the faeries?" she teased, with a gently mocking smile.

"Yeah, yeah." He grinned, embarrassed. "You know what I mean, Molly, it's not the same around here somehow."

Molly could only nod her agreement, for she missed everyone too. She was a kind-hearted soul and fooled nobody with her brusque, no-nonsense manner. Apart from her lifelong friend, Morgan, she found she missed Luke most of all, and Cissy and Penelope too, of course, both of whom she'd become very fond.

And the fact that Alessandro was off gallivanting with that sister of Aeryn's – Molly clicked her fingers as she recalled her name, *Daraproud* – meant that the food quality had diminished quite remarkably. Oh, Hans did his best and he was a very good chef. It was just that Alessandro had been, well, a wizard in the kitchen, obviously. And anyway, Hans had to have some time off and that meant she had to either put up with Wallace's truly awful attempts at cooking or risk her own, which were even more awful.

"Moth and Velveteena could have cooked us up a decent meal," she mused aloud.

"Yep," he agreed, not at all surprised to find she was thinking of her stomach, "but would you trust 'em?"

"Probably not," she admitted, and a grin broke over her face, lighting it up so that, for a brief moment, she resembled the pretty young witch she'd once been. "C'mon, how about I nip into the mortal world and get us a takeaway?"

"You can't!" Wallace was aghast. In truth, he had no idea what a takeaway was, but he did know there were strict rules against *nipping* into the mortal world. "Morgan would be furious if he found out." Even as he spoke, Wallace knew he'd have to find a more compelling argument.

"I can't?" Molly was thoroughly enjoying his discomfiture. "Why not?"

"Well,"—he searched desperately for a more compelling reason—"you just can't!"

Molly tilted her head to one side and regarded him seriously for a moment. Then she grinned once more and winked. "Watch me."

Chapter 15

Logan could hardly remember a time when he hadn't felt angry. The resentment he had first felt before he was even old enough to recognize it as such had, over the intervening centuries, twisted and warped his soul until it had become black and rotten. And now, as always whenever he found a new source for this emotion, he ruminated far into the past, mulling over every individual grievance in a manner he found almost pleasurable. He had experienced it first at a very young age toward his twin, born mere minutes before him. Morgan, whom he'd loved deeply yet, confusingly for one so young, also detested with increasing hatred as the years of their childhood passed by.

Morgan! First born! Stronger! Cleverer! Popular! As always when he thought of his brother, Logan felt the hot flush of anger creep up his neck and onto his face. *You had everything! Just because you were lucky enough to leave our mother's womb first! Why was I the unlucky one? Why me? Always me!*

The age-old cry of the weak.

Even our father favored you! Loved you! Hated me!

Never by a look, gesture or word had the twin's father shown favoritism between the two boys. Owain had been a good man and respected by all. He had struggled and fought to raise two boisterous children as best he could while coping with the grief of losing the woman he'd loved beyond measure but who had died in childbirth. Yes, a good man, who had not deserved the obscene manner of his death.

Thinking of his father's death always raised an emotion in the Dark Wizard, one he disliked and thrust away hastily; guilt! But even as the old familiar thoughts swirled around his mind, Logan now had another grievance to add to the list.

The Landlord.

That accursed wizard of no real power (or so Logan had thought) who had stolen his wand thus forcing him into this never-ending journey to the goblins. He fumed when he considered how he might, at this very moment, have been sitting comfortably, back in the old Victorian mansion, basking in the knowledge that he and he alone had had the courage and cunning to finally destroy the Demon King.

As ever, Logan found he could transform lies into truth with very little effort and he neatly glossed over the fact that he had captured the Landlord intending to torture and kill him for no real reason except that he wanted to.

Having been escorted courteously but firmly back along the main street (which this time took only a few minutes, he'd realized sourly) and seen safely across the border, his way had been easy and uneventful for the past few hours. But now he panted as he toiled up a particularly steep and rocky incline.

As he finally reached the top and paused to recover his breath, he looked back at the ridiculously short distance he had traveled and his heart sank. It would be a long time before he at last reached the high hills that covered the caverns of the demon world.

Or what used to be the demon world, he thought with satisfaction as he set off down the incline, refusing to be daunted by the distance ahead. The glow of pride at being the instigator of the Demon King's demise would sustain him for a while yet. Nor was he unduly worried about how he would get back through the maze of tunnels, now blocked by thousands of tons of fallen rock.

My new wand will show me the way through, he thought smugly, *it is a powerful one; the goblin queen promised. A few fallen rocks won't slow me down and soon I will be home and then... Well, my brother had better beware.*

He took out his new wand for the umpteenth time and looked at it proudly. He knew it had none of the frills of some wands, yet it shone brightly in the pale sunlight. He thought about the goblins and the respect they had shown him.

No doubt they were a little scared of me and my reputation, he mused with condescension, *particularly now I have a wand again.* Logan enjoyed that someone was in awe of him; it didn't happen often.

Even that goblin queen treated me with deference. No more than I deserve though. Ahead, Logan thought he saw a movement, some animal perhaps. *But she and her kind will be rewarded when I defeat my brother. They will be exactly the kind of allies I can use.*

Logan began a daydream where everyone, mortals, goblins, wizards and witches, would kneel before him, and Morgan would at the head of the queue. He was just in the process of bestowing forgiveness for his brother's many sins when he saw the movement again and raised his wand.

"Who is there? Show yourself if you value your life!"

*   *   *   *

The door crashed open and a strong wind gusted into the room, causing crockery to rattle violently and sparks to leap from the fire onto the hearthrug. The Landlord, dragged from his slumber, jumped up quickly and stamped them out before it was ruined.

"We had a marvelous time!" Penelope followed the wind into the room and the Landlord winced at the sound of her voice, loud and strident, irritating after the silence. "Oscar went swimming and swam for miles!" The excited girl exaggerated and, on cue, the dog ran inside just in time before the Landlord slammed the door closed.

"Then he chased a seagull, but it flew away! Sorry about the rug by the way," Penelope added as she belatedly noticed the half a dozen or so little black holes, some of which still smoked slightly. "But then it dived at him and it was huge too! But luckily Oscar barked, and it flew off!" She paused at last, partly to catch her breath and also at his lack of response. "Are you okay, Landlord? I'm sorry if I woke you."

"No, you didn't wake me," he lied and smiled at her. He stretched his long arms up until they touched the ceiling and yawned widely. "But I think I might get a breath of air myself." As the door closed behind him, he breathed a sigh of relief. He was very fond of the girl but, my goodness, she talked a lot!

The wind whipped around him as he turned down the narrow lane down to the lighthouse and the sea. If anyone had seen the unnaturally tall, gaunt figure, with his long legs and long black coat, they would have imagined he'd come from the pages of a Dickens novel. But the Landlord didn't want to see anyone or for them to see him; he still had some thinking to do and he didn't want to be disturbed.

He had to follow her story to the end, however painful he found it; he owed Mitra that at least, and so, muttering a few simple words, the glamour enveloped him and he was hidden from view. As he neared the cliffs, the area became more crowded with mortals, so he chose a spot a short distance away, facing the sea. He sat on the springy grass, enjoying the sight of boats on the water, some so distant they looked like children's toys.

It was all so peaceful, so normal...

Ashamed of his reaction, he'd risen to his feet almost immediately, but when he tried to offer comfort, Mitra turned and ran. Taken by surprise, Cornelius tried to follow but slipped and fell headlong on the grassy slope, and by the time he could recover, his friend was far ahead.

"Mitra! Please, wait!"

He saw her turn and look at him, but she did not stop, and her manic giggling carried clearly to him on the wind. And so began a game of cat and mouse that would live long in his memory and torment him for centuries to come. On and on it went, hour after hour throughout that night and all of the next day and the next. At times it seemed she was tiring at last and he was drawing close and he would be re-energized, filled with new hope. But then he would round yet another valley or scramble to the top of the latest in a seemingly endless number of hills, only to catch a glimpse of her, far in the distance once more.

But toward the evening of the third day, he hauled himself wearily over the top of a rocky ridge and there she was, waiting, not a dozen meters away.

"Mitra!" He stopped abruptly and almost tripped over his feet, so surprised was he to see her. "Mitra, what happened?"

"Why do you follow me?" Her voice was soft, normal, sounding only mildly curious. "What is it you want?"

"Want? I don't want..."

"Or perhaps it's guilt. That's it, isn't it? You feel guilty!" Now her voice was rising again, becoming shrill and out of control. "Admit it! You know you're to blame! You abandoned me!"

She was screaming, her reason gone, and it seemed to Cornelius that she didn't recognize him at all. Suddenly the tirade stopped but the silence was somehow just as loud. Then she made a curious gesture, one that unnerved him far more than the screaming had. Mitra cupped a hand beneath her chin and placed her index finger across her lips, tapping slowly. It was a classic thinking pose, but the way she put her head coquettishly to one side and her sly, calculating look gave it a sinister twist that made him wary.

"Or perhaps not." She was crooning now, mouth curving into a rictus smile full of cunning. "I think it's me you want. That's the truth, isn't it, Cornelius?" She moved a little closer. "You lust after my body. Your thoughts are unclean, I can smell them. I can even taste them!"

Cornelius was shocked at her words, repulsed. He couldn't reply. He wanted to hold her close, to stem the filth that issued from her lips and banish whatever evil spirit possessed her. But he couldn't speak, couldn't even move.

Now she was closer still. "Do you want me?" Almost a whisper now.

Mitra tugged at the tattered remains of her dress so that it fell from her shoulder and hung at her waist, leaving her breasts exposed. She squeezed each nipple in turn until they were engorged and hard, and thrust her hips at him provocatively. "You can have me if you want…"

"Mitra! Don't! Stop it, please, please, stop it!" The words were ripped from him with such passion that for a moment it seemed they had taken effect and that her face softened slightly. "It's me, Cornelius, your friend. Just let me help." A tiny flame of hope kindled inside him and he forced himself to speak more calmly. "Come back with me, I can…"

"Liar!" Her features were once again as hard as granite. "Do not abuse me with your lies!" And from somewhere within the folds of her dress she took out her wand. "Necromancer!"

A stream of glittering witch fire hurtled toward him and, without conscious thought, his own wand was in his hand and he deflected the blow just in time. But its power knocked him to the ground, and he lay there, dazed, for fully a minute. When, at last, he raised his head, Mitra was gone.

Cornelius sat for a very long time, deep in increasingly troubled thoughts. It wasn't the power of the blow that had shocked him, although he knew he should have been able to withstand it more easily. No, it was something else.

That something terrible had happened to her was obvious but he'd believed he could somehow make it right, heal her from whatever possessed her. But now, with mounting horror, he realized she had suffered some unspeakable evil.

Cornelius thought back to the many times he'd witnessed witches fire; countless times!

And it was silver, always silver, like the glitter that mortal children like to play with. Whether the witch be good or bad; silver. Always silver.

The fire cast from Mitra's wand had been black.

Black as polished anthracite.

It was a long time before he felt able to carry on. There was no urgency now, for he knew, with sudden clarity, where Mitra was going. The day had been cloudy and overcast, the sun peeping through only occasionally, yet he'd had an inkling of their direction. Now, in the clear night, he could navigate by the stars and he knew with certainty.

For some reason he couldn't fathom, Mitra, after escaping the horrors she'd suffered, had returned to Wales. Perhaps drawn to the place where she'd known such happiness. But now they were traveling exactly northeast, toward the portal which would take her to the place of her birth.

Like a wounded animal, Mitra was going home.

Chapter 16

Created long ago and made not just of wood but of stone, the wand's surface was inlaid with precious metals, each with their own peculiar magical properties and only found on the farthest planets of the most distant galaxies. What gave this particular wand its immense power though was its core, or rather what had been placed there. The key elements of Earth, Water, Fire and Wind were not unusual, for it was always useful for the holder to have mastery over these. But this one was rich with incantations and that *was* unusual. To place powerful, magical spells into a wand required both time and effort and was extremely expensive; even the best might contain only two or three.

This one had far more than that, some said as many as seven or eight, and nobody remembered why it was instilled with such power. It was fitting, of course, that the queens of the goblins across the ages should possess the ultimate, what had come to be known as the *Queen's Wand*. Goblins are, after all, the absolute authority in the art of wand-making.

It was much too powerful for everyday use and so, in times of peace, it sat on its raised dais, resplendent and magnificent. All were welcome to come and marvel at this magnificent example of the goblin art. Provided, of course, one did not touch…

It had become a game between them, a cat-and-mouse game that she usually enjoyed. Myla was the mouse, forever evading her sister to continue her mischief; she was the cat, trying to catch her at it.

And she, Maisey, was smart, always thinking, keeping one step ahead and finding ever more inventive ways to thwart her. Like the time, knowing Myla would avoid the fifth, seventh and fifteenth steps because they creaked, she'd enchanted the third, eighth and eleventh to scream like banshees when they were stepped upon.

Or the time she'd animated all the wood carved animals and birds throughout the house and made them scamper into her room should they see her sister sneaking around at night. But if Maisey was smart, Myla was smart *and* devious. Sure, the staircase trick had caught her out the first time, but on the second occasion she'd deliberately stepped on the three steps. When they screamed like banshees this time, all the other steps began to laugh, maniacal and deafening, enough to drive you crazy if you had to listen for too long. Certainly, their father had gone crazy at being dragged from his bed in the middle of the night.

As for the animals and birds, their mother had been furious at their loss. Uncharacteristically, this trick had caught Myla out twice, but on the third occasion she'd enchanted the door to the house to open if they appeared. Thus, a steady stream of mice and mistle-thrushes, foxes and finches, badgers and blue tits had streamed out into the fields and the air, never to be seen again.

On this particular night though, Myla had not resorted to magic or sorcery but to good old-fashioned skulduggery; she'd spiked her sister's drink. It would have worked too had she been as adept at sleight-of-hand as she was at enchantments. Oh, she was quick, certainly, but not quite quick enough. Maisey had very sharp eyes and she'd seen her drop the tiny purple pill into her drink. So after a while, noticing Myla become increasingly impatient but aware of how intently she was watching, Maisey raised the glass to her lips and began to drink. Except that at the same time she gave a discreet twitch of her wand beneath the table and caused the liquid to evaporate the instant it entered her mouth. When it was all gone, she wiped her mouth and sighed a little sigh of satisfaction, preparing for the next part of her act.

Presently she'd begun to yawn widely and slur her words. Then, confessing she really didn't feel very well, she'd retired to bed and soon the sound of soft snores could be heard from behind her bedroom door. Maintaining the false snores whilst sitting up in bed reading was a bit of a chore to be honest but she managed to keep up the pretense. She was rewarded a couple of hours later by the sound of feet, treading softly along the passageway outside her room. Maisey hurried silently to the door and listened until the footsteps receded, then she opened it noiselessly and slipped from the room.

Outside, the moon was bright and she easily spied her sister, already far ahead as she looked furtively around before disappearing round a corner. She hurried to catch her but, turning the same corner, there was no sign. *Where are you hiding, sister?* Maisey cursed her inwardly. *What are you up to now?*

Having traversed the next few blocks without success, her

annoyance was turning to puzzlement. Usually by this time Myla would have allowed herself to be seen, if only to ensure the chase continued. Turning down yet another block, she saw, halfway down, a green light that splashed the street from an open doorway and her stomach knotted with apprehension.

"Noooo," she muttered as she approached, instinctively knowing it was Myla who'd opened that door. "Please tell me you didn't..." She pushed the door wider and stepped inside, then gave a low moan and sank to her knees in disbelief and already-burgeoning terror.

"Myla, what have you done?" she whispered. Then, as the shock took hold, she screamed, "What have you done!" She closed her eyes for a long moment, hoping somehow she was dreaming. But when she opened them again, the dais that held the Queen's Wand was still quite, quite empty.

*   *   *   *

"You won't hurt anyone with that!" Myla stepped from behind a rock and indicated the wand scornfully. "It's useless."

"You dare to speak to me thus?" Logan snarled at the goblin, stung by her impudence. "Give me one good reason why I shouldn't blast you right now!"

It was an idle threat of course; he was still deep inside goblin territory after all. *There are probably hundreds more of them nearby,* he thought.

"Well, one good reason would be that you can't. Not with that thing anyway," Myla replied insolently. "Try it and see, why don't you?" And, seeing the red flush of anger creep up the neck of the

Dark Wizard, she added, "Go on, I dare you!"

This was too much. *If there are more of them about, I'll kill them too!* He raised his wand high above his head, into what is known among wizards as the killing stance. *And if that so-called queen doesn't like it, I'll kill her too.* The he hurled a bolt of fire at the goblin.

Or rather, a blob of fire. No bigger than a match flame. A flame which flew – well, *sauntered* – about half the distance before it went out, falling to the ground with a sizzle, like a drop of candle wax.

"What the...?" Logan tried again and this time the tiny flame managed only a quarter of the distance. And the third time it didn't ignite at all but simply dropped, painfully onto the back of his hand, and he cursed loudly.

"Why won't it work!" he demanded. "What have you done?" There was murder etched into his face as he ran toward the goblin.

"I haven't done anything." Myla allowed him to get within a few meters then disappeared, causing Logan to stop.

"You dare to use a glamour? You think to evade me? I'm the Dark Wizard!" Even as he spoke, he felt something brush past him and grabbed at it, but in vain.

"But the goblin queen has." The voice, now behind him, was matter-of-fact. "Done something, I mean."

"Show yourself!" Logan howled as he spun around, clawing wildly at the empty air.

"As you wish." From the side this time and a little more distant, ten meters away, Myla faded back into view.

"You think you can..." He spluttered and choked in his anger. "You, a mere goblin?"

"Now, now." Myla folded her arms and wagged a finger as if at a naughty child, and this only incensed Logan more, as it was intended to do. "There is absolutely no need for rudeness!" Her hands went to her hips, akimbo style, and she thrust her chin forward. "None whatsoever!"

Logan gaped, incensed and shocked that anyone would dare speak to him in this way, but before he could articulate, the goblin had vanished again. Then reappeared seconds later, tapped him on the shoulder, then quickly disappeared again, remaining hidden while Logan raged and cursed. Only when he ceased at last, spent and exhausted, did he see the goblin perched, chin resting on her raised knees, on a nearby boulder.

"Look." Myla jumped down and held out her arms in a placatory gesture. "We could keep this up all day." She ventured a little closer, but not *too* close. "Or we can talk."

"I'm listening," Logan grunted, determined to seize the creature if it got too close. "Get on with it."

"Fine," she agreed, still keeping a prudent distance. "So it's like I said; I haven't done anything; I had nothing to do with making the wand." Now she did risk a step forward. "That was the work of our worst, our most rubbishest apprentice. It was he—"

"Wait, wait," Logan interrupted, anger making way for puzzlement, "I thought it was your queen who made..."

"It was she who put the magic, or the *lack* of it, into the wand but she didn't—"

"But I don't understand! Why would she do that? Why give me a wand with no power? Why would she trick me?"

Myla sighed wearily and covered her eyes for a second. *He really does have limited intelligence. No wonder his brother always wins.* The meaning of the gesture was not lost on Logan and he swore silent retribution.

"Because you are the Dark Wizard, Logan." She risked the use of his name; the first overture of friendship. "You *do* have something of a reputation." Myla smiled to herself at the incongruity of such a massive understatement.

The use of his name was also not lost on Logan, and he wondered at it. *What does this idiot want from me?* "Yes? So? I have a bit of a reputation; what of it?"

"So, there's no *way* the queen was gonna give you loads of power. Obviously. We goblins have no use for the arguments of wizards and mortals; we just want to live in peace. Well, most of us do, except that I'm really, really bored, which is why..."

"I see," snapped Logan, his anger returning. "So I've wasted my time. This journey has all been for nothing! This wand; useless!" He flung it away in disgust.

"Well,"—Myla grinned—"not exactly. It does contain enough magic to get you back through the demon world and into your own." She looked on, amused as Logan scrambled down the steep, rocky slope to retrieve the wand which had rolled to the bottom. Scornfully she watched him slip and slide, losing his balance at last so he traveled the last few meters on his backside.

Bet your arse is sore, she thought gleefully as she followed, skipping lightly across the stones. But when she saw Logan's scuffed and torn clothing, she thought it prudent to mask her amusement.

"Of course, I could show you a much quicker way."

Logan had been busy shaking loose stones from his shoes, but suddenly his attention was riveted on the goblin. *A chance to get out of this forsaken place!*

"You could?" he asked sweetly.

"Oh yes, certainly,"—Myla hesitated—"and I could maybe get you a slightly better wand." She winced at the understatement.

"A better one?" Logan smiled his most charming of smiles. "It seems we got off on rather the wrong foot." He stood and brushed himself down. "And for that I am truly regretful."

I'm bloody sure you are. Myla's expression didn't change.

"But I would very much like to take you up on your kind offer." Logan smiled ingratiatingly. "Very much."

"Well, naturally. I never doubted it for a second." The goblin scratched the side of her nose delicately. "But I do have certain conditions..."

Maisey was too far away to make out what they were saying, but it seemed that her sister and the wizard were getting on very well indeed, and she didn't like it.

What's she up to? she mused, worriedly. *Why has she followed this evil Dark Wizard?* And the thing she had asked herself so many times throughout their lives, *Why does she play these dangerous games?*

Maisey had long ago learned to sense when Myla was contemplating mischief. She knew her sister wasn't bad; goblins rarely are, but she *was* mischievous. Mind you, *all* goblins are mischievous, it's just that Myla was more mischievous than most.

She loved her dearly, but absolutely despaired of her sometimes; well, most of the time really. She knew Myla's mischief stemmed mainly from being bored and dissatisfied with the life of a goblin, which she viewed as mundane. But oh, how she wished she wouldn't get into *quite* so much trouble.

They were twins and almost identical, but two sisters could not have been less alike in nature. Maisey was placid but with a personality that sparkled. Her hair was long and many shades of red, like the colors of trees in fall, and her face was oval in shape, her chin pointed and delicate. She had the slightly elongated nose of all goblins but this enhanced, rather than marred, her features, and her ears were rounded, like a mortal's but much smaller.

Myla's hair was slightly darker, which was often the only way to tell them apart. Except that her personality was darker and her dissatisfaction often made her argumentative and confrontational. Not that she was an unhappy child, but sometimes she just *knew* there had to be more to life than being an *ordinary* goblin.

But now Maisey's features were marred by a worried frown. *Come back,* she willed as the Dark Wizard came scrambling down the slope ahead and she was forced to duck out of sight. *Come back with me and I'll speak to Kamontip. We can fix this!*

But instead, she could only watch in horror and amazement as her sister and the wizard faded into the distance. Maisey lay down and curled into the fetal position, her tears falling freely. "You are lost," she whispered, her sobs coming quickly now. "You are truly lost."

Presently, the young goblin regained control and looked first in the direction Myla had gone, then toward her town where life continued as normal so far as she knew.

I have to go back, she thought morosely. *But I dare not. I cannot face the queen and tell her what my sister has done.* As her tears threatened to return, a rabbit popped its head from a nearby burrow, scampered up and jumped into her lap.

"I'll run away," she told it. The idea had some merit, but the rabbit merely stared and blinked. "You're right," she admitted. "Where would I go? And anyway, I have to save Myla; it's always me has to rescue her from trouble."

Her companion curled up and went to sleep. Maisey looked at it fondly and stroked its fur, taking comfort from its presence. "I'll go back," she said softly. "But not yet. I daren't. Not just yet."

*   *   *   *

The small matter of Myla's conditions was dealt with in minutes. There was only the one really; that the Dark Wizard show her a little of his darker magic.

Oh, playing pranks and creating mischief here and there was all very well, but to be honest, Myla was so bored with all that. She wanted something with a bit more bite; nothing that would do any real harm, just something a little, well a little *darker.* She knew she could have real fun in the mortal world with a few tricks up her sleeve. Myla, young and foolish, had simply no inkling of just how dark the Dark Wizard's magic really was.

Logan, of course, had agreed readily; he would break the promise once he was safely back in his own world. He'd glanced slyly at the goblin. *If she's lucky I might even let her live...*

So now they walked in a silence that was hardly companionable, neither one trusting the other, until they reached the foot of an extremely steep, rocky outcrop.

"It's up there?" The Dark Wizard's gaze traveled slowly upward; it looked awfully high. "That's the way out?" he asked, and looked at the goblin suspiciously.

"Yep." Myla was poker-faced. "Up there."

Actually, there were several much easier ways she could have chosen but for sheer entertainment value this was the best by far. She waited until Logan had climbed a few meters then began her own ascent. In seconds she had passed him easily and skipped nimbly to the top.

Showing more common sense than usual, Myla neither laughed nor commented when Logan arrived at last, face hot and sweaty, his chest heaving. Instead, she took out her wand, keeping the Queen's Wand carefully hidden, and spoke the incantation that would summon the doorway and allow them to leave this dimension.

It faded into view; just an ordinary looking wood paneled door, set in a wooden frame. All around it and beyond the scenery was unchanged, but when Myla turned the knob and pushed it inward, Logan saw the darkness of a passageway and stepped forward eagerly.

He'd hardly dared believe the rumors to be true. A door connecting different worlds! Logan didn't know how such a thing were possible!

There were two passages which lead from the circular room beneath the lamppost.

One was the passage-between-the-worlds and it linked the mortal world with the Sanctuary, which has existed, in its parallel world, for countless centuries, providing protection to mortals throughout the ages.

The other, the Corridor of Dimensions, was for a long time hidden, except from the leaders of the Sanctuary. For the last few hundred years this had been Morgan and he had guarded the secret as jealously as his predecessors.

It contained many doors, some of which led to other worlds, planets taken by the ancient council of witches and wizards from their newly inhabited solar system. Each world was placed in its own dimension, thus hidden from the eyes of mortals and given to those who had also fled; witches, demons, goblins and the like.

But times change. The Necromancer had been diminished, unseen for many centuries, and the demon race was finally annihilated by the blood moon. Relations between Queen Aeryn and Morgan had been repaired and it seemed the time had come at last to reveal the existence of the corridor. Old suspicions had been put to rest and the love between them, denied for two hundred years, had been allowed to rekindle. Morgan had shown her the secret passageway and the decision had been made to reveal it to all.

Hidden away in his dark mansion, in the months following the defeat of the demons, Logan knew nothing of its existence and, with trepidation, he forced himself to breathe deeply as he stepped fully into the Corridor of Dimensions with Myla following hurriedly behind.

As soon as they were through, the door closed and they were plunged into momentary darkness before torches set into the walls burst into flame and filled the passage with flickering light. Even with pauses to touch some of the doors they passed, which seemed painted onto the walls, it took only a minute to reach the bottom. Filled with curiosity, Logan looked cautiously into the passage-between-the-worlds.

Even now, they're in there, plotting against me no doubt. For a crazy few seconds he considered hammering on the door of the Sanctuary and declaring battle there and then. Fool that he often was, Logan didn't know that the door was invisible and shown only to those who needed to know its exact whereabouts.

Easy there, have patience. They will all die when the time is right, he cautioned himself as he turned left into the circular room, closely followed by Myla.

"I don't like it in here," the goblin complained, her voice echoing around the room.

"Quiet!" Logan whispered nervously. "Keep your voice down, you don't know who might be listening."

Just then, as if on cue, a small, white rectangle appeared somewhere near the ceiling of the circular room. Logan realized instantly what it was. *The door at the base of the lamppost!*

But the goblin reacted first and dragged him back into the Corridor of Dimensions so neither of them witnessed the amazing spectacle of someone *oozing* into the circular room. They just had time to scuttle up the corridor and flatten themselves against the wall, unseen in the relative gloom, as a solitary figure appeared briefly then continued up the passage-between-the-worlds.

The witch! What an opportunity! Logan reached for his wand before realizing it would be of no use against the witch's power. "Quickly!" He took hold of the goblin's arm and urged. "Get after her! Kill her! We may not have another chance!"

"What? Are you stupid? I'm not going to kill anybody!"

But in that moment Logan had gone momentarily mad; the chance to rid himself of one of his enemies was too much to resist. Myla was still holding her wand ready to enter the mortal world but now, quick as a cobra, Logan snatched it from her hand…

… and was thrown five meters back up the corridor. To his cost, he had forgotten that nobody could command a wand made for another and Myla's wand had not been pleased at Logan's attempt. Still, knowing the need for secrecy, it had not wished to draw attention and so, while it delivered a shock of epic proportions, this wasn't accompanied by the usual loud bangs and flashes. Unfortunately, Logan could not fully stifle a scream of pain and the sound had carried.

Molly, intent on balancing a pile of pizza boxes, had failed to sense the presence of intruders but she stopped, puzzled as her sharp ears picked up the sound. She walked cautiously back along the passage-between-the-worlds and into the circular room. Seeing it was empty, she took a few paces up the other corridor and peered into the gloom.

It had taken all of Myla's strength to half carry, half drag Logan, still doubled up with pain, further up to where it curved slightly to the left, out of sight of Molly's searching gaze.

Please, please don't come any further! the goblin willed and, obligingly, the pizza boxes chose that moment to teeter dangerously and crash to the floor.

"Oh, you have got to be bleedin' joking!" The sounds of cursing rushed up the corridor and Myla sniggered quietly.

Still grumbling loudly, Molly put the slices back into the boxes as neatly as she could and scraped bits of meat and vegetable from the floor, throwing them on top. *Wallace will never know,* she thought as she gingerly lifted the pile of boxes once more. Then, still muttering darkly, she retraced her steps back up the passage and into the Sanctuary.

Chapter 17

The Landlord stirred and got to his feet. With a quick glance round to make sure no one was looking, he removed the glamour. Here, in the present-day mortal world, this was a popular place; people walked their dogs along the cliff tops, and in the summer months tourists came to see the lighthouse, visit the nearby tin mine or travel further down to Land's End.

He drew curious stares as he strolled toward the lighthouse and the cliff edge a dozen meters or so beyond. All around him were the excited cries of children as they kicked footballs, threw frisbees, licked their ice creams and ate their picnics. Nearby, a family was playing a version of baseball while another had begun a game of cricket. As he watched, a boy of perhaps ten or eleven threw his hands in the air and shouted *owzat!* as he threw the ball past his father's bat and knocked over the stumps.

The Landlord smiled indulgently. Much as he preferred the solitude of his home in its other dimension, he did enjoy visiting the mortal world now and then. He liked mortals, for all their faults. They were like children, blissfully unaware of the existence of a parallel world, one where evil lurked and threatened their very existence.

And that's how it should be, he reminded himself, *just as they are oblivious to the existence of those who strive to protect them.*

He shook his head in wonder as he thought of the girl, half child, half woman, who'd been blessed – *or cursed,* he thought wryly – with immense power. It had been thought Luke would fulfill the prophecy but it was Cissy who'd done so. Now, after Morgan's retirement, she had become leader of the Sanctuary.

Retirement? He sniffed with disapproval and neatly glossed over the fact he had done so long ago. *How can a wizard retire?* But Morgan had gone to be with Aeryn in her own world. *Time to let the young ones have a turn,* he'd said. But to be fair, Morgan had served the Sanctuary well, protecting this world of mortals, and this time it had been a close call; so close! The Demon King had nearly overcome them, and this world of mortals had never been in such peril.

Aeryn and her army had arrived just in time and they had Penelope to thank for that. Even then, the combined might of Aeryn, her sister Daraproud and son Dominic might not have been enough until again it was Penelope who'd reminded Aeryn of her power to invoke the blood moon.

The demon army had perished in their thousands, yet Kanzser had escaped to his mountain lair and the chance to rid the world of his menace had gone. But now the Demon King was dead and in the unlikeliest of ways.

Strange how things work out, he mused, *that the Dark Wizard should work against his brother Morgan for so long yet be the one to finally rid the world of the Demon King.*

Logan had shown initiative, he had to admit. The Landlord still wasn't sure how Logan had achieved it or why, but he did not care. In the end, Logan had done what he himself had longed to do for centuries; he had unwittingly avenged the death of Mitra.

The Landlord had been moving slowly nearer the edge and now he looked down at the sea crashing onto the rocks below, then round at the pleasant scene being enacted around him. It had all looked very different three thousand years ago, of course; no village, not even the occasional dwelling, just a wild and rugged landscape, breathtakingly lovely in its austerity...

... It had taken almost two weeks to get there and she'd been so exhausted near the end he'd almost caught up, but some inner strength drove her on. When at last he crested the hill and began the short walk down, she was already there and had been for several hours, standing almost at the very spot where the Landlord stood now, many centuries into the future.

"Mitra... you're too near the edge." He spoke hesitantly, expecting a torrent of abuse, but she merely smiled and spoke in the gentle, musical tones he knew and loved.

"Are you worried I will fall, Cornelius?"

"Of course," he said, relieved she seemed a little calmer, "please come away, come with me." He was pleading now. "Whatever has happened to you... well, we can fix it; we can make it right."

"Ah, no, Cornelius, that's where you're wrong," she contradicted, shaking her head sadly and looking at him for the first time. "The things that have been done to me..." She hesitated, and he strained his ears to hear her next words, so quietly were they spoken, "I can never tell

a living soul of the shame I've endured."

"Mitra, surely we can..."

"No, my love, it is too late. I have unleashed an unspeakable evil upon the world."

"Mitra..."

"Goodbye, Cornelius, I'm sorry I blamed you. Truly, the blame is mine. Please don't judge me too harshly.

She'd taken another small step backwards and time slowed as he realized her intent. He rushed toward her, but it was of no use; for Mitra it was too late, had been too late from the instant the Demon King entered her tiny cottage.

From the instant the Landlord had murdered the demon to create the blood moon.

"Goodbye, my darling."

And with arms outstretched, just out of reach of his despairing grasp, she allowed herself to fall backward into the void.

"Steady on, mate."

The warning brought him back to the present and he felt a hand grip his arm. He looked gratefully at his rescuer; it was the same mortal who'd been playing with his children earlier.

"You okay?" The man looked curiously at him. "I thought for a minute there you were gonna topple over the edge."

"Yes. Thank you, I'm fine. I just felt a little dizzy for a moment." He managed a weak smile. "I'm very grateful to you."

"Yes, well," the man persisted, "you wanna be more careful, mate." He gestured toward the cliff edge. "It's a long way down."

The Landlord looked down at the rocks, far below. "Yes," he

agreed, "it's a long way down."

Safely away from the edge, the Landlord stared out to sea for a long time, lost in his memories. When at last he returned to the present, he was surprised to see the sun had painted a palette of red and orange across the sky. Behind him, the cliff top, so recently full of holidaymakers, was now almost empty.

As he made his way back up the hill to the cottage, he experienced a sudden longing to be back home. The encounter with the Dark Wizard, brief though it had been, had left him feeling dirty, soiled somehow. Beautiful as this part of the mortal world undoubtedly was, he wanted nothing more now than to be back amongst his friends, Ffranc, Catrin and the villagers, and to leave the protection of the mortal world to Cissy and the Sanctuary.

He decide he would spend a few days at the cottage then return home, and felt a resurgence of his spirits having made the decision. Yet still he couldn't get Mitra entirely from his mind. It had taken him many months to find out what had happened to her and when he did, the horror of it defied belief...

PART TWO

Chapter 18

Since the creation of the blood moon, he had known it would eventually kill him and all of his kind. So, for as long as he could remember, Kanzser, Demon King, had been careful to the point of obsession, keeping note of the moon's phases, not daring to venture out in the days before and after it was full. Still, despite his caution, the possibility he might one day be caught unawares began to lay heavily on his mind, his uneasiness increasing as the centuries passed.

And so, a plan gradually took shape in the Demon King's mind, a plan to create a new being; a non-demon that could withstand the blood moon. He would make it stronger, fiercer than the best of his demons, and its evil would surpass even his own! Then he would make another, and they would breed, again and again so that soon...

In his warped imagination, the Demon King created a super-race, an army so invincible that, with himself at its head, none could withstand it. There arose an image of his enemies kneeling before him in supplication, pleading for their lives, an image in which he conquered the other dimensions before he moved into the mortal world to spread his evil far and wide.

Some plans were simple, some not so. This one was appalling in its intricacy, containing as it did layer upon layer of death and misery. But any plan, good or evil, must start somewhere and Kanzser's began with a journey to the Plains of Desolation, where the most malformed, depraved examples of his kind existed.

They cowered before him as he passed, avoiding his eye lest they attract his notice. But he regarded them with contempt; he did not need these sniveling, pathetic creatures. On another occasion he might have lingered while his guards rounded up a few of them for his amusement. Then he might have had them fight, tear each other limb from limb while he watched. Or perhaps he might have used some of the less ugly ones for his own pleasure, participants in the deviant sexual games he so enjoyed.

But he was in a hurry to begin his quest and so it was that, unable to find what he needed, his growing frustration turned to anger, and any who strayed too close paid the ultimate price, and soon he had left a trail of bodies behind.

He might have missed it, such was the anger that clouded his senses, but at last the faint sound of chanting and cheering intruded upon his consciousness. He followed its direction and began to hurry as he heard other sounds which, with growing excitement, he recognized as those of violence and chaos. He heard curses, bones breaking, creatures dying, and the pleasure it brought him was intense until finally it was simply a crescendo of indistinguishable sounds so loud, they would have rendered any human insane.

Tripping and stumbling in his haste, his pleasure was orgasmic as he drew closer to the source. Then, without warning, he rounded a sharp bend and Kanzser halted in his tracks, staring in wonder at the spectacle before him.

The creature was magnificent. Stunning, fabulous, although no adjective was sufficient to do it justice. It towered more than twice the height of any of its attackers, almost God like in the firelight, which reflected and danced off the great slabs of muscle coated in sweat from exertion as it fought off the swathes of demons that beset it from all sides. Yet the creature made it look easy, nonchalant as the pile of its victims grew higher, though it held no weapon other than huge fists that struck like bony hammers.

Kanzser felt saliva jet into his throat then drool dripped from the sides of his mouth to form tiny pools of acid on the rocky floor. All at once his anger returned and he realized, a little sardonically, that he was envious, jealous even; jealous of the demons who buzzed and irritated this creature like so many flies around rancid meat. Jealous of their proximity, envious of them touching him, those few who managed to get close enough.

Gradually, they became aware of his presence and the cacophony dwindled as they froze in terror, all except the creature. He killed a couple more demons then slowly turned and looked at Kanzser.

"I was enjoying myself," he challenged insolently. "Why do you disturb me?"

There were gasps of horror from some, but instead of being angry the Demon King laughed and clapped with delight. "Leave us."

The demons surrounding the creature scuttled thankfully away, hardly able to believe their good fortune, while those who'd gathered to watch simply melted into the shadows.

"Now, demon, what is your name?"

The creature towered over him, yet such was the aura of power surrounding Kanzser he was not dwarfed.

"What is your name?" he repeated. The creature said nothing but the look he gave was both defiant and unafraid.

He does not fear me! thought Kanzser, as something like exultation flooded through him. *Well, he will learn fear but there can be no doubt he is the one I've been searching for!*

"What is your name?" he repeated again, and this time the creature answered in a deep, rumbling bass.

"Who is asking?"

Now anger *did* threaten to overcome him. *Such insolence!* Yet he allowed no trace of it to show. "You don't know who I am?"

"I know," admitted the creature, sounding bored. "What is it to me?"

"Maybe nothing, maybe everything," replied Kanzser, and was rewarded with a spark of interest flaring in the creature's eyes. "Now, you were about to tell me your name?"

The creature hesitated, but then his curiosity got the better of him. "I have no name," he announced cautiously and, in a more conciliatory tone, "Why do you deign to speak to the likes of me?"

Kanzser paused before he replied. *This must be handled cautiously; this creature has pride, too much for its own good.* "I've seen you fight. You are talented, strong. I do not waste such talent. So, I have an offer for you."

"An offer?" Suspicion oozed from him. "What offer?"

"Not here." Kanzser managed to hide the slyness in his voice. "Accompany me back to my chamber and we will eat, drink and talk."

The creature opened its mouth to refuse and then stopped. It was many days since he'd eaten anything other than demon meat. He nodded. "So be it."

A short time later, they were sat at the huge dining table in the ornately decorated room where, centuries into the future, the Demon King would entertain the young Logan, manipulating him, turning him into the Dark Wizard he would become.

"So, Kanzser, what is your offer?" The creature used his name as if they were acquaintances, but he let it pass.

"Eat first, then we will talk." As if on cue, two servants entered bearing plates piled high with meat; deer, horse and others he'd never seen before. The creature noted with satisfaction that there was no demon meat; he was heartily sick of eating demon. As soon as the plates were on the table, he leaned forward eagerly then recoiled in disgust at the aroma of heavy spices.

Kanzser noticed the reaction and, like lightning, his hand shot out and took the nearest servant by the throat.

"How dare you serve this filth?" he growled dangerously. But the servant hardly had time for terror as its body went limp, the life squeezed from it. Kanzser dropped the body nonchalantly to the floor, already forgotten.

"My apologies." He regarded the creature with cunning. "You can kill the other one if you like."

The creature contemplated the pathetic figure of the remaining servant who now cowered before him. Fully a minute passed before he shrugged in a bored fashion.

"Go," he commanded at last, "bring more food, this time without the spice." But as the terrified demon scurried from the room, he snapped his fingers and it froze, shaking uncontrollably, certain its end had come. The creature pointed to the body on the floor. "And have someone get rid of that."

Excellent. Kanzser smiled secretly. *Already he learns to enjoy power!* He lifted a large jug from the table and proffered it to the creature. "Would you like wine?"

Chapter 19

The room swam before his eyes and the edges of his vision was beginning to star and go black. He became aware of a loud, thumping noise in his ears and a sound like waves rushing along the seashore, getting louder and louder.

He shook his head irritably, trying to clear his vision but only making it worse. Across the table he could dimly make out the figure who sat silent, watching. Suddenly he didn't feel well, and vomit surged into his throat. He swallowed it back, hurriedly and painfully, the acid scorching and corrosive.

What's happening to me? he thought, feeling the panic rise. He tried to stand but the floor tilted and he fell back into his chair.

"Is everything alright, my friend?" Kanzser's voice was rich with false concern. "You seem a little... disoriented."

"What have you done to me?" He felt detached, barely able to speak the words as a new wave of sickness overtook him.

"Oh, nothing really." The reply seemed to come from far away. "Just a little something in the wine."

The creature screwed his eyes and managed to bring Kanzser's features into focus. Then he lunged.

He shouldn't have been able to do that! Kanzser thought exultantly. *He is mighty indeed!* But the effort had taken the last of the creature's strength and even though he'd managed to get a hand around Kanzser's throat, he could not muster even the slightest squeeze. Kanzser laughed mockingly and swatted the hand away. "Sleep well, my friend."

And the creature crashed, unconscious, to the floor.

It wasn't the light that penetrated his subconscious, for in this rotting dungeon deep within the demon lair there was little, save that which came from the two burning torches set into the walls.

Nor was it the stink of rotting flesh from the hundreds of dead rats carpeting the stone floor, or the old blood that decorated the walls, a legacy from scores of the Demon King's victims. It was the sound of tapping, the clack-clack-clack of fingernails on wood. They were long and tapered almost to a point, encrusted with dried blood and excrement. As he tapped impatiently with one hand, its owner lifted the other and pushed a finger up into its large, hook-like nose and scooped out a big ball of mucus. As he sucked it with relish, he watched the creature gradually awaken.

At first everything was blurred, indistinct, but the creature's gaze was drawn immediately to the sound. Clack-clack-clack, repeated over and over, monotonous, penetrating. Then it stopped, and there followed a long pause.

"I see you are awake."

The words seemed shockingly loud in the now silent room and his head whipped toward the speaker. The movement caused a new sound, of chains rattling, and for the first time he became aware of the dull ache in his arms and shoulders. His vision cleared, and he saw the unmistakable figure of Kanzser sitting before him on a large, ornately carved wooden throne.

"What have you done, demon?" the creature hissed, his voice venomous, hatred pouring from his eyes. "What have you done?" He pulled violently against the chains, only to stifle a cry of pain as the manacles around his wrists bit cruelly into his flesh.

Kanzser flinched and pushed further back in his chair. He glanced uneasily at the chains that held his victim, relieved to see they were attached securely to the walls, embedded deep into the stone.

"Relax, my friend." The words rolled from his tongue as smoothly as castor oil and just as bitter. "I've simply made you my prisoner."

The creature howled with rage and thrashed violently from side to side in a futile attempt to escape. Soon the blood ran down his arms, but he was oblivious to the pain as he strived to reach his tormentor, becoming increasingly infuriated, eyes wild and blazing, teeth gnashing, and a torrent of incoherent threats and insults filling the air. Kanzser laughed and left the room.

At last he had the physical specimen he needed and now it was time to begin the second part of his plan. The idea had come to him long ago, when the demon had escaped the clutches of the wizard Cornelius and warned him of the creation of the blood moon. He'd killed it of course, strangled it actually; Kanzser didn't like bad news. But the idea had been stored, ready to use when the time was right. Now, he had the vehicle into which he would instill the most powerfully depraved magic imaginable, but he needed a source for that power.

Of course, the wizard would be ideal, but Kanzser had dismissed the impossibility. The legend of the wizard Cornelius had rung far and wide for many centuries; few had not heard it. But the making of a blood moon? Even Kanzser had not imagined such power.

But the witch? Powerful too. It was said that Cornelius's friend and companion was the most powerful of her kind. Kanzser had spat a huge gob of phlegm at the thought of those vermin. But he sensed her power was different; purer than the wizard's. It would need to be corrupted before he stole it from her.

She'd been relatively easy to find even though her name was unknown to him, and he'd soon learned of the estrangement between her and the wizard. Kanzser had grinned at that; it would make his task much easier.

He had used some of his rudimentary magic and all his vast cunning to disguise himself as a mortal and mix freely in all the villages far and near. By these means he'd soon learned her name, Mitra, and how enormously powerful she really was. Far from being daunted, he'd rubbed his hands together with glee, for he knew the more power she possessed, the more he could steal for his creature and the more successful his plan would be.

He'd entered her cottage as silently as a cat, yet she'd sensed his presence instantly and turned, standing from the fire she'd been tending. Mitra saw through his disguise immediately, for it could not hide the almost palpable aura of evil that surrounded him.

But years of peace in her land had made her careless and her wand, which should have been close by, was sitting out of reach on the kitchen table. And Kanzser was quick – oh, so very, very quick – and before she could cover even half the distance, he'd crossed the room and dealt her a vicious, back-handed blow which sent her crashing to the floor, unconscious.

By the time she awoke, it was already too late and she was doomed. It would have been kinder if she could have remained unconscious for longer, and kinder still if she'd never awakened at all.

Chapter 20

It was the suffocating warmth of the room and the cloying, alien stench of demons that woke her. As Mitra came slowly to her senses, she found she was laying upon something hard, a table perhaps, but her mind felt hazy, her thoughts detached. Her head felt heavy and it ached dully. She kept it still in an effort to ease the pain but in her peripheral vision she could see a network of thin tubes with some kind of red liquid coursing through them. Mitra glanced down at her body and realized she was naked; she instinctively tried to cover herself with her hands but found she couldn't move.

"You can't move." The voice came from somewhere to the side. "You are quite helpless." A figure moved into her vision, a vile, hideous-looking creature. Mitra knew instinctively who it was.

The Demon King, she thought, and all hope left her. *I will not leave here alive.* He looked at her lasciviously and drool fell from his mouth as he licked his lips. *I will not cry,* she told herself, determined despite the humiliation, which was almost worse than her terror at what he might do to her.

"There, there," he crooned softly, "don't look so upset, there really is no need." He stroked her head in a parody of tenderness and she felt the scraping of his hand, the rasping sound in her ears.

Rasping.

Scraping.

My hair, they've taken my hair. And now, unbidden, the tears ran silently down her cheeks. Mitra allowed them to fall for only a moment before blinking them away angrily, for she refused to let this monster see how much he frightened her. But when he approached, coming fully into her vision, and she saw his mean, cruel eyes with their calculating stare, his flaking, scaly hide with its suppurating sores, her spirits quailed.

He leaned close and she gagged at the stink of his hot, fetid breath. "Do not fear me." He had noticed her reaction. "I will not hurt you."

The lie was so obvious she felt an insane urge to laugh and it gave her momentary courage. "Liar!" she spat. "I am Mitra! Witch! I do not fear the likes of you!"

Kanzser threw back his head and laughed, a high-pitched cackle that rang out into the maze of passages that was his realm. "You do not fear me?" His laughter faded gradually. "Perhaps not." A long, rough finger stroked her cheek then moved to her neck, and she shuddered as it came to rest on the softly pulsing vein in her throat. "But soon, you will."

Mitra had almost forgotten her nakedness but now she tensed as that same finger traced a long, red welt between her breasts and onto her abdomen. There his hand rested lightly and somehow that was even worse, but her torment was only just starting as she felt him almost idly caress her navel. Again, tears squeezed from the corners of her tightly closed eyes, but this time they were tears not of fear but of humiliation and anger that he would violate her so.

"You can never hurt me, not ever! You and your kind,"—she rolled to one side and spat on the floor—"are nothing!"

If she'd hoped to illicit an angry response, Mitra was disappointed. Her tormentor merely grinned, displaying sharp, rotting teeth. Mitra had never wished for death, not once throughout her long life, but she prayed for it now, fervently and with longing.

But then, suddenly and without warning, he removed the hand and chuckled contemptuously. "You think I want that from you?" He gazed at her with his small, pig-like eyes and she shrank away, wondering what was coming next. "I have no interest in using you in that way; I have a much deeper plan in mind."

She had barely time to speculate what that might mean as he took two long strides to the door and flung it open.

"But they might."

Outside in the passage, clamoring for entry and prevented from doing so only by the will of their master, were about a dozen demons.

All naked.

And Mitra began to scream, silently, deep within herself.

Again, she prayed that death would intervene.

She was brought back to her senses by the sound of the door slamming back into its frame, so that the clamoring was abruptly stilled.

"Lift her." The Demon King's command was harsh and guttural and Mitra felt herself hauled roughly into a sitting position, legs still outstretched upon the table. For the first time she noticed the servant, who now placed rocks behind her to keep her upright, and could see the full extent of the room in which she was trapped. It was small and circular, without windows, lit only by candles made from the fat of dead demons, of which Kanzser's slave pits provided many. They emitted only a little light, mostly hidden by wisps of thin, black smoke. But poor though it was, she thought she could see another figure standing across the room and she strained her eyes to make it out.

"Ah, it is dark in here; you cannot see." The Demon King snapped his fingers and the guard moved to light more candles. "We must have more light! I need you to see exactly what awaits you."

But Mitra did not answer for she was retreating into that inner space that each of us has; that place deep inside our minds where nothing can harm us, and where we feel safe.

"Wake up, witch!" He snarled as he gripped her chin, causing his nails to dig painfully deep into her skin, drawing blood. "I said look at your fate!"

There was enough light now to see that the figure was huge, mostly demon but obviously part human. But it was motionless, unconscious or perhaps even dead; what harm could it do her?

"I don't understand," her voice croaked through dry, cracked lips as she glanced involuntarily at the door.

"You fear them?" Kanzser cackled with mirth and his gaze swept slowly along her nakedness, but she found she hardly cared anymore. "Well, so you should, witch; you really should!" He leaned in close to her once more and again she couldn't help shrinking away. "Can you smell them?" he whispered, almost gently. "Smell their desire? More candles!" He stood suddenly. "We need more light!"

And as the room brightened, she could see properly the tubes she had noticed earlier and she took in the scene with disbelief. Across the room stood a large tank filled with a red liquid she quickly realized was blood. From it, several thin tubes led to the demon, inserted into different orifices of his body. Her puzzlement lasted mere seconds as she followed the tube's path and saw that one led directly into her wrist. For the first time a horrified awareness began to dawn.

"Yessss... I see it begins to make sense." He walked over to the creature who still hung motionless by its chains. "This is what I call, affectionately I might add, the creature. And he is nearly dead; loss of blood you see."

Kanzser grinned evilly and Mitra turned even colder if that were possible, for she instinctively knew what he would say next. "He needs your blood," he said, immediately confirming her suspicions. "Oh, don't worry, he doesn't need all of it. You won't die. Not just yet." He turned a small tap at her wrist, and she felt a stinging sensation as her blood began to flow.

Chapter 21

The body of an average-sized woman holds around nine pints of blood. If one of these is lost, she may feel a little weak, dizzy perhaps, but it will pass; recovery is certain. Lose two pints though and things look very different; much more serious. Her body may go into shock and the organs start to fail. So if help doesn't arrive...

Three pints? Well, by now the organs are in big trouble and though she may still be alive, death is pretty much around the corner.

And more than three pints? Forget it.

In contrast, the average demon, be it male or female, requires much less, for their brains are smaller and they have fewer internal organs. They can afford to lose much more – as much as half even – and when this happens, they do not die, but enter a kind of suspended animation that gives their bodies time to replenish. Only when around three-quarters of the blood supply is lost is death guaranteed; it's one of the many reasons they are so hard to kill.

And it is why the creature, far from being dead, was merely unconscious, awaiting a fresh blood supply.

"You see, Mitra, it's a very delicate balance, mixing his blood,"—

he waved a hand at the creature—"with all its inherent wickedness, with your blood, it having such magical power." Kanzser shook his head in mock perplexity and hopped from side to side, lifting each upturned palm in turn as if weighing options.

"Too much wickedness, not enough magic?" He paused on one foot and lifted a questioning eyebrow. "Or..."—he hopped to the other foot and raised the opposite palm—"not enough wickedness and too much magic? Although you can never have too much magic, I suppose."

He nodded, satisfied, then slapped his hand hard against his forehead. "But you can never have enough wickedness either! My dear, I simply don't know what to do! It's such a conundrum!" He giggled, a mad, sinister sound. "What a predicament! And, of course, you human forms are so fragile; always the danger I might take too much and kill you!" He placed a mock-horrified look on his face. "Accidentally, of course, nothing personal!"

He stroked her cheek, which was cold and clammy to the touch, but she barely felt it. "How are you feeling? Not dying just yet, I hope!" He turned off the tap and the blood flow from her vein abruptly ceased. In truth, Mitra was feeling extremely nauseous and ill. She was cold and starting to shiver. But her spirit was as yet undimmed and she glared at him defiantly.

"Oh, okay,"—he shrugged—"not in a talkative mood." He patted her hand. "No matter." He turned the tap back on. "Now, let's see, I've taken about..."—he shrugged again—"well, who knows how much I've taken; it's not an exact science, is it?" He continued talking but she had begun to zone out.

Prattle on, you ridiculous creature, she thought, *you might kill me but you won't win. Cornelius's blood moon will get you in the end.* And, for the very first time in her long life, the thought of another living thing losing its life gave her pleasure.

"But I do applaud you for your gift," he was saying jovially. "Your blood is reviving my experiment. Look!"

Mitra looked up and, sure enough, now that most of the shadows had been banished, she could see the creature was indeed stirring, while she felt weaker by the second. She watched as her lifeblood flowed through the tube and into its veins, but now she was having difficulty concentrating and for the first time she experienced a sense of impending doom.

"Not long now," he whispered softly, almost crooning, into her ear. "It's a shame, witch, that your agony couldn't have lasted longer." He stood abruptly and clapped his hands. "But, hey-ho," he exclaimed loudly in a sing-song voice, "can't have everything!"

The creature was fully awake now, aware of its surroundings and beginning to thrash against the chains with which it was held.

"Quiet, you!" he snarled at the creature, who took no notice and thrashed even harder. "No consideration for others." Kanzser shook his head as he turned back to her. "But as I was saying, your agony, not finished yet." He winked. "The best is yet to come; or the worst." He shrugged. "Depends on your point of view."

His attempts at levity were wasted, for Mitra no longer cared; his words were meaningless. Her breathing was shallow now and her heart rate had slowed to almost nothing. She was close to death.

"No! No, no!" Kanzser was suddenly frantic. "No you don't! Not yet anyway!"

And almost at once, Mitra felt herself reviving, but far from being a pleasurable sensation, she felt no relief, only horror. Strange feelings of hatred were entering her mind and she, who had never harmed a living soul, began fantasizing about killing and causing pain, suffering and misery.

Kanzser, seeing his captive on the point of death, had quickly snatched the glass tube still attached to the creature, broke it in two, and jammed the end into his own artery.

Now it was his own blood that revived her. Suddenly, what was left of the contents of her stomach gushed into her throat, acidic and scalding, before it vomited from her mouth and hit Kanzser full in the face. Far from recoiling in disgust, he grinned delightedly and licked it away with his long, snake-like tongue. Where it had gone into his eyes, he wiped it away almost daintily with a fingernail, which he then sucked with relish.

"That was close!" He pulled out the tube and summoned one of the guards to come nearer. "But we need you full of strength if you are to enjoy the next bit!" Without preamble, his hand shot forward and tore a long, jagged wound from right to left across the guard's chest and Mitra gagged when she saw the exposed heart.

"Shove that in and stay there," he ordered, and the guard, without so much as flinching, rammed the end of the glass tube into the red, pulsing organ. He watched dispassionately as now his own blood poured into Mitra, but powerless to prevent it, she could not bear to watch. "Now you,"—Kanzser moved toward the creature—"shut up and listen."

Chapter 22

A fortnight had passed and still Mitra lived. He had not, of course, allowed his demons to harm her; she was far too valuable for that. Having no further use for her, it had been the Demon King's plan to dispatch her immediately, but somehow, the knowledge that she lay there in his darkest dungeon, terrified of the fate which awaited her, was all the more pleasurable. His anticipation was building nicely but soon he must be done with it for he had a more pressing problem at hand, and he needed no distractions.

Tomorrow, he promised himself. *She will die tomorrow.*

Kanzser thrust her from his mind and considered the difficulty he was having with the creature. Gradually during the previous two weeks, it had become apparent that he had bestowed upon it far more power than he had intended, or was wise.

It's not an exact science.

The words he had spoken to the witch were coming back to haunt him and the creature was becoming – had *become* – a real problem. Oh, it had been quiet enough in those first few days while it fully regained its strength and as its body adjusted to the massive influx of magic it had received.

But then... Kanzser shook his head ruefully... the magic had begun. Low level to start with, making things disappear, causing objects to levitate, that kind of thing. But soon the creature had learned to use his magic to control things; living things.

How long before he learns to control me?

It had started with solitary demons spontaneously bursting into flame or turning on each and fighting, neither stopping until it had murdered the other. Soon a pattern developed as Kanzser realized these occurrences only happened when he himself was nearby. *As if the creature seeks to prove a point,* he thought. *Or send a warning...*

*   *   *   *

How long will he keep me here, alive? And why?

Mitra did not lack courage and she knew her death was approaching, had long since resigned herself.

But when? And how?

The latter was the hardest, not knowing how she would meet her fate. No doubt it would not be pleasant and trying to anticipate what the Demon King intended tested her courage most of all.

Following his departure with the creature, still weak and leaning heavily on his shoulder, Mitra had taken stock of her predicament. As the blood from the demon guard still poured into her veins, she'd looked around for a means of escape but quickly realized there was none. Even if she hadn't been strapped down, the door was made of iron and would be heavy to open. Anyway, she had distinctly heard the sound of the lock turning as the Demon King left.

She'd felt another flutter of panic as she realized the guard would have caught her anyway, before she could cover half the distance. And what if, by some miracle, she did escape into the passage? She didn't know the way out of this cursed place, and she was alone amongst goodness knew how many of these vile creatures.

If she'd had her wand, it would have been different, but it was gone; even the Demon King was not so stupid as to leave that within reach. A witch and her wand have an inseparable bond, each lost without the other, and she realized, sadly, that she would almost certainly never see it again.

These thoughts had flashed by in seconds and before she knew it the guard had pulled the glass tube from his own heart and from her vein. He released the leather straps that held her arms and legs, not so much unfastening them as tearing them apart as if they were no more than paper. For a wild moment she thought, *this is my chance!* But the guard read her thoughts accurately and gripped her arm painfully, shaking his head in warning. The opportunity, not that there had been one really, was gone. Still, her strength had returned and she'd felt better able to face whatever the Demon King had in store for her.

But now that seemed an age ago and since then her spirit had eroded, little by little with each day that passed. Her witch senses enabled her to keep a reasonably accurate track of the movements of the sun and moon, even though it seemed an age since she had last seen either. She knew with relative certainty that thirteen days had passed since she'd been taken from that room and thrown into this deep, dark cell.

Thirteen days!

When will it end?

The superstitious might say she should not have tempted fate. The more rational-minded might have pointed out her fate would have come to her sooner or later anyway. As it was, it was at the precise moment these thoughts entered her mind that she heard a noise.

A noise she recognized, for she had heard it before.

Thirteen days ago.

Her entire body went cold as the sounds of clamoring and grunting excitement grew louder. She hurried to the door of her cell and peered through its tiny, barred window. The passage outside was thronged with demons.

And Mitra began to scream.

Not silently this time but loud and shrill so that it rang across the entire demon world.

Kanzser was sitting in one of his personal chambers when he heard the scream. Behind him stood one servant, kneading and massaging the knots in his shoulders, while another knelt before him and oiled the muscles of his thighs, each touch sending waves of contentment and pleasure through his body. Yet another servant fed him sweet cakes, especially made for him, and held to his lips a great goblet that brimmed with wine.

Yet, pleasurable as all this was, it paled into insignificance at the ecstasy he felt from hearing that scream. He considered rousing himself to go and watch but really, he was just far too comfortable...

Just then, the door slammed open and the creature stormed in. Kanzser sat up hurriedly and, not wishing the servants to witness his fear, dismissed them. They scurried quickly and thankfully past the creature, who noticed them not at all.

"Demon, no more! I have shown forbearance, but enough! Acknowledge me as your Lord and master or I will prove to you that I am!" His face was centimeters from Kanzser, who flinched and shrank away from the snarling creature. "I want this realm," he continued in a low, dangerous growl. "It has been yours for too long. Now it is mine!"

With that final shout, he placed a finger under the table's edge and flipped it, sending it spinning violently across the room to smash against the far wall.

Despite his fear, Kanzser was stung. "Never!" he cried. "It is *mine!* You will never—"

The sentence was cut off abruptly as a huge hand clamped around his throat and squeezed. Kanzser was no weakling; all demons were immensely strong but even he was powerless to resist.

"Stop. Please," he croaked as his vision began to star. "There is no need." And a final, desperate gamble, "Remember it was I who gifted you your power!"

Whether it was this timely reminder or perhaps his plea for mercy, the Demon King didn't know; he cared only that the creature chose that moment to release him.

"You remind me of the need for gratitude," it said softly, "and for that I am sorry."

Kanzser gaped in astonishment. Demons never expressed gratitude or sorrow, it was utterly alien to them. Despite his near brush with death, he began to laugh and the creature waited patiently as he wiped tears of mirth from his eyes.

"You're joking, right? Gratitude? You feel gratitude? It's not poss—"

"You see, Kanzser," the creature interrupted, "you have no inkling of what you have created." It sat and helped itself to the goblet of wine which Kanzser, somehow, still held in his grip. "You have destroyed the witch, who did you no harm. And in doing so you have given me immense power to add to my already prodigious strength."

He took a deep drink from the flagon. "In doing what you did, you gave me an infinitesimal amount of her goodness too; her humanity, if you will. I don't want it and will find a means to eradicate it, but for now it is a part of me." It was a long speech and the creature's face turned red with the effort, giving him an even fiercer aspect.

"You should be thankful, Kanzser; it's the reason I haven't killed you. Yet." He paused to let that sink in before he continued, "You had no idea just how much power she possessed, did you? But she was the most powerful witch of her age, perhaps of any age. How ironic that you should seek to create an equal, someone to continue your line should the blood moon strike you down; which it will, by the way. You sought to make me part demon and part witch in equal measure so that I would be immune."

The eloquence of the creature was almost as frightening as its power it. Kanzser had sought to create something unintelligent and pliable, easily bent to his will; it was dawning on him just how badly he had failed.

"And you have succeeded! The blood moon cannot harm me!" He stooped and prodded him in the chest. "But you have also failed; I am more witch than demon or human." He stood abruptly and, for the first time, raised himself to his full height. With arms lifted high above his head, he shouted, "And I have *power!*"

The word resonated around the room with such force that tiny cracks appeared in the stone walls.

"Now watch demon. Watch and learn!"

The room was suddenly cast with a deep, red glow and Kanzser flinched, knowing exactly what it was. *Treachery! He has tricked me! He invokes the blood moon! I am betrayed!* As these crazed thoughts raced through his mind, the stone walls faded to reveal the maze of passages that was his kingdom. Except it was crumbling into dust and the very ceiling above was crumbling, falling, crushing him...

And the room returned to normal. There was the creature, intent on refilling the wine goblet as if nothing had happened. He glanced at Kanzser sardonically.

"Mere illusion, but prophecy also, for what you have just witnessed will come to pass. But it is far in the future; do not look so stricken!" He glanced pointedly at the large pool of urine by the Demon King's feet and said with mocking sympathy, "There is really no need to panic. Not yet."

"Why you!" Kanzser reached for the knife in his belt and prepared to throw it, only to find himself flung across the room to crash with such force against the wall it would have killed a weaker being.

"I did that with a mere thought, Kanzser. It is useless to try and kill me, you cannot win." This was said with such certainty that Kanzser needed no further convincing. Nevertheless, the creature hadn't quite finished. "Watch."

A huge crack appeared across the floor and from it belched flames and acrid smoke and the room was filled instantly with overpowering heat. Deep inside, Kanzser could see his slave pits with its hundreds of creatures wielding their picks and spades, their hammers and knives.

Once they entered the pits, the average lifespan of these doomed demons was a mere month or two before their flesh melted from their bones in the stupendous heat and their once great strength failed them at last. Yet still they worked without surcease, morning and night, seeking to eke out another few hours of their miserable lives. But even the braver specimens soon lost their will to fight back as the endless quest to remain alive continued.

But now they weren't working; they were looking up. And some had begun to climb, as Kanzser saw to his horror, at great speed, scaling the sheer walls and getting closer by the second.

"If they reach the top, they will kill you," the creature informed him matter-of-factly, but Kanzser had no answer, rendered speechless by his approaching doom. Then the first of the slaves scaled the top and were upon him, wielding great hammers and knives which began to rain down upon him relentlessly. Yet he felt no pain and heard the creature laugh derisively as each figure faded into nothing and the illusion disappeared and the crack closed.

"See? You cannot win; do you accept that now, demon? Will you give me your realm?"

Kanzser was no fool and knew he was beaten, at least for the moment. With his innate sense of self-preservation, he knew how to wait and fight another day. And just then, that same self-preservation presented him with an idea, one so audacious...

He lowered his eyes and bowed his head slightly as if in submission. "Certainly, I did not dream you held so much power... stupid of me not to realize... you may take my world; it is yours."

There was a long pause while the creature assessed him suspiciously, searching for trickery or deceit. With perfect timing, Kanzser waited until he was about to speak then broke in with a single word; now looking the creature straight in the eye. "But." The creature stiffened. "You said yourself you are more witch than demon,"—he sensed the creature was about to interrupt and went on hurriedly—"and witches prefer to see the sky, to dwell in wide, open spaces, not in dark, cramped tunnels." Kanzser took a deep breath. "What if I could show you such a world? Give it to you?"

The creature had been about to shout and scream his frustration, possibly even to kill this devious demon. But now he paused. "Go on. Supposing there were such a place, what would you want in return?"

Kanzser took another deep breath. This really was now or never, for he realized with sudden clarity that he could never willingly give up his realm. He would keep it or die in the attempt.

"I keep my world, you have yours. We live side by side but in different dimensions, never to meet again."

The creature turned away and was lost in thought for many minutes while Kanzser waited. He thought he might expire in an agony of suspense, but the creature finally nodded.

"Show me," he commanded.

It did not take long for them to traverse a way through the network of passages until they stood in a small, circular chamber which, unlike those of the Demon King's realm, had been formed naturally when the dimensions were created, long ago.

But, unknown to its creators, it contained a flaw, a tiny crack less than the width of a mortal hair but which, had it been wider, would provide a gateway between two dimensions; one that should never have existed.

And of course, it did get wider; Kanzser had made certain of that. After all, one never knew when such a gateway might come in useful. And now at last it had and this creature definitely looked interested! Kanzser had never been through, for he'd never been certain of getting back. For all he knew, doors between dimensions might be one way or something.

Let it find out for itself, he thought. *All I need to do is find a way to stop it coming back.*

"What do you think?" He tried and failed to keep his anxiety from showing. But the creature appeared not to have noticed and was nodding slowly.

"The sky is blue, the sun is shining," he said. "I like that." There was another long pause until, at last, the creature nodded decisively. "I accept your offer, demon."

Well, thank goodness it wasn't raining, Kanzser thought illogically, as he almost wept with relief.

"But."

I knew it was too good to be true.

"If I find you have misled me, if this world does not live up to your promises, I will return." The look he gave was cold and devoid of emotion. "And there will be no mercy."

"Relax,"—Kanzser tried to look nonchalant—"you will find it exactly as I described." He winced inwardly. "I have visited it many times."

"Well then,"—the creature nodded, satisfied—"pray we do not meet again."

"Wait."

The creature's head turned slowly, lithesome as a cat. Even now he suspected trickery and raised a questioning eyebrow.

"What is your name?"

The question seemed too random and the creature's eyes narrowed suspiciously. "You waste my time, demon. I have no name, or if I do it is long forgotten. Why do you ask? If you plan falsehood at this late hour..."

"No falsehood," Kanzser assured him earnestly, "simply that such a magnificent being as yourself has never been seen before. You are indeed a wondrous creation. Thanks to me," he added, pointedly.

"Your point?"

"My point is you *do* owe me a debt and I would have you repay it by ensuring that history remembers you are my creation. And for that to happen, you will need a name."

"Yes, I owed you a debt," the creature agreed, "and I've repaid it by allowing you to live. And to keep your kingdom." He turned half away but his curiosity was piqued. "You've already thought of a name, I suppose?"

"As a matter of fact, I have," Kanzser confirmed, modestly. "It is a name to encompass your immense power, your vast array of talents, your—"

"Yes, yes," the creature interrupted. "What is the name?"

"You shall be called Necromancer!" Kanzser flung the name out proudly. "It is a name that hints at your magnificence."

The creature ignored him and tried out the unfamiliar word. After he had repeated it several times, he looked long and hard at the Demon King before he nodded. "I like it," he admitted, "except for one thing."

Now it was Kanzser's turn to raise a questioning eyebrow.

"I am an individual, a one-off. There has never been, nor will there be in the future another such as I. And therefore..."—he turned and faced his new domain, and he was a formidable, fearsome spectacle —"I am... *The* Necromancer!"

Chapter 23

Kanzser watched for a long time until the Necromancer was a tiny dot in the distance, for he was taking no chances on him breaking his promise. As one who lived by lies and deceit, Kanzser did not trust that the Necromancer would not, after all, return to claim the demon world for his own.

But how to prevent it? Therein lay the problem.

Post guards? Pointless.

Raise an army against him? The idea had some merit but...

The Necromancer has such power! What if my army is not sufficient?

Cause a cave-in? Collapse this room and all the tunnels around it? Again, pointless.

Kanzser shook his head in frustration. He could do nothing to prevent the Necromancer from entering his realm, should he wish.

How did I get into this mess? I regret the day I found that creature and plucked it from obscurity. And this is how it repays me!

By this time Kanzser was almost nearing his own suite of rooms, a servant, who should have recognized its master's bad temper and kept out of the way, paid the price for its stupidity as Kanzser took it by the throat.

"Why does he repay me thus?" He shook the servant violently. "Why?" But the demon was already dead and he flung it to one side in disgust. "Stupid! Stupid! Stupid!" He slammed the side of his head with his fist at each word. "Stupid!" Feeling slightly dizzy, he entered his chamber and flung himself into the chair. "Nothing short of magic can prevent him from coming back. Magic I do not possess!"

The table lay in ruins against the far wall, but the flagon of wine stood on the floor beside the chair, remarkably still intact, and he poured a generous measure.

My magic is rudimentary at best.

It was a rare admission for one who despised weakness, particularly in himself. He raised the goblet to his lips but before the first drop of wine could touch, he stopped as a thought slammed suddenly into his brain. He threw aside the goblet and sprang to his feet.

Kanzser ran more quickly than he had in a very long time, down the series of passages that led to the very lowest depths of his realm. He was still a hundred meters away when her screams, little more than whimpers now, reached his ears and his hopes surged.

The witch still lives!

Kanzser crashed through her cell door and was confronted by a crowd of laughing, leering demons gathered around the bloodied and bruised, barely recognizable figure of the witch.

The demons were taking it in turns to throw Mitra to each other, like a bizarre and twisted game of Pass the Parcel. The winner would take her as its prize. Only an hour previously the sight would have delighted him, but now he was incensed, and the unfortunate demon who was about to throw her next felt the full force of his fury. It had no time to react as Kanzser, with a scream of anger, took hold of its head with both hands and twisted violently. Then, before its lifeless body had even hit the floor, he had gathered the witch in his arms and ran from the cell, leaving the other demons to look at each other in puzzlement and terror.

Mitra had just enough presence of mind to grab her robe from where it had lain beside her and she concealed her nakedness. As Kanzser reached the upper levels and stopped, panting for breath, he dumped her to the floor.

"You can walk from here," he snarled. "Get on your feet."

As she lay there, too weak to move, she wondered, dully, *what new torture does he have for me now?*

"I said, get up, witch!" He kicked her viciously.

Despite her exhaustion and despite the pain that racked her body, Mitra found the strength to smile at him, a smile filled with hatred and contempt. "Make me, demon. Make me or kill me."

Kanzser howled angrily, snatched her by the arm and yanked her half to her feet. Mitra bit her lip, determined not to cry out at the excruciating agony of tearing ligaments as he dragged her along and at the humiliation when he kicked her each time she fell.

He howled again with frustration as she fell once more, and this time he left her where she lay and stomped furiously up the corridor to find his servants.

"You!" he yelled at the first two he came across. "Carry her and follow me!" They scurried hurriedly to obey as Kanzser spied another servant. "And you,"—he flung a large, iron key—"my chambers; fetch her wand. Quickly!"

And with that, he walked swiftly to the room where he had bid farewell to the Necromancer, his servants frantically trying to keep pace, terrified of his anger.

Chapter 24

"Stand up."

Mitra felt the sting of the knife at her throat and thought about refusing his demand. Not so long ago she had longed for the blessing of death but now it seemed there was a chance for life and her unquenchable spirit was urging her to grasp it.

I want to live!

But she had her pride.

No! Do not give him what he wants!

But Mitra, despite the horrors she had endured, really, *really* wanted to live a little longer at least. Even if it was just long enough to see her friends once more, to see Cornelius, to explain why she could never see him again, even though she loved him still.

"Remove your knife. I will do as you ask."

"You will do it with the knife at your throat, witch," Kanzser snarled. He pressed the knife more firmly into her skin and a thin trickle of blood ran down her neck. "Make one false move and you will die." He nodded to the servant, who unfolded the cloth in which her wand had been wrapped and handed it to her, gingerly, careful not to touch the wand itself.

Mitra took it, and for a few moments basked in the comfort it gave. Momentarily she forgot her surroundings, the horrors she had endured and the bleakness of her future. But she was only allowed a brief respite before he barked, "Get on with it."

Jolted back to reality, she nodded. "This door you want, what shape would you like it to be?"

"I don't care. Just *do* it." The knife pressed deeper, cutting cruelly into her flesh. "Do not think to distract me, witch. I can cut your throat faster than you can raise a wand against me."

Perhaps, you fool. Perhaps not. Mitra forced her mind to go still, to dull the pain and forget the precarious thread that kept her from death. Then she began.

First she drew a circle, encompassing the gap in the rock wall, ensuring she did it very slowly, emitting a high-pitched screech. As expected, the demons cowered away, hunched on the floor, trying to drown out the painful cacophony. Kanzser, of course, was holding the knife and could not do so. When the din finally stopped he was sweating profusely.

"Quietly." He gripped her arm painfully with his free hand. "Do it *quietly*."

"Or you'll do *what,* exactly?" she mocked. Kanzser's only response was to twist the knife in the open wound on her neck and she gasped with pain.

Touching her wand against the rock wall, the incantations began to take hold, slowly at first then quicker and urgently. Soon her body swayed, undulating gracefully as she became totally lost in the spell. As she drew the pictures that formed in her mind, her wand flowed up, down, sideways like a conductor controlling the most exquisite of orchestras. In her mind's eye her hair, now only a stubble, flew wildly and passionately as she moved. She remembered fondly how Cornelius had liked to immerse his hands deep within its soft luster as he kissed her.

Faintly at first, then brighter until they were incandescent silver, lines appeared within the circle.

It's a lock, thought Kanzser. *She's actually done it; a door with its own lock.* Until then he hadn't been completely certain the witch could do it.

Pretty good, she thought, admiring her handiwork for a moment as, with a final flourish, she completed her task. Then, with an almost dismissive flick of her wand, the lines became invisible and there was just solid rock once more.

"You have done well," he admitted. *What it is to have such power,* he thought jealously. *Too much power. She cannot be allowed to live.* "But how does it open? The lock is invisible."

"*Of course* it's invisible," she replied. "You asked for a *hidden* door." Mitra found she was enjoying herself. *Now for the best bit.* She laughed silently.

Kanzser flushed. "Of course I understand that," he hissed. He was sorely tempted to hit her, or even better, give her to one of his demons. But he dared not remove the knife from her throat.

"Put your hand into the rock."

"Why?" he asked, suspicious.

"It is the only way to reach the lock mechanism."

Tentatively, he placed his free hand on the wall and found, to his surprise, that it was soft and yielding as he pressed. He thrust his hand further and was met with an excruciating, scalding sensation.

"You bitch!" He hugged his hand to his body as he soaked up the pain, almost losing control of the knife in his other hand.

She smirked. "Well, you don't want anyone to be able to open it easily, do you?"

"Very clever," he admitted sourly. "You are right."

"You saw how the mechanism became visible?" Her eyes challenged him. "Put your hand in again and turn the lock."

Bracing himself, he did so, and once more the agony was immense. But the door swung open and daylight flooded the chamber.

"It's incredible." Kanzser was impressed, despite himself. "You have done well."

Mitra tensed, ready to act if, as she expected, the knife was thrust into her throat.

"Now, throw your wand to the floor."

"No."

"You dare defy me?" he shouted. The blade cut more deeply and her blood flowed freely. "I could kill you now!"

"You could," she agreed. "But I would blast you into a trillion atoms before I died." There was silence as Kanzser weighed up the threat. "Got yourself into a bit of a predicament, haven't you?" she goaded. Lightning fast, Mitra spun away from the knife, performed a perfect pirouette and leveled her wand at the Demon King. "Are you ready to die, demon?"

Kanzser glared, hatred dripping from his eyes. "It seems you have the upper hand." He laughed easily, then shrugged nonchalantly, playing for time as he half turned away. Then with equal speed, the knife hurtled toward Mitra's head, but she knocked it to one side with a casual twitch of her wand.

"Oh dear." She smiled. "It seems you've played your *final* hand."

"Kill me then, witch!" Kanzser challenged as, terrified and desperate, he tried to prolong his life. "But there is another, stronger than even I. Will you kill him also? Will you, when he is a part of you?"

At his words, there was a sudden roaring inside Mitra's head. The events of the last weeks ran with perfect clarity, like a movie in her mind, and the grip on her wand tightened. Every act of torture she'd endured, every humiliation was played in vivid technicolor as the roaring increased and became unbearable.

Kill him! Do it! Kill him! The voices in her head urged her, becoming louder and more insistent. *Kill him!*

Mitra raised her wand and the words of the incantation crowded into her mouth, clamoring to be let out.

But as her mouth opened, another image entered her vision. An image from long ago. It was a demon, naked and terrified. And blood. And the moon turning red as the creature died. And her words, "*Why Cornelius, why?*"

She breathed a long, shuddering breath and clamped her mouth shut. Her wand lowered slightly. "No," she said, a little shakily. "Your end will come, demon, that much I prophesize." Kanzser flinched at her words; a witch's curse was not to be taken lightly. "But not at my hand. I will not murder. I will not become like you." With that, she stepped backwards through the open doorway, flung a last triumphant look at the Demon King, and slammed it shut.

All need for defiance gone, Mitra sank to her knees and gripped her head, squeezing it hard in a futile attempt to make the images disappear. This only made them more persistent and she clenched both hands into bony fists and hit herself, repeatedly, until her face was a bloody mask of cuts and bruises.

And at last, as it dawned on her the images would never give her peace, all she could do was scream.

Watching her from a short distance away, the Necromancer felt a curious regret at the witch's anguish, knowing that he could not have been created without her. Eventually her screams faded and she rose to her feet. Swaying in her exhaustion, she hobbled unsteadily away from the door.

Realizing that even her great mind had been unable to withstand this fresh onslaught, the Necromancer allowed her to leave his realm, knowing she was broken at last and could never pose a threat to him.

And there the story of Mitra ended; except it had remained in the Landlord's mind for many centuries, often lying dormant, deep within his consciousness but always ready to surface when least expected. And when it did, he would replay the events over in his mind as he was doing now, as he had done so many times. The guilt never lessened, always there to haunt him.

To his surprise, Cissy and Penelope had already left the cottage; she would return to her parent's home before returning to the Sanctuary. The Landlord hoped the girl would be allowed to return with Cissy rather than having to stay with her parents in the mortal world which, in his opinion, was really rather boring.

He sighed and looked around the little cottage for the last time. He would miss it, he supposed; it was lovely here. But soon he would be back in his beloved world, away from the doings of wizards and the like. He thrust the last remnants of his memories deep inside, closed the cottage door behind him, and walked out onto the village street.

Soon he had left the small collection of houses behind and clambered over dry stone walls and into the fields. The sea was an iridescent shade of blue and he had to shield his eyes from the silver speckles of sunlight on the water. For a while he watched the brightly colored fishing boats as they bobbed along, eager for their next catch, then he turned his attention to the lighthouse which stood, as it had for centuries, overlooking the ocean.

He reached it with a few strides of his long legs and, checking to see he was unobserved, spoke the incantation. With a final look around, he pushed open the small, iron-studded door that had appeared and ducked into the portal that would take him to 17th Century Wales, and home.

PART THREE

Chapter 25

It was around mid-morning on a Sunday in the mortal world and there were few people about on Old Kent Road when Logan and his new companion, Myla, stepped cautiously from the Corridor of Dimensions and into the circular room.

It is strange, is it not, how a person's entire life can be determined by the most innocuous of circumstances? Our whereabouts at a particular time, not a minute earlier or later, the events that place us there and what we happen to be doing the exact moment something else happens. All of these can and do alter the course of our lives without us even realizing it.

And that's how it was for the little girl in the red coat.

She was a pretty child with her blue eyes and blonde curls. Nine years old and so very excited at today's birthday treat: a visit to the *Harry Potter* studio in Watford.

Of course, if her mother had been paying more attention, it might not have happened, but perhaps she shouldn't be blamed. She'd got home late from her part-time job in the pub a mile or so from her home, fallen into a deep sleep, only to be awakened what seemed minutes later by the strident, piercing alarm of her iPhone – which she promptly snoozed, not waking up again until fully two hours later. Much later than she had intended. And much later than fate had decreed. Or perhaps fate had decided to play a monstrous joke.

So now she was quite unable to enjoy her daughter's excited chatter. Instead, she peered into the shop window at her reflection, hairbrush in one hand, lipstick in the other, trying to make herself presentable.

If only she'd had the time to do that at home.

If only she hadn't accepted that extra shift; but money was so *very* tight.

If only she hadn't snoozed the alarm.

If only… two of the saddest words ever spoken.

And so, on this quiet Sunday morning on the Old Kent Road in the heart of London, the pretty little girl in the red coat just happened to be in the wrong place at the wrong time. Nine years old today, chattering excitedly, bubbling with happiness; ignored by her mother who had too much on her mind.

Had she been looking along the road, in the direction they'd just come, or the other way to watch for the arrival of the eagerly awaited bus… instead of staring at the lamppost across the road. The lamppost that was old and different, not like the ones she was used to. Different enough to excite a mild curiosity.

Curious enough for her to stare at the tiny door near the bottom. The door which was starting to open.

If only.

It wasn't until he was halfway through the doorway into the mortal world that the Dark Wizard remembered he hadn't used a glamour, nor did he have a wand with sufficient power to make one. Even he, uncaring as he usually was, knew the importance of hiding the existence of his kind from the mortal race.

"Quickly!" He grabbed the goblin by the arm and pulled her bodily through. "We need a glamour!"

While Myla fumbled for her wand, Logan noticed the two mortals. The woman had her back to him, engrossed in something in the window, but the girl was staring right at him!

Unlike Morgan, who dedicated much of his life to protecting the mortal race, his brother detested them as inferior beings and hated them disproportionately. So it was that, far from feeling threatened at being seen, Logan felt anger; anger and the need to cause harm.

Without a wand, his shape-shifting abilities were drastically weakened but still he made a fair attempt at frightening the girl. His face twisted horribly, his eyeballs almost popped from his skull and his ears became elongated and pointed. It was enough to send the girl scuttling behind her mother's legs to hide beneath the folds of her coat. When she summoned the courage to look again, Logan had disappeared beneath the glamour.

Hmmm... he thought. *Not quite the reaction I was hoping for.*

He felt cheated somehow as he watched, dissatisfied, as the girl stepped warily from behind her mother and looked up and down the road, a puzzled expression on her face. Impulsively, he retook Myla's arm and led her across the road. The girl noticed a slight shaking of the air, caused by the glamour, and stared at it intently. Thus, when Logan chose that moment to reveal himself by thrusting his shoulders forward, she saw only a head. A head without a body, a head that hovered in the air, its eyes jet black, eyebrows arched above them, giving the face a demonic aspect.

But it was the mouth that was most terrible. It grinned, revealing a row of long, needle-like incisors, and as her eyes widened in shock, those terrible teeth snapped forward suddenly as if to bite her. As she jumped backward, the pretty little girl with the blue eyes and blonde hair saw deep into its throat, to the fire that burned there and the tiny people, naked and hairless, trapped within the flames, arms outstretched toward her, clamoring to be set free.

It was then that the girl began to scream, and it was at that moment, as her young mind began to fragment, that the little girl in the red coat, with an insight beyond her years, knew she would feel neither young nor pretty nor happy ever again.

Unheeding that he'd condemned the girl to a life of misery, Logan immediately forgot her, suddenly anxious to be back in the lonely, derelict mansion he called home.

Alerted by the screams that rang out in the still morning air, a crowd gathered, buzzing with excitement, eager to know what had happened. Some were keen to be heard, casting their judgments about cruelty and child abuse. Others nudged each other and nodded wisely in agreement.

One woman made the mistake of approaching the little girl, only to be met with a further barrage of screams. The woman scuttled back to the safety of the crowd and attempted to hide her embarrassment by shouting at the mother.

"What have you done to that child? You should be ashamed of yourself!" Others immediately took this up as the herd mentality clicked securely into place. "Yeah, you bitch!" and "Hanging's too good for the likes of you!"

The few braver souls who tried to caution reason found some of the abuse redirected upon themselves and, as the scene threatened to become ugly, several police cars and an ambulance arrived. A hurried discussion took place, then the paramedics took charge and one scooped the girl into his arms and into the waiting ambulance. The doors slammed and it slowly forced its way through the reluctant throng. With nothing more to see, the crowd dispersed to their homes, the pleasing prospect of their Sunday dinners, and the even more delicious anticipation of an afternoon's gossip.

*   *   *   *

Cissy closed the door of her home behind her with a faint feeling of relief. It seemed an age since she used to wish her father, who'd worked very long hours, could spend more time at home. Now he hardly left her side and even more unusually, neither did her mother, who'd always been a no-nonsense, slightly aloof kind of parent.

She knew the reason for it of course and she couldn't really blame them. Involuntarily she looked up at her bedroom window where she had crashed through in the grip of the demon who had kidnapped her and taken her to the Dark Wizard.

How long ago it seems!

No, she couldn't blame her parents, and she did love them dearly, but the atmosphere at home had quickly become stultifying; there they were now at the living room window, waving, her mother bravely holding back her tears.

Cissy's mother had argued fiercely against allowing their daughter to return to the Sanctuary, but as he often did, her father had supported her.

So, there she was, waving to her parents, sad to leave them but excited at the thought of seeing her friends again. She closed the garden gate, gave a final wave, and walked off down the street, her strides lengthening as soon as she was out of sight of the house.

Before long she was almost running, but even so, she'd hardly reached the end of the street before a car passed by, beeped its horn and pulled in front of her. Cissy grinned as she opened the door and got in. "Hi, Dad."

"Hey, sweetheart." He looked a little embarrassed. "I didn't see the point in you walking all that way."

"Dad, it's not far."

"Yeah, I know, but your mother..." He didn't need to finish the sentence and they drove silently for a while. Presently, they turned onto Old Kent Road and after a hundred meters or so he slowed the car so Cissy could look across at the shop doorway, still in shadow with no sign of life inside, where Molly had first met Luke and all their adventures had begun.

They drove on, but gradually the car was forced to a crawl by the crowds of people, many of them walking on the road.

"What's going on?" Charles was puzzled. "There isn't a soccer match today, is there?"

"It's football, Dad," Cissy corrected. "And no, I don't think so." She turned to watch as an ambulance passed them going the other way, also at a crawl. Then the crowds thinned and at last Charles Hamilton stopped the car and turned to his daughter.

"Well, this is it." He smiled bravely.

"I guess so," she agreed brightly, hoping he wouldn't embarrass them both by crying or something.

"Anyway," he said, "final instructions from Mum." He held up his fingers. "Number one, make sure you get your five-a-day; plenty of fruit and veg. Number two—"

"Dad," she interrupted, half annoyed, half amused, "we don't have time. And you're parked on a double yellow line."

"I know. But what's the worst that can happen? Anyway, if I were you, I'd worry more about how you're gonna manage to get inside without being seen. There are still quite a few people around."

Cissy smiled at her father's clumsy attempts to delay her. "But you're forgetting something," she said, knowing he hadn't forgotten at all. "I'm a witch now." She took out her wand. "I can make a glamour."

He grinned. "Oh well, you can't blame me for trying." He became serious. "Just promise me you'll be careful, Cissy."

"Of course I will, Dad." Her eyes filled with tears and suddenly they were in each other's arms. Before the tears could fall, she broke away, muttered a few words and waved her wand. As she disappeared, he felt her kiss his cheek, then the car door opened, closed again a moment later with a soft click, and she was gone. Charles watched as the tiny door at the base of the lamppost opened and he imagined her squeezing through. Then, thirty seconds later, it closed again, and he knew she had left his world.

Chapter 26

A few days after Logan's departure, Kamontip awoke with a strange feeling of disquiet that grew stronger as the day continued. Not knowing its source, she said nothing, but it was soon noted how she was unusually terse and that a cloud hovered across her usually pretty, carefree face. At last, Gnerx, the wise old wand-maker, came to sit beside her and after a respectful silence, spoke.

"My queen, it is clear something troubles you. Could it relate to the stranger who, not long ago, entered our land? I know you think of him often." Having said what he needed to say, the old goblin withdrew, but Kamontip stopped him with a gesture.

"As ever, Gnerx, your wisdom cuts to the heart of the problem." It was true, she realized; she did think of Logan often but why this sudden feeling of doom?

I miss him a little but...

And suddenly, the old goblin's words were like a light illuminating her mind.

"Gnerx," she said slowly, "approximately how long is it since the wizard left our land?"

"Approximately, my queen?" He paused to consider. "It is approximately three days,"—he looked up at the sun, which was just beginning to set, and smiled modestly—"and nineteen hours."

Despite her sudden urgency and the panic enveloping her, she felt a flicker of amusement at his tendency for exactitude.

"And how long since you last saw the Queen's Wand? Quickly now, think!"

"Let me see." He stroked his chin reflectively. "I last saw it…"

"Never mind!" The old goblin's exactitude could also be infuriating. "Check on it. Now!"

At once he called to his apprentice who, as ever, was not far away, and whispered in his ear. The apprentice ran from the room and there was silence for a while, one which grew longer until Gnerx spoke hesitantly, "You suspect the wand is gone?"

She nodded tersely, wishing he would be quiet.

"And that the stranger is the thief?"

"Yes, yes!" she exclaimed. "Who else could it be?"

"But he was always observed, was never left alone."

The expression on the queen's face suggested it might be prudent to stop, but still he offered what he hoped were words of comfort. "Anyway, my queen, we do not yet know that it is gone, and I really don't see why—"

Before the angry retort could leave her lips, the door crashed open and the apprentice ran into the room, red-faced and panting. "It is not there! The Queen's Wand, it is stolen!"

"Logaaan!" Kamontip screamed. "You are a dead man!"

"But it can't be him," Gnerx insisted, running after the queen as she stormed from the room. Risking her wrath, he argued, "I tell you, it's impossible!"

She rounded on him, her eyes blazing, and he cowered. But Kamontip was no tyrant and the sight was enough to stem her anger somewhat. She turned from him and took several deep breaths. When she faced him again she smiled a little sheepishly. "I'm sorry, Gnerx, that was unforgivable. I should not unleash my anger upon you." She indicated he should walk with her. "It was just a shock to find the wand gone. It has been with the goblins for, oh I don't know how many thousands of years."

Gnerx opened his mouth to supply the answer but she forestalled him with a hand on his arm.

"Never mind, it does not matter. Tell me why you think the Dark Wizard did not commit this atrocity."

"Simply that he was never alone. It was on your instruction, my queen," he reminded her, "that someone be with him at all times during the day and that his lodging be watched at night. I can assure you your wishes were followed most assiduously."

Kamontip heard the defensive note and kissed him gently on the cheek. "I trust you, Gnerx, as I always have. So, if it's not the wizard, then who?"

Not really expecting an answer, she was about to walk on but Gnerx didn't move, but stared fixedly beyond her right shoulder as if he had spotted something fascinating. Kamontip half turned to see what he was looking at before she recognized the evasion and realized he was struggling with his conscience.

"Yes, Gnerx?" she asked gently. "What do you know?"

"I don't know anything; not *exactly*," he demurred. "But..."

"Go on!"

"Myla has not been seen for quite some time." He hesitated. "Nor her sister Maisey."

"Myla? Surely even she wouldn't dare?" Kamontip stared at him. "Gnerx, exactly how long has she been missing?"

His answer was a hammer blow.

"So, Myla stole the wand and gave it to the wizard? Do you think? Has she betrayed us all?"

Gnerx had no answer but his silence was eloquent.

"No," she said at last, "I refuse to believe it. She is young, bored and restless. Stupid!" She almost shouted the last. "But she is no traitor!" She slammed her palm against her thigh in frustration. "So why, Gnerx? Why take the Queen's Wand, the most sacred relic of our kind? And why is Maisey involved? She has always been the level-headed one of the twins; why allow herself to be mixed up in Myla's wild schemes?"

They had reached the palace gardens and, spying a stone bench, Gnerx indicated they should sit. He was silent for a long time and Kamontip did not interrupt. If anyone could unravel the mystery, it was he.

"I think you are correct, my queen," he said at last, "the goblin child is young and foolish. I believe that she took the wand to do great mischief in the mortal world and then, being unsure how to do so, used the wizard as a means of getting into their world."

In his wisdom, Gnerx had identified almost precisely what had happened, but Kamontip immediately saw a flaw in his reasoning.

"But why take the Queens Wand?" she insisted. "She has a perfectly good wand of her own with which to perform her mischief."

The old goblin shrugged. "Perhaps she hoped to do greater mischief with it; which indeed she could, as well as great harm."

"Nonsense." She shook her head irritably and jumped to her feet. "She is not seeking to perform higher magic; the wand would consume her if she tried." She sat down again, all at once exhausted. "Myla desires only to play her petty tricks on the mortals and her own wand is perfectly adequate for that."

Gnerx did not answer, for he knew that Kamontip was not yet thinking clearly, had not yet realized the obvious danger.

"We just have to hope she keeps it safe until she returns, although the young fool will probably lose it."

Still he remained silent but, in his mind, he willed, *think, my queen, please think!*

"No," she announced decisively, after they had remained silent for almost a minute, "she is irresponsible but not stupid. She will realize she cannot use the wand and return it to me."

Gnerx could have screamed with frustration. *Think!*

But Kamontip was remembering the other question. "But Maisey; why has she involved herself in her sister's schemes?"

He shrugged dismissively. "Perhaps she has not, my queen. Is it not more likely she saw Myla take the wand, or at least learned of it? I would say she has followed her into the mortal world to protect her or, more probably, try and limit the damage she might cause." He stopped, realizing he had sounded irritated – which he was. *Why is she so blind to the obvious danger?* "My queen, there is something you have not yet considered."

"No, Gnerx." She rose to her feet much more calmly this time. "I feel reassured. I'm sure Myla will..." She paused at the expression on his face. "My friend, something troubles you, your manner has been one of irritation and even agitation."

"I meant no disrespect!" He flushed. "I apologize!"

"There is no need, my friend, and please, speak freely before me, without fear." And then, Kamontip, goblin queen, paled visibly as the truth finally came to her. "The Dark Wizard," she said dully, "he will discover Myla has the wand and…" She faltered as this further, even greater shock rendered her momentarily speechless. "Gnerx," she said at last, "we gave the wizard a useless wand, only to then gift him one with almost immeasurable power. If he discovers Myla has the wand—"

"Which he will," he interrupted.

"Well, yes," she agreed. "*When* he discovers the wand, the mortal world will be in great peril."

It was no exaggeration to say that queen and subject felt frightened at that moment. But had they known what the Dark Wizard was even now contemplating, they would have been terrified.

Chapter 27

"Cissy!" Molly enveloped her in a giant bear hug, nearly squeezing the life out of her. "Thank goodness you're back! It's been so boring around here!"

"Hi, Molly." She grinned. "Good to see you too."

"Where's Penelope? I miss that girl."

"Molly, she's at school; I *explained* this to you, like, fifty times." Cissy rolled her eyes. "Mum and Dad, well, Mum mostly, don't want her spending all her time with *'those strange people in the otherworld place.'* She grinned. "Mum thinks it's unhealthy and that you're all a bad influence; you especially, Molly."

The old witch grinned back. "I do my best to be, Cissy, I do my best."

"Anyway, she'll be here tomorrow."

"Why tomorrow?"

"Because it's *Saturday,* Molly. And all next week as well; it's half-term." She held up a hand to stop Molly from asking what that was. "Don't, Molly. I already explained that too!"

"Ha!" Molly exclaimed and her eyes twinkled. "You've got much too big-headed since you became leader of the Sanctuary."

Cissy flushed, embarrassed; she still hadn't got used to the idea of being the leader. It seemed scary that she might have to make big decisions to save the mortal world. And it was *ridiculous* that she might have to tell people like Molly and Wallace what to do.

Just then Luke appeared, and the two teenagers looked at each other a little shyly. He hadn't gone with Cissy and Penelope on their holiday, and although they'd texted and spoken on the phone *all* the time, they hadn't seen each other for a few weeks. Anyway, this was different, and both found the situation a bit weird. When they'd first come to the Sanctuary everyone assumed it was *he* who'd fulfill the ancient prophecy and inherit incredible powers. But it hadn't worked out that way and at the battle with the demons it was *she* who'd suddenly been transformed into a witch of fearsome ability.

Luke had been worried she'd be a bit standoffish, a little too grand to bother with him anymore, but he should have known better. She was exactly the same as always, and she proved it now.

"Luke!" she exclaimed. "I've missed you so much!" She flung her arms around him and kissed him hard on the lips, much to his embarrassment. Molly rolled her eyes and Wallace, who chose that moment to enter the room, turned around and went back out again. Cissy grinned. "Am I in time for breakfast?"

"Only if you make it yourself; Hans is visiting relatives and Wallace is cooking."

"Wallace?" She shuddered. "That's a disaster. We'll order in; we can get it delivered to the lamppost."

"You can't do that," objected Molly. "It's bleedin' irresponsible."

Cissy looked at her in genuine amazement. "Hang on, *you're* talking about being irresponsible? *You?*"

"Yes, but you're the leader now. You should be setting an example."

It took a few seconds for Cissy to realize Molly was joking, then she laughed. "Anyway, didn't you nip out for pizzas once?"

"Well, yeah," she admitted. "More than once, actually."

"Well then," replied Cissy, firmly. She took out her phone, opened the app and began to order. "What are you gonna have, Luke?"

Once Luke and Molly had decided, she went in search of Wallace, then once the order was complete, hopped out into the passage-between-the-worlds, through the circular room and onto the Old Kent Road.

As she waited for the meals to arrive, she sensed a strange atmosphere, like a pall of disquiet hanging over London and which she hadn't noticed when her father dropped her off less than an hour earlier. Perhaps she was already back in *witch mode* but her instincts seemed to warn her to be prepared, that a great evil was coming.

Order in hand and back in the passage, she walked thoughtfully back to the Sanctuary but once inside she said nothing, thinking she'd probably imagined it. They ate their food and she soon forgot it as she and Luke headed to her room and spent most of the day downloading and listening to music, just as they'd loved to do when they first got together, in the days when they had no idea of the existence of this parallel dimension, nor of witches and wizards, faeries, demons and other weird and wonderful things.

The following day, Penelope arrived and brought her usual excitement, noise and chaos, so happy was she to be there. Then, after the initial onslaught of her arrival, things began to quieten down and they all settled once more to life in the Sanctuary.

Chapter 28

Despite the shock, Kamontip slept well and awoke the next morning feeling calm and clear-headed. "Gnerx, come," she summoned the old goblin. "We must plan a course of action, quickly." They sat and she continued, "I must enter the mortal world immediately, retrieve the wand, and Myla can hope I don't throw her into prison for the next thousand years!" Realizing she was becoming overwrought again, she said, more gently, "As for Maisey, hopefully I will..."

"But you cannot! Think of the danger! If the wizard has the wand, he can use it against you!"

"But it is the Queen's Wand, made for the goblin race, specifically for its queen! Surely it will refuse to do me harm?"

Gnerx shrugged. "Perhaps, but think, *please* think of the repercussions if you are wrong!" Now it was his turn to feel agitated. "Your own personal wand against the Queen's Wand? It would be no contest!"

"Certainly, you are right,"—there was a hint of disdain in her voice—"but would you have me send another in my place? Should I send someone else to attempt a task which I dare not?"

Stung, he snapped back at her, "This is no time for your pride. You are the queen! Your safety cannot be risked!" He breathed deeply. "And anyway, if you just go marching in, go anywhere within the vicinity of the wizard, he will most certainly sense it."

She was about to interrupt but he pressed home his advantage, hurriedly. "My queen, wait. Who knows if the wand might even react to your presence and warn him, however inadvertently?" He shook his head fervently. "No, my idea would be to send not one, but two, perhaps even three of our younger goblins into the mortal world, then through the window into the dimension where the Dark Wizard can be found." Gnerx stopped her protests with an almost peremptory hand. "My queen, you exude power. You would be much too conspicuous. It is better that—"

"I know, I know," she interrupted, "I was merely trying to expedite matters." She knew from experience that he would waffle interminably and, having made the decision, she was anxious to get things moving. "Do you have any thoughts on who we might send?"

It wasn't in Gnerx's nature to make quick decisions but rather to weigh up the options, consider the pros and cons, and then weigh them again.

"Bip, perhaps?" she prompted.

"Too fat." He shook his head, emphatically. "Wouldn't be able to run away fast enough if needed."

Kamontip nodded; he did have a point.

"Anyway, he would never fit through the door in the circular room."

Where does he get his information from? She shook her head in admiration. *I wouldn't have a clue how big the door is or even know it's in a circular room.*

"I was thinking more of someone like Gsan."

A good choice, she conceded, *the quest will need intelligence.* "Good," she said aloud. "Who else?"

He hesitated. "Blort?"

"No! Too stupid!"

"But strong," he pointed out, "immensely so. And brave too."

"Not brave," she argued, "just too stupid to recognize the danger."

"Well, perhaps," Gnerx conceded, "but his strength may be needed."

"Alright," she agreed, amused at his stubbornness, "we will send him also. And the third?"

"Perhaps two will be sufficient."

"Three." She was emphatic. "There should be three."

They both lapsed into silence for a while then burst out, in perfect unison. "Gree!"

They laughed together; it had been so obvious.

"The perfect choice!"

"A born leader!"

"Intelligent and brave!"

"Fetch them to me, Gnerx." She laid a hand on the shoulder of the old goblin. "They must be ready to leave as soon as possible."

He arose and gave a slight bow. "Of course, my queen, I will send someone to find them."

"No! Wait!" They turned, startled, as Maisey entered the room. "Send me! Please!"

Gnerx was the first to react, looking at the girl so fiercely she took a step backward. "Where is your sister? Did you aid her in this atrocity?"

"I didn't!" Recovering herself, Maisey glared back angrily. "But, but..."

Kamontip rose and motioned Gnerx to be quiet. Taking the young goblin's arm she guided her to a chair. "Sit down, Maisey," she said gently. "Tell us all you know."

It didn't take long to describe the events of a few nights ago, how she'd followed Myla from the house but been unable to find her, and how she'd discovered the theft of the wand.

"But I guessed she would follow the wizard." She stopped, tears filling her eyes. "She's so stupid. Stupid. Stupid!" Calming herself, she went on, "And I was right. I found them talking; they didn't see me." She looked up at Kamontip, her eyes frightened. "They were planning to go to the mortal world. And then, they just disappeared."

Kamontip and Gnerx exchanged worried looks, their suspicions confirmed.

"And then,"—Maisey hesitated—"I hid, outside the town." She looked shamefaced. "I was scared, you see. Scared to face you and tell you what Myla had done."

Gnerx looked at her sharply. "That was silly. And cowardly. We might have stopped them before they entered the mortal world!"

"I know. I'm sorry. I shouldn't have. But I can make amends! Let *me* bring her back, please! I can stop her from doing any real harm. Please. Send me instead! Oh, and you won't punish her too much, will you? Myla only meant to do mischief. She doesn't think of consequences. She doesn't think at all, really." Her tears were falling freely now and she stared beseechingly at the queen.

Despite her sympathy for the girl, Kamontip forbore to answer the last question.

"Give me your wand," she ordered. "It will need more power if you are to enter the world of the mortals. Go home now to your parents; they are distraught. I will summon you when your wand is ready."

Chapter 29

The Landlord was once again enjoying the peace of a life totally absent from wizards or witches. For sure, he'd enjoyed seeing Cissy again and Penelope always made him smile. He was sitting in an old armchair on the station platform, enjoying the warmth of the sun, when a familiar friend bounded up to him.

It was the squirrel who had freed him from his cell in the witch's land, so long ago; a young squirrel then but old and gray now. He whispered his message to not awaken Oscar, who was dozing in the sunshine. He loved the dog dearly but had no time today for playing, which Oscar would surely want to do.

The Landlord whispered a few terse questions but the squirrel knew no more, only that the Queen's Wand had been stolen. He accepted a few nuts, which the Landlord found at the bottom of one of his deep pockets, then scampered away.

I suppose I should let Cissy know right away, he thought glumly, and immediately began to talk himself out of it. "They'll know soon enough; probably even before I could get there," he justified himself to Oscar, who still hadn't stirred. The dog opened his eyes, shook his head at the Landlord's latest bit of nonsense, and went back to sleep.

You're making excuses again. As always, his conscience intruded and he shook his head impatiently.

No I'm not, he told it firmly. *Well, not much anyway. Re-forging the link between here and the Sanctuary isn't a five-minute job, you know; not least because I have to find the Conductor – goodness knows where he is at the moment – and make sure he's even willing for the train line to be diverted into another dimension. He has quite enough of those to manage as it is!*

Uncomfortably aware he was having this conversation entirely inside his head, which even he realized might seem a little crazy, the Landlord picked up a ball and threw it for Oscar to chase. Oscar opened his eyes again, debated whether he could be bothered to play, and decided he could.

We really must get a phone line put in, the Landlord thought, as Oscar retrieved the ball and dropped it at his feet. *Then I could just phone the Sanctuary. Better still, get one connected to Aeryn's world, then Morgan can be the one to run the errands!*

"Anyway,"—he threw the ball again—"perhaps it hasn't been stolen; perhaps Kamontip just lost it." Oscar skidded to a halt, turned and regarded him with skepticism.

"Okay, okay," he agreed, "that's a bit unlikely. More likely Logan has something to do with this." It wasn't hard to put two and two together. *If Logan is behind this, Morgan must find out what he's up to!* But then he remembered his friend was no longer the leader of the Sanctuary.

The Landlord didn't really know why he was so reluctant, but he sighed, knowing he was going to have to go see whether Logan did indeed have the Queen's Wand. But which way? It would take at least a week and probably more to re-open the link.

Through the Corridor of Dimensions, or whatever silly name it's been given? he wondered. *Then up into the mortal world? That would be the quickest and easiest.* He nodded, glad to have made the decision. *Then all I have to do is get through that window in the wall, which Logan probably thinks I don't even know about.*

The Landlord strode purposefully toward the patch of shimmering air which marked the portal into the witches' land, but then the unwelcome thought that he would need to pass near to the Sanctuary if he chose that way, began to niggle at his mind.

If I go that way, they're bound to sense my presence; Molly especially. Nobody knew better than he that a witch's senses were incredibly finely tuned. *Then they'll want me to come in and be –* he shuddered *– sociable.* Another thought struck him, and he shuddered again. *And they'll probably want me to stay for tea...*

Back inside, he quickly threw a few items for the journey into a pack. He contemplated taking his wand and looked enquiringly at Oscar, who nodded firmly. He quickly removed it from its hiding place, put it in his pocket, and strode out the back door. "C'mon Oscar," he called, "looks like we're going the long way around."

And the door slammed shut.

The sun was hot and there was not a breath of wind to disturb the smoke which meandered lazily upwards, covering the village with a faint haze that smelled pleasantly of woodsmoke. The Landlord always enjoyed this quiet time, gazing down as he had done countless times before upon the people who were as dear to him as if they were his own family. But it had not always been this way; there had been a time when this was a place of penance not joy, because nearby stood the place where he'd created the blood moon, an act designed to protect the mortal race but which had contributed, so many years later, to Mitra's death.

So long ago!

The sight of Mitra casting herself into the void had rendered him helpless with grief for a long time and the urge to follow her had almost overwhelmed him. But, despising his own weakness, the Landlord had made himself return to her home in her chosen village. And though it was truly a penance, in that place with all its familiarity but which he would never again share with her, he found a kind of perverse comfort.

Then came the time for him to return to the Sanctuary, to face his friends.

And to find I could hate even them!

It had been too much to bear and he found that, as well as blaming himself, he blamed them also.

What does it mean to be a witch, a wizard? he asked himself. *If Mitra and I had been ordinary people, without power, she would never have suffered such torment!*

Yes, he found he could hate the world in which he lived; this world which existed to protect the mortal world.

Yet it doesn't protect its own! It couldn't save Mitra!

As his anger had turned to rage, the council of witches and wizards became wary and, for the first time in many centuries, decided to intervene in worldly affairs. In his present state of mind, the wizard Cornelius was extremely dangerous. It was decided he must be imprisoned, until his sanity returned.

Until his sanity returned – that, at least, was the party line.

Never, was the reality.

But one voice stood alone in support of him. One witch, distant ancestor of Mitra herself, and one who did not blame Cornelius for Mitra's death; not nearly as much as he himself did.

"One day he will escape," Siwaraksa had argued. "He is too powerful not to. And when he does, his fury will know no bounds." The council had considered her words, troubling as they were. "Send the wizard Cornelius home to recover," she urged. "He does not deserve this treatment. He simply needs time to grieve."

And the council had readily agreed, for if Cornelius turned against them, they knew the consequences could be catastrophic. He was returned, this time choosing an old inn, deliberately close to the entrance of the demon world and to the place where he'd created the blood moon. Cornelius would not allow himself to forget his crimes and this place served well for the penance he craved. The people of the nearby village welcomed him into their bosom, tending and nurturing him as they would one of their own. Eventually, the name Cornelius was forgotten except by those who knew him well or those with long memories...

Oscar had sensed the Landlord's mood change and barked sharply, jerking him from his reverie.

"You caught me daydreaming again, my boy." He laughed and patted Oscar's head, then straightened and pointed. "Look, there's Ffranc." The little dog squinted through the haze but could make out nothing except indistinct figures; the Landlord's eyes were far sharper than any animal's.

"Come on; race you!" The Landlord's long legs took him several meters in front before even Oscar could react. Then the dog barked joyously and chased after him, and they reached the bottom of the slope together.

"I'll need a horse."

"Of course." Ffranc nodded. "I'll speak to Dai, the blacksmith."

Just then, Catrin burst in and overheard the last part of the conversation. "Why do you need a horse? Where are you going?" Then she remembered her manners and grinned. "Hi, Landlord."

He grinned back, as ever completely entranced by her spirit and sheer joie de vivre. "Got to go to London." He knew she would be fascinated by this, and sure enough, he was not disappointed.

"London! The big city!" she breathed excitedly. "How marvelous!"

"Yes." Her excitement was infectious. "London two centuries or more in the future!"

"Really? Can I come?" It was Grufydd who burst in and interrupted, somewhat selfishly forgetting Catrin.

The Landlord smiled at the boy, whom he'd known from childhood. He was a good lad and some company would be nice. "I don't see why not," he hedged, "but you'll need to speak to your—"

"And me!" Catrin hopped from foot to foot in excitement. "I'm coming too!"

"No!" Ffranc cut in sharply. "You are not."

"Oh, but—"

"No, Catrin," Franc repeated, "it's far too dangerous. Last time you encountered the Dark

Wizard he made you mute."

"We're going to encounter the Dark Wizard?" Grufydd exclaimed. "Cool!"

"We're only going to have a look," the Landlord demurred. He muttered softly, glancing at the old man.

Ffranc glared at him. "Cornelius, I said no and that's my final word. I'll thank you not to try and change my mind."

"I wasn't," he objected mildly. "I merely pointed out I'm not planning to encounter Logan, just to have a teeny-weeny little look."

"Nevertheless." Ffranc sealed his lips and folded his arms.

The Landlord was on the point of arguing further, but he stopped himself. It was not his business to go against Ffranc's wishes.

"Sorry, Catrin." He shrugged. "Not this time."

Someone less spirited might have given up, meekly hiding their disappointment. But not she. "You sexist pigs!"

The three of them blinked, particularly Ffranc and Grufydd, who had no idea what the word meant. *Sexist* was a word she'd picked up from Cissy during one of their brief meetings; Cissy had been talking about Luke at the time.

"It's because I'm a girl, isn't it?"

"Of course not," Ffranc said, attempting to mollify her. "It's because of what happened." "And you're as good as any boy!" interrupted Grufydd generously.

The Landlord, probably wisely, remained silent.

"Fine! Whatever!" she exclaimed. "Enjoy your *trip!*" Catrin injected every ounce of scorn she could into the final word before she flounced from the room.

Too easy, thought the Landlord, and glanced again at Ffranc. *You should know that, my friend.*

Catrin appeared once more in the doorway, her face still flushed with anger. "And *you,*" she pointed at Grufydd, "are as bad as the other two." She gave the three of them a look that should have turned them to stone. "Well, the wedding's off!"

"But it's not even my fault!" he protested. But she was already gone.

"Wedding?" The Landlord looked at Grufydd in surprise. "What wedding?"

"Catrin finally agreed to marry me." He grinned. "It's our betrothal party soon; the villagers have already begun preparing."

"You mean it *was* your betrothal party; she's just called it off," the Landlord pointed out, tactlessly.

"Oh, it's okay. She calls it off at least once a month when something doesn't suit her. It's her way of letting off steam."

The Landlord smiled at the boy's confidence. "Well, congratulations, Grufydd; to both of you."

"Will you come to the party? We'd like you to come. I think Catrin just forgot to ask you, what with her getting mad and all."

"Of course!" the Landlord promised unthinkingly until he remembered the journey they were about to undertake. *Anyway, if Logan does have the Queen's Wand, and if the mortal world is in peril, it's the Sanctuary's problem, not mine,* he told himself. *I'm only making this trip as a favor.*

"And Morgan?" the boy persisted. "Do you think he'll come too?"

"I'll ask him. I'm sure he'll be as excited as I am."

The next morning, the Landlord and Grufydd were up and saddled before daybreak and there was no sign of Catrin as they trotted from the village.

Chapter 30

"We're being followed." The Landlord and Grufydd were nearing the end of the third day and had just crossed the border into England. Ahead lay the village of Shrewsbury where they planned to shelter for the night and rest their horses. He'd been aware of their clandestine companion almost from the outset, mostly because he'd been expecting it.

"You may as well join us for supper, Catrin!" he called loudly, unable to suppress the laughter in his voice. "And a comfortable bed for the night!"

For a few moments nothing stirred but then, from the midst of a nearby copse, a horse appeared, its rider grinning broadly.

Grufydd's mouth dropped open. "What's she doing here? And how did you know it was her?"

"What, you weren't suspicious when she meekly accepted she couldn't come? It was obvious she planned to follow us! And anyway," honesty forced him to admit, "I saw Dai the blacksmith fitting new shoes on her horse."

"It's too late to send me back now!" Catrin grinned triumphantly as she caught them up. "Hi, Grufydd." She winked. "You might want to close your mouth."

The boy snapped his jaw closed and blushed. Catrin laughed and the Landlord rolled his eyes.

"Who says it's too late?" he enquired, keeping his expression stern, and her grin faltered.

"Really?" she asked hesitantly.

"Yes, really. It's very naughty of you to disobey your grandfather like this." But he couldn't help letting his mouth quirk upwards slightly.

She breathed a sigh of relief. The Landlord would never use a word like *naughty;* he was much too cool for that.

"I know, but I did leave him a note, so he knows I'm safe."

"Oh, well I suppose that makes it alright then!" he said with heavy irony.

She laughed. "I know!"

"But shouldn't we let Ffranc know Catrin is safely with *us?*" Grufydd asked anxiously.

"We'll send... an email, or something," the Landlord replied, a little vaguely.

"I told you," said Catrin, having no idea what an email was, "I left him a note. I bet he was so angry! C'mon, Grufydd, race you to the town!"

The Landlord watched fondly as the pair galloped ahead. He continued at a more sedate pace so they were forced to wait for him.

"Come on, Landlord!" complained Catrin. "We're hungry!" She leaned across and kissed his cheek. "Thanks for letting me stay," she said, feeling a little self-conscious.

"You're welcome." He in turn tried to hide how ridiculously pleased the kiss had made him feel. He had always been inordinately fond of the girl, seeing in her the daughter he and Mitra might have had if things had been different; if Mitra had been able...

He shook his head. This was not a time for sadness, and together they rode down the hill toward the lights, which welcomed them through the falling dusk.

Catrin and Grufydd were up early the next morning, eager to go. The Landlord was less eager, and they waited impatiently while he ate breakfast.

"Come on, Landlord! Are you being so slow on purpose?" and "Surely you've had enough to eat by now?" they nagged until eventually he gave in and they could start the day's journey. Each new day started like this and each one brought new sights to amaze and thrill the teenagers. From Shrewsbury to Ludlow they traveled, and from Tewkesbury to Witney then St Albans, until at last, weary and saddle sore, they approached the walls of London. Unfortunately, night was falling when at last they arrived, and the curfew was already in place. The Landlord made a half-hearted attempt to gain entry but the night watchman, a genial red-haired giant, was having none of it.

"Oh well," he said, resigned, "it was worth a try, but it looks like we're spending the night in the open. Good thing the skies are clear." He sent them both to gather kindling, muttered the spell that would ignite a small fire and they gathered closely, for the night air had grown chilly.

There was still food in their packs and the ground, although hard, had yet to become uncomfortable. For a while they were lulled by the dancing flames and the crackling of the wood, but before long it was Catrin, ever the restless one, who asked for a tale.

The Landlord stared into the flames for a long time, as if transfixed, and she wondered if he hadn't heard. But eventually he looked up and smiled.

"A tale you say?" He reached into his pack and took out an apple. "Well then,"—he took a bite—"I could recite legends of wizards and witches, of strange beasts; some real, some mythical. I've met faeries and—"

"Demons?" interrupted Grufydd, hopefully. "Can you tell us a tale about demons? About where they come from, I mean?" Grufydd had lived in the shadow of the demon world his entire life, as had Catrin and everyone they knew. But the boy had developed an unhealthy fascination.

"No!" The Landlord reacted more sharply than he'd intended. "No," he said again, "the subject is... painful." He lapsed into silence and the mood soured, but for moments only until he looked up and saw the glum expression on the boy's face.

"But I can tell you the very strange, but totally true – well probably – story of how the goblin and the horse came to be entangled with the..." And he began a long and completely fictitious tale which sufficed until their eyelids drooped, and they fell asleep at last. He smiled fondly and felt glad, despite himself, for he usually preferred his own company, that they were with him. Determined, as the flickering flames captured him once more, not to let the shadows of the past enter his mind, he thought about nothing, and soon he slept also.

They passed through the gate early next morning and Catrin's first impression was of how noisy and smelly London was; and how crowded. Never before had she seen so many people and the noise felt deafening. It seemed that nobody spoke; everyone shouted. Costermongers competed, cheerfully trying to out-do each other. Disagreements turned into arguments, which turned into fights that attracted excited on-lookers, eager to bet and shout the odds on the outcome.

There was music everywhere, from ballad singers and barrel organs to bands with their trumpets and trombones, French horns and flutes; others with their cornets and clarinets, bassoons and bass drums. They all raised an out-of-tune, discordant din that the two teenagers found thrilling.

They looked around in wonder at the street performers, contortionists and clowns, jugglers, fire eaters, rope walkers and dancing bears. Sheep being herded to the shearing pens, pigs and cattle to the slaughterhouses, cows from which a jug of milk could be bought for a penny. The clacking of horses' hooves on cobbles, the clucking of hens in pens and cockerels in cages added to the cacophony. There were chickens everywhere, strutting about and getting underfoot, ready to trip the unwary into a bath of fresh animal dung, which literally carpeted the street. And dogs, so many dogs! Barking, squabbling, whining and generally contributing to the mayhem.

And the smells were almost as overpowering, for mingling with the smell of dung was the smoke from the countless fires cooking sizzling slabs of steak and, occasionally, the delicious aroma of baking bread. Catrin and Grufydd were accustomed to such smells of course, it was just that these were magnified a hundredfold.

"Isn't this marvelous?" Catrin shouted, her eyes shining.

"What did you say?" Grufydd yelled back.

"I said it's marvelous!"

He nodded, his own eyes reflecting her excitement. "I know!"

"I wonder where we're going!"

"We know where!" Grufydd rolled his eyes sarcastically. "To the Dark Wizard's mansion!"

"I know that," Catrin said, annoyed. "I meant how will we get into his dimension? He's in a different one to this, you realize?"

"Well, kind of,"—a deep frown furrowed his forehead—"but different how?" Grufydd, although not exactly stupid, was perhaps not the brightest either. "The Landlord did try to explain but, well, it's difficult to work out, isn't it? I mean, all he went on about was doors, doors and more doors. What does any of this have to do with doors?"

"Well," she began, wondering how she could explain how they were to travel two hundred years or so into the future, "the doors are... look, Grufydd, we can't keep on shouting like this; it's making my head spin! Let's talk about it when things have quietened down!"

And right on cue, the Landlord, with a perfunctory glance over his shoulder to ensure they'd not been followed, made an abrupt left turn down a much narrower side street. The noise ceased as if at the flick of a switch and their ears rang in protest at the sudden silence. They had moved so swiftly from bright sunshine to shadow that they were momentarily blinded, barely able to stumble after the blurred shape of the Landlord whose pace had slowed not one bit.

Gradually, as their eyes became accustomed, they could make out tall buildings on either side, unlike any they'd ever seen. They stretched so high it seemed they might touch the clouds and they seemed to lean inwards. *As if they're trying to block out the light,* thought Catrin with a shudder.

Suddenly she gripped Grufydd's arm. "Look!" she whispered excitedly. "The buildings, they have windows!"

"So?" Grufydd whispered back.

"They have glass in them!"

Grufydd had heard of glass but, like Catrin, had rarely seen it. A novelty for sure, but he really couldn't see why she was getting so excited about it. *Honestly, girls can be so weird...*

"Why are we whispering?" he whispered.

"I don't know," she whispered back, "this is just one of those places where you feel you should."

"Oh, that's not right at all!" boomed the Landlord, the sound so shockingly loud they both jumped. "Absolutely nothing to be frightened of down here, the neighbors are very friendly!" They looked at him skeptically and he smiled. "Honestly, I mean it. Look through the windows, tap on them and wave if you like. Clean them while you're at it too!"

Sure enough, the windows *were* grimy and thick with dirt and soot.

Which is odd, thought Catrin as she peered through the first one, seeing the inside was beautifully spotless. And so it proved with the next one and the next. Again and again, she rubbed a small spyhole, delighting in its bobbly, uneven feel, and peered through the patterns of tiny air bubbles. Each room revealed a scene of domesticity.

"Come and look!" she urged Grufydd yet again, but he demurred disinterestedly.

A good lad, that Grufydd, thought the Landlord who was keeping a very close eye on both of them, *but singularly lacking in imagination.*

"I don't get why these people would keep their houses so clean but not wash their windows?"

"Good question, Catrin," he acknowledged, "and the answer is, that they cannot."

"Why not?"

"You tapped on a few of the windows, didn't you? Yet nobody answered."

"They never even noticed!"

"Exactly," agreed the Landlord.

"Well, why not?" Grufydd joined the debate.

"It was like they didn't know we were here," Catrin continued.

"Almost as if they were in another world...."

The Landlord looked at Grufydd with approval. "See? You can use your brains, if you try!"

"Yeah, but I still don't get it."

"Me neither," added Catrin.

"Just tell us!" they chorused, loudly.

"Well, what have I told you about the Sanctuary?"

"That it's in a different dimension?" asked Catrin.

"And that it can exist in any time throughout history, depending on which door you use to enter it?" added Grufydd.

"Doors... dimensions.... hang on! Those people and how they dressed, it was different in each house!"

"So? What does that matter?"

"No," she said excitedly, "I mean *really* different, the rooms themselves too, and the furniture!" She looked triumphantly at the Landlord. "Those houses are in different dimensions, aren't they? In fact, each one *is* a different dimension!"

He smiled, delighted they'd got there in the end. "Almost right, Catrin. Except that they are all mortals, and so they inhabit the same dimension, but at different times in history.

"But I thought that only happened with the Sanctuary. Why this place too?"

"I'm confused." Grufydd thought he should contribute.

"No time to explain now," replied the Landlord, "we're almost there, and you should both cease chattering." He led them into what was little more than an alley. "Down here you should be at least a *bit* frightened. Even maybe a lot. Probably." His eyes sparkled with mischief, but Catrin had the uncomfortable feeling he wasn't entirely joking.

"Don't worry,"—he saw Grufydd had turned slightly green— "only a little bit. Definitely. But the neighbors are most certainly not friendly," he added. And very softly, so they would not hear, "There is much danger here."

Chapter 31

“It’s too quiet,” Molly announced.

“What is?” Luke asked.

“I’m not sure exactly.” Molly weighed her words. “But I don’t like it, something is brewing, I can feel it.” She looked up as Cissy entered the room. “I sensed a disturbance out in the passage that day I sneaked out for pizzas.”

“You went for pizzas? To the mortal world?” Luke grinned.

“Yeah, well. Never mind that now,” she answered. “Mark my words, you two,”—she shifted her ample bosom into a more comfortable position—“it’s definitely too bleedin’ quiet.”

“You’re just grumpy.” Luke winked at Cissy. “As usual.”

“Don’t be so bleedin’ cheeky.” Molly forced a grin but deep down she felt greatly disquieted, as she had for several weeks. “Actually, I’ve had this feeling since the day Cissy arrived back at the Sanctuary.” She lapsed into silence and thought back to that day, to that sudden cramping of her stomach, that unaccountable feeling of trepidation.

Sensing her mood, Cissy sought to distract the old witch. “You remember you promised to show me the laboratory where you made

Peter's potion?" Molly grunted. "Well how about now?"

"I'm not in the mood."

"Aww, c'mon," Luke joined in, "it'll be fun!"

"There was nothing bleedin' fun about the trouble caused by those faeries." But she spoke without heat, happy to let herself be persuaded.

Soon, Cissy and Luke had climbed the staircase to the upper corridor. At Molly's signal, they stopped outside Luke's bedroom and waited as she raised her wand and muttered an incantation. The walls shifted apart, revealing a dark corridor, and she motioned them to enter.

"And this is the thermometer," Molly was saying as she held it up to the light. Cissy peered at it, curiously.

"Are those... horses?" she exclaimed in wonder.

And sure enough, there they were in the bulb at the bottom of the glass tube. Those same tiny, silver horses Luke had last seen charging frantically up and down, trying to reach the temperature needed to create the potion that might save his father's life.

Now they trotted sedately in and out of the little lake of quicksilver to graze on miniscule, almost indiscernibly delicate strands of silver hay.

"Incredible," she breathed, "the most beautiful creatures I've ever seen."

"Aren't they just?" Molly smiled. "This thermometer is many thousands of years old. It was built, so it is believed, by the great witch—" She stopped abruptly as her stomach cramped with pain, making her wince.

Luke moved toward her. "What's wrong?"

"I'm okay,"—she held up a hand—"but we have to get back into the Sanctuary."

"Aren't we still there?" Cissy asked, puzzled.

"Technically, at this moment, we are nowhere; in between dimensions, if you like," Molly answered shortly. "Now please, come on!"

Back in the Sanctuary, Molly went to the lounge, where Wallace still sat, and stood at the door that led to the passage-between-the-worlds. There she listened, her nose twitching.

"What is it?" the old wizard asked, but Molly held up a hand irritably.

After a minute, she put her hands on her hips and announced indignantly, "I knew it. I just bleedin' knew it. There's someone outside."

"That can't be good!" Wallace jumped to his feet. "Luke, bring your sword!"

"Wait!" ordered Cissy. "This might require magic too."

"Fine! Molly, come on!"

"Oh, relax, Wallace." Molly grinned; it was rare to see him move so quickly. "We can leave this to the youngsters." The truth was, her instinct wasn't screaming *danger!* and she suspected whoever was out there presented no great threat. He began to object but she cut in, "And you should remember, Wallace, that Cissy is the leader of the Sanctuary now."

The girl gave her a grateful look, but Luke had already opened the door and within seconds they were both in the passage-between-the-worlds. The two friends proceeded quickly but cautiously and in silence. Soon they spied a young girl creeping furtively into the circular room.

"Who are you? State your business or die!" Luke challenged, sword held aloft, ready to strike.

Cissy had her own wand poised but even so, she couldn't help a flicker of amusement at the clumsy pomposity of Luke's challenge.

He really does need to learn to chill a little, she thought. *She hardly looks much of a threat.* Aloud, she said in a more reasonable tone, "Who are you? And why are you here?"

"I am Maisey, of the goblin race. As to why I'm here, that's rather a long story."

"If you are a goblin, you obviously have a wand." None of the harshness had left Luke's voice.

"I do," she agreed carefully.

"Then hand it over." The order was peremptory but Maisey hesitated before turning to Cissy, who she deemed the more reasonable of the two.

"I understand your need for caution," she said slowly, "yet it is no easy thing for a goblin to give up her wand."

"Tough," Luke interjected.

"Luke, stop," Cissy admonished gently. "Imagine how I would feel if I had to give up *my* wand, or you your sword." She turned to the goblin. "You may keep it, but it must remain on your person."

Maisey bowed. "Thank you," she said. "So perhaps I may continue on my way?"

"Continue where, exactly?" Cissy asked.

"Oh, just to the mortal world."

"I'm afraid we cannot permit that." As she spoke, Cissy noticed

Luke's knuckles whiten around his sword handle.

"It is my understanding that it is the wish of the great wizard Morgan and his queen, Aeryn,"—Maisey was annoyed and unable to hide her sarcasm—"to *permit* use of the Corridor of Dimensions providing no harm is intended."

Cissy forced herself to relax. "You speak truly, but these are troubled times and we do not yet know your intent. It is our *request,* therefore, that you are our guest within the Sanctuary until these matters can be ascertained."

Despite Maisey's inclination to argue, and goblins were *always* inclined to argue, three things persuaded her against it.

One was the sword, which Luke still brandished menacingly. Another was the obvious ease and familiarity with which the girl held her own wand. But the third, far more compelling reason was curiosity. No goblin, so far as she knew, had ever stepped inside the Sanctuary. It was a place of folklore and legend, a mysterious, magical space. And now she had the chance to see it!

Maisey nodded, smiling. "I guess I'm at your mercy."

*   *   *   *

Something very strange was happening in the middle of London. Traffic was at a standstill from Marble Arch to Trafalgar Square to Westminster Bridge to... seemingly everywhere. Oh, wait. Nothing unusual about that; this was London, after all. But what *was* strange was that all across the capital, drivers were opening their doors to see why, all at once, they weren't moving. And as they stepped from their cars and lorries, as riders dismounted from their motorbikes and cycles, their feet encountered not hard tarmac but black, glutinous treacle.

Passengers on buses, themselves unable to move forward, watched in bewilderment the rapidly escalating chaos; those on the top decks in particular were able to see just how far it reached in both directions. Those lucky enough to be on the pavements laughed at the sight of them all painstakingly lifting their feet from the sticky mess and wobble, precariously, or better still, topple into the thick goo.

Not wanting to miss out on the fun, children escaped their parents' grips and dived into the sticky swamp, relishing the opportunity to get absolutely, thoroughly dirty. And the noise across the city grew steadily until it could be heard from far away. Screams of laughter and fear, happy shouts, angry yells amid the cacophony of thousands of horns, the high-pitched wails of cars competing with the rumbling, low-pitched bellows of lorries, all contributing to the general chaos.

Soon, a hundred helicopters buzzed across London as the camera crews inside tried to get the best coverage for their news networks. And when they swooped down low, the wind from their rotors caused successions of treacle waves to rear up like herds of black horses and chase each other down the streets of the capital.

From her vantage point, high up in one of the trees that overlooked The Mall, Myla sat with tears of mirth rolling down her cheeks. The black waves that swept along the width of the promenade were split briefly into two streams by the fountain then joined together again as they poured into the grounds of Buckingham Palace. Even she was amazed at the mayhem she had caused.

She'd already had such fun earlier that day when she'd spotted the London Eye. She had no idea why the mortals were so excited to climb aboard those little cages and rotate slowly upwards then back to the ground, but she'd instantly seen the opportunity for more mischief.

In her opinion, the wheel turned much too slowly, but she'd soon rectified that and had it spinning so fast it was impossible to make out the individual cages anymore and the whole thing was a vertiginous blur of dizziness. Only when the wheel had begun to shake in its foundations had Myla halted its rapid rotation; she had no wish to cause real harm. But she'd delighted in the sight of so many mortals staggering around like groggy, distinctly green goblins, and she'd watched, fascinated, as a horde of mortal vehicles, something that didn't exist in her world, came screeching noisily to a stop, their pretty blue lights flashing.

Myla watched as the black treacle rose to the first-floor windows of the huge building near the fountain and then the second. Reluctantly, she twitched the Queen's Wand and its progress stopped, then began to recede. She didn't want anyone *drowning* in the stuff, for goodness' sake!

Satisfied at an excellent day's work, she was about to leave when she heard a sound from behind her.

Chapter 32

"You've got a damned nerve, wizard, ain't you?" a voice snarled from the shadows. There was the sound of someone scuttling away.

"Who was that?" whispered Catrin.

"Doesn't matter," the Landlord said in a low voice. "Some people just *have* to bear grudges. I mean, it was two hundred *years* ago, for goodness' sake." They walked on and as the alley walls seemed to close in, Grufydd took Catrin's hand. Strange faces with haunted eyes watched from dimly lit windows as they passed.

The Landlord pulled them swiftly aside as someone emptied a bucket of some unidentified but obviously disgusting liquid from above. "Nearly got you!" an old crone cackled as a window high above them slammed shut.

"I think we're unwelcome here, don't you?" He winked, trying to reassure the frightened pair.

Behind them, a small boy appeared and shouted an obscenity. He threw a stone, which hit Catrin painfully on the arm. Grufydd made to give chase but the Landlord's bony hand clamped his arm tightly.

"Be quiet now, there's someone up ahead. Stay close to me."

"You dare to show your face here, Cornelius?" The man was tall, his face pock-marked with disease, and most of his teeth were missing. He held a large, dangerous-looking club. "I swore vengeance if you came here again. You remember that?"

"Relax, friend, we're just passing through." The Landlord withdrew his wand and held it by his side. The man took the hint and, after muttering something unintelligible – but in Catrin's opinion probably not very nice – stepped aside and let them pass.

"How long does this alley go on for?" Grufydd tried to stop his teeth chattering as he looked fearfully at the Landlord.

"Don't worry, Grufydd." Catrin grinned, trying to sooth her own nerves. "I'll protect you."

"Not much further." The Landlord smiled. "Just to that pub over there."

"You're joking!" hissed Grufydd. "You want us to go *inside*? Where we can't run?"

"Nonsense," he replied cheerfully. "We'll be quite safe in there."

"*Safe?*" Catrin scowled. "It will be full of *people*. None of whom seem to like you!"

"You'll see." He grinned infuriatingly and pushed open the door. "Follow me."

To their surprise, they found themselves in a cheerfully lit interior, filled with music and the hubbub of happy chattering. The place was packed but apart from one or two shady looking characters who immediately scurried out, most greeted the Landlord warmly.

"Cornelius!"

"What are you doing here?"

"It's been too long!"

As he made his way to the bar, his path was interrupted by handshakes and lipstick filled kisses. Catrin and Grufydd were welcomed with friendly smiles and curious stares, and they began to relax in the convivial atmosphere.

They reached the bar at last, to where a pretty, fair-haired woman with laughter lines around her eyes was busy serving huge jugs of dark, foaming beer.

"Cornelius," she chided with a smile as she turned to him, her eyes shining. "Where on earth have you been all these years!" She took a cloth and wiped away the smears of rouge that painted his cheeks before kissing him fully on the lips.

"What's all *that* about?" Catrina whispered, nudging Grufydd. "Look, he's *blushing!*"

"On this earth?" The Landlord ignored their whispers. "Well, that's a complicated question, Marica." He grinned. "What year is it here at the moment?"

"Oh, stop it," she said with a laugh. "You know what year it is. The same as yours in Wales. Presuming you've come from the back door and not the front. I think..." She shook her head, laughing. "Now, who are these two?"

Marica soon had the teenagers feeling right at home and their earlier fears were quite dispelled. Catrin poured tankards for the customers, who still crowded around, while Grufydd took a sip of beer and pretended he liked the taste, much stronger than that of his native Wales. The Landlord went off to chat to a few old friends, no doubt catching up on the gossip. It was a while before they noticed he was now huddled in deep conversation with Marica, in a dark corner of the bar.

"You've kept it open?" he asked, his expression tense. "The portal, I mean."

"I know what you meant." She nodded. "And yes, of course I have. I don't forget the debt my family and I owe you."

"No, you never owed me a debt, Marica. You should know that. Your great-grandmother was"—he paused—"a remarkable woman."

"I wish I'd known her." Marica sighed wistfully. "And I know it's pointless for me to wish you could stay longer. I presume there is trouble in the future mortal world?"

"Trouble perhaps," he agreed. "When is there not? But you are right, I must not tarry longer." He stood and looked round for Catrin and Grufydd. Catching their eye, he motioned them to follow.

Unseen by anyone, Marica took them behind the bar and opened a small wooden door. On the other side was a long corridor filled with empty barrels, waiting to be taken back to the brewery. At its end was a bookcase which she slid aside easily, revealing a dark chasm with, someway in the distance, a hint of daylight.

"Come back soon," she whispered, tears glistening in as she embraced the Landlord. Turning to the teenagers, she smiled bravely. "Look after him," she said, her voice bright and false. "You have no *idea* of how much trouble he gets himself into!" She pushed them gently after the Landlord and closed the portal quickly. Fixing a smile, she returned to the bar where a clamor of customers waited to be served.

"Who is she? Is she a witch too?" Grufydd rattled out the questions.

"She didn't sound like she was from around here," added Catrin. They had already stepped into the daylight and the Landlord was hurrying them along the busy London streets, eager to reach their destination. They were staring around at the traffic, wrinkling their noses at the stink of the pollution. "How do they move?" Catrin whispered and nudged Grufydd. "They don't have horses to pull them!"

"Marica?" the Landlord smiled. "No, she's not a witch. Well, not exactly. And you're right, Catrin; actually, she's from Holland, although her distant family were Londoners, born within the sound of the Bow Bells."

"What's Holland?"

"What are Bow Bells?"

He held his hands up in mock surrender at the barrage of questions. "Not now! We'll be here all day. Look it up on the internet!"

"What's that?" they chorused.

"Enough! Really, it doesn't matter. All you need to know is that she is a good friend of Molly's and has been custodian of this portal for many years, and her ancestors for centuries before her."

"How does she know Molly?" Catrin asked immediately and the Landlord sighed.

"They helped Molly when she was young, after her parents were killed in the witches' rebellion; before she met Morgan. The great witch Siwaraksa managed to send her to safety only minutes before she herself was captured and... well, never mind that."

This, of course raised a whole new barrage of questions.

"What was the witches' rebellion?"

"Who was Siwaraksa?"

The portal had been placed far from the Dark Wizard's mansion to avoid discovery and they had a long walk ahead of them. The teenagers, thirsty for knowledge, were determined to make the most of their time with the Landlord.

"So, you're saying there are mortal witches who have the same power as, say, Morgan and Molly? And even you?" Catrin was incredulous.

"Well, hardly!" He pretended to be affronted. "We're only talking tiny amounts of power in comparison, but enough to set them apart from their fellow mortals. And when mortals don't understand something, they feel threatened, and when they feel threatened, their impulse is to kill." He shook his head sadly. "It is not so long ago that such people were burned alive, as punishment for being different. Ironically, most of those who died had absolutely no power whatsoever!"

"Burned *alive!*" exclaimed Grufydd. "That's horrible!"

Yes, and in the time you both live, the Landlord thought, *it is happening right now.* But he had no wish to horrify them further.

"The mortal race can be a cruel one," he agreed. "We should be quiet now. Logan's house is close. Can you not feel the change in the air, now that night has fallen?"

They hadn't noticed it before, but now it seemed obvious. The atmosphere was silent and ominous, and no birds sang. Indeed, there were none to be seen, just as no animals roamed abroad. Unconsciously, Catrin and Grufydd moved closer to each other, their arms touching. Suddenly, they turned a corner, and there it was.

The Dark Wizard's mansion was a large, black-stone, gothic pile and it looked its most magnificent and sinister on this dark night of intrigue. The moon shone brightly on its many slated roofs and reflected in the diamond panes of every window, disguising whatever might lurk within. Its score of tall chimneys cast elongated, arm-like shadows across the lawns, and its chimney pots transformed into fingers that appeared to seek out the unwary.

Many years had passed since Logan had discovered, quite by chance, the anomaly which lay right at the very top of one of the two remaining circular towers (the third one he'd destroyed during a fit of temper back in 1837.) The anomaly of the room at the top was that it hid anyone and anything from view of even the most powerful witch or wizard.

Logan watched now from that room as the Landlord and his companions crept furtively around the mansion outside.

Him! he thought, his forehead furrowing into a fretful frown. *What's he doing here?* Not for the first time he regretted not having killed the Landlord when he'd had the chance. *And who does he have with him? Why are they snooping around?* But the reason was obvious. *They think I have the Queen's Wand and fear what I will do with it.*

"Well, I don't have it yet," he said to the large black bird, his constant companion, "but I know all about the goblin's little games. She *must* have the Queen's Wand."

He glanced at the cages containing three of his lost souls, ready for his experiments, and felt a frisson of excitement. He stroked the crow's feathers absently. "And soon it will be mine, and then let the fun begin!"

Logan hadn't yet decided what to do with his captives, except his determination to cause the utmost amount of damage and horror possible. He leaned from the window, secure in the knowledge he couldn't be seen, and peered intently at the three intruders outside.

And, all at once, he knew who the wizard's companions were. The last time he'd seen the girl he'd robbed her of speech. *Such a satisfying memory! The look on her face!* But he flushed with anger when he remembered how she'd dared to defy him.

And suddenly he smiled as the most delicious idea came to him. He crossed the room and stood before his lost souls again, delighting in how they cowered at his approach. He stood for a while, saying nothing, his mouth drooling at the pleasure these creatures gave him.

When the Dark Wizard returned to the window, the intruders were gone.

Nervous, cold and bored, the teenagers were becoming fractious.

"And what about that witch you talked about? Siwa... Siw..."

"Siwaraksa!" Catrin nudged his ribs, painfully. "Everybody has heard of Siwaraksa!"

"Well I haven't," he argued crossly. "You think you're so clever!"

"That's because I am!"

"Quiet!" hissed the Landlord. "Anyone would think you were children! How can I concentrate with you two squabbling? I'm thinking I shouldn't have let either of you come!"

They sobered instantly and Grufydd blushed beetroot red while Catrin looked shamefaced. "Sorry," they both muttered, which might have been more convincing had Catrin not winked at Grufydd and he smirked back.

"There is great evil being practiced here," he continued, "but what it is, I do not know." He sighed. "I suspect our journey has been fruitless; it doesn't seem that Logan will appear." He turned his back on the mansion and led them down a side street. "Something tells me he is not far away though; hiding, probably. Come quickly now, we must leave this dimension and reach the Sanctuary."

"Will we go through the lamppost?" Grufydd asked.

"What's the lamppost?" Catrin whispered.

"It's the way into the Sanctuary from the mortal world," Grufydd whispered back, proud to know something she didn't.

"We *could* do," the Landlord agreed. "But I rather think we'll do this in style. By the front door!"

They continued, out of breath as the pace quickened and they had to run to keep up.

"How do you even *make* a portal?" the boy said after a while.

"You cannot exactly *make* a portal, Grufydd," replied the Landlord, "but there are natural weaknesses between the dimensions, which can be exploited. It would take too long to explain now."

There was silence for a while and by the absorbed expression on the boy's face, the Landlord could tell he was trying to process the information. But it wasn't long before he had yet another question.

"That still doesn't explain why mortals chose to live right next to the demon world; that's stupid."

"Not stupid, Grufydd. Just unfortunate. The demons had lain dormant for many centuries and no one suspected they were still there, albeit in another dimension. It was just bad luck, particularly for your village."

They had reached an alleyway, which ended in a brick wall with three windows set high up.

"At last." He heaved a sigh of relief. "This is the way out of Logan's realm." He took out his wand, murmured an incantation, waved it at the teenagers, then grinned broadly at the shock on their faces as their feet left the ground and they found themselves propelled upwards towards the middle window, which was swinging open as if to greet them.

Chapter 33

Cissy had already stridden ahead, followed at a more sedate pace by the shorter-legged goblin, with Luke bringing up the rear. By the time they had caught up, Cissy had already used her wand to reveal the door into the Sanctuary. As it swung open, they all jumped through, much to the surprise of Molly, who leaped to her feet and reached for her wand.

"Relax, Molly, it's okay." Cissy gestured to the girl. "This is Maisey, the reason you almost wet your knickers earlier."

Wet my knickers indeed, she thought indignantly, but was prevented from an acerbic response as Maisey gasped. "You are the great witch, Molly?" There was wonder in her voice and her eyes shone.

Molly looked for any hint of mockery but clearly there was none, and the flattery went some way to mollifying her. "I am. What were you up to in the passage-betw—"

"And the great wizard Morgan? His name is legendary too. Is he here?"

"Morgan is no longer the leader of the Sanctuary; that burden has passed to Cissy, here. Now, what were you doing—?"

But Maisey had clapped a hand to her mouth in mortification. "I'm sorry!" She turned to Cissy. "I meant no disrespect. When we met, I had no idea of who you were! The tales of your exploits during the battle against the"—Maisey had to consciously prevent herself from spitting on the floor in disgust—"demons are already legendary in our town."

Cissy smiled. "Thank you, Maisey. You are very kind. But really, you must tell us why you were going to the mortal world."

"The mortal world!" Molly exclaimed so loudly that Maisey took an involuntary step back. "Why the bleedin' 'ell are you going to the mortal world?"

Molly's cockney accent, always more pronounced when she became agitated, was totally unintelligible to Maisey, so she remained silent. In the end it was Luke, always hungry, who spoke.

"How about we have something to eat and you can tell us all about it?" he suggested.

"So, we knew the stranger was coming long before he reached the town." Maisey munched on sandwiches and cake as she looked around at her surroundings. "We let him go down the main road of our city until the queen – she's called Kamontip – was ready to meet him."

"Okay, go on," said Luke. "What then?"

"Well,"—Maisey was enjoying being the center of attention—"you'll never, ever guess who the stranger was!"

But Cissy, of course, had already put two and two together. "The Dark Wizard," she replied dully. "Logan. He needs a wand."

"Oh," said Maisey, a little deflated, "you already knew."

"Never mind." Cissy was desperate to know whether Logan had succeeded. "What happened next?"

"So, he was Kamontip's guest for all the time he was there." Maisey paused to think. "And he was shown all around the town." Faintly uncomfortable at the three pairs of eyes fixed intently upon her, the young goblin tried desperately to remember more. "Oh, I know! He was never left alone either. That's why Gnerx didn't believe it was he who stole—"

"Yes, yes," interrupted Luke. "But did he get a wand?"

"Oh, well yes, he did."

The collective hearts of Cissy, Luke, Molly and now Wallace, who had just joined them, sank at this unwelcome news.

Maisey grinned at their crestfallen faces. "But don't worry, Kamontip is far too clever to give power to someone like him. The wand he got had only enough power so he could get home through the realm of the Demon King, the way he came in. And then he would have a long, long journey back to the dimension in which he lives."

"But none of this explains—" began Luke, before Molly cut in.

"The demon world? So that's how Logan got to *your* world; I had wondered." She stopped, her expression even more puzzled. "But how did he get through the demon world? It doesn't make sense. Unless..."

"Unless he wiped out the remainder of the demon race," Cissy breathed. "Those who escaped the battle?"

"Which includes the Demon King," Luke reminded them.

"But how?" Cissy aimed the question at Molly. "Surely he doesn't have that much power?"

"No," the witch replied. "I don't think any wizard would; not even Morgan." She lapsed into silence before admitting, "I've no idea how…"

"It was the blood moon."

Everyone stared at Maisey in astonishment.

"How?" said Cissy at last. "How did he conjure it?" As far as she knew, only Aeryn had that power.

"Actually, how the blood moon got inside the demon world might be the more pertinent question," Luke pointed out.

"Oh, I didn't think of that." Cissy was puzzled. "Maisey, could you be mistaken?"

"Dunno," she admitted, "maybe I could." She thought for a moment. "All I heard was that he caught some of the moon's poison in a jar. You know, on the night of the big battle."

"Captured some in a jar." It was a rare contribution from Wallace, who found himself chuckling.

Cissy was skeptical. "Is that possible, Molly?"

The witch grinned. "I've no idea, but the Demon King's bleedin' dead, isn't he?"

"Okay, okay, that explains how Kanzser died." Luke felt they were straying from the point. "But it doesn't explain why you want to go to the mortal world."

"That's true," Cissy agreed and looked at Maisey. "I think you'd better start from the beginning."

"Start from after the Dark Wizard got his wand; we don't need to know how he got there, you've already told us that bit," Luke interrupted quickly. "Go on."

Maisey sighed. This was the part she hadn't been looking forward to. She stared for a moment at the four expectant faces. "Well," she said at last, "it's to do with my sister. And the Queen's Wand."

By the time she had finished talking, nearly an hour later, the expectant expressions had changed to ones of concern. Molly had realized immediately how serious this was, for she alone knew of the wand, and was aware of its power.

"How much harm could this wand do in the wrong hands?" Luke asked, impatient to form a plan of action.

"It's one of the most powerful wands that ever existed." Not unusually for her, Molly's tone dripped with sarcasm. "*That's* how much harm it could *actually* bleedin' do."

Luke flushed. "Okay, okay, don't get upset," he muttered, "I was only asking."

"Sorry, love," said Molly, "I didn't mean to—" Her head whipped around as the front doorbell rang. "That never rings." She looked at Wallace. "The last time was in,"—she thought for a moment—"nineteen eighteen."

Wallace nodded. "You're right, that was when—"

"Err... is anyone actually going to answer that?" Luke enquired with a studied sarcasm entirely aimed at Molly, who realized it and grinned.

"I'll go then!" And she was on her feet and leaving the room before anyone else could react.

"I'll go with her," Wallace announced, "make sure everything's okay."

Molly, wand in hand, cautiously opened the enormous front door of the Sanctuary, Wallace behind her, sword drawn. Then they both jumped back in surprise as a tall figure bounded through.

"Molly!" exclaimed the Landlord, kissing her on the cheek. "And, Wallace, my dear fellow,"—he grabbed his hand and shook it vigorously—"how are you?"

"Why use the front door?" Molly complained. "We never bleedin' use the front door."

"Oh, I just fancied a change. And just because something is never done doesn't mean you should never do it." He paused for a moment and his brow furrowed. "At least, I think that's right. Anyway, if I'd come the other way, along the passage, you'd have sensed it, Molly, and spoiled my surprise." He winked infuriatingly. "Come on in, you two." He gestured to Catrin and Grufydd. The boy had been there before but Catrin looked around in undisguised curiosity.

"Hans! The very man!" The chef had just appeared, wondering what all the commotion was, and the Landlord smiled at him. "Is the kettle on? And I would love some of your hot buttered toast!" Out of breath, he turned to the bewildered witch and wizard. "Now, where's Cissy? I have news." But as he strode into the large sitting room he stopped when he saw the goblin. "Ah," he said slowly, his face becoming serious. "I see my news has come too late. You know already of the loss of the Queen's Wand."

"Yes," said Cissy, "we've just been told. Maisey is on her way through the mortal world to retrieve it."

"A wise move," the Landlord approved, but he was suddenly worried and distracted.

"Hi, Grufydd, good to see you again." Cissy pecked him on the cheek and he blushed scarlet. "How's life in seventeenth-century

Wales?" Tongue-tied as always with this girl who seemed to him like a force of nature, he smiled awkwardly, but was rescued from answering as Cissy had already turned to Catrin. "It's good to see you again!" She grinned at the girl. "Any news from the village? How's Ffranc?"

Catrin smiled back. "He's fine, and the big news is that Grufydd and I are betrothed." She blushed slightly and her eyes shone with happiness.

"What?' Cissy exclaimed. "That's fab!" She turned and sought out Luke. "Luke, guess what? Come here, quick!"

"What?" he replied, hurrying over. "What's happened?"

"Nothing yet," she said, grinning, "but Catrin and Grufydd are betrothed. Isn't that marvelous?"

"Err ... yes." He looked uncertainly at the couple. "Fantastic. Well done!" Turning, he muttered in Cissy's ear. "What's betrothed?"

She nudged him in the ribs and he winced. "It means they're engaged to be married, silly."

"Oh! Right, of course." He grinned at them, embarrassed. "Honestly, that's fantastic news. Congratulations!"

Cissy rolled her eyes and decided to save him from further embarrassment. "Come on, I'll give you a tour." She grabbed Catrin by the hand and whisked her away.

Just then, Hans appeared again, suspiciously quick, with the tea and toast. It was black; totally incinerated. "Hans," the Landlord admonished with mock sternness, "you've tried using magic to make this." He handed the plate back. "Would you mind?" As the burned offering disappeared toward the kitchen, he continued, "As I was saying, I can help you a little. I've just come from the Dark Wizard's mansion."

"His mansion?" Molly interrupted. "Don't be so bleedin' silly. Why would you?"

"I am never silly," he admonished, "well, hardly ever. And I have been there. Logan was out though."

"Out? What do you mean out?"

"Out. As in not at home. On vacation. Gone to the shops. Whatever."

"Molly, shut up,"—Wallace saw her about to argue—"let the man tell his tale."

"I was not long back from visiting the realm of the witches," the Landlord went on, "when I was told of the removal of the wand. Don't!" He saw Molly about to ask what he'd been doing there. "So, I sensed the theft and then it was no great feat to surmise who had taken it. We know Logan has been to the goblins." He looked around at his captive audience and weighed his next words carefully. "And it has been used."

He allowed the exclamations of dismay to die down before he continued. "Not by anyone of any great power, I don't think; I would have sensed its use more strongly. I surmise, therefore, that it was not by Logan. But perhaps,"—he glanced at the goblin—"our friend here might shed some light?"

Again, Maisey related her story and the Landlord smiled, pleased at the confirmation of his theory. "I had thought the wand was stolen by the Dark Wizard and my heart is eased to know it was not. It is my belief then that Myla has used the wand to perform some act of minor mischief. No great harm seems to have been done. Not so far..."

"What would happen if she used the wand to do something more serious?" Maisey asked, fearfully.

The Landlord answered as reassuringly as he could. "Myla would unlikely have the knowledge or skill to perform great magic." He hesitated. "But if she does..." He shrugged. "It is possible..."—he shied away from the word *probable*—"that the wand may consume her. In other words, kill her."

"Then I must follow and find her quickly!" exclaimed Maisey, horrified.

"Yes," the Landlord agreed, "you must."

He did not add that should the wand find its way into the hands of Logan... But a glance at Molly's troubled expression confirmed she understood all too well.

Cissy and Catrin returned, still hand in hand, to be met with an awkward silence as nobody knew what to say or do next. Puzzled, Cissy looked at Molly, but the witch shook her head and it was Catrin who broke the silence.

"I forgot to ask, Landlord, is Morgan coming to our betrothal party?" Now it was Molly's turn to look surprised; she'd heard nothing of this. "Oh, and you of course, Molly, and everyone else. You're all invited."

"Of course he is!" The Landlord cursed inwardly, having completely forgotten to mention it to Morgan. *I'll drop these two off at the village then swing by and see him, he promised himself.*

There was a further silence and a thunderous look swept across Molly's face. *I'm happy for them, but how can he contemplate going to a party when the mortal world is in peril?* she mused angrily. *It's... it's bleedin' inconsiderate.* She glared at the Landlord, a red flush rising from her neck and onto her face.

The Landlord stared back, accurately reading her thoughts. *I swore long ago to have no more to do with the doings of mortals,* he thought firmly, avoiding the sudden guilt that entered his mind.

They continued to stare for embarrassingly long moments, but the Landlord eventually lowered his eyes. "Well, this has been a complete waste of time," he complained to no one in particular. "And it took ages to get here!"

"Well, if you'd re-opened the link like you were supposed to," replied Cissy, pointedly.

"And when did you get so bossy?" he enquired. And under his breath, but pitched so she would hear, "Worse than Morgan already."

Cissy grinned. "That's a compliment, I think!"

He smiled back. "Probably. Well, take care everyone!" He paused, aware that he should possibly say something else. *Don't want people to think I'm strange.* "So, Mousey will keep looking for the Queen's Wand? Why do they call you Mousey?" He raised an eyebrow at the goblin. "You don't look at all like a mouse."

"It's Maisey." She smiled. "And yes, I will."

"Excellent!" He clapped his hands together. "And I suppose you Sanctuary lot can sort it out from there." His face already wore a distracted look that told everyone his mind was at least halfway back home. "Well, we mustn't delay any longer!" He was halfway to the door when he remembered and turned around. "You two coming then?"

"You could use the Corridor of Dimensions," Maisey pointed out. "Then use the portal from the witch's land; it would be much quicker."

The Landlord glanced keenly at the goblin, wondering how she knew about the portal.

"Oh, we goblins have our ways and means of knowing many things," she answered his unasked question. "It was just a thought."

Cissy and Luke followed this exchange with surprise, having no idea what it meant. Molly and Wallace did know, but they kept silent.

"Thanks for the reminder," the Landlord said. "But I don't think I'll bother; too many memories."

Maisey noticed the sad little smile on his face and was sorry for her teasing. She wanted to speak up, but he was already disappearing through the door. Catrin and Grufydd followed closely behind.

So it was that the Landlord made the mistake of ignoring the strange disappearance of the Dark Wizard, a decision that would plague him for the remainder of his life, even though he couldn't have known the repercussions it would have.

Nobody could have foreseen that.

Chapter 34

"Psst!"

Myla stared but saw no one.

"Pssst! Over here!"

This time she almost fell off the branch in shock as there, sitting directly opposite, in a tree on the other side of The Mall was the familiar face of her sister.

"Maisey! What are you doing here? How?"

"Never mind me! What about you!" she hissed back. "Why are you in the mortal world? And what's the meaning of this?"

Myla looked at the river of black treacle which had now receded back to the first-floor windows of the palace. She grinned. "I know! Isn't it fabulous?"

"No! It isn't! It's...it's..."

"Oh, lighten up, sis! It's only a bit of fun!"

"Fun? Fun! You've exposed the mortal world to magic! Goodness knows how this is going to be cleared up! All the glamours in the universe can't hide this!"

"Well," retorted Myla, defiantly, "the Dark Wizard doesn't mind when I go out and cause chaos. In fact, he encourages me to!"

"The Dark Wizard? What do you mean the Dark Wi..." Comprehension dawned and she felt herself go cold. "You're still allied with him? Oh, Myla! You fool!" Maisey held her head in her hands and rubbed her eyes until they were red, then looked blearily at her sister. "Logan, in our world, seemed a bit of an idiot, I admit, although I'm sure it was largely a pretense. But in this world, he is a different person altogether. Myla, he is evil!" She sighed. "Well, at least he doesn't have a decent wand..." She stopped, aghast. "Oh, no, please tell me he doesn't..." Myla was avoiding her eyes and Maisey was suddenly very scared. "Please, Myla, please tell me you have the wand safe. Just tell me you didn't give it to the Dark Wizard."

"Of course I didn't! I'm not that stupid! Anyway, I couldn't make chaos like this with my own wand, could I?"

Reassured, Maisey nodded at the truth of it. "So give it to me."

"No."

"Myla, you must! If it falls into his hands..."

But Myla had already jumped nimbly from the tree and was running.

Just as quickly, Maisey gave chase, but suddenly, Myla stopped, turned and grinned triumphantly.

All at once, Maisey's feet were enveloped in a glutinous mass of black treacle. The words that issued from her mouth were very un-goblin-like indeed.

*   *   *   *

"So, he wanted to make a creature that was immune to the blood moon. I think he planned using it to breed a new army. But the Demon King badly underestimated the witch's power and instead of a being he could manipulate, he created a monster. A monster he couldn't possibly control."

Myla was sitting in the Dark Wizard's mansion, filling in some of the blanks in Logan's knowledge about how Kanzser made the Necromancer all those years ago.

"Interesting," he replied vaguely. Truthfully, Logan was hardly listening; he was hungry, and the mansion, being unoccupied for so long, was freezing. He waved his wand toward the big open fireplace and spoke the incantation in his mind that would light a fire. But nothing happened and he looked furtively to see if the goblin had noticed. Myla pretended she hadn't. *This wand is useless!* he thought. *I will make that goblin queen pay!*

"Never mind all that," he ordered. "Light some fires. Then cook me something. I'm hungry."

Myla quailed at the thought of having to cook; she was so *useless* at it! But she wasn't about to tell him that and she wandered off, curious to explore the place anyway. Soon, she found the kitchen where a drawer of rotting vegetables was in the fridge, in a soup of their own slush, an opened tin of tomatoes with a green, furry topping, and half a dozen eggs.

These will do, she thought gleefully as she poured the whole lot into a bowl, adding a good measure of salt to hide the taste. In no time at all, and with much help from her wand, she had fashioned something resembling a passable vegetable omelet.

"This is *good,*" Logan admitted. "I might keep you around if you can cook like this!"

Myla smiled, inwardly. "So, as I was saying, Kanzser used the witch, Mitra; did awful things to her." She shivered. The goblin race were a kind-hearted one; they did not make war, nor did they hurt or kill without reason. Myla could not conceive of how one living thing could be so cruel to another.

Perhaps this naïveté had led her to join forces with Logan in the first place, for after all, what harm could it do? This poor young creature, completely out of her depth, had been hoping to cause a bit of mischief but was about to unleash something, the consequences of which she could never have dreamed and for which she would never forgive herself.

"The Demon King created the Necromancer? I didn't know it was he."

"Oh yes." The goblin nodded slyly. "And some say the Necromancer, though long gone thanks to your brother, cannot truly by killed."

Mention of Morgan had the desired effect and Logan lapsed into a brooding silence. But what Myla took for anger was, in fact, excitement.

The Demon King thought himself the stronger, but it was I who survived! If only I could resurrect this creature! He looked thoughtfully at Myla. *My brother will bow down in allegiance to me and the mortal world will be mine to rule at last!*

"So what would it take, do you think, to recreate this monster?"

"The Necromancer?" Myla was appalled. "You couldn't!"

Logan put down his fork and looked at her coldly. "You presume to tell me what I can or cannot do?" His eyes flashed dangerously.

Oh, be quiet and eat your rotten, slushy omelet, she thought.

Hopefully you'll get food poisoning. "No, of course not," she said. "I just meant you don't have a wand powerful enough."

"No, but *you* do."

"What?" She took out her wand. "This old thing?"

At that moment, a large crow flew in through the window and landed on Logan's shoulder. It pecked fondly at his ear and fixed the goblin with a sharp, beady-eyed stare.

"You haven't met my spy, have you?" Logan stroked the bird's sleek, purple-black feathers. "He's been watching you."

"W-watching me?" Myla stammered. She sensed a change in the atmosphere, which had become cold and sinister, and for the first time she felt frightened.

"You see, goblin, you made the mistake of thinking me a fool."

As Logan unwittingly echoed the words Maisey had said to her only hours ago, Myla groaned inwardly. *Why didn't I listen to her? Why!*

"I know all about the chaos you've been creating in the city." His voice was soft and crooning. "And you didn't use *that* wand, did you?"

"How else do you think I did it?" She fixed a smile on her face and spoke brightly. "It's an excellent wand, you know."

"You're lying to me." Logan shook his head in mock sorrow. "Do so again and I will have my spy peck out your eyes. Then I will throw you into a dungeon where you will live out your days in darkness."

Shaking now, for she had no doubt he would carry out his threat, Myla reached inside her coat and drew out the Queen's Wand. "Sorry," she said, probably unwisely. "I'd forgotten all about this one." She held it out but Logan hesitated. "It's ok, the Queen's

Wand was not made for just one person, do you see?" She tried to keep the scorn from her voice. "It's been handed down through the generations. It won't harm you."

Knowing she wouldn't dare lie again, Logan took it eagerly, and his eyes lit with a strange, glittering light. He could sense its power, the strength of which he'd never felt before.

"How... how will you do it? Raise the Necromancer, I mean." Myla was not only curious, she fervently hoped that, even with the power he now held, the Dark Wizard wouldn't succeed.

"Oh, don't worry, goblin. I have a book with some *very* nasty spells in it." He laughed in triumph. "And I have something else. Follow me."

It was the Dark Wizard's habit to seek them out as avidly as any other collector, although this particular hobby wasn't quite as harmless as most. His *lost souls* had been sacrificed during a skirmish with his brother, while he, Logan, made his escape. Now they were back, these people for whom society had no answers and no compassion for the personal hell they found themselves in.

Their only succor lay in companionship, so they grouped together throughout London; safety in numbers, you might say. But it made them easier to find and Logan already had a dozen or so locked in the cell which had once held Luke's father, Peter, and Cissy. And outside he had three of the stronger looking ones digging a hole in the grounds of the old Victorian mansion; a big, wide, deep hole. This would keep the many more of their kind he intended to capture. That it was reminiscent of the Demon King's slave pits bothered him not at all.

At the noise of Logan's approach, the vain shouts for help from those in the cell faded and they cowered in the corners, each trying to look as inconspicuous as possible.

"See how they fear me?" Logan gloated. "And so they should!" He stooped and draped a casual arm across her shoulders; she had to force herself not to cringe from his touch. "You see, Myla," he continued, "my experiments are not an exact science, and the mortal race is weak." He shook his head disgustedly. "They have no stamina; that's why so many die!"

Myla was aghast at his casual talk of murder and she felt overwhelmed with guilt. But, thankfully, she was saved from finding an answer to his boasting; she felt she'd probably have slapped him.

"But come, I have some upstairs I've already prepared. Oh, raising the creature you call the Necromancer may be a little too ambitious, but I'm still going to have such fun!" He smiled and stroked the Queen's Wand reverently. "Come on," he said, and she hurried to follow him up the corridor. "Laters!" he called as he passed the cell, went out into the hallway and up a narrow, circular staircase that led to the top of the tower.

By the time they reached the top, Myla was out of breath and it was a moment before she saw what was kept in that room. But when she did, her knees buckled and she sank to her knees in horror.

The three men in their cages moaned in terror as they sensed the moment of their doom was at hand. And for the first time, this goblin child, who never really meant to harm anyone, realized the full extent of what she'd done.

"I plan to send these three out to cause a little mischief." Logan grinned maliciously. "They just require a little adaptation first." Myla groaned as he picked up the Queen's Wand and prepared to begin. "You like mischief yourself, don't you, goblin? Perhaps you can go along with them!"

Myla was weeping copiously now as she stared at the lost souls beseechingly, her eyes seeking some kind of absolution for her crime. But, of course, there could be none.

"No?" Logan shrugged. "Well, it's up to you." He moved to the cages and raised the wand. Looking back over his shoulder he winked at Myla. "Time to begin."

Chapter 35

After centuries of living beneath the shadow of the Demon King, peace had come at last to Ffranc's village. Today was one of particular happiness and joy as all came together to celebrate the betrothal of Catrin and Grufydd.

"I'm glad you could be here." Ffranc surveyed the scene and nodded approvingly at the joyous throng of chattering, singing, dancing people. "They deserve this. After living under the shadow of evil for so long, they deserve these moments of happiness."

"And many more to come, I hope." The Landlord smiled down at his friend. "And you, Ffranc, you must be very proud today."

"Of course, how could I not be. They look well together, don't they?"

"Well, it's long been expected they will marry, and Grufydd is a good lad, if a little..." The Landlord bit his tongue, embarrassed.

"A little dull?" Ffranc chuckled. "But loyal and true, which counts for a lot. And anyway, he has emerged from his shell since he visited the Sanctuary." He turned to Morgan, who, true to form the Landlord had only at the last minute remembered to invite. "And I have you to thank for that, old friend. I'm delighted you could come today, and so is Catrin, although she barely remembers you, so long has it been since your last visit."

Morgan accepted the rebuke for it *had* been too long, and the two men stepped forward to embrace. "It's good to see you again, Ffranc." He hesitated and looked at where Catrin was talking animatedly to a group of villagers. "That precocious child has grown into a beautiful young woman. I'm glad. Well, glad doesn't even begin... I mean,"—he shook his head in frustration—"what I'm trying to say is, I'm happy the harm done to her by my brother is no more. I feel responsible and..."

The words *my brother* hung heavily in the air for a few seconds before the Landlord opened his mouth, ready to break the suddenly awkward silence. Yet it was Ffranc who spoke.

"I'm glad too, but you bear no responsibility, Morgan. You should not answer for Logan's crimes." Ffranc did not add that there would have been fewer of these had Morgan killed his brother years ago as many, himself included, believed he should have done.

And as the three of them walked companionably to where the village was gathering en masse, none knew that Logan was about to commit his most horrendous crime yet. Ffranc left them as he wanted to speak to the young couple and agree on final arrangements. As the village elder, he had performed countless ceremonies over the years but this one was different and he felt strangely nervous.

The Landlord and Morgan were left alone and, each reading the mind of the other, began to weave their way toward where two teenaged lads, clearly relishing the importance of their role, were handing out huge tankards of the delicious, if somewhat lethal beer brewed by Dai the blacksmith. Their progress was slow as, with every few steps, someone stopped them to greet the Landlord and share a few words.

Morgan was viewed with curiosity and even suspicion by some of the younger folk who did not know him but could sense he was someone of great power and importance. But many remembered him and from these he received just as warm a welcome as the Landlord. Before too long, each held a tankard of the rich, frothy beer. Still, before they could be finished, the ceremonial horn blew, which called all to gather in a circle around the couple, and the betrothal ceremony began.

It started with a rather long-winded speech from Ffranc, and the Landlord, who was easily bored, allowed his attention to wander. His gaze meandered around, taking in the faces of smiling or sniffling women, the fidgeting of the young children already wanting to go and play, and the men, each on their best behaviour but equally anxious to escape the proceedings and for the party to begin.

That one there, the short, fat one, already perspiring, doesn't look comfortable at all, he thought, amused. *And him there, swaying from side to side; too much beer already, probably.* His eyes continued to follow the circle round. *What about that one, the tall one? He looks angry, a bit shifty and out of place.* The Landlord's reverie was interrupted by a loud cheer and, realizing he'd not been paying attention, wondered hopefully if it was all over and the couple were betrothed. It all seemed rather long-winded to him. *I wonder how long the actual wedding will be, when it comes,* he thought, *probably twice as long.*

But no, Ffranc was talking again and with a small sigh, he glanced at Morgan to see if he was equally bored, but to his annoyance his friend appeared to be enjoying the ceremony immensely. Unsure why his mood had suddenly soured, the Landlord looked around more intently, not realizing it was now an examination, rather than idle curiosity.

There's another who looks out of place. He was looking around the circle more quickly now. *And him, even taller than the other two... all of them taller than anyone else here... unusually tall...* And, suddenly aware of a growing sense of unease, he realized he knew absolutely everyone present except for these three men.

He nudged Morgan and whispered, "Those three, over there,"—he pointed discreetly—"and over there; they don't seem right somehow."

"What?" Morgan frowned. "What do you mean?"

"Just look at them! I don't know them!"

Caught by his urgent tone, Morgan cast a brief glance at the men. *Yes, a bit odd looking,* he supposed, *very tall, almost as tall as I am, but no...*

"Nothing wrong, as far as I can tell. A bit strange looking perhaps, but really, just because you don't know them doesn't mean—" He stopped abruptly.

"What is it, Morgan?" Although the Landlord's power far exceeded that of his friend, his senses had not been as finely tuned for a long time and he waited impatiently for a response. "Morgan, what is it, what have you seen?"

"Wait!" he whispered back, irritably. "Just wait!" Morgan peered slowly, intently at each of the three strangers in turn.

Yes, he thought, *there it is again!*

Unmistakable now, so that he wondered how he hadn't seen it sooner, was the faintest of shimmers around each of them.

"Something's very wrong," he agreed at last. "They certainly aren't human, that's for sure, at least not any longer." He grabbed the Landlord's arm and pulled him backward, out of the circle of watchers. "Come on, we must find out what's going on."

Whether the intruders sensed something or whether it was mere coincidence, at that moment the forms of all three seemed to dissolve and then transmogrify into grotesque parodies of the human form. And they had wands. Not the kind of wand a witch or a wizard would have, sleek, beautiful and enriched with the history of their kind. These were crude affairs, twisted and knotted like miniature branches.

But deadly.

One of these was already aimed toward the not-yet-betrothed couple and both wizards realized, with horror, its intent. Morgan unleashed a bolt of fury toward the creature, who easily ducked it. The Landlord reached for his own wand, the wand which was absent and had been for countless years; it was the first time he'd ever regretted not having it.

Instead, he shouted, a deep, thunderous roar that contained all the power he could muster; it was enough to distract the creature, who turned toward him as he fired. The killing bolt, already leaving its wand, narrowly missed Grufydd and hit a young woman beyond him – a pretty woman, beautiful even – before she sank to her knees, then forward, face down in the dirt, already dead, her body a torn and mangled ruin.

The scene, so placid and happy only moments before, was now one of panic and chaos. The creature continued to search for Catrin and Grufydd, increasingly hampered now by the melee around it, and any who came close or hindered their view were simply cut down with a casual, dismissive flick of its wand. The others focused on the fast-approaching wizards, sending a steady stream of impending death toward them, and the Landlord could do little except try and keep himself alive as Morgan used his wand to shield them both and answer with his own fire.

As they ran, he screamed at anyone he passed to prostrate themselves on the floor, to avoid the lethal barrage. But none listened; their panic was too great and, adept as Morgan was at catching and deflecting the bolts of fire upward and out of harm's way, he could not catch them all. Some, only a few, escaped him and more people died.

So intent was Morgan on deflecting the merciless, staccato-like bolts, he had little chance to direct his own with any great accuracy. But then he got lucky as one of his bolts struck home, tearing one of the creatures almost in two. The Landlord, turning to congratulate him, lost concentration for a second and nearly paid for it with his life. When he became aware of the fire hurtling toward his head, it was already far too late to avoid it. It was then that the man cannoned into him, whether by accident or design, the Landlord would never know, but shoving him violently out of the way and taking the full force across his abdomen, zipping it open like a purse, his entrails spilling out.

As they continued their charge, the wizards had no time to spare him a glance. Suddenly, from the corner of his eye, the Landlord spied Grufydd running toward the two remaining creatures, the sword he had taken to proudly wearing on his hip held high above his head. Cursing the boy's foolhardiness, the Landlord veered away to intercept him and saw, to his horror, that Catrin was following him.

Morgan was unable to help, beset as he was by the creatures' relentless fire. But, no longer having to protect his friend, he could concentrate his efforts on fighting and, infinitely more powerful that he was, it was his opponent who soon fell to its knees, desperately fighting for its life. But then, to Morgan's own horror, he spotted a figure creeping stealthily up behind the creature, a big man who gripped the shaft of a huge, murderous-looking axe.

Dai! Morgan realized as he tried to increase the intensity of his own fire. The creature couldn't last much longer and was hardly able to resist at all now, its attention focused on merely staying alive. *Don't!* Morgan screamed inwardly as he saw the blacksmith raise the axe. The creature was weakening, could only last seconds more.

"Dai, don't!" he now screamed with all his might. "I have him!"

But the axe was already arcing down toward the creature's neck, striking but only half-severing it so the head hung to one side, grotesquely resting on its shoulder. And before it died, its face became transfixed with anger and rage as the creature turned to meet its tormentor. With its final act, it fired one last bolt of power, weak now but so close it disintegrated Dai's body into a hundred pieces of bloody tissue and bone.

"No. No. No!"

Morgan could hardly take in the magnitude of what he had just witnessed, what he was witnessing all around. For this was no battle, but simply the slaughter of innocents. The remaining creature was suddenly acutely aware that it was alone and its tiny, primitive brain registered that it might be in trouble. Those precious seconds of panic gave the Landlord the time he needed to reach Grufydd. He flung himself forward and wrapped his arms around the boy's legs, tackling him to the ground.

They'd be proud of that at the rugby in Cardiff, he thought illogically as the firebolt whistled harmlessly above them. But the creature was already aiming at Catrin, who had almost caught up with them. It was then that Ffranc, showing a remarkable turn of speed, ran past, deliberately placing himself in the line of fire, protecting the girl.

And for a few seconds, a few paltry, agonizing seconds, it seemed he would, knife in hand, reach the creature and rip out its throat...

The first bolt of fire took him high in the chest, leaving a gaping hole. And as the old man continued his run, hardly faltering despite the terrible wound, the scene turned to slow-motion for the Landlord and everything went silent.

He saw chips of bone fly in all directions followed by a cascading, fountain spray of scarlet. At the same time, he was aware of Morgan trying desperately to turn and level his wand. And of Grufydd, jaw drooping with shock, a bewildered expression on his face which might have been comical at any other time.

And Catrin's face, already contorting, twisted out of shape, mouth open so the Landlord knew her screams had already begun.

Then the sweet relief when a stream of pure, white power arrowed from Morgan's wand, incinerating the remaining creature.

And the utter despair upon realizing it had come a millionth of a second too late. Even as it died, a second bolt of fire left its wand, and while Ffranc might have survived the first, this second hit him squarely in the chest, killing him instantly.

Then that the scene clicked back into real-time, and the Landlord flinched as Catrin's anguished screams pierced his brain.

Chapter 36

From the cold, ice-bound wasteland of the planet he called home, Anarkus had watched with scorn as the Dark Wizard experimented on the mortals. *If I'd been there, I'd have raised the Necromancer itself,* he mused. But it had been fun, he had to admit, watching those, creatures, *whatever* they were, that the Dark Wizard had managed to summon, as they wreaked havoc among the mortals. The sight of dead and dying mortals had thrilled him – and that girl, how she had *screamed!* Anarkus smiled at the memory.

He despised mortals and had been tempted to intervene when the Sanctuary battled the demons, just to see Morgan and his cronies lose. He couldn't abide those sanctimonious custodians with their do-gooding ways, and their wish to protect the mortals was something he'd never understood. Mortals were vermin; only slightly less disgusting than the demons themselves. But if he *had* intervened, he'd have had to get rid of the demons himself, which would have taken more effort than he was prepared to expend.

If I'd been there... the thought had taken root in his mind. *Perhaps my time has come,* he mused. Yes! He felt a sudden surge of excitement and he knew he couldn't spend another *minute* on this lonely, uninviting planet. He went to his star scope and stared at the mortal world for a long time. He saw everyday domesticity, which made him feel a little sick, good deeds that made him want to vomit! But then he also saw crimes and unhappiness, tragedy and heartache, and the surge of excitement returned.

At last, he thought, *this is a world I would like to rule.*

*   *   *   *

It lurked silently in the shadows, alone and afraid; abandoned in this strange, unfamiliar place. All its kindred were dead and it had no idea in which direction lay home, only that it was very far away.

It wasn't the noise that frightened the demon; it was familiar with noise. Nor was it this place, with its strange dwellings, narrow streets and alleyways; it welcomed these, for they provided darkness and places to hide. No, it was the knowledge he was the last of his kind that filled him with terror, yet he was determined to survive.

Each night he crept from his hiding place to hunt for food; the occasional dog or cat made a welcome change to the endless supply of rats. Unseen in the shadows, he watched with envious eyes the steady stream of mortals as they passed by, totally oblivious to his presence. Their smell set his senses tingling and his mouth drooled with desire to taste their succulent flesh.

For now, he would content himself with easier prey; would not, *could* not attack these terrifying mortal creatures. Not yet. But soon, perhaps, when his hunger grew and the temptation became too much.

Tonight though he would feast well, for as he crept from the shadows he spied two skinny, mangy-looking dogs, themselves searching for the scant pickings from the piles of trash littering the alley.

With lightning speed, he shot forward and gripped one of them by the neck, preparing to engulf its head within his huge, drooling, stinking mouth. But the other dog, fiercely protective of its mate, leaped and bit the creature's arm, hanging on determinedly until it was flung away with such force it crashed into the wall at the other side of the alley. Instantly it was back on its feet, growling menacingly, at the same time yelping with pain.

But the brief respite had given the other dog, still held firmly by the pincer-like hand, the chance it needed. Twisting its head at an impossible angle, it sank its teeth into its adversary's forearm. Reflexively, the hand opened and it was free. Both dogs fled their doom, disappearing like thieves in the night into the darkness.

Screaming with frustration, he paced angrily up and down the alley until his heart ceased hammering and he could look around for easier prey. It wasn't long before he spotted the dozens of gleaming eyes; rats who'd enjoyed the show immensely but who dared not move from their imagined safety.

These at least were no match, and he soon had a pile of the sleek, black bodies arranged before him and he sat down to eat. First, he plucked out the eyes, setting them aside for dessert, knowing they were the tastiest morsels. Then his teeth ripped into the succulent flesh, warm blood spurting over his hands and dripping down his chin.

Crunching the last of the tiny bones and picking out those that had lodged in his teeth, he licked his hands until the last of the blood was gone and turned his attention to the eyes. Scooping them up, he crammed them all into his mouth, sucking greedily. They really were the most delicious part.

Sated at last and too full to move, he presently felt the need to urinate. Not bothering to stand, he did so where he sat until a pool of foul-smelling liquid surrounded him. Its stench permeated the air and drifted up into nearby streets, causing mortals to close their windows hurriedly and complain about *those bloody drains*. But the wildlife who had made these grimy London streets their home knew better. They recognized the stench of something evil in their midst and determined to stay well away.

The demon, now dozing in *after dinner* contentment, was initially unaware of another smell that had entered the alley, but gradually he lifted his head and breathed in the aroma with pleasure. His thought processes were not the finest but if they had been he'd have recognized the smell as human-like but *not quite human*. But he did have instinct, and as a tall figure became apparent in the gloom, his senses screamed *danger!* As the smell grew stronger, it was no longer enticing but menacing, and the demon shuffled backward into the shadows, hoping fervently it hadn't been seen.

Its hopes were dashed as a loud, amused voice rang out, "And where do you think you're going, demon!"

Terrified, it could not have answered, even if there'd been time. All he saw was a white-hot bolt of liquid fire before it slammed into him and he collapsed, unconscious, in a crumpled heap.

Returning his wand nonchalantly into his robe, the figure grasped the demon by its long, straggly hair and flung it over his shoulder.

Then, whistling a bright happy melody, it walked from the alley, its long strides taking it swiftly toward his next destination; a date with the Dark Wizard.

Chapter 37

The screams that disturbed the stillness of the morning were an ugly cacophony of horror, disbelief and anguish and were yet to be replaced, as they soon would be, by a cold and unrelenting lust for revenge.

The Landlord raced across the village square in a vain attempt to intercept the girl, but he was already too late. He slowed to a walk and watched helplessly as Catrin threw herself down beside Ffranc's lifeless body, and now the screams were replaced by sobs, her tears falling onto his cheeks, so it seemed as if it were he, not she, who cried.

"Ffranc!" She frantically shook his shoulders as if determined he could only be sleeping. "Grandfather, wake up!"

The sight of the young girl, vulnerable and waif-like in her simple, white betrothal gown, tore at the Landlord's heart. He'd lived for thousands of years and seen many things; yet, at that moment, he believed he'd never witnessed such a horrific scene. Desperate to somehow change what he saw, he propelled himself forward until he stood beside the girl. Yet he made no attempt to intervene, knowing it would be as pointless as it would be unkind. These last moments with her grandfather were the start of a long and painful grieving, one that would never truly heal.

The Landlord placed a tentative hand on Catrin's shoulder and glanced around at the devastation. He saw Morgan moving slowly, dazedly around, squatting beside the prostrate bodies, checking pointlessly for life. Further away, someone had already dragged away the bodies of the creatures and was piling logs on top in preparation for burning, wood intended for a betrothal feast but now serving a much darker purpose.

It was a long time before Catrin ceased sobbing but, emotionally spent, she was nearing exhaustion. At last, as her sobs subsided and became soft, kitten-like whimpers, the Landlord drew her gently to her feet. But, devoid of strength, her legs buckled, and she would have fallen had he not stooped quickly and gathered her into his arms. There, she snuggled into him, her thin arms snaking around his neck, and she was instantly asleep.

Morgan had at last finished his grisly task and, as expected, found none of the fallen still alive. He straightened from his stooped position and flexed his back painfully. The Landlord watched and his face was inscrutable as he caught Morgan's slight shake of the head. He did not react and no one, except perhaps for Morgan himself, would have suspected the rage that burned within his heart. It was Morgan who, once Catrin lay safely in her bed, cast a spell that would cause her to sleep for many hours. Then he and the Landlord left, for they, with the help of the villagers, had another task to perform.

The afternoon was well advanced and the sun was beginning its descent before each of the bodies, except that of Ffranc, had been raised upon biers of wood. By the time the village children, those who remained, had draped each one with the garlands of flowers they had made only the day before, darkness was upon them.

As was the custom, the oldest remaining member of the village took a flaming torch and led the others on a slow procession past each of the biers, pausing at each one to pay silent respect. Once they had all passed, he stepped forward again, then paused, unable or unwilling to go further. The torch shook violently in his hand and the tension in the air grew as his struggle continued and people began to mutter their disapproval at this lack of respect. Eventually, prompted by a nudge in the ribs from Morgan, the Landlord approached the new village elder and gripped the torch, steadying its erratic meandering, and together they approached the first of the biers.

The bodies of the murdered burned long into the night and the smoke obscured the moon and the stars. As dawn broke, the stench still permeated the air as Morgan and the Landlord were in a heated, whispered debate.

"She's been through enough! She shouldn't be made to face this as well!"

"And if we don't wake her, allow her to say her goodbyes to her grandfather, she will never forgive either of us!"

"No, Morgan, I won't have it! I simply will not—" He stopped as the wand in Morgan's hand flicked sharply toward the girl and she began to waken.

"Oops." The innocent expression on Morgan's face was completely spoiled by the smirk that tinged his lips. "That was accidental."

The Landlord was spared the need to respond as, at that moment, Catrin sat up and yawned loudly. "Hello, you two." She looked at them sleepily. "Where's grandad?"

And with the look on both their faces, realization dawned and the memories came flooding back. Abruptly, she turned and flung herself back onto the bed, the pillow muffling the sound of her cries. The Landlord made as if to go to her but was prevented by Morgan's hand on his arm.

Leave her, he mouthed, and after hesitating, the Landlord nodded, and together they left the room. When Catrin emerged an hour later, puffy-eyed but calm, from the small house she and Ffranc had shared, the preparations were complete. The usual custom after a death in the village was that they be bathed and dressed in white linen, before their final journey to meet the flame. But so many had fallen yesterday that there had been no time for such niceties and now Ffranc also would not receive that which had been denied his friends and neighbors.

So, there he lay upon his own funeral bier, dirty and bedraggled yet serene and proud, and encircling him was his village, each one waiting, needing to say their farewells to this man who had guided them for so long. At Catrin's approach, they parted to allow her through, though none were able to meet her eyes.

Head held high, she accepted the torch from the village elder and lay it amongst the wood. Instantly the flames leaped up around Ffranc's body, the heat so intense that those nearby had to move swiftly back. The villagers looked at each other, puzzled; no wood could possibly burn so quickly. They little suspected that there had been help from Morgan who, along with the Landlord, had determined Catrin should not be subjected to her ordeal for any longer than was necessary.

And then something curious happened. As Franc's disintegrated into ashes, smoke arose into the air, not black and foul-smelling, but pure white and sweet. This time however, it was not of Morgan's doing. Perhaps it was caused by the small amount of wizard blood that had flowed through Ffranc's veins. It did not matter, for amongst the villagers, the legends were already being spoken.

*   *   *   *

It wasn't until they'd returned to the old railway station nearly a week later, that the Landlord allowed his rage to spill over.

"You know who is responsible for this, don't you?" He jabbed a bony finger into Morgan's chest and glared accusingly.

Morgan neither flinched nor stepped back, although even he was astounded by the extent of his friend's anger. Instead, he stared intently, trying to see beyond the eyes and into the mind, searching for a clue as to what was wrong. For something was *very* wrong, that much was obvious.

"Demons," he said at last, "three renegade demons who somehow survived the blood moon, out for revenge."

"Demons? That's what you think? *Demons?*" He laughed incredulously, a mean, nasty laugh, so unlike him and one Morgan didn't like. "Oh, Morgan, you misguided fool! Those were not demons!"

"They must have been. What else?"

"Think!" The Landlord shook his head angrily. "Morgan, use that brain of yours and think! Who hates you and would do anything in his power to cause you harm? Who delights in mischief for its own sake, whenever, wherever he can? Who has a new wand, the Queen's Wand at that?" This was a long speech and he was forced to pause for breath. "And lastly, who would be so foolish as to attempt the recreation of..." He paused again when he saw comprehension dawn at last.

Morgan stepped backward, staggered, and sat down heavily into the nearest chair. "The Necromancer," he guessed. "He tried to recreate the Necromancer." His voice was flat, without emotion. "I find it hard to believe that even he—"

"Well he did!" The Landlord could feel his rage rising again. "But instead, he created those worthless spawn. And what? You think they just *decided* to murder my friends?" He bent low so that his face was close to Morgan's. "But I swear to you now, no more excuses for that accursed brother of yours. You should have killed him years ago, but you have persisted in trying to find good where none exists. And now look at the heartache your hesitation has wrought!"

He stood abruptly and there was something akin to scorn in his voice. "But no matter, Morgan, for when I next see your brother, and I promise it will be soon, I will do it for you."

Morgan knew the Landlord did not make empty threats, but he also saw his friend's rage and knew it would eventually pass. When it did, so would his urge for revenge, for it was beyond the Landlord's comprehension to commit murder. It had been done to his old love, Mitra, a guilt the Landlord had lived with for thousands of years and a guilt that rendered him incapable of committing the same act.

Morgan sighed and thought of Cissy and the others. He knew he couldn't abandon them to face the trials that were surely coming, alone. But for now, it would have to wait. He had a wedding to attend.

Chapter 38

At first, Logan didn't recognize the doorbell chimes; as far as he recalled, it had never been used before. Aghast that someone would have the absolute temerity to disturb him, he marched angrily to the door and flung it open. Whoever it was would pay dearly.

"Logan!" A tall figure pushed past him. "So glad to meet you at last!"

Logan gaped, his angry words trapped like hot coals in his mouth.

"Your attempts to raise the Necromancer were admirable. Truly. Really good. Honestly. Well done!" Receiving no reply, the stranger grinned. "Sorry, sorry. Rude of me to barge in like this. We haven't been introduced. I'm Anarkus."

There was a long pause before, finally, Logan spluttered "I'm... I'm..."

"Yes, yes." Anarkus patted his hand kindly. "You're Logan and you're wondering what I'm doing here." He waited as Logan nodded, still unable to speak. "Quite right, too! Awful of me to disturb you like this. Honestly, my manners! Well, you see, it's like this. Your attempt to raise the Necromancer – wonderful. Simply quite *fabulous.*" Suddenly, the smile left Anarkus's face and he pierced the wizard with a searching look that sent a shiver down his spine.

Logan swallowed, uncertain, sensing that he was in some kind of danger. This stranger exuded menace. *Why is he here?* he thought. *And what does he want?*

"But amateurish. Not what I'd have expected," Anarkus continued. Then the smile returned, which confused Logan even further. "But no matter, we're going to do it together. And we'll need this."

Logan had hardly noticed the demon draped across Anarkus's shoulder, so stunned was he by the intrusion.

"That your servant?" Anarkus dropped the demon to the floor and indicated the goblin, who was unsuccessfully trying to hide behind a nearby hat stand. "Have it take *that* up to the secret room in your tower." He grimaced with distaste. "Then get rid of it. It's of no use to us. Send it away. Better still, kill it. Or something." Anarkus waved a hand airily to indicate he didn't really care. "Whatever."

How does he know about that room? Logan wondered as he indicated frantically, that Myla should obey.

"You're wondering how I know about the room." Anarkus watched with contempt as the goblin crept from her hiding place, head lowered almost to the floor in an attempt to remain anonymous. He'd never liked goblins back in the old part of the universe with its dying sun. And there there'd been a planet *teeming* with them.

Vermin, he thought. *I'll use it in the experiment. That'll be fun. And there'll be one less of them polluting the universe.*

"I *know,*"—he turned to Logan—"because I've been watching you for a long time. And your brother. And... well, everybody actually." He grinned sardonically. "They call you the Dark Wizard, don't they? I've never understood why, tbf."

While Logan tried to work out what *tbf* meant, Anarkus continued, "You're not that dark and certainly not so powerful."

"Why are you so certain you'll succeed where I could not?" Logan dared, stung by the stranger's arrogance.

"Really? You need to ask?" He cocked a surprised eyebrow. "Because it will be me making the spell rather than you." He paused as an angry flush appeared on Logan's neck. "Oh, you don't agree?" He smiled condescendingly. "I've told you, you're really not that powerful in the grand scheme of things. And it takes a mighty wizard, as well as wand, to raise the Necromancer. Understand now?"

"Yes," Logan grated, not daring to release his anger.

"Anyway, you tried to raise it from scratch and you were never going to succeed. I, on the other hand, will not do so."

"What are you talking about?" Logan was already sick of this braggart who, if he hadn't disturbed him so much, would long since have been flung out the door.

"Oh dear." Anarkus shook his head. "You really don't understand, do you?" By now they had wandered into an opulent lounge filled with old Victorian furniture. He sat on a *chaise longue,* his boots deliberately smearing mud on the delicate fabric, and indicated Logan should sit opposite. Logan did so, determined not to show his annoyance. But Anarkus noticed anyway and sniggered.

"There are three reasons why I will succeed where you could not. One, I have true power." He counted on his fingers. "Two, the flesh of that demon will make this *so* much simpler. And three,"— he looked keenly at Logan, wanting to see his reaction—"I will not be attempting this from scratch. You see, Logan, it is *I* who will be transformed." He laughed triumphantly. "I see you are surprised. But it's obvious when you think about it. I'm already the most powerful wizard, like... ever. So who better than I to do it?"

Logan shook his head slowly and his mouth dropped open.

"I'll be quite fearsome, don't you think?" He paused. "Well, I'm already fearsome, obviously. But when the spell is complete and I am transformed, I will be truly the master of all." Anarkus's eyes were lit with madness. "Then I will pay a visit to that accursed witches and wizard council." He allowed himself to daydream briefly before turning to Logan again. "That is going to be such fun! And then it will be the turn of the mortals. I have a fancy for this world and I'm tired of being so far away on my cold, dull planet. So I've decided to take over this one. Shouldn't take long."

Having long harbored a similar dream, Logan could only stare at him in appalled silence.

"And, if you're lucky, I might take you along for the ride. Make you my second in command, so to speak. Or I might not. Perhaps I'll just get rid of you. I haven't yet decided."

*　　　　*　　　　*　　　　*

With difficulty, Myla at last managed to drag the demon up the stone spiral staircase and into the room at the top. Panting heavily, she weighed her options, knowing she had only minutes before Logan summoned her to return.

And then what? The goblin wondered. This new stranger frightened her in a way that Logan did not. One certainly wouldn't underestimate the Dark Wizard, but Myla felt he quite liked having her around. But this new stranger was different and Myla didn't fancy her chances of surviving much longer. From downstairs she could hear laughter and it chilled her to the bone. She wondered if the two wizards were already planning her demise.

But how to escape was another problem entirely. Obviously not by the front door; she'd never make it. *And Logan keeps every window in the place locked.* The goblin felt the first flutter of panic. Involuntarily, her eyes went to the narrow window of the room where she stood. It was the only one in the castle that wasn't glazed. Being so high off the ground, Logan had presumably not thought it worth bothering.

Myla forced herself to stick her head through the gap and look down. Immediately the ground seemed to rush up at her and she leaped back in fright, dizzy.

"Goblin!"

She jumped at the shout and looked around with big, scared eyes, feeling like a cornered animal, but there was nowhere to hide. Shivering with fright but seeing no other way out, Myla was about to climb through the window when an awful thought popped into her head.

The Queen's Wand! I can't go back without it! Summoning her courage, she walked back to the top of the spiral staircase just as another shout summoned her.

"Goblin!" Logan bellowed again, sounding angry this time. "What's taking so long?"

Myla ran down the first flight of steps and shouted, "I'm coming!" But instead of continuing down, she veered left into Logan's chamber.

She knew this was where he kept the Queen's Wand.

But where? She looked round at the clutter in the room and her heart sank.

Frantically pulling open drawers and cupboards, Myla knew she had only seconds before Logan – or worse, the stranger – came to investigate. Sure enough, the moment the thought entered her head, she heard footsteps coming rapidly up the steps.

She looked around, forcing herself to slow down, almost sobbing now with fright. *And there it was!* High on a shelf, almost out of sight and certainly out of reach. But Myla hadn't risked so much to give up now. Taking a run, she jumped onto the table, sideways onto a cupboard, and forward onto a wardrobe. Then, pausing only for a short breath, she leaped for the shelf, just managing to nudge the wand and send it falling to the floor as she fell.

She landed nimbly on her feet and caught the wand just in time, then in a flash she was out of the room and hurtling back up the stairs just as someone's shadow approached the final bend. Without a thought, she was out of the window and climbing down the wall, her hands and feet scrabbling desperately for purchase.

Maisey stared up at the Dark Wizard's mansion, wondering how on earth she could get inside and find her sister. As she walked stealthily around the outside looking for a way in, she was startled to see a small figure clinging high up on the outer wall of the turret. Drawing closer, she was even more surprised to see who it was.

"Myla!" she hissed. "What are you doing!"

"What does it look like?" she called back, sarcastically but softly. "I'm escaping!"

"Well get on with it! I'm nervous! We need to leave!"

"I can't! I'm stuck!"

Maisey rolled her eyes and, not for the first time, cursed her sister for the ridiculous amount of trouble she brought upon herself. Drawing out her wand, she thought for a moment then smiled and pointed it at the trees that populated the area. She formed an image in her mind and, with sounds of creaking and cracking, branches began to elongate, growing thinner before intertwining, forming a ladder that snaked up to where Myla clung. Nervously, she clambered on and scrambled quickly down, relieved to be on firm ground again.

"You are such an idiot!" Maisey whispered.

"I am not!" Myla whispered back sulkily. "I just like adventures. I can't help it if you were born boring!"

"Well, I'd rather be boring than have to face Kamontip and tell her the Dark Wizard has the Queen's Wand!"

"Oh, but he doesn't." Myla grinned triumphantly and pulled the wand from her pocket.

Exasperated and undecided whether to scold her further or hug her, Maisey opted for the latter. "Now come on! Let's go!"

"Wait!"

Maisey stopped and turned slowly as she strived for patience. "What now?"

"He keeps people imprisoned in his dungeon!"

"What are you talking about?" Maisey said impatiently. "We can't hang around here. Come on!"

"He calls them his lost souls. We have to free them!"

Maisey stared at her, horrified. "We can't! We have to get away! They'll just have to take their chances," she said firmly, avoiding

Myla's eyes.

"Maisey, he uses them for his experiments!"

"But—" She was about to refuse again when she felt a bitter sensation in her stomach which she recognized as shame. "Okay," she agreed. "But we have to be quick. Show me where."

Within minutes, Myla had led her halfway around the building and pulled at the undergrowth. Soon she had uncovered a small, barred window.

Inside were about twenty people, imprisoned in unbearably cramped conditions. As light filtered into the room, they shielded their eyes; it had been a long time since any of them had seen daylight.

"Help us!" they clamored, reaching up to the bars. "Please! Set us free!"

"We will!" whispered Maisey. "But you have to be quiet! Now stand away from the bars."

Within a minute, the bars were a pool of molten metal on the cell floor and its occupants were clambering out to safety. There were a few puzzled looks at this strange-looking pair followed by hugs and brief whispers of thanks. Then they melted into the shadows and were gone.

As for the two goblins, they ran, as fast as they possibly could.

Chapter 39

The castle was festooned with purple banners, Daraproud's favorite color, and outside the crowds gathered, dressed in their finest clothes and holding flowers ready to throw for the new couple. Roses, gladioli and orchids already covered the yellow cobbled streets of the town through which the procession would pass.

Flags fluttered in the breeze from the tallest turrets of the castle; not just the standards of Aeryn and Daraproud but as a mark of respect and peace, those of the half-dozen important families invited to the festivities. Draping the whole area was an eiderdown of delicious aromas as dozens of street vendors cooked their wares. The scents of roasting meat and baking bread competed with that of the flowers, perfumes, tobacco smoke and incense. Jugglers and acrobats entertained the quickly amassing crowds and children skipped and played amongst it all, excited to see the princess.

Inside, the sun streamed through the wedding room's long, many-paned windows, lighting it with a soft, golden ambiance. The low hum of conversation from the hundred invited guests added to the sense of suppressed excitement that was steadily building. Alessandro had got his wish and representatives from the Viangg tribe had indeed been invited. Whether this would promote peace between the two families was debatable.

Morgan thought of Catrin's betrothal party and thrust it quickly away, lest his sadness sour the occasion. Aeryn, as ever, read his thoughts accurately and drew him into a brief embrace.

"Peace, my love. They will be avenged. Cornelius will see to it."

Her words were well meant, but they jarred and tugged at his conscience. He had decided not to lend his aid in retrieving the Queen's Wand because, after all, Cornelius would need no help in wresting it from Logan's hands and returning it to its rightful owner. *And I have a family now. They need me. Daraproud needs me here on this, the happiest day of her life.* His decision made sense. *So why do I feel so guilty?*

"Yeah, lighten up." Molly nudged him. "This is a wedding not a bleedin' funeral." Aeryn winced at her lack of tact, but Morgan smiled; he was used to it. Molly was already on her third glass of wine and slurring her words a little. He recalled the last time she'd been thoroughly drunk.

It was what... about seventy years ago at that party celebrating the however many thousands of years since the creation of the Sanctuary? He chuckled. *It was hilarious. The chaos she caused!* Seeing Molly's empty glass, he removed it from her fingers and replaced it with a full one from a nearby table.

"Thanks!" she said, surprised at his solicitousness. "Be right back." She had spotted someone she knew across the room and went to resume an argument they'd started in the 1870s.

"Daraproud looks amazing!" Penelope came running up, her face flushed with excitement at being included as one of the bride's attendants. "Hi, Aeryn!"

"Penelope, hello! Welcome to our castle." She bent and kissed her cheek. "At least this time you came with an invitation!"

Penelope grinned. "I know. I was so scared when I just turned up like that!"

"Nonsense, child. You were never in danger. Well, not really." She nodded at Morgan. "Unlike him."

"Oh, hush." He smiled. "You were happy I was there." Their eyes locked and they were momentarily lost in the love they held for each other.

"Ha! So you say. I was happy *and* angry," she reminded him, turning to the girl. "It's a pity Cissy couldn't be here. Luke and Wallace also, of course."

"I know," agreed Penelope, remembering how she'd begged them to come. "But they couldn't leave the Sanctuary *completely* unguarded. Molly and I will go back in a few days."

"Well, no matter. Now, I understand my sister has *another* surprise for you."

"What? Tell me!" Penelope jumped up and down with excitement. "What is it!"

"Have patience!" Aeryn laughed. "You will find out soon enough! Anyway, I think the celebration is about to begin."

Sure enough, as if by telepathy, the noise had ceased and moments later two figures appeared at each end of the room. Alessandro, immaculately groomed and wearing a robe of pure dark blue silk, held with a belt of fine-spun silver at the waist. On his feet were shoes of silk velvet of the same blue.

But it was Daraproud who drew everyone's eye, for she looked even more beautiful than usual. Perhaps it was the flush of happiness in her cheeks and the sparkling excitement in her eyes. Or the simplicity of her gown, a sumptuous shade of dark green, which molded to her every contour, down to her ankles. Or her hair, jet black and so sleek it looked wet in the torchlit room, like a seal's fur as it rises from the sea. It reached to her waist, threaded through and caught at the end with the same fine-spun silver.

Slowly, they approached each other and met in the middle. Alessandro sank to his knees and intoned formally, "Accept me as your companion in life until death."

Daraproud drew him to his feet and said, equally formally, "I accept." She in turn lowered to her knees and the words of the ancient ceremony were repeated.

Then, turning to their guests, they announced, "We accept each other."

"Again," the crowd demanded, as one.

"We accept each other!" Louder this time.

"Again!" This time the demand was deafening.

"We accept each other!"

There was a short pause, and then the chanting began. "Kiss. Kiss." Slowly at first but quickly gathering momentum. "Kiss, kiss, kiss!" The chant gained such volume they were heard by the waiting crowds outside, who looked at excitedlyat each other. They knew the ceremony was almost complete and their princess would soon be amongst them.

"Kiss!"

And the newlywed couple obliged, thus sealing their pact, and the gathering erupted into cheers and whistles of congratulations.

A short time later, two pure white stallions, manes threaded with flowers and coats shining in the blazing sun, were led to the castle gate. Daraproud and Alessandro appeared, hand in hand, to a tumult of cheers. They both mounted – she flamboyantly, he rather more nervously – and the procession began.

But almost immediately, Daraproud reined her horse to a stop and nodded to Penelope, who stood between Aeryn and Morgan. "Penelope," she called, "come here a moment!"

Wondering if something was wrong, the girl approached with trepidation. But when Morgan hoisted her into the saddle, she screamed in delight.

"So this is the surprise!" Daraproud's arms locked around her waist, and she looked up at her, eyes shining. "Thank you!"

Then, with the noise and cheers even louder than before, the procession continued on its way.

Chapter 40

"*That's* your wand?" Anarkus laughed. "Seriously? Logan, you really are pathetic."

"Very funny," said Logan dourly. "I was a fool to trust the goblin."

"You were indeed. All goblins are vermin. Although," he added, "their queen certainly played *you* for a fool." He sniggered. "I like that. Perhaps I should pay her a visit."

"Don't!" Unaccountably, Logan detested the idea of this monster sullying Kamontip with his presence.

"I see!" Anarkus laughed gleefully as comprehension dawned. "You like her, eh?" The smile left his face. "You disgust me. No wizard should associate with the likes of them."

"This one isn't so bad," Logan objected. "She's been quite—"

"I don't agree," Anarkus interrupted. "But that reminds me, have the vermin fetch the Queen's Wand. Well, it's *my* wand now. We'll need it soon."

Not daring to argue, although he'd so badly wanted to keep that wand for himself, Logan went to the bottom of the narrow spiral staircase. "Goblin!" he shouted. He was met with silence.

"So, your little vermin friend is hiding. Now why would it do that?"

"Goblin!" Logan called again. "What's taking so long!" Logan knew with a sudden, dreadful certainty that Myla had escaped.

"I wouldn't stand for that! Really, Logan, do you have *any* power at all?" Anarkus pushed him aside and ran up the stairs. "Come on. If it wants to play hide and seek, let's go find it!"

At that precise moment, Maisey and Myla were already heading for the lamppost and the safety of the circular room. Soon they'd be back in their own world and Myla was contemplating what she would say to the queen; what excuses she could possibly concoct. She'd always been able to talk her way out of trouble but this time she suspected it wouldn't be so easy. After making her sister beg a little, Maisey had offered to go on ahead and smooth the path for her return.

"Taking the Queen's Wand." She regarded Myla severely as they oozed through the tiny door. "You are in *so* much trouble. You know that, right?"

"Helpful. Thanks, Maisey, that's really helpful. Of course I know I'm in trouble." Myla regarded her sister hopelessly. "Just try and stop her from executing me," she said tremulously.

"Oh, Myla!" Maisey took her into her arms and hugged her fiercely. "She won't execute you, silly; she's not a monster." She walked quickly into the Corridor of Dimensions, anxious to be on their way and get it over with. "But,"—she winked—"I bet your punishment will be *pretty* terrible."

"So, you let it escape," said Anarkus sourly, watching from the turret window as the two goblins disappeared into the distance. "Is there no end to your incompetence?"

"It... it doesn't matter," Logan stammered. "We still have the Queen's Wand. I'll get it for you." He started for the door, eager to escape Anarkus's anger.

"No, we don't," Anarkus said softly, his tone dangerous. "It's gone too. I can sense it."

"But it can't be! I hid it well!"

"Why do you think the second goblin was here? Did you think the goblin queen would stand idly by and not send someone to get it back?" He lunged forward and took Logan by the neck, holding him against the wall, his eyes ablaze. "Give me a reason not to kill you right now!"

"Because... because you need me?" Logan choked, terrified.

Never before had the Dark Wizard's life hung by such a fragile thread, but suddenly Anarkus released him and laughed.

"Need you?" His was a cold, cruel laughter that continued until tears of mirth ran down his face. "*Need* you? No! I let you live because you *amuse* me!"

The spell was not a particularly difficult one for a wizard of Anarkus's undoubted skill, even though it would take most of the night to complete. He began by tracing a complex series of symbols with his wand onto the naked skin of the demon which now hung from the ceiling of the turret room. When he'd finished, he replicated them onto his own.

"That's the easy part done," he muttered, almost inaudibly. "Now for the rest."

"There are still the mortals I keep imprisoned," Logan ventured. The *easy* part had already taken two hours and he was getting bored. "You can use them?"

"They're gone too. Be quiet."

"But surely..."

Anarkus opened his eyes and regarded him, momentarily lowering his wand. "If you speak again, I will cut out your tongue."

Not knowing whether he meant it, but suspecting he did, Logan lapsed into an uneasy silence. Anarkus reached deep within and the incantations came quickly into his mind. He let them remain there, gathering momentum until, as the pressure built inside him, they escaped his lips, quietly at first.

The sound was curiously melodic and Logan felt himself relaxing, and presently he dozed. But the incantations were eager to be heard and soon they poured from Anarkus's mouth like wild animals bursting from a cage, free at last.

Logan jerked awake, annoyed at the interruption of a rather pleasant dream he'd just begun. *Can't he do it more quietly?* He thought grumpily and was about to complain when he remembered how much he valued his tongue. But now the demon's limbs were jerking spasmodically as the outrageous power Anarkus was creating flooded into them.

No wonder I couldn't raise the Necromancer myself, Logan thought, impressed despite himself. *I have literally no idea what he's saying.* He watched, fascinated as the demon began to speak, mirroring the incantations in a low, guttural tone.

They continued for most of the night, shouting the words at each other as if they were gladiators, each vying for supremacy. All at once, the demon's eyes snapped open and it gave a shattering roar which shook the room. The ceiling, which held its shackles, began to crack and stone dust drifted down. The demon glared malevolently at Anarkus.

"You fool!" it rasped, fighting to free itself of its chains. "You dare give me such power?" A large chunk of stone fell from the ceiling as it crumbled.

Anarkus knew the demon did not yet have the intelligence to use that power to free itself. But it would soon. This was a delicate balance and he relished the task. *Hopefully that ceiling will last long enough,* he thought, mildly concerned.

"Power?" Anarkus taunted. "You don't *look* powerful. How powerful are you?"

The demon was nonplussed, trying to come to terms with the thoughts it had in its head; it had never had thoughts before. "Why should I tell you?" it hedged.

"Oh, c'mon, humor me. Go on. How powerful?"

It took a while but the demon answered at last. "I am like the Necromancer, yet not like him." It considered for a moment. "No, I am even *more* powerful."

"Excellent!" Anarkus smiled triumphantly. "That's good then!"

"Release me and I will make you my servant," it offered, oozing malice and cunning. "I *promise*."

"Oh, I don't think so," Anarkus said, coldly. "You might be powerful, but you're still a dirty demon. I cannot *abide* your kind."

"You dare?" The demon thrashed against the chains and a massive piece of masonry narrowly missed Anarkus's head.

"Oops. That was close!" Anarkus hopped out of the way. "You do realize the sacrifice I'm making," he observed conversationally to Logan. "Oh, it's okay. You can talk now." He waved a hand at the wizard as more stone crumbled from the ceiling.

"Sacrifice?" Logan stared upwards in terror. "If you don't do something soon, we'll *both* be sacrifices!"

"Nervous?"

"Anarkus, stop it! That thing is nearly free!"

"Oh, for goodness' sake, Logan, if you insist." He raised his wand and pointed it at the demon. "Watch this."

Suddenly, the words changed and the incantation became faster and more intricate. Taken by surprise, the demon could not react quickly enough and watched in horror as its flesh began to draw from its body like thin, wispy strands of smoke.

"You see, Logan," Anarkus panted as he fought to draw the demon's flesh closer, "my blood is the purest it is possible to be. Did I ever mention I'm descended from the original wizard himself?" Boasting, he half turned to Logan and his concentration lapsed for a second. The demon lunged for him but was dragged back by its chains.

"But you see," he panted as he exerted control again, "now it will be. Forever. Tainted." His breaths were coming in short gasps; even he'd not realized how difficult this would be. "By this dirty, disgusting creature." The demon was now almost wholly engulfed in wand fire and its flesh was drawing closer to Anarkus, at the same time turning translucent.

"But,"—he yanked his wand back like a fisherman striking as his fish took the bait—"imagine the power I will have!"

The first of the demon's flesh entered his body and then more. As it weakened, it tried in vain to resist but Anarkus had no intention of letting it off the hook. Now though, he became aware of the pain, faint at first, barely noticeable but growing quickly.

The demon was powerless to resist, unable to mirror the incantations and prevent this assault upon its body. More of its flesh melded with that of Anarkus and, with a rare flash of insight, it realized it was doomed. But now Anarkus had a problem.

"Logan! It's still attached to the ceiling!" Anarkus saw the flaw in his plan, almost too late. "I can't use my wand, it's a bit busy! Use yours!"

"I can't either. It's rubbish, remember? *Pathetic* I think you called it."

"No. I called *you* pathetic. Now stop messing around and pull the chains from the ceiling!

Better do as he says, thought Logan. *He'll only complain if I don't.* He leaped up and grabbed one of the chains still securing the demon. The last of the stone around it crumbled away and the demon, Logan and half the ceiling came crashing to the floor.

With his free hand, Anarkus reached into his robe and drew out the knife he always carried. With two swift strokes, he cut through each of the demon's wrists, freeing them from the shackles. As Logan was drenched in blood from its severed arteries, the demon was engulfed entirely within Anarkus, who screamed at the agony of it and fell, writhing to the floor.

Spitting blood and dust from his mouth, Logan watched with interest as Anarkus wriggled around and wondered whether he would die. *I hope so,* he thought, *that would be so funny.*

But Anarkus had no intention of dying. He emitted scream after dreadful scream, trying to soak up the pain and, gradually felt it diminish. Then, with another scream, this time of triumph, he felt a new, ecstatic power rising within him.

"Am I not magnificent!"

"Yeah, wonderful. But never mind that, just look at my clothes. They're ruined!" Logan complained. "Do you mind if I go to bed now? It's been a long night."

"*You* may go to bed," Anarkus agreed. "I, on the other hand, have plans to make."

"What will you do now?" Logan was curious. "Murder all the mortals?"

Anarkus laughed scornfully. "Don't be stupid, Logan, I want to *rule* the mortal world, not kill it. No, I will create a virus."

"Don't the mortals have loads of those already?"

"Oh no, my useless friend, not like this one." Anarkus felt power and energy coursing through his veins. "The name of the virus I will create is much more dangerous and it will spread throughout the mortal world." He went to the window and looked out. "It is called"—and the word left his lips and rolled across London— "Mistrust!"

Chapter 41

It was a beautiful, sunny Wednesday as Anarkus strolled across Westminster Bridge with its gaily colored railings and stately, black-and-gold painted lamps. Below, the sunlight dappled the Thames and pleasure boats cut through its gently rippling water. To his right, the London Eye was stilled as engineers sought to solve the mystery of its mysterious high-speed spin, but the place still thronged with excited children and tourists, some queuing for the aquarium, others, the already packed restaurants.

At the far side of the bridge stood the magnificent edifice of the Houses of Parliament, seat of the government. The Elizabeth Tower soared nearly a hundred meters into the sky and just then the tower clock, Big Ben, chimed, announcing to the city that it was noon.

The air was filled with children's laughter, the deep throbbing notes of boat horns and heavy traffic crossing the bridge. After the silence of his own world, the cacophony assaulted his senses.

Ahead he spied a young couple approaching, hand in hand. Clearly very much in love, they paused every few steps to exchange kisses and secret smiles. Anarkus smiled also, but one of cunning and malice. He withdrew his wand discreetly and muttered an incantation.

Now, with every step he took, the ground fractured into a spider's web of cracks and the painted railings blistered. The sun no longer reached the water, which became dark and uninviting. Everything behind him turned gray and people began to stop, stare and point.

The young couple, oblivious to anything but themselves, passed him and as they did, the girl stopped and turned to her lover.

"You bastard!" She flung his hand from hers. "I *know* you're having an affair! Did you think I wouldn't find out?" With that, she stormed off, tears running down her cheeks as the man stared after her, his face etched with anger.

Just then, there was a minor collision between a car and a lorry. Within seconds the drivers had leaped from their vehicles and were arguing furiously. Pedestrians intervened, not to quiet things down but to add their own opinions and blame. In no time, dozens were involved and the first punches were being thrown.

Seeing this, ordinarily law-abiding citizens joined in the melee, eager to fight and cause harm. Furious at the hold-up, other drivers began fights of their own. Tourists abandoned their plans to visit aquariums and poured onto the bridge.

Inevitably, the chaos attracted the attention of the police who ran onto the bridge from both ends. But they were not intent on restoring order. Their mission to keep London safe forgotten, they joined in the fighting, truncheons raining down on exposed heads, and now people were being seriously injured.

Anarkus laughed in delight. This was only a small start to his plan but clearly his virus was working already. Walking nonchalantly through the crowd, he reached the magnificent gothic entrance to the Parliament building and went inside.

The place was busy with parliamentary employees scurrying around and excited tourists curious to see inside the seat of government. Within seconds the excited atmosphere changed to one of silence and fear as everything turned gray; the stained glass, the mosaic floor and the intricate stone and wood carvings. Frightened people streamed to the door, pushing and shoving to get out. An elderly lady fell to the floor, screaming as she was crushed underfoot. Her husband of sixty years thought about trying to help then decided it was too much trouble and ignored her, intent on reaching the outside.

Still inside, aides and employees who usually paused to pass the time of day ignored each other, hurrying past and casting suspicious glances. Two MPs, from opposite sides of the house but friends for years, accosted each other at the top of the broad, stone staircase. Soon they were brawling until one had the other bent backward over the stone balustrade, striving desperately to send him tumbling to his death on the stone tiles far below.

Anarkus ignored them all and made for the commons chamber where the Prime Minister's question time was already in full swing. In his black long-tailed coat and white bowtie, the doorkeeper moved towards him, ready to challenge if needed. But before he could get close, Anarkus's hand twitched and a small tornado of gray dust arose from the floor and enveloped him. There was only time for a stifled scream, cut off as his lungs turned to ashes before he died, transformed into a desiccated statue of dust.

Interesting, thought Anarkus. *I didn't know they did that.* Satisfied, he delicately touched the statue's nose and it collapsed like a house of cards into a small pile at his feet. Ignoring it, he moved forward and put his ear to the door. From inside could clearly be heard boos and jeers as the opposing sides tried to out-shout each other, with cries of derision and calls of *Here! Here!*

Anarkus smiled sardonically. Humans really were the most ridiculous creatures. Pushing the door lightly, it swung open and he stepped inside. At first he was unnoticed and it was already too late by the time he was. As the grayness of the virus swept across the chamber, good-natured catcalling turned into the beginnings of violence.

At first, shouts of *Order! Order!* could be heard as the Speaker of the House tried in vain to muster some decorum. But these soon ceased as he, suddenly full of scorn for these buffoons, leaped from his platform and laid in with his fists to whoever stood in his way. Soon, the entire place was a mass of seething bodies kicking, biting punching and scratching.

Stooping, Anarkus whispered into the ear of the Prime Minister who abandoned at once his tussle with the shadow Foreign Minister and left the chamber, clicking his fingers and summoning his private secretary to follow. Minutes later he was in his office reaching for the telephone.

"Get the President of the United States on the line," he ordered. "And the leaders of..." he reeled off the names of several of the most despotic leaders on the planet. Turning to his private secretary he barked, "Get me the heads of each of our armed forces. And the secretary for defense. I want to know the strength of our weaponry." He paused to think. "Particularly how many missiles, bombs"—he waved a vague hand—"and stuff, we have."

When the man had scuttled away, the Prime Minister sat, head in hands. He just *knew* attacks were being planned; that vast stockpiles of nuclear weapons were armed and ready all over the world.

And all of them aimed at us, he mused. *Even in the US, no doubt. Bloody Yanks; never did trust 'em.* He raised his head and looked out the window with desperate, paranoid eyes. *Well, I'll push the damn nuclear button first and not think twice.*

A short time later, he was engaged in a heated discussion with the US President, who sighed angrily as he slammed down the receiver. "Goddamn Brits!" he shouted, startling an aide who'd just entered the Oval Office.

Anarkus stepped from the portal in Times Square, New York City, and grimaced with distaste at the crowded mass of humanity and the smells of car fumes and hot dogs that pervaded his nostrils. He briefly considered taking one of the many bright yellow taxis that were simply *everywhere* but then reminded himself he wasn't a tourist. Anyway, he didn't have far to walk.

Down West 46th Street he went, then onto 6th Avenue, and within minutes he'd entered number 30 Rockefeller Plaza, where a famous news anchor was delivering the latest NBC news. He marched past directors and producers, past lighting technicians and camera operators, and glared at the special guest who was pontificating about the government's stance on foreign policy. Unaccountably, the guest, who was known as a radical and no pushover, stood meekly from his seat and, head bowed, vacated the studio.

Anarkus took his seat and turned to the cameras. The news

anchor, herself famous after many years as one of the highest paid TV personalities in the US, sat and watched, astounded but quite unable to protest. Live to millions across the US, Anarkus spoke softly and hypnotically for nearly thirty minutes. His compelling message was simple; you cannot trust your neighbors, nor your friends.

"Even as I speak," he told them, "they plot against you. They will steal your money and your homes. They will not rest until they have taken everything you have; not until you live, destitute and homeless, facing only a slow, lonely and painful death."

And across the globe people realized it was true. Just as they saw how handsome this stranger was, how caring and how.... *trustworthy!*

"You cannot trust *anyone,*" the handsome stranger continued, "and you must attack, before they attack you! But,"—and the smile he gave them was so filled with love that nobody doubted him for an instant—"you can trust *me.*" Everywhere, people smiled and nodded; many cheered as the stranger delivered his final message. "Get rid of your bosses, presidents and prime ministers, your dictators and overlords. *I* am your leader now and you know you can trust *me!*"

From New York to Nebraska and Los Angeles to Little Rock, the message fired across the airwaves. Within seconds it was being shared across the globe. Now, from Thailand to Tahiti and from Morocco to Mexico, friends, neighbors, loved ones, work colleagues looked at each other with a suspicion that quickly turned to hatred. Thoughts of violence infiltrated the minds of everyone, whether they'd seen the news broadcast or not, and law and order across the mortal world began to fail.

Satisfied, Anarkus left the studio and decided he *would* take a taxi after all. He stuck two fingers into his mouth and attempted to whistle one, but no sound came out. With a flicker of annoyance, he flicked his wand at the nearest one and it screeched to a halt, causing a cacophony of car horns and angry shouts. Its passengers, and the driver, got out and walked away in a daze. Anarkus settled himself behind the wheel and, unsuccessfully, tried to work out the controls. In the end he used his wand again to set the car in motion, then he settled back to enjoy the four-hour drive to 1600 Pennsylvania Avenue...

At the White House, the President was walking in the rose garden, trying to assuage his anger, which still threatened to overwhelm him. At first, he failed to notice the tall figure who approached. When he did, he instinctively looked for his aides and secret service guards, only to find they'd mysteriously disappeared.

I'll have someone's head for this, he thought, his anger intensifying. *I need that goddamn nuclear football.* He was referring to the briefcase, always kept within easy reach and which contained everything he would need to start a nuclear Armageddon. But all at once, his instinct told him something was very wrong. It was then he realized the flowers, the lawns, *everything* had turned gray and that the sky was almost black like the herald of an approaching thunderstorm.

What the hell? he wondered, staring as the tall figure tipped him a mock salute and walked away. Dazedly, the President of the United States returned to the Oval Office and sat at the famous old desk. He pressed a button on the intercom and spoke, "Get me the defense secretary. We're going to war!"

And so it continued throughout the mortal world. Across

America, racial tensions flared and murders increased a hundredfold as the bigoted realized their crimes would no longer be investigated.

In Northern Ireland, tensions between the opposing sides were magnified once more and the killing began anew, while in South America, drug lords flooded the streets with their entire stocks of narcotics, no longer interested in profit, seeking only to bring death and misery as quickly as possible.

There were riots on the streets of Paris and gender-based violence and discrimination in the Middle East intensified to even greater levels.

In Europe, far right groups took advantage of the unrest to spread their message of hate with even more venom than usual and people began to *listen*. And across the entire globe, the fingers of world leaders everywhere hovered over their nuclear buttons, each wondering with mad, paranoid desperation, which of them would be the first to strike.

In a mere two days, the world was in chaos, and the virus spread so quickly that those in the Sanctuary had heard nothing.

Chapter 42

"You bitch!" Lucy Hamilton sat astride her neighbor's chest, pinning her arms. "I've never liked you! Take that!" And she delivered a resounding slap across the woman's face, grinning in triumph at her look of utter shock and the already reddening cheek. "And that!" Now the woman's cheeks resembled two rosy apples. "And th—" She looked up, outraged, as her husband grabbed her wrist to prevent the blow.

"What are you doing, Charles? This bitch deserves it. The number of times she's complained of petty nonsense over the years! Do you remember—?"

"Lucy, stop!"

At first, he'd watched with satisfaction as his wife stormed up to the neighbor's door and demanded loudly she *get the hell outside!* And even more satisfaction as the woman had appeared, incensed at the intrusion and ready for battle. Then, as the argument escalated and deteriorated into violence, he'd egged them on gleefully, inciting them further.

But all at once, the wrongness of it had crept into his mind and the sight of his usually gentle wife screaming at the top of her voice, hair awry and her tights a shredded mess, sickened him.

Charles dragged her to her feet and bundled her into the house while she, powerless to prevent him, flung insults over her shoulder at her prostrate victim.

"What are you doing?" she screamed, pummeling his chest and trying to push past.

"Lucy! Wait. It's like we're infected or something!"

She continued to struggle for a minute longer before relaxing against him. "You're right." Suddenly she could sense it and she put a hand to her forehead. "What's going on, Charles? What came over me?" She buried her face in her hands and began to sob quietly.

"I don't know, darling." He enveloped her in his arms. "But there's a wrongness in the air. I can feel it now. Can't you?"

Her sobs subsided and she regarded him. "Yes, yes!" Anything to assuage the guilt she already felt. "I should apologize!" She made for the door.

"Perhaps now isn't the time," he suggested softly. "I doubt she'll want to listen."

"Of course," she agreed, sinking onto the sofa. "But what are we going to do?"

"*We* aren't going to anything," he told her, gently. "But I need to get to the Sanctuary and warn them."

Lucy knew it was pointless to argue with her husband, who could be awfully stubborn sometimes, and she assented meekly. "Go then, I'll wait here. But promise me you won't get involved in anything."

He nodded distractedly as he took his jacket and ran up the stairs to the bathroom. Reaching behind the hot water tank, he took something out and secreted it. Within minutes he had left the house and was walking quickly toward the lamppost.

She gave him a few minutes head start, determined to follow, but then she caught a glance of her ruined hair in the hall mirror and looked down at the missing buttons on her blouse and the destruction of her tights. Lucy Hamilton *never* left the house looking anything but perfect.

*   *   *   *

Peter and his wife had just returned from a short holiday at a remote country cottage and knew nothing of the events that had swept across London and the world. Already restless, he couldn't decide what to do for the best.

Still recovering from the demon poison that had almost cost him his life, he'd been moved to safety before the battle with the Demon King and had not returned to the Sanctuary since. Actually, Morgan had forbidden it and, truthfully, Peter had needed that time to fully recover. Now, apart from a slight ache in his chest where the demon blade had pierced him, and even then only when the weather was cold, he suffered no ill effects.

But still he delayed, for he valued the time to get to know his wife and son. Luke had been a baby when Logan imprisoned Peter, and his wife had believed him dead these many long years. Now, though, he was feeling restless, secretly envious of his son who'd returned to the Sanctuary a week earlier.

Nonetheless, Peter had stayed steadfastly away and been happy to do so, for he loved his wife very much and they had so much time to catch up on. But she'd noticed his restlessness and steeled herself to say the words she knew he wanted to hear. And hard though it had been to let Luke return to the Sanctuary, this was even harder. The last time her husband had left he'd not returned for sixteen years. Now she took hold of him and drew him close.

"Go, return if you must. I understand." Her voice became a whisper as she looked up at him. "But please, promise you will return soon." She turned away so he wouldn't see the tears filling her eyes, but he pulled her back.

"I will go soon," he agreed, "but not just yet, a few more days at least."

And she nodded, grateful. But that evening, as they sat relaxing together in the lounge, her nostrils twitched suddenly as an unpleasant smell entered them.

"Can you smell burning?" She was already out of the room and halfway up the stairs before he could reply. Seconds later the scream came. "Peter!"

He sprinted upstairs to find thick smoke billowing from their bedroom and a chest of drawers ablaze. "Get water!" he yelled as, thinking quickly, he hauled the duvet from the bed and began to smother the fire. Seconds later, she returned with a bucket of water.

"What happened?" she gasped as the last flames were extinguished. She opened the window and the smoke began to clear.

"I've no idea, I... Oh my God!" he exclaimed. "My wand!" Frantically he pulled open the top drawer, the charred remains crumbling in his hands. Inside were the remnants of socks and underwear, and in the middle, totally unharmed, his wand. He breathed a sigh of relief and took it from its box, holding it tightly.

"I don't know how…" He stopped as an idea struck him. *Had his wand caused this? But why?*

A gust of wind blew through the open window and slammed the door shut. Instantly, streams of tiny, silver sparks flew from his wand, three, four, five of them, impossibly bright, twisting, swirling, reaching. *Like tendrils,* he thought, and watched in fascination as they merged together and reached toward the door. *No, like fingers,* he realized as they gripped the knob and turned it.

Peter set out for the Sanctuary, unaware he was walking into tragedy. It was quite a distance to the lamppost, but it didn't occur to him to do anything other than walk; he'd spent too long in a tiny, cramped cell, courtesy of the Dark Wizard. With his strength fully restored, he relished any chance to be outdoors and free. But as he rounded the corner, he could see in the distance there was a figure leaning against the lamppost.

Damn it, he cursed silently, *why did he have to choose that one to lean against? It's gonna be difficult to get past, even with a glamour to hide me.* So, it was with surprise that, as he got nearer, he recognized who it was and ran the final few meters.

"Charles!" he exclaimed. "What are you doing here?"

"I'm coming with you," Charles replied without preamble, "and once inside I'm going to need your help to get inside the Sanctuary."

"Get inside? Help? What are you talking about? How *can* you help, you don't have a wand!" *Brutal but true,* he thought guiltily.

"Because of this." Charles drew the object from inside his jacket.

Peter stared at his friend in amazement. "The Knife of Chiang!" he exclaimed, forgetting to talk quietly. "Morgan showed it to me once. It was hidden away in the Sanctuary; hidden because it's precious and *extremely* perilous. How did you get it? *And why!*"

"I followed Morgan once, years ago, when we were boys." He smiled at Peter's incredulous look. "We'd been there about six months, I think. I couldn't sleep one night and I sneaked to the kitchen for something to eat. Alessandro was there preparing the next day's dinner; you remember how he hardly ever used to sleep?"

Peter nodded. "Go on."

"Well, as I passed the door to Morgan's chamber, it was slightly ajar and I heard voices. They were Morgan and Molly's, so I peeped in. They were talking about the knife and Morgan was hiding it in a secret place. I was just in time to hear him say the incantation. And I memorized it." He shrugged. "That's it."

"What do you mean, *that's it?* What happened then?"

"I bided my time and stole it just before I had to leave the Sanctuary," he replied, matter-of-factly. "It seemed important to do so somehow."

"You *stole* it? Like for a souvenir? You stole the Knife of Chiang for a souvenir? Why, Charles, and how? How did you get away with it without anyone knowing?"

"Not a souvenir," he denied. "I told you, it felt as if I had to do it, a sort of compulsion. As for how, well it was easy; I just walked into the room, said the words, and helped myself." Charles blushed slightly at the confession. "Nobody knew it was gone and they probably still don't." He stopped as a sudden thought occurred and gripped Peter's arm in excitedly. "That's it! It was meant to be! That's why I felt the compulsion to steal it. I've always wondered. I've had it hidden behind the hot water boiler in the bathroom for all these years!"

"The Knife of Chiang." Peter shook his head in wonder. "One of the most sacred relics from the elder years, hidden in a bathroom in the mortal world." He had to smile. "Charles, I can hardly believe it. You are a dark horse, I must say." Peter felt envious that he'd never done anything remotely close to breaking the rules.

"That's not the point!" Charles was almost beside himself with agitation. "The point is, why? Don't you get it? What if fate decreed I steal the knife to defeat this... whatever menace threatens the mortal world?"

"That's ridiculous, there's no way—"

"Why? Why is it ridiculous?" He lowered his voice as people began to look at them. "Peter, please," he urged, "I need your help. I *have* to get into the Sanctuary." He saw his friend waver and pressed home his advantage. "Look, I do know the words to get through the lamppost. If you won't help, I'll simply go in and wait for someone who will."

"But you've no wand," his friend said weakly, "and you won't get even close to whatever this... this *thing* is with that knife. Charles, it's suicide, you know it is."

"Perhaps," he agreed, "but this is my daughter we're talking about. She needs my help! And ask yourself why *you're* going, Peter. You can pretend all you like that it's for the good of the Sanctuary but we both know you're doing it for Luke. So you of all people should understand my position."

Peter could think of no answer, so he simply nodded. He *did* understand, he understood all too well what Charles was going through. He looked around at the busy scene around him.

Far too damned crowded, he thought worriedly, then shrugged.

But what the hell.

"Come closer," he instructed Charles and embraced him. He stared defiantly at two old women who'd been affecting not to eavesdrop on their every word and silently dared them to say something. They stared back for a moment then turned away, either in embarrassment or disgust.

One of them sniffed and both men distinctly heard her say, "I knew it, Mary, I bloomin' knew it. Homos, a pair of bloomin' 'omosexerals."

Not knowing whether to be amused or annoyed, Peter decided not to use a glamour. *It will give those two a shock they'll never forget!* he thought, as he gripped his wand and muttered softly. Within seconds they had entered the circular room.

*　　　　　*　　　　　*　　　　　*

Lucy knew where the lamppost was, for Charles had shown it her many times over the years, but another surprise awaited her when she reached her destination on the Old Kent Road. After so many years of believing him dead, Lucy now knew that Peter Simpson was, in fact, very much alive. But this was the first time she'd laid eyes on him in seventeen years and now, here he was, meeting with her husband. From her hiding place in an alleyway across the road, she watched as their conversation became increasingly animated. Her husband seemed to be trying to persuade Peter of something and he was just as adamantly refusing.

If only I could get closer and hear what they're saying.

But she knew she could get no nearer without being seen, and anyway the two men were huddled together speaking urgently and in low tones. They were being watched by a couple of elderly women close by and it appeared Charles and Peter were acutely aware of their presence.

So, with no chance of getting any nearer, Lucy could only watch, curiously as a small door at the base of the lamppost opened, then disbelieving as the two men disappeared into the tiny space. Charles had described it many times, yet to see him shrink to a fraction of his size then somehow ooze into the lamppost was something her mind couldn't comprehend.

A trick of the light, she assured herself, *that's all it was, a trick of the light.*

And all the while she was blissfully unaware of the eyes that watched her...

Chapter 43

Molly, having drunk far too much wine at the wedding, was still in bed nursing a monstrous hangover, when Charles and Peter were greeted with surprised delight and welcomed into the Sanctuary. The smiles soon faded when they described what was happening in the mortal world.

"What do you mean, *gray?*" asked Luke.

"Just that; *everything* is gray," Peter replied, "but it's worse than that. Everyone is fighting each other. The pictures on TV, honestly you should see them. It's awful."

"Yeah, even your mother had a fight in the street earlier," Charles added to Cissy.

"Mum had a fight?" To Cissy, this was the most unbelievable thing she'd heard so far. "Did she win?"

"And according to the news, the government is on the verge of collapse." Charles chose not to think about his wife fighting. "Worse, we've fallen out with America. There's even talk of war between half a dozen countries at least. Including the UK!"

"What's happening down here? Can't you keep the bleedin' noise down?" Then Molly noticed Cissy's father and her look of annoyance changed to one of concern. "Charles! What are you doing here?"

"Hi, Molly. Well, it's like this," Charles began.

"We should go have a look," decided Cissy when Charles had finished, and they all nodded, even Molly, who was feeling very ill and longing for her bed.

"But still, we cannot handle this alone," said Peter. "I'm telling you, you haven't seen it yet. We're going to need Morgan and Cornelius."

"I'm sure we can manage," replied Cissy, a little defensively. As leader of the Sanctuary, she felt she hadn't yet made her mark.

"This is no reflection on you as leader," Peter advised gently. "But this menace... it's powerful. I think we'll need all the help we can get."

Charles shifted uncomfortably, knowing there was nothing *he* could do to help. "Peter's quite right, sweetheart. You don't have to do this alone. Fetch them as quickly as possible."

"I could go!" offered Penelope.

"No, Penelope, you couldn't," said Molly firmly.

"Why not?" she argued, a mutinous expression on her face. "You'll all be out destroying this... whatever this is. It's not like you'll let me join in *that!*"

"I think Penny *could* go," Cissy ventured.

"And it's not like she hasn't done it before," added Luke. Penelope looked at them both gratefully.

They all turned to Wallace, but he shrugged, always content to go with the flow.

"See?" Penelope went on. "Even Wallace doesn't object!"

"Well, you lot do what you want then," Molly said, bad-temperedly, seeing she was outvoted. "I'm off back to bleedin' bed."

*   *   *   *

Kamontip, whose annoyance at Myla's actions had diminished somewhat with the return of the Queen's Wand, was prepared to be forgiving.

"Go back and tell the silly girl to come and see me." She smiled at Maisey's worried face. "Don't fret so much," she said kindly. "The punishment I've devised is not harsh."

"Wh-what will her punishment be?" she asked.

Kamontip, seeing the girl's pain, drew her into an embrace. "I said don't *worry*, Maisey!" She grinned. "Although, when I said the punishment isn't harsh, I suspect Myla will think differently."

"What is it?" Maisey asked again.

"Your sister will enter my service. I will give her tasks of the utmost boredom. She will rise each morning at dawn and retire at sunset and each task I set will be tedious and utterly pointless. For a period of, say... one year? That will certainly cramp her style!" When their laughter subsided, Kamontip became serious. "But now I have another task for *you*, Maisey, if you are willing. I need to know what is happening in the mortal world. I have no doubt it is something bad, and I need information. After your success in retrieving the Queen's Wand, for which I am eternally grateful, I can think of no one better to do this."

Back in the mortal world, Maisey had been shocked to see what had happened, how everything had turned *gray*. Clearly, the Dark Wizard's companion had transformed himself into something very powerful indeed. She witnessed first-hand the arguments, the violence and the aura of evil that overhung this mortal city. And from the conversations she overheard, it seemed to be spreading across the entire world.

Maisey knew she needed to tell Kamontip at once, so it was with annoyance that she saw two men standing there, talking animatedly as she approached the lamppost. Her frustration grew as they showed no sign of moving on, until she seriously considered using her wand to … well she didn't quite know *what* she would do. But it didn't matter because suddenly, much to her surprise the door of the lamppost opened and they disappeared inside.

Her relief was short-lived though as a woman now approached the lamppost and began to kick and pull at the tiny door.

This is ridiculous, Maisey fumed inwardly as she stood and marched toward the woman, who was intent on her task.

"Psst."

Lucy jumped and stifled a small scream. It was one shock too many to see this small figure looking up at her, pretty and childlike in size but quite clearly *not* a child. And although its features looked human, Lucy knew she most certainly was not.

"Don't come any closer." She raised her handbag in a threatening manner, which Maisey found comical.

"You want to follow?" the goblin asked. "You can if you want." Before a second scream could escape Lucy's lips, Maisey took out her wand and waved it so that the scream emerged as a whimper instead of being loud and piercing.

"Sshhh!" Maisey hissed. "We can't draw attention to ourselves any more than we have already!" She glanced at the two old women, still there, staring incredulously.

"Can't draw attention?" Lucy stammered in reply. "What? Who are you?"

"Doesn't matter!" Maisey whispered. "Are you going to the circular room?"

"Circular room? I don't know what that is!"

"Really? So you're not a witch?"

"No, of course not. I'm—"

"Doesn't matter," Maisey interrupted rudely. "If you're not a witch you can't come in."

"Oh, and you're going to stop me? You're like, two feet tall or something."

"Exactly," Maisey grinned as she opened the door and stepped inside, her body shrinking as she did so. "See ya!" And with that, the door slammed shut.

Lucy kicked the door angrily and cursed loudly. The two old women looked at her disapprovingly and she glared back, defiantly. Then, she could do nothing but trudge forlornly back home.

Chapter 44

At least I didn't land ages away from the castle this time, thought Penelope as she crossed the drawbridge and banged on the door.

"Hi, how are you?" She beamed at the guard as the door swung open and she marched inside. "Where's Aeryn?" Receiving no answer from the slightly stunned soldier, she strode forward, following the sounds of music and laughter that filtered from somewhere up the wide staircase.

Memories flooded back as she entered the large, sunlit room where she'd first met the queen. *How frightened I was that day!* she remembered, then faltered, suddenly worried she would be refused aid, *again.*

But Aeryn had already spotted her and, as the harassed-looking guard came running into the room, panting heavily, his face beetroot red, she dismissed him with a gesture.

"Penelope! It's good to see you again!" Aeryn was fond of this child who'd had the bravery to seek her help in defeating the demons. "But you do have a penchant for turning up where you're not invited." Her eyes twinkled, making a lie of the reprimand. "But, child, what has happened?" Aeryn was alarmed at the wild look in the girl's eyes.

"*Cara Mia!*"

Penelope was prevented from replying by a loud cry in an exaggerated Italian accent and she turned, startled. "Alessandro!" She ran to him and flung herself into his arms. "I've missed you so much!"

"I have missed you too *mia carissima,* but what is wrong? You were here only a few days ago! Tell me and I, Alessandro, will endeavor to fix it." The old reassuring laughter was in his voice, but he cast a worried glance at Aeryn.

"I've come to ask for help..." Penelope faltered, aware of the irony in this statement. It was not so long ago when she'd last turned up here unannounced, asking for help. "Oh! But this time I was *asked* to come." She looked beseechingly at Aeryn, hoping she wouldn't be sent away this time. "By Cissy. And Luke. And Molly, well kind of. And—"

"Hush, child. You are a welcome guest here." Aeryn smiled reassuringly. "Come, we will find Morgan and you can tell us your story. Surely nothing so bad can have happened since we saw you last."

But soon, Aeryn and Morgan were exchanging grave looks. "I must go," the wizard said flatly, expecting protests from Aeryn. But she knew him well; better perhaps than he did himself.

"Of course, you must." Oblivious for a moment of anyone's presence, they moved into each other's arms and hugged for a long time. "Please be careful and come back to me," she whispered as tears moistened her eyes.

"I could come too." Alessandro hesitated and ignored Daraproud's look of outrage. "There might be something I can do."

Morgan smiled gratefully. "Thank you, old friend. I know you do not make the offer lightly." He glanced at Aeryn, and an eyelid dropped into a half-wink. "But I need you here to protect the queen. And, of course, your new wife. Keep them safe for me, please."

Daraproud rolled her eyes and Aeryn smiled, amused like her sister at the thought they might need protecting. But she said nothing, touched as she saw Alessandro's chest fill with pride at the task he had been given.

The Landlord should have been at the wedding. As Morgan's closest friend, he'd certainly been asked, but had resolutely rejected all of Morgan's entreaties. He would forgive him in time for the death of Ffranc, but he couldn't yet make himself do so. But it had been hard to miss Daraproud's day, for he'd long been a friend to both sisters, as he had to their parents and even their grandparents. He knew he was acting unreasonably, that Morgan was not truly responsible. *But if only he'd silenced Logan long ago, as he should have done!*

"What do you want?" said the Landlord in a tone that would have frozen mercury. He winced as Penelope looked at him with big, round eyes, confused and upset at the rift between the two men whom she loved so much.

"How is Catrin?" Morgan ventured tentatively.

"She has disappeared and I cannot find her," replied the Landlord. "Is that what you came to ask? You're a little late."

"No," Morgan admitted, disturbed at this news. "I came for your help. Not for me," he added hurriedly. "The mortal world. It's in trouble."

The Landlord leveled a steely gaze at Morgan. "So?"

Watching, Oscar rolled his eyes in frustration. He loved the Landlord with all his heart and was utterly loyal, but sometimes... honestly! He scampered out onto the station platform, unnoticed by either wizard.

Morgan flushed, annoyed at his friend's intransigence. "*So,* the Sanctuary needs our help. Some evil has permeated the mortal world and without us they are lost. Do *not* pretend to me you don't care, Cornelius!"

The Landlord stared at him for a long moment, fighting his instinct to refuse, then turned abruptly and went to the cupboard on the wall. Oscar had already anticipated him and was holding the key in readiness. The Landlord took out his wand, feeling it nestle into his palm like the old friend it was. He turned once more to Morgan.

"Lead the way," he invited.

Chapter 45

"We must find its source!" Cissy felt desperate and out of her depth. *How can we fight this when the culprit is invisible? What do I do?* she wailed inwardly. "Molly, help me."

Wasting no time after their initial shock at the appearance of their respective fathers, Cissy and Luke, along with Molly, had quickly hatched a plan and hurried from the Sanctuary. Charles had moved to follow but was quickly forestalled by Peter. "Let her do this, Charles," he advised, "she's the leader now. Let her lead."

But Cissy, encountering the new, gray London had no idea what to do next. *Surely Morgan never had to deal with anything like this?*

"Wait." Molly lay a calming hand on the girl's arm. "Stop bleedin' panicking and let me think." This was said with some asperity as Molly tried to fight her own burgeoning panic. She forced her mind to relax, allowing her senses to explore the air around her.

What's she doing? Luke mouthed and Cissy shrugged, frowning. She put a warning finger to her lips.

For the next hour, there was silence and, in that time, not a person or animal came into view nor vehicle pass by. At last, Molly spoke as the answer came to her in a rush of clarity.

"It's a virus," she announced. "Someone has created the nastiest, most dangerous bleedin' virus imaginable."

"A virus!" Cissy exclaimed. "What kind of virus? The only ones I know are like colds and flu and things."

"Well, it's not that kind," Molly replied, worry etched into her face. "If only it were." She giggled at the image of everyone in the mortal world coughing and sneezing; wiping their noses with big white handkerchiefs. She giggled again and, as Cissy and Luke looked at her curiously, recognized her panic was rising again. "There must be something," she muttered, imagining what her old teacher Siwaraksa would have done. Taking out her wand, she touched it to the street. Nothing happened.

C'mon, c'mon, think. Angrily, she reached back in time to the far depths of her memory until she found a solution. Then she tried again and this time the web-like cracks disappeared, the blistering of the paint on the railings reversed and their colors returned. Above, a thin ray of sunshine penetrated the thick, black clouds.

"Thank goodness!" exclaimed Cissy. "You can reverse this!"

"Yeah," Molly agreed, "just so long as I can walk across the entire bleedin' world."

"Oh. So, what do we do?"

Striving to control her impatience at the girl's haste, Molly replied, "There's an incantation."

"Which is...?" Luke asked.

"That's what I'm trying to bleedin' remember," she snapped.

*　　　　*　　　　*　　　　*

Many times, across the millennia, Rosalind had spoken to the witch and wizard council of her concerns about the rise of Anarkus. And just as they refused to involve themselves with the doings of the mortal race, neither would they acknowledge her fears.

"It is not our concern," she was told, "we are merely observers." When Rosalind had tried to argue, she was met with condescension. "You are the youngest of us, by far," they said kindly, "and the most inexperienced. Understandably, you are frightened."

She'd appealed directly to its leader, hoping to circumvent the attitudes of the council, which, it seemed to her, were designed to hinder all progress.

"If the mortal world is under threat, then it is the role of the Sanctuary to save them," Portia had reminded her. "And if he chooses to attack us,"—she'd shrugged, unconcerned—"then we will deal with him."

The thought flashed through Rosalind's mind that the council hadn't *dealt* with him the last time. And as for her inexperience, wasn't she the only one who'd come *close* to preventing Anarkus's escape after he'd murdered Laiis?

Much of her time over the centuries was spent at the star-scope set high up in the council chamber. It had always been this way, for she was fond of the mortals and enjoyed watching them go about their everyday lives. To see them develop as a race had been a delight, even if that development came at a cost.

From the balcony, she watched as one after another of their enemies attempted to rain misery and suffering on the mortal world, only to be defied each time by the Sanctuary. How Rosalind would have loved to fight by their side! She'd always been curious and a little hurt, that she had never been asked to take her place as its leader and had always suspected Portia took secret pleasure in denying her. She'd repeatedly pleaded to be allowed to go to their aid and always she'd been refused. Not only that; she had been warned that the punishment would be dire if she disobeyed. Rosalind was no coward but she dared not defy the council on this.

And so, when Kanzser had subjected Mitra to the most depraved of tortures, she had not intervened, though it had broken her heart not to do so. And when the demons attacked the Sanctuary, still she had not interfered.

And when Ffranc was murdered, the screams of the girl Catrin had wrenched her heart almost in two and she wondered how her fellow council members could bear to stand by and do nothing. And for the first time she wondered not just how, but *why*.

Her distrust, which had begun as an embryo, centuries ago, was suddenly fully formed and she realized she could no longer remain passive. And now here was Anarkus, the latest in a long line of threats against the mortal world. Secretly, she had gone to see Cornelius, her departure unseen by those who would have prevented her. But he had advised caution, scared what the consequences for her might be, and extracted her promise that, whatever happened, she would not try to help, *at least for the moment.*

Anarkus, meanwhile, was having *such* a good time; he'd particularly enjoyed his stint in front of the TV cameras. Knowing that billions of mortals were hanging onto his every word and quaking with fear had brought a feeling of excitement he'd never known before. And the knowledge that soon they would all kneel before him was the best feeling of all.

So, his happiness was marred one day when he sensed his grip of power on the mortal world had weakened. Someone somewhere was taking back control, and Anarkus knew *exactly* who that someone was. It was somewhat annoying; he'd just engineered a small war between two small countries and had been about to cause oil tankers in the Gulf of Mexico and the Persian Gulf to explode, thus causing massive loss of marine and other wildlife.

But rather than being disheartened, he merely smiled.

It is time the Sanctuary came to an end, he thought. *They think to defeat me, but they do not know the power I wield over them!* Anarkus spoke the incantation that would open the portal and within minutes he was speeding back to England and its capital city, London.

Chapter 46

Morgan had always known that Charles had stolen the Knife of Chiang and now, there it lay on the table before them. After he and the Landlord had arrived, it hadn't taken long for them to learn of the atrocities being committed in the mortal world. On the short journey back to the Sanctuary, Penelope had told them most of it anyway.

"Molly is searching for the incantation?" he asked.

"Yes, with Cissy; they're in the library," confirmed Wallace.

"I'll go help!" exclaimed Penelope. "I'm good with libraries. I bet *I'll* find it!" Before anyone could comment, she had rushed from the room.

"She probably will, too." The Landlord smiled.

"I know," agreed Morgan. "Never did I know a more precocious child. Now, let's get down to business." He picked up the knife and laid it carefully across his palm. "Is it not beautiful?"

"It is!" exclaimed Luke, fascinated. "Can I hold it?"

"You can." Morgan handed it over. "But be careful not to cut yourself; this is no ordinary knife."

"So," Peter asked, "is this what you'll use to defeat whatever is doing this to the mortal world?"

"It will help," said Morgan. "But not me. I will not wield it."

"Who then?" he replied. "You, Cornelius?"

"I doubt it," the Landlord declared. "I'm rubbish with knives; I'd probably miss."

"In any case, it has to be you, Peter," Morgan said. "I believe you have a crucial role to play if we are to defeat this menace."

"*Me?*" Peter shook his head. "That doesn't make sense! You and Cornelius—"

"No," Morgan interrupted gently. "For the first time in history the entire mortal world is in danger of being consumed by evil. If we cannot stop it, then they are lost." He took the knife from Luke and studied it. "Perhaps this is the only means of defeating this... whatever it is. No ordinary knife can do it."

"Necromancer?" the Landlord enquired.

"Perhaps," Morgan agreed. "Although I find it hard to believe Logan was able to create something so powerful."

"I know." The Landlord frowned. "And that's what worries me. This thing is powerful and far beyond Logan's control, if indeed he did create it."

"Yes, and anyway, I believe destiny has decreed that Peter and the knife will be needed if we are to save the mortal world. We will know for sure in a moment."

"But you haven't answered." Peter was agitated at the responsibility it appeared he was being given. "Why me? I don't understand. You're both much more powerful than I am."

Morgan thought for a moment, then said to the Landlord, "The blood thorn found its way into the cave entrance of the demon lair when you created the blood moon, right?"

The Landlord nodded; this was old news.

"Yeah, and did you ever wonder why it lay there for thousands of years, unnoticed, until it was needed for Peter?" Molly entered the room just in time to join the discussion.

"Never crossed my mind," the Landlord admitted. "Aren't you supposed to be in the library?"

"Oh, Penelope kicked me out." She pretended to look affronted. "Said I was rubbish and I'd never find the incantation in a hundred years with my old-fashioned ways."

"She has a point," agreed Morgan.

"Yeah, very funny. She's too bleedin' cheeky for her own good. Anyway, you were saying?"

"Yes, what are you getting at, Morgan?" Peter looked at his friend, still puzzled.

"Just this," Morgan continued. "That the blood thorn didn't *accidentally* find its way into the cave entrance. It did so for a purpose and that was to save the life of someone far in the future. Someone important."

Wallace looked sympathetically at Luke, who was remembering those dark days when his father lay close to death.

"That's right," Molly took up the story. "Haven't you ever wondered why it chose *you*, Peter?"

Even the Landlord, never the most tactful of beings, winced visibly.

Morgan smiled, amused as ever by Molly's bluntness. He looked at Charles. "And didn't *you* ever wonder why Molly and I put the knife in that cupboard?"

"And why we made the incantation to open it again so easy," Molly added.

"And why we put it in just as you were passing the door, which was wide open?"

"Well, not really," answered Charles. "It just seemed the right thing to do, somehow. To steal it, I mean."

Morgan nodded. "It should have been Peter who took the knife, but of course fate had decreed he would not be able to guard it. Fate already knew he would become a prisoner of the Dark Wizard."

"So it had to be *you,* Charles, so you could keep it safe until needed and, most importantly, give it to your closest friend when the time was right." Molly grinned. "But at the back of a hot water tank in your house? *Really,* Charles?"

"Look," said Peter, "I get all this. But I still don't understand why you can't do it. Or Cornelius."

"Well, he probably *could,* but Cornelius is about the clumsiest wizard I've ever known." Morgan was only half joking. "And he's right; he'd probably miss and stab himself. Anyway, neither Molly nor I have the power to use that knife."

"Nor I," added Wallace.

Morgan nodded. "We all tested it but none of us could get so much as a spark."

"Where did it actually come from?" Luke asked, and Morgan looked embarrassed.

"Alessandro found it one day, at the back of a knife drawer in the kitchen."

Molly smirked. "Been there for centuries, apparently."

"I knew it was there." The Landlord's smirk was even wider.

"Show off," she muttered.

Morgan handed the knife to Peter and, as soon as he touched it, its blade shone brightly and there was a faint humming, like bees on a hot summer's day. A pleasant sound, as if the knife was glad to have been awakened at last.

"I see," he breathed, awestruck. "So I'll kill it with this?"

"Yes," agreed Morgan, and he looked around at them all, gravely. "You all know it is not the Sanctuary's way to kill if it can be avoided, but in this case ..."

"I don't know if I could take a life; even one such as this," Peter stared at Morgan, worriedly.

"Yet you must." The sympathy in Morgan's eyes was evident to all. "You must plunge the Knife of Chiang deep into this creature's heart. For only then will his menace be gone forever."

"Yeah," agreed Molly with a grin, "you'll need to stick the knife in good and bleedin' hard."

Frowning, Morgan placed an arm around Peter's shoulders, drawing him away from the others. "I want you to go on ahead of us; soon actually," Morgan told him. "The rest of us will try and lure this creature to an open space, hopefully where there won't be many mortals. Do not use the knife until I tell you; that's most important. And your aim must be true, remember that. Now, I think you will know the place; it's called..."

As their voices faded, the Landlord sat next to Charles. "By hiding the knife, you have done the Sanctuary, and the mortal world, a service you cannot imagine; you realize that, right?"

Charles looked at him gratefully, but Penelope came hurtling into the room waving a piece of paper before he could reply.

"We found it!" she yelled. "It was easy in the end!"

"Easy for a computer genius like you, you mean." Cissy followed close behind, grinning.

"Excellent!" Morgan exclaimed. "Well done, both of you." He looked at the words on the paper. "We must memorize this. Peter, you should go now."

"Take care, Dad, don't go getting yourself killed." Luke embraced his father, who hugged him back tightly.

"Charles, I cannot thank you enough for bringing the knife," Morgan continued. "But now you must go home; there is nothing further you can do to help and I would not have you placed in unnecessary danger."

Charles was disappointed but knew it was pointless to argue. "And you," he said, taking Cissy into his arms, "be very careful. No heroics, understand?"

"Oh, don't be an old fusspot, Dad." She laughed, hugging him back. "I'll be fine."

Charles nodded then followed Peter to the door, and moments later they had entered the passage-between-the-worlds.

After a few moments spent memorizing the incantations, Morgan beckoned Penelope to him. "Now," he said, "Hans is busy in the kitchen, cooking up something special for you." He winked. "Don't give him too hard a time while we're gone, okay?"

Penelope nodded, but tears appeared in her eyes. "You're all coming back though, right?"

"Definitely," he promised, "aren't we, Molly?"

"Course we bleedin' are." She lifted the girl and gave her a sloppy kiss. Penelope giggled and wiped her mouth.

"So, that's settled then. We're coming back," the Landlord deadpanned. "Come on. Let's go do this thing."

Chapter 47

Morgan and the Landlord exchanged glances, their expressions grim. As far as the eye could see, everything was gray. Streets, buildings, cars, people. Even the sky. All a dull, uniform gray.

The few mortals they met shuffled along, heads down, unaware of their surroundings. The only animation they showed was at seeing other mortals. Then a few words would be exchanged, quickly turning into pushing and shoving, and within seconds into fighting.

"This is bleedin' awful," Molly said, voicing all of their thoughts.

"But we can sort it, right?" Luke asked in a hushed tone. "Please tell me we can fix this."

"Course we can." Cissy took his hand and gripped it tightly. "Whoever, *whatever* caused this doesn't stand a chance."

Just then, a smartly dressed man in a pin striped suit and fancy shoes stumbled across the road towards them. Except that now the suit was crumpled, the shoes muddy and scuffed. His hair was awry and matted and he clearly hadn't washed or shaved for several days. He cannoned into Wallace, gave him a hostile look, and swung a punch, which the wizard avoided easily. The Landlord twitched his wand and muttered softly, then caught the man as he slumped to the ground in a deep sleep.

They continued toward central London, witnessing a dozen similar sordid little scenes, which saddened them further.

"This is where it started." Molly stopped suddenly. "Right here."

"How do you know?" Morgan asked, though he knew her instincts were rarely wrong.

"Dunno," she answered with a shrug. "I just do."

"Then this is where we should begin to mend it." Cissy took out her wand.

Luke and Wallace were not experienced with their wands, preferring swords. But the others spread out, each facing a different direction. Then, as one, they shouted the incantation.

A blinding white light burst into the air, spreading quickly outwards, and everywhere it touched, the grayness created by whatever disease had touched London dissolved and disappeared. There was a perceptible easing of tension in the atmosphere as natural colors were restored and mortals lifted their shoulders, yawned as if waking from a deep sleep, and continued briskly on their way.

But now there was a problem. Their faculties returned, some mortals were staring at them in bemused surprise. Most kept a safe distance but a few of the more curious were moving nearer.

"We need a glamour!" shouted Luke but Molly shook her head.

"We can't do such strong magic from beneath a glamour. Cornelius, what will we do?"

The Landlord shrugged. "Nothing we can do. You lot will just have to sort it out later. Erase their memories or something."

"Erase their…" Molly glared at him. "You really are the bleedin' limit, Cornelius."

"There's a bigger problem," Luke announced. "Despite your impressive show of power, it didn't get very far." Sure enough, the restoring of color and of life to the mortals had reached only a few hundred meters. In the distance, everything was untouched and still very, very gray.

"We need to get higher!" yelled Morgan. "Make it reach further!"

"How?" Molly was doubtful. "Do you realize how bleedin' *high* the buildings are in London? If you think I'm climbing millions of bleedin' stairs…"

"No need!" Cissy grinned. "Come with me!" She ran down the short flight of steps toward the London Eye and, shouting a short incantation which gave wings to her feet, leaped on top of the first pod. Then the next and the next until in no time she was standing at the top and the whole of the city lay before her. "Come on!" she yelled, her voice faint on the breeze. Morgan and the Landlord grinned, ran, and within seconds stood beside her.

Molly, meanwhile, watched in open-mouthed outrage. "You've got to be bleedin' joking."

"Go on, Molly," Luke teased, "you can do it easily."

She gave him a look that could have soured milk and made cheese. "Now that,"—she looked once more at the figures, high up in the distance—"is just bleedin' inconsiderate."

Although they now had one less wand, the power they generated caught on the wind and spread across London. Gradually they were aware of the sounds of traffic building once more as normality returned. Below, a large crowd had gathered, watching as the three tiny figures sent out a shimmering wave of light. Many filmed them on their phones, and as social media got up and running again, the scene quickly went viral.

Back on solid ground, the crowd surged towards them. They concealed themselves beneath a glamour, disappearing suddenly and adding more fuel to the wealth of footage, now being seen worldwide.

Leaving the crowds behind, they found themselves in Oxford Street where a mass of shoppers proved life was returning to normal. Only the dozens of abandoned vehicles, as yet unclaimed, hinted that anything unusual had occurred.

"Where now?" asked Luke.

"Hampstead Heath," replied the Landlord. It's high up and we need to see how far the spell has reached. It's only about eight kilometers. We can walk."

Molly stopped in her tracks. "Walk?"

Luke didn't fancy it either. "Can either of you drive?"

"Really?" Morgan rolled his eyes. "D'ya think?"

Wallace shook his head also and as for Molly, Luke didn't bother to ask.

"Well, I can steer," he said doubtfully, looking at the long lines of abandoned cars. The only one large enough was a black London taxi. Luke opened the door, hoping there'd be keys, but there weren't.

"Look, we have wands," Cissy said, impatiently. "How hard can it be?" She touched hers to the hood of the taxi and the engine burst into life. In a long series of kangaroo hops and many engine stalls, with Luke at the wheel, they finally reached the park gates. Their spell had reached this far, and much further they saw, as they approached its highest point.

"Now what?" Luke asked.

"Now," Cissy told him, "we wait."

The wait was long, and they spent an uncomfortable night, but at least it gave time for the creation of a glamour. Not a fool-proof one – the park was too large – but one that would at least provide some protection for witnesses of the battle that was to come.

For a battle there would be. The Landlord and Morgan had realized whoever was doing this wouldn't stand idly by as his handiwork was undone. It was only a matter of *when* he would come to claim back what the Sanctuary had regained.

*　　　　　　　*　　　　　　　*　　　　　　　*

He'd been a young boy, many thousands of years past, when he'd last seen the man who now approached, but the Landlord recognized him immediately.

His arrival had been heralded by an unnatural graying of the sky. Unnatural because it wasn't just the clouds, it was the *entire* sky. And it was accompanied by a graying of the grass and trees around them, so it felt like they were standing in a world drawn with charcoal.

"Anarkus," said the Landlord, "I had thought you long dead. Yet here you are with your mischief. What did you do?"

"Mischief?" Anarkus laughed in delight. "Rather more than that, I think. I invoked the spirit of the Necromancer. Used a bit of genuine demon blood. And here I am. I already had power, Cornelius, but now you should grovel before me. You cannot *imagine* the transformation I have endured."

"Grovel?" The Landlord pretended to think about it. "I don't think I've ever actually done that."

"But you will now!" Anarkus flung a bolt of white heat that staggered the Landlord. He had never imagined such power and knew at once they were in trouble. It was followed by a staccato barrage such as they'd never experienced and they were forced to their knees in desperation. Only their skill prevented a quick ending to the battle, but there was hardly time to return fire of their own.

But then the barrage stopped and Anarkus stepped back, laughing. "That is just a taste," he mocked. "You cannot win." He sent a searing bolt of fire arcing into the sky, which ripped through the glamour, tearing it to shreds and revealing hundreds of mortals, watching, mouths agape at the spectacle.

"Join me now as my servants," Anarkus crooned softly, "and I will let you live." He smiled cruelly. "Or else I will kill you." He gestured toward the mortals. "And them."

Their response was a concentrated stream of ardent fire, but he swatted it aside. Angrily, he pointed his wand at the crowd and twenty or so mortals turned to ash where they stood.

"I warned you!" Anarkus screamed. "I will kill them all!" His anger consumed him as entirely as lava engulfs the mountain from which it spews and he felt his strength double, then triple. And with it, his power was magnified tenfold. He sensed it at once and gave a primeval howl of triumph.

But suddenly a bolt of wand fire hit him squarely between the shoulder blades. As planned, Peter had remained hidden, awaiting his opportunity. Now, seeing his friends on the brink of defeat, he acted desperately and, taken by surprise, Anarkus was thrown to the ground. At once, a coruscating stream of hot agony from five wands engulfed him and only his supernatural speed saved him from death.

"Well done, Peter!" shouted Morgan as they assailed their foe from all sides. Only Luke and Wallace searched desperately for an opening to use their swords, but none existed. And Anarkus, with the combined power of the Necromancer in his blood, was an adversary unlike any they'd ever faced. Even in his agony he managed to stand and deliver a curse of such magnitude it could not be countered and was barely avoided. The three wizards did so, as did Molly, but Cissy had far less experience and she was an instant too slow. A sliver, just a hairsbreadth of the curse, entered her temple, piercing her brain. Curiously, she felt no pain, just a sudden, strange dreamy detachment from all that was happening, and she sat, her wand cast aside on the grass.

Barely able to make sense of the melee around her, she thought she recognized the very tall man who twisted and turned, coat swirling this way and that, wand doling out sparkling bolts of death which spun like Catherine wheels in all directions.

He's the Lan... Landlord. I wish he would stop; she was having difficulty concentrating. *He might hurt someone...* She was also having difficulty moving, her muscles tightening, limbs becoming stiff. Cissy did not know it, but she was fortunate that only the minutest sliver of Anarkus's curse had touched her brain. But for that lucky chance, she would already have been dead.

Yes, fortunate to still be alive, only rather quickly going insane...

What's happening to me, why do I feel so strange? She tried to shake her head and clear her senses, but somehow it would no longer move.

Her eyes switched from the Landlord to the other figure, the one everyone seemed intent on killing.

Who is he? she wondered as she watched Anarkus, undeniably magnificent, twisting and turning in the showy dance he loved to adopt when fighting. *He's beautiful,* she thought, feeling a spark of interest. *So strong, so powerful.* Her attention switched back to the tall man. *Don't hurt him, please don't...* She tried to rise, go to the man's aid, but it was just too much effort.

Don't you dare hurt him... she slumped sideways and closed her eyes.

"No!"

With no intention of obeying Morgan's order to return home, Charles had followed Peter surreptitiously to the park. Since the glamour had failed, he'd watched in an agony of suspense as his daughter battled for her life, and with a sense of his own failure as a parent at his inability to help.

But as he saw his daughter fall, he feared the worst and, uncaring of the danger, rushed to her side. Instinctively fearing another assault, Anarkus sent a bolt of power, which caught him in the chest. Luckily for him it was weakened – Anarkus's full power was needed elsewhere – but it was enough to send Charles unconscious to the ground beside his daughter, his head resting in her lap.

Oh, Charles, you fool! Morgan thought, despairingly. *Cissy isn't dead!* Why did you interfere! But his momentary distraction allowed Anarkus to gain the upper hand again and, knowing that without the power of Cissy's wand it was only a matter of time before victory was his, he gave a primeval scream of triumph.

"Now you are mine!" he gloated. "And there will be no mercy!"

He raised his wand arrogantly, certain now of his victory.

"Cornelius, do something! We cannot prevail!"

Wallace had been frustrated and ashamed at his inability to help, but now he was terrified because never in all his long life had he seen anything so powerful and he knew the end had come. But his desperate shout, although well-meant, was catastrophic in its timing. The Landlord's head turned slightly and that thousandth of a second was all Anarkus needed to send a stream of fire-filled invective from his mouth, so drenched with evil it would have killed any other wizard. And the Landlord might have succumbed instantly had it struck where aimed, in the dead center of his forehead. But, lightning fast as the invective was delivered, the Landlord's reflexes were quicker and as he dipped his head so that it glanced off his scalp, furrowing a long, ugly burn through his hair. But weakness was already invading every strata of his body and, as he fell to his knees, he knew their last, faint hope of victory was gone.

Awake again but unable to move as the curse held her firmly in its grip, Cissy watched dispassionately as the battle went against the Sanctuary. Then she felt a new emotion, one of elation as she saw the Landlord fall.

I hope he dies; I hope they all die. She looked across at the figure of Anarkus, tall and magnificent, and her lips peeled back into a rictus grin. *Kill them all, my love,* she willed. *All of them.*

She looked down at the man whose head still lay in her lap. *Familiar,* Cissy thought, uncaring, *perhaps I knew him once.*

She looked again at the Anarkus. *Yes, kill them all, my love.*

Fighting against his nausea, the Landlord looked at the scene before him and felt a wave of desolation. *We have failed,* he thought, trying desperately to stave off the darkness that enveloped him. *For centuries we have protected the mortal world but, ultimately we have failed them. Now, there is no hope.*

Chapter 48

Almost no hope. But at that moment, Kamontip appeared.

It was unlike the goblins to involve themselves in the affairs of others, but when Maisey returned, Kamontip had listened to her story with increasing dismay. She was astute enough to realize the demise of the Sanctuary might well be imminent and that it would not stop there. Whatever this creature was, it would not be satisfied with the mortal world. Sooner or later, it would turn its attention to hers.

Anyway, that fool Logan would undoubtedly get himself killed and Kamontip hadn't finished with him yet. *Nobody else will save him from himself if I don't,* she'd mused, wondering why she cared.

Extravagantly, she leaped into the fray, somersaulting once, landing in a crouch, her body bathed in a golden, sparking glow – all of which was totally unnecessary, but Kamontip had style and was determined to make an entrance. Although she couldn't see Logan, she knew he was probably watching from somewhere.

And as well as style she had intelligence. Seeing immediately what the others had not, she knew intuitively it was pointless to try and kill this creature. Instead, with a contemptuous flick of her wand, she sent Anarkus's wand flying from his grip, and with another she sealed his lips, preventing the curse he was already forming. Astounded at how quickly the tables had turned, his eyes widened in shock as he heard Morgan shout, "Peter, now! The knife!"

With Anarkus still powerless in the grip of Morgan, Molly and Kamontip, Peter ran forward, knife held high, and plunged it toward his chest. His aim was true but at the very last instant Anarkus twisted away and it sank into his flesh, narrowly missing his heart.

He felt his power draining away with such speed he was astounded. The knife's existence had been kept secret from the witch and wizard council for centuries, and Anarkus had no idea how to counter its unique power. The knowledge that such a weapon existed left him shocked and, for now at least, quite unable to muster whatever little strength remained to fight back.

Certain Charles was dead, the Landlord staggered to his feet and looked across at the body of the man who'd done nothing wrong except love his daughter. *I should have prevented this,* he thought sadly. *Morgan is too trusting as always. I should have made sure Charles went home. I should have laid a spell to prevent him from coming here.* He suddenly felt old and tired, and his shoulders slumped in a rare gesture of defeat. *Yet more guilt to add to my collection,* he thought with uncharacteristic self-pity. *I wish...* He shook his head to rid himself of the thought, angry at his weakness.

"Yes, and if wishes were fishes, we'd all cast nets," he muttered as Molly, who understood perfectly what was going through his mind, came over and enveloped him in a huge bear hug.

"This is not your fault," she said softly.

The Landlord, who really didn't do hugs at all, submitted for a moment, then squeezed her shoulders briefly and stepped away. "Thank you, old friend. As always, you understand me." He paused and looked across at the heart-breaking scene being enacted before him; at the girl, for the moment not the powerful leader of the Sanctuary but simply a daughter weeping over the body of her father.

"It's hard, isn't it?" Molly acknowledged. "So very, very hard."

As Anarkus's power diminished, Cissy was returning to her senses. Her confusion faded and recognition of her friends of the Sanctuary returned. The curse within her edged slowly from her brain and soon it would leave her body entirely. She looked down and saw the unmoving form of her father, his head still cradled in her lap. Convinced he was dead, she let out a plaintive scream and gathered him into her arms, sobbing hysterically.

Morgan watched sadly. "I must go to her..."

"Morgan, don't!" Molly called after him. "It's too soon..." Her voice trailed away as she watched him crouch beside Cissy and awkwardly place an arm across her shoulders.

"I'm sorry, Cissy," he began, "so unutterably sorry."

She reacted with rage, her eyes blazing as she shrugged away his arm. "Sorry?" she screeched. "Sorry? This is your fault! How can you say you're sorry when it's your fault!" She was panting heavily and spittle flew from her mouth as she struggled to contain the torrent of words. "And you,"—she looked at Molly—"I trusted you most of all!" She gestured at her father. "He didn't deserve this; he was a good man! A brilliant dad!"

"Cissy," Morgan tried to interrupt, "your father isn't dead!"

"Liar!" She fell into another bout of sobbing, but nobody knew what to do and Morgan shrugged helplessly. Even Molly, stung by the accusation, dared not approach. She hovered uncertainly and Cissy spoke to her again, softly this time, almost a whisper. "But I should have known, shouldn't I?" Her voice dripped with contempt. "You all just use people." She jabbed a finger at the witch. "After all, *you* started this when you tricked Luke into going to the Sanctuary."

"Cissy, it isn't Molly's fault, you know that!"

"Oh, you're right, Morgan, so right. It isn't Molly's fault; not *just* her fault anyway." She stood suddenly and her face was a mask of hatred. "It's all of you!" Screaming again, now tinged with hysteria, she went on, "All of you with your secret worlds and your fucking Sanctuary!"

It was Luke who hurried forward and gathered her in his arms. She collapsed with him to the floor, sobbing hysterically.

All at once the Landlord was filled with a burning rage. Still weak, he lurched toward Peter, who still held the Knife of Chiang.

"Give it to me," he rasped, and his eyes were terrible.

"Cornelius, I..."

It took only a thought for the knife to fly like a dart into the Landlord's grip and Peter stared at him incredulously. The Landlord ignored him and, with the knife held high, approached Anarkus who could only watch, powerless to prevent his doom.

"Cornelius, don't! I forbid it!" But Morgan would not – *could* not – raise his wand against his friend. And he doubted whether, at this moment, he could have prevented him anyway.

But the knife didn't fall and remained hovering in the air as the Landlord's hand trembled violently. For a voice was filling his mind, one so compelling that everything around him became dreamlike.

And it was the one voice he could never have ignored.

"Do not kill in anger," it told him. "Once, you murdered a demon. Oh, my love, I understand the necessity, I always did, and perhaps I should have been more forgiving."

The Landlord shook his head to dispel the hallucination. He so badly wanted to kill Anarkus. *He needed it!*

"I forgive you now, Cornelius." The words were more urgent. "But if you kill this creature out of revenge, with hatred, you will be consumed and become him. Let him go; he is weakened and can no longer harm you. Do not commit a second murder, I beg you."

Slowly, the Landlord lowered the knife and the air began to shimmer. No longer certain he was hallucinating, he watched as the tall, proud image of the only woman he had ever loved appeared before him, blurred and indistinct. The guilt that rose within him was almost more than he could bear.

"Forgive me, Mitra," he said. "I have failed you so often and now I have done so again." The darkness closed around him and for a long moment he imagined he was dreaming.

"Wake up, Cornelius, wake up."

He opened his eyes to find she was close and no longer indistinct. She was beautiful again, as she had been in her youth and as she had been before... his mind shied away from the memory.

"Ah, Cornelius, there you are." Her voice was musical, as he remembered so well. Her smile was filled with delight at seeing him again and her eyes brimmed with her love for him. "Never have you failed me, my love, for the evil deeds wrought upon me were not of your doing."

"I should have protected you." He shook his head. "If I hadn't created the blood moon, and if…" He was having difficulty gathering his thoughts. "And the mortals, they are doomed. I cannot…"

"You always did worry too much, Cornelius," she chided gently. "Always tried to take the world's troubles upon your shoulders."

"But the mortals!" he insisted. "*You* would have found a way to save them."

"Shhh." She placed a finger on his lips and, to his surprise, he could feel her touch.

"Have I gone mad?" he whispered. "Are you real, Mitra?"

Now her laughter rang out, as clear as a mountain stream. "No, my love, you are not mad." She bent and kissed his forehead. "Now, rest and sleep, for I have work to do. When you awaken, I will be gone, but I want you to remember something and do so for the rest of your days."

She kissed him again, this time on the lips, a long, lingering kiss. And when she finally drew away, he heard her softly say, "I love you, Cornelius. I will love you for eternity."

For a few, precious seconds he fancied her tears mingled with his own. She left him at last and as she faded into the distance, he saw her raise a hand and he thought there might have been words upon her lips, but he could not be sure. And then he sank to the ground and slept.

Anarkus had almost been forgotten but he'd been watching intently, awaiting his chance. He'd been surprised to witness the rise of the witch for he knew she was long dead; indeed, he'd watched in delight, centuries ago, as she'd endured the Demon King's torture. As she disappeared and the wizard slept, he seized his opportunity.

The power of the Necromancer, which he had briefly held, was gone forever but he'd managed to retain just a little of his own, weak though he was. Leaping to his feet, he grabbed his wand, shoving Peter violently to the ground. Turning, he fired a last bolt of fire, but not randomly; he knew exactly where he wanted it to go. It hit Cissy's head, driving the curse sliver back into her brain, so deeply she screamed in silent agony. Then, knowing he had seconds only to escape, he staggered drunkenly away, his vision already beginning to star.

His strength ebbing fast, Anarkus fought his way through the crowd until he finally reached the edge of the park and wandered, light-headed into the road. At once there was the screeching of brakes as cars narrowly avoided him and the air was filled with honking horns and shouts of abuse. Unheeding, he reached the other side and into an alley where, thankfully he sank to the ground amongst the welcoming shadows and lost consciousness.

There had been no time for pursuit as Cissy rose to her feet and they stared, astounded, as she trod a lurching, twitching, circular path around her prostrate father who lay face down and uncared for on the grass.

"Morgan!" Molly hissed, seeing her friend's uncharacteristic indecisiveness. "Tell us what to do. You have to lead us now!"

It was like the flicking of a switch as the wizard's brain began to engage again. "Luke, you and Wallace carry him inside." He nodded at the still unconscious form of Charles Hamilton. "Quickly, before he awakens."

"But what about Cissy? I want to—"

"Do as I say!" he snapped. "I will deal with this!"

But Luke was staring at his friend, horrified as she walked slowly and stutteringly toward them, her legs jerking and her body twisting awkwardly with each faltering step. Attracted by the sound of Luke's voice, Cissy's head jerked upward and her gaze latched on to his.

I know him, she thought, *I'm sure I do… I shouldn't kill him.* Then, curiously, one eyeball remained fixed on Luke while the other rolled to the side and fastened upon Morgan.

But him—she'd never felt so sure of anything in her life—*him I should destroy.*

Her arm suddenly began to move upward, still outstretched, each movement accompanied by an audible click like a cog wheel turning, slowly but inexorably. And in her hand, she held her wand.

Luke still hadn't moved and now it was too late as Cissy's arm continued to ratchet upward, her wand now almost pointing at Morgan's chest.

For a split-second, Morgan considered throwing a spell to knock it from her grip but decided the risk of removing her arm as well was too great. Molly, however, had no such scruples.

"Sorry, Cissy." The spell came flying past Morgan's ear, almost singeing his hair, then she watched in amazement as it hit Cissy's wand and deflected away. Simply *bounced* off and dissipated into nothing.

"What the bleedin'…?" Molly looked incredulously at the girl. "How?"

"Kamontip!" Morgan called. "We need some help here!"

But the goblin queen considered she'd more than done her bit already. She ignored the shout and continued to scan the crowds of mortals who still watched from a safe distance, in fascinated awe.

Where are you? she wondered. The possibility that Logan wasn't there after all was somehow... disappointing.

Cissy, wand now level with Morgan's head, sent her own bolt of fire back at him. But it was slow, matching the lethargy of her limbs which were still in the grip of Anarkus's curse, and he easily dodged.

"Molly!" he urged. "We must contain her and get her inside!"

She nodded and, their minds working in unison as always, each sent a stream of power that locked around Cissy's upper arms. But they were sent casually, almost gently, neither willing to risk harming the girl.

And she simply shrugged them off, as if the shackles were made of paper.

"What the bleedin'...?" Molly repeated and looked incredulously at Morgan. "Again!" This time the restraints were sent with more force and Cissy couldn't shake them off so easily. But her strength was rapidly returning and the ratcheting motion of her limbs disappeared and she could move freely.

With a wild, high-pitched cackle of triumph, she plucked each of the fiery ropes from her arms and ran at them, her wand raised against Morgan. They responded instantly and this time, didn't hold back. The shackles attached themselves again and remained intact. But the power Cissy exuded was shocking and Morgan almost faltered as he felt it.

"Steady on!" Molly struggled to catch her breath. "If either of us fall, we've bleedin' had it."

Always stating the damned obvious, Morgan thought. But they were stuck; Cissy didn't yet have the strength to escape her bonds, but neither could Morgan or Molly move her. And they could feel the girl's strength and power increasing with every second.

Luke and Wallace had sheathed their swords for fear of harming Cissy, and now they circled the arena, clawed hands outstretched, ready to make a grab should the chance arise. To Molly the sight was suddenly hilarious, despite their predicament, and she choked, partly with mirth, mostly in exhaustion.

"So, obviously you *do* have a bleedin' plan, Morgan?" Molly gasped. "Even fighting the Demon King wasn't this hard."

"Then"—Morgan could barely speak himself—"we must try harder!" He sent even more power channeling down his wand.

And Cissy simply resisted, smiling sardonically.

It's no good, he thought, desperate, *she's too strong!* But then a third stream of power joined theirs, one which even Cissy, with her own strength fast returning, could not match. She hung there, held within the triumvirate of power, quite unable to escape.

Startled, Morgan turned and, to his unutterable relief, saw it was the Landlord, back on his feet, his legs trembling slightly, but the hand that held his wand was rock steady.

"Cornelius! Thank goodness you're alright. For a minute there—"

"We shouldn't delay, Morgan," came the terse reply. "Let's get going."

"Of course," the wizard agreed. They began to guide Cissy toward the door just visible far down the slope. Then they were into the Corridor of Dimensions and taking her quickly, careful not to let the streams of power slip for an instant, down toward the passage-between-the-worlds.

Chapter 49

Logan's mood was not helped by the fact he'd been forced to watch the battle surrounded by crowds of *mortals*. Thankfully, now the spectacle had ended, they were drifting away.

So, my brother wins again, he thought sourly. But his rancor was muted by his undeniable relief that Anarkus was gone. His musings were interrupted by the approach of the goblin queen, and he felt an undeniable lifting of his spirits.

Before he could speak, Kamontip slapped him hard across the cheek, the sound echoing across the park. "That's for stealing my wand."

It wasn't actually me who stole it, Logan thought illogically.

"And in any case, you will never defeat your brother."

Her words shocked him, so blatantly spoken were they, but then a wondrous thing happened. The goblin queen smiled.

Not a smile of hatred or of mockery.

Nor one of derision or contempt.

But a smile so full of tenderness and understanding it quite literally took his breath away. And as he looked into her eyes, he found the same emotions mirrored there, and something else; something he couldn't quite fathom.

Liking? It was an idea so alien to Logan that he couldn't be sure; to the best of his knowledge nobody had actually liked him before. Confused, he stammered, "I can beat him yet." But even to himself he sounded unconvincing.

Kamontip shook her head firmly. "No, you can't; you have no weapon." And thus she made it easy for him to pretend this was the only reason he couldn't. "And it would be such a shame for you to die."

He'd been about to protest he needed no weapon, but his mouth snapped shut and he looked at her, searchingly. "You mock me."

She sighed heavily. "No, Logan, I do not."

The honesty in her eyes was so transparent that even he, the consummate liar, could see it was true. "But..."

"No buts, Logan." This time the use of his name seemed to hang between them, and he was uncharacteristically lost for words. "You know, if you got over this ridiculous jealousy of your brother, which is unfounded by the way, you might actually find yourself enjoying your life."

"Unfounded?" Her words stung and he began to protest but again she interrupted.

"Well, it's hardly his fault he was the firstborn, right? You've let your jealousy ruin your life for far too long, you know."

Logan could find no answer to this, and they sat for a long time, watching as the sun began to set, both lonely but unwilling to give up that loneliness. For both of them, it felt safer that way.

"Personally, I find him a bit priggish," Kamontip said eventually.

"Your brother, I mean." She paused, musingly. "I don't know, he's just a bit *too* good for my liking."

As far as he knew, this was the first time anyone had ever criticized the sainted Morgan. "You don't like him?"

Kamontip shrugged. "He's okay, I guess. I like you better." This time he stared at her, no longer doubting her honesty. "C'mon. It should be safe by now; they'll be back inside the Sanctuary." She took his hand as if leading a bewildered child. "Let's get you home."

"Home? Your home?"

"Don't flatter yourself." Her face was neutral and gave nothing away. "I said I *like* you; get over yourself." But she squeezed his hand to take away any harshness from the words. They walked in silence for a time until eventually, she stopped and pointed ahead to where the ground rose.

"Race you!" Kamontip was way ahead before he could react, but nevertheless he joined in the game and ran after her, collapsing, out of breath, beside her on the grass as they reached the top. "See? You *can* have fun if you try hard enough!" She took out her own wand, keeping the Queen's Wand safely hidden. *Best not to expose him to temptation.* She spoke the incantation and a door appeared, then she stepped through, turned and beckoned him to follow.

In the Corridor of Dimensions, Logan hesitated, suddenly unsure. He knew this was a parting of the ways, that she would return to her world, he to his. On a day of unfamiliar emotions, he now experienced another. Regret.

"Okay then." She gave him a small shove. "You know the way."

Certainly, I know the way. Return to the mortal world, into the dead-end alley and through the window. Then back to that lonely old mansion. The idea did not appeal to him. *Probably forever,* he thought, morosely.

"Go on!" she hissed. "It isn't safe for you here!" Another push, harder this time. "I don't want you to be caught!"

"I could always..."

"Goodbye Logan." *For now,* she added silently. She spun on her heel and marched up the corridor, disappearing quickly into the gloom. Within seconds, he heard a door opening and closing.

Back in her world, Kamontip smiled, albeit a little regretfully, but mostly with relief. She knew Logan liked her and she'd enjoyed the flattery but really, he was trouble; *big* trouble.

And goblins, as we know, do prefer a quiet life.

But Logan wasn't destined to go home. Back in the mortal world, lost in thoughts of Kamontip, he was oblivious to the unnatural quietness, caused by the glamour created by the three members of the witch and wizard council.

"Going somewhere, Logan?" one drawled sardonically as all three raised their wands against him.

Startled, Logan jumped. "Who are you?" he stammered, but even as he spoke, he knew the answer.

"You've been *very* naughty, Logan. Trying to raise the Necromancer, what were you *thinking?*" said another.

"Foolish, too," agreed the third.

He looked around wildly for a means of escape, knowing there was none. "What are you going to do?"

"Well now, *we* aren't going to do anything. Unless, of course you try to escape. But Portia would like a word."

"She's the council leader," added another.

"And she's *very* annoyed with you," finished the other. "Now, will you come quietly?"

Defeated, Logan's shoulders slumped and he nodded, resigned.

*   *   *   *

"Where are we going to put her?" Molly panted, red-faced and sweating. "I can't think of anywhere safe enough. Alessandro's storage cellar perhaps, but even then..."

They were halfway along the passage-between-the-worlds and Cissy remained trapped within the strands of their web, her frantic attempts to escape thwarted by its power. Still, she kept up a steady stream of insults and taunts, snarling and spitting viciously like a rabid animal, her body twisting and writhing violently.

"We're not going to the Sanctuary." Morgan himself was panting slightly with the effort. "We're going through"—he led them another half-dozen steps before he stopped again and faced the wall—"here."

But they had a problem that had been troubling Morgan almost from the moment they'd begun this surreal journey, and now even he hesitated, unsure what to do next.

"You need your wand to open the door." The Landlord smiled in understanding, for he'd also foreseen the problem.

Statement of the obvious is always irritating and this time was no exception. A caustic retort formed on his lips, but Molly got in first.

"Well, ain't that just bleedin' marvelous." She gave them both a furious look. "You didn't have a plan for this?" Her voice was incredulous. "I mean, bleedin' 'ell, Morgan!"

It was such a typical Molly kind of remark that the tension

lightened immediately and they all laughed, even Molly herself.

"Bleeding hell indeed," he agreed. "Any suggestions, Cornelius?"

"I think,"—his friend thought for a moment—"that Molly and I can hold her long enough for you to work the spell." Instinctively they both glanced at the old witch, who was clearly struggling now though, unusually for her, uncomplaining. "The problem is of course," he continued, cheerfully, "that it will take much longer to open the other door."

Morgan blinked in surprise. "You know about that door?"

The Landlord shrugged. "Of course."

"Well, I've no bleedin' clue what you're both talking about and I don't suppose you're gonna tell me either." *Men and their secrets,* Molly thought sourly, *so bleedin' inconsiderate.* She gave the pair of them a stony look. "C'mon, let's get her to her knees."

"What?" Morgan was nonplussed.

"Oh, just do it," she snapped. "For once in your life, Morgan, let someone else be in charge." There seemed to be nothing to say to this and the three of them exerted more pressure. As gently as they were able, they lowered Cissy to her knees.

Curiously unresisting now, the girl's upper body slumped forward a little so that her head fell onto her chest and her long hair cascaded down onto the floor, exposing the back of her neck. Molly shuddered at the image, for Cissy suddenly resembled a prisoner awaiting the executioner's axe. Quickly, she reached into her pocket and drew out a slightly grubby handkerchief. She tapped it quickly with her wand, muttered a few words, and waved it beneath Cissy's nose. Instantly her eyelids drooped and she fell into a deep sleep.

Despite her bulk, the old woman stooped quickly and caught

the girl, lowering her carefully to the floor. Then she rose, panting heavily and looked at each of them in turn. "See? Sometimes it just takes a woman's touch."

"Unorthodox but effective," Morgan admitted, turning to face the wall. "Now, let's see about this door."

It took only seconds for it to appear, complete with key, on the wall before them. Morgan turned it and the door swung open to reveal a short corridor, unlit, with walls of rough-hewn stone, unlike the smoothness of the passage-between-the-worlds.

"What are you doing?" It wasn't that Molly doubted her friend. After all, she'd been there when he'd adopted a similar pose and opened the way into the old railway station, *eventually,* when she'd gone to meet the conductor.

"Trying to open the cell," he replied curtly.

"What bleedin' cell?"

"Molly, shut up."

"He's so touchy sometimes," Molly whispered to the Landlord, ensuring Morgan would hear. "There's definitely a cell behind that wall, right?"

"Oh yes." He nodded. "Well, not behind it exactly. It's more a case of summoning it."

There was silence for several minutes.

"So why is it taking so long?"

"Because it's complicated. It's not really there. Kind of."

Another long silence descended as Morgan tried every incantation he could think of, without success.

"So who made it?" Molly asked loudly. "Oops, sorry, Morgan, you're concentrating." She looked at the Landlord, who smirked.

"So who made it?" she whispered.

"The wizard and witches council. Millennia ago, when they first created the Sanctuary. It's only ever been used once."

"Who *for?*" Molly was intrigued, but still remembered to whisper – as loudly as she could.

"A wizard. Centuries ago. You won't have heard of him."

"What happened?"

"I'm not sure but it must have been serious. Anyway, he tricked his jailers and escaped. Ran off with a witch from the Far Lands."

"Ha!" exclaimed Molly scornfully. "Those witches from the Far Lands were always a flighty bunch; no morals at all."

Not all of them, Morgan thought indignantly. *I knew a very nice witch from the Far Lands once.*

"Come on, Cornelius." She nudged him. "You *must* know what happened to them!"

"I don't!" He laughed. "Really, I—"

"If you two could just be quiet for a minute?" Morgan could stand it no longer. "This is really, *really* difficult!"

"Oh, for goodness' sake, Morgan." The Landlord grinned. "How hard could it be?" He touched his wand to the wall and instantly a door appeared.

"That's just not fair!" Morgan huffed. "That's like me almost opening a bottle of ketchup that refuses to open, then you doing the last bit and making it look easy!"

They sobered and looked down at Cissy's prostrate form. Then Morgan picked her up and, with infinite gentleness, laid her inside the cell. The three of them looked at her in silent tribute for a few moments, then the door closed, entombing her inside.

Chapter 50

Looking back across the years of his long life, Morgan thought this might be the hardest thing he'd ever had to do. He had waited as long as possible, partly to allow Cissy's father time to recover a little, but more, he had to admit, because he needed time to gather his own courage. Now, the look Charles Hamilton gave him was one of anger, despair and unutterable loss.

"More than ever before I wish I was a wizard of note." He paused but Morgan remained silent. "Why?!" He took hold of the wizard's lapels and shook them violently. "Why didn't you teach me how to have power?"

Morgan shrugged helplessly but made no attempt to remove Charles's hands. "My friend, this serves no purpose, I can't..."

"Why?" He pushed so hard that Morgan stumbled backward.

"Charles," he said sharply, "even if your power was great, you couldn't have stopped Anarkus. You saw what happened out there!"

"Damn you," Charles growled, completely altered from the genial, good-natured man he'd been. "Damn your arrogance, Morgan. I'm not talking about Anarkus, I'm talking about *you*. You and the misery you have brought to my family, the death and destruction you leave behind you, wherever you go! And for what?" He moved threateningly towards the wizard, hands raised, but still Morgan made no move to defend himself.

"So you can work your devious machinations, no matter the cost? You don't care, do you? You have everyone dancing to your tune, thinking you're some marvelous savior, protecting the human race." He was panting, out of breath. "My daughter was almost killed out there!"

And all at once he broke, slumped sobbing against Morgan's shoulder, great heaving, racking sobs that tore at Morgan's heart. He raised his arms to put around the man's shoulders but stopped, hesitant and unsure.

It was Charles who drew away, wiping his tears with an angry gesture and straightening his shoulders. "But no more," he said proudly. "I will take Cissy with me, back to my own world and do... do what is necessary to care for her." Tears welled again in his eyes.

Morgan hesitated. "I want to help, it goes without saying—"

"Never!" The single word ripped from deep within him. "I require no help from you, Morgan, I've seen what your *help* can do. All I ask is your word that we will never meet again."

There was a silence before Morgan nodded sadly. "Of course, if that is your wish. But it is my hope..."

"It is my wish." Charles looked at the wizard for what he hoped would be the last time. "I'm going now and taking Cissy with me; I will ask Molly to fetch her." He went to the door but Morgan's next word, although softly spoken, halted him in his tracks.

"No."

He turned, incredulous, and stared. "No?"

"Charles, Cissy is... unwell, affected by the battle. She is..."—he temporized, for how do you tell a man his daughter is insane?—"She is overwrought by what happened out there."

"Overwrought? Of course she is *overwrought!* Take me to her. Please, Morgan!"

Guilt flooded through him as he looked at the tortured man before him, a good man who'd had the misfortune to be the father of a witch. A man whose progress Morgan had followed almost since birth until the age of sixteen when he'd been drawn into the world of the Sanctuary and then rejected.

All well and good for those who have talent, Morgan mused, his eyes momentarily downcast, *but what of those who haven't, like this man? To what end do we subject them to pain and danger, only for it all too often to end in heartbreak?*

And a small voice deep within his mind, the voice of reason, replied, *So that the mortal race may survive; that is the end we seek.* Morgan could not deny the truth of it. He gathered his resolve again. "Perhaps in time, Charles. But not now."

Charles opened his mouth to object but he knew there was no point and his shoulders slumped.

"I'm sorry," Morgan said as he turned and left the room.

*   *   *   *

"I don't see why you just can't bleedin' stay," Molly grumbled. "It's not as if you have much to do back in Wales, is it?" Collectively, Luke and Wallace winced at her lack of tact. "I mean, you look after

354

a railway station where no trains ever go; how hard could it be?"

"That's a bit unfair, Molly," the Landlord chided gently. "I *am* the custodian of the portal, after all." He should have been offended but he understood the root of Molly's unease and for the Sanctuary to have no natural leader was not a good thing.

There was a slightly awkward pause and even Molly, who had no filter, thought she might have said too much. But in his good-natured way, the Landlord quickly smoothed over any difficulty.

"You miss Morgan very much, don't you?"

"Yes," she admitted, "it's not the same around here since he went to live with Aeryn. No offense," she added hastily to Wallace and Luke. "Nor to you either, Cornelius."

"None taken," the Landlord said. He had not yet had time to examine the reasons for his newly found sense of peace, but when he did, he would realize that seeing Mitra again, no matter how briefly, and knowing that she forgave him, was worth more than all the riches in the universe.

"I dunno," Molly continued, "I'd kinda got used to him being in Aeryn's world, and he did come and visit quite often. And Cissy was doing such a good job..." Her voice faded away and they were all silent for a moment.

Morgan chose to enter the room at this point, and he pretended not to have heard Molly's last comment. "Charles has returned home," he informed them. "He's not good."

Nobody answered. They were all secretly relieved that, at Morgan's advice, they'd not had to face him themselves.

"What about Cissy?" Luke spoke up, nervous. "Is there hope?" Morgan turned and looked at the boy, mature beyond his years, and realized the effort it had taken to voice those words. He remembered a time, not so long ago, when Luke had asked the same question about his father.

So much heartache for one so young, and in such a short time.

"There is always hope, Luke." And to himself, *while ever I have breath in my body, there will be hope.*

The next day, Luke and his father returned home. Peter was worried for Charles's state of mind and wanted to be close by his friend. And Lucy would need his support too. Luke would return to the Sanctuary in a few days; he wouldn't be parted long from Cissy, even though there was nothing he could do to help her.

The Landlord was also eager to return home, as was Morgan, although he would remain for several weeks yet. But first there was something to be done.

The thought of Cissy remaining in that cold, dark cell was anathema to them all and Molly had spent most of the night preparing her room, which lay next to Luke's. Preparing it so she'd be unable, however hard she tried, to escape.

It still contained her possessions; clothes, books – including the extremely old copy of *Wuthering Heights,* of which she was so proud – the slightly bedraggled teddy bear she'd been given for her first Christmas, and her prized collection of *Shadow High* dolls. But it was a prison, the doors and windows warded so powerfully that, even with the might of Anarkus lodged in her brain, she'd not be able to get out.

So, while Wallace was in the kitchen with Hans, preparing Cissy's favorite meal in a vain attempt to make her new prison more palatable, Molly, Morgan and the Landlord stepped into the passage-between-the-worlds.

They heard her, alternately snarling and giggling maniacally, before they saw her. And when they finally plucked up the courage to unlock her cell door, a horrific scene awaited them.

In her torment, Cissy had gouged her face, leaving deep, bloody scratches, and large clumps of her hair lay on the floor. Her eyes were lit with madness and she had soiled herself, the rank stink of feces and urine permeating the air.

Her first instinct was to attack, but when the three streams of wand fire enveloped her, she screamed; not in pain but with anger and hatred as, quite unable to resist, a torrent of vitriol and profanity poured from her mouth.

Wallace had already put the food in her room and he watched, astounded but helpless to assist, as they brought her inside. Somehow they managed to bundle her fully clothed into the shower of her *en suite,* then run from the room before she could attack them, Molly shouting the words that would seal the door shut.

Chapter 51

The Landlord had been home for two days when there was a knock at the door of the old railway inn. It was the *back* door which meant it was coming from 17th Century Wales and if it was who he expected...

"Catrin!" The Landlord, who *really* didn't do hugs, lifted her off her feet and pulled her close, tears filling his eyes. "I've been so worried!" He released her at last and his attention turned to the witch behind her. "Rosalind." He smiled. "How can I possibly thank you?"

"She took some finding, Cornelius, I can tell you." The witch grinned. "And at first she refused to come back." She smiled fondly at Catrin. "But now we're great friends."

Later, as they ate dinner, he regarded the girl solemnly. "What will you do now, Catrin? Return to the village?"

"No!" Catrin shook her head vehemently. "No, Landlord, I couldn't. There's nothing there for me now."

"There's Grufydd," he ventured, but she avoided his eyes.

"I know. But that was before... before." She was unable to say the words and she looked helplessly at him.

"I understand." For a moment, sadness threatened to overwhelm him. "But life does have to continue." He winced at how prosaic the words sounded.

"I know. And maybe one day …" She shrugged. "But right now I just can't." She gave him a challenging look, thinking he might argue.

But he was the Landlord and he understood perfectly. "What will you do?"

She took a deep breath. "Rosalind says she will guide me to the land of shades."

The Landlord looked sharply at Rosalind, his mind working overtime. "Siwaraksa," he said at last. "You hope Siwaraksa will cure Cissy."

Catrin nodded. "Rosalind told me it's almost certain the Sanctuary can't cure her. Not even Molly."

"That's true. But…"

"I need a purpose. I can't go back to the village, I really can't!" Catrin sounded worried he would try and persuade her. "And I liked Cissy; I want to help if I can."

He nodded, his expression troubled. "But you must know Siwaraksa can't return to the living, Catrin."

"I don't intend her to come back with me. I want her to *teach* me."

"When will you go?" the Landlord asked Rosalind later. Catrin had gone to bed and they could speak freely.

"As soon as the trial has ended," Rosalind confirmed. "Well, as soon as I can get away; naturally, I will need to leave secretly. Which reminds me, I must return before my absence is noticed."

"Ah yes, the trial." The Landlord nodded. "Logan's luck has run out at last and he will receive the punishment he deserves."

Rosalind's expression was troubled. "That's what I'm worried about."

"You fear they will demand his execution?"

Rosalind sighed. "I know they will. I will argue against it of course. But…"

"But Portia is hard to argue against," he finished for her, sympathetically.

"Will you speak for him, Cornelius?"

It was a dilemma that had been worrying him, for much as he had always believed Logan deserved death, now that he was to face trial, he feared the impact it might have on Morgan. "Perhaps," he said evasively. "The truth is, I just don't know. Why will you argue for him? He has committed many crimes."

"I know," she pondered slowly, unsure how to answer. "I'm not sure. Except that life is sacrosanct, whoever you are. Doesn't executing someone make us just as bad as they are?"

The Landlord didn't know how to answer; it wasn't quite how he viewed it.

"Anyway," she stumbled on, "Logan is weak and not always responsible for his actions." She flushed as he raised a skeptical eyebrow. "No, Cornelius, he has long been consumed by his jealousy of Morgan. And the damage done by Kanzser, the Demon King, is incalculable!"

"Perhaps." He nodded. "Anyway, we will just have to see what happens at the trial."

And with that, Rosalind had to be content.

Chapter 52

Amelia had no idea what happened to the red coat she'd liked so much. Nor did she care, for it belonged to her other life, the one when she'd been a child. Because to Amelia, childhood seemed a long time ago and she could barely remember those happy, carefree days.

After the incident on the Old Kent Road, she had been taken first to an Accident and Emergency department and then, when they didn't know what to do with her, a psychiatric hospital where she underwent numerous psychological tests.

Gradually she improved slightly and even began to talk a little, although she'd never be drawn into talking about *that day*. After a few months she was allowed to return home and, eventually, school. But the other children were wary of this strange, silent child, much changed from the one they'd known and who looked at them with lifeless eyes.

One day a supply teacher arrived in class, a tall man with black hair and gaunt features. It was raining heavily and he was unfortunately wearing a long, black raincoat. In Amelia's mind, this was the tall stranger, back to haunt her, or worse.

When her screams didn't drive him away, the obscenities that vomited from her lips sent him running from the school as he realized that perhaps teaching wasn't for him after all.

Two weeks later at assembly, which began each day with the school song, Amelia had taken out a sharp knife, stolen from home. As the child next to her sang happily along, she'd attempted to stab her in the mouth.

The police were called and she found herself back in the hospital, this time for a much longer stay. She refused to talk about the incident except to ask her social worker whether the child was dead. The social worker reported later that Amelia had seemed disappointed she wasn't. When her distraught mother had asked why she'd done it, her daughter had replied, "I didn't like the demons inside her mouth. They scared me."

Young and small in stature though she was, the other patients were scared how she watched them with calculating eyes. Amelia exuded a sense of menace and evil and, although the heavy medication she was forced to take made her movements slow and clumsy, nobody was careless enough to get too close. Soon she had nothing to occupy her mind except the memories of what had happened; memories of demons and tormented souls from the very depths of the inferno. The nights were worse, for that was when the demons came out of hiding, wanting to play.

When her mother committed suicide, no longer able to bear the sight of her distant, damaged daughter, Amelia hardly registered the news; all she wanted was to see again the tall, dark stranger. She felt desperate to look inside his mouth and see the demons that both fascinated and terrified her.

When she took a pair of scissors from a nurse's pocket she was finally segregated after slicing her arms and wrists to ribbons, then entering the bedroom of the girl next door and attempting to do the same to her. As the girl fought in vain, Amelia bit her deeply in the neck, then sat on the floor, quietly licking the blood from her fingers with obvious relish.

But what nobody knew, and Amelia wasn't telling, was that she hadn't picked the nurse's pocket, she'd simply willed the scissors into her hand. Soon she realized she could perform other feats like this, but she was already learning cunning, and told nobody.

Now she was watched, constantly, and not once in the years that followed did she come into contact with another human being, except those who brought her meals and cleaned her room. Or the doctors who still occasionally tried to help her.

Now, about six months after *that day,* she stood looking through her window at the world passing by. She felt happy where she was; didn't want to be out there where the demons lurked, waiting for her.

Well, not exactly *happy* perhaps, but content. Because Amelia knew something with utter certainty. That one day, the tall stranger would return.

Chapter 53

For the first time ever, mortals were aware of the existence of wizards and witches; this was a crime the council could not ignore. They had successfully hidden the existence of their kind for thousands of years but now, because of Logan's actions, it was a secret no longer.

For the past year, the Sanctuary, along with the wizard and witches council, had done all they could to limit the damage but even they could not take back the thousands of images and videos that bounced around the world via the internet.

Morgan looked back over the last twenty-four hours with a sense of unreality. Just before midnight on the previous day, he'd been shaken roughly awake, startled to find the Landlord standing over him.

"What's going on?" Morgan struggled to sit up.

"Shhh!" the Landlord hissed. "We need to be quiet!" He crossed the room and grabbed a handful of clothes from the wardrobe, flinging them onto the bed. "Get dressed, quickly! You have been summoned!"

Morgan was already alert to the urgency in his friend's voice and had been swinging his legs from the bed, but now he paused. "Summoned? By whom?"

The Landlord grinned wickedly, pleased to have the advantage over the usually unflappable Morgan. "By the council." His tone implied it should have been obvious. "Now, c'mon,"—he flung open the door—"I'll be going with you."

"You will? Why?" This was all happening too fast.

The Landlord turned and winked. "Because I've been summoned too."

They had made a stealthy exit into the passage-between-the-worlds to be confronted by a door that had certainly never been there before, so far as Morgan knew. The Landlord spoke words in a language that even he, Morgan, had never heard and he had the uncomfortable, alien feeling of things being completely beyond his control.

The door swung inwards to reveal an inky black void. Without hesitating, the Landlord took his arm and they walked through. And began to fall.

After his initial shock, when his stomach had seemed to shoot up into his throat, Morgan began to relax. He'd heard of portals like this, although he'd never experienced one, and he knew exactly where it led. Feeling a sudden excitement, despite the ordeal that lay ahead, he was curious to learn what the planet of the witch and wizard council would be like.

The silence was absolute as they plummeted at, what seemed to Morgan, a tremendous speed. *Blissful,* he thought as he allowed the feeling of peace to wash over him, all his cares seeming insignificant. For all he knew, the journey might have lasted hours already. But he had rarely known such contentment and didn't want it to end yet. Then, of course, the Landlord had to ruin it.

"Don't you think it's strange." he said conversationally, "how so many have yearned to rule the mortal world?"

Morgan grunted.

"I mean, think about it. Logan, Kanzser, Anarkus; and that's just recently! Don't you ever wonder why they've coveted what would seem to me a most thankless job?"

Morgan remained silent, trying to cling onto his contentment.

"Not that they couldn't *do* with a ruler; they can barely be trusted to look after themselves!"

All at once, that contentment had disappeared, replaced by apprehension and a sense of impending doom. Their journey through the portal was no longer silent, but noisy and uncomfortable.

What's wrong with me? Morgan wondered. But he knew what it was, of course. Despite the magnitude of Logan's crimes, and all the associated, irrational guilt Morgan felt as a result, he had not yet reached the stage where he wished his brother to pay the ultimate price. But now, for Logan, time was running out.

"And as for those who call themselves leaders, their presidents and dictators, those who think they are kings and queens, don't get me *started!*"

How I wish he'd stop prattling on!

"Anyway, that's why the Sanctuary was created, to protect mortals from evil, because they can't be protected from themselves."

Morgan sighed; statement of the obvious was *so* irritating!

"For goodness' sake, lighten up, Morgan! It's not us on trial here, you know!"

"Sorry." He smiled and patted the Landlord's arm condescendingly, knowing it would annoy him. "I was thinking of Cissy," he lied, "and whether I did the right thing in leaving her to lead the Sanctuary. Look what's happened to her; imprisoned and insane, and all Molly's attempts to cure her have failed."

"Of course you did the right thing," the Landlord said, troubled by his friend's mood. "It *was* the right time, for you *and* for her." There was silence for a while. "Anyway, Cissy will be cured eventually."

"Why, do you know something?" Morgan asked.

"Oh no," replied the Landlord, unwilling to mention Catrin's quest, which would likely end in failure anyway. He was saved from saying more by an almost imperceptible lightening of the inky blackness. "Almost there," he announced cheerfully.

"We can't be," Morgan objected. "We're still going *really* fast."

"Nevertheless. Any second now..." Sure enough, just then a rectangle of shimmering white light appeared before them and, to his surprise, Morgan realized they were no longer plummeting.

"Told you," boasted the Landlord. "Come on." He bounded through the door and Morgan followed more cautiously, but their way was blocked by two rather large, intimidating guards.

"If you don't mind, sir," said one in a deep, gruff voice. "We do not allow weapons here."

"Weapons?" the Landlord replied incredulously. "As if I would!" He smiled sweetly and he and Morgan submitted themselves to a thorough search. "Portia!" the Landlord exclaimed when they were released. He strode towards a tall, handsome woman who turned, her face breaking into a smile when she saw him.

"Cornelius." She held out her hand for his kiss but he ignored it and hugged her tightly. Then he thrust her aside and made for another, much younger woman. "Rosalind!"

Portia looked after him with a rueful smile and turned to Morgan. "Welcome," she said with a twinkle in her eye. "It is not often one gets to meet the leader of the Sanctuary."

"It's not often one gets to meet the leader of the witch and wizard council either," he returned politely.

"True." She inclined her head. "But be welcome here. You are a friend to this council."

"I'd heard there was a protocol for meeting the leader. Cornelius explained it in minute detail and said I should follow it on pain of death."

She laughed. "And you believed him? He's inclined to exaggerate, you know."

"Yes he is," Morgan conceded. "But shouldn't he have shown, oh I don't know, a little more respect?"

"He should, but he's Cornelius. He gets away with far more than he ought. He always did."

Morgan bit back a smile. "This is a nice room. Is it where the trial will take place?"

"It is beautiful," Portia agreed, avoiding the question. "It is our council chamber; one of my favorite rooms in our old home. This is an exact replica."

They looked around at the three-sided room with its shelves, which he knew contained ancient histories of the witch and wizard races, and its balcony open to the stars. Morgan walked over to the balustrade.

"And this is where Anarkus fell; in your old home I mean."

"It is." Portia nodded. "Unfortunately, Rosalind's aim was not quite true. A little further to one side and who knows?" She sighed. "I would have hoped you'd have more success when you met him recently."

Morgan looked over at the woman who was now conversing with the Landlord. *She doesn't look like a killer,* he thought.

"It was unfortunate," he agreed, shortly, annoyed at the criticism.

"Yes, Morgan, *very* unfortunate. He will be back to cause trouble for the world you protect. And mark my words, it will be *soon.*"

"I don't think so. I was there, remember? Anarkus is finished."

"If you think that, then you are naïve. I was *there* when he fell from that balcony. Do you have any idea how far that drop is?"

"What's your point?"

"My *point* is that he walked away from it. Sure, it took him years to do it, but he returned. He will do so again."

"You seem angry."

"Angry? No, Morgan, I'm just tired of this whole damned business. Now, if you'll excuse me, the trial is about to begin. And it will take place here." She looked at him with something like sympathy.

"I hope you will look favorably upon him," Morgan ventured, and her demeanor altered.

"Favorably?" she said coldly. "The actions of your brother are yet to be judged. That is the *point* of a trial." She walked quickly to the ancient stone table and sat at its head. Moments later, the other judges walked into the room.

It was seldom necessary to bring the entire council to proceedings such as these but it seemed Portia was taking no chances on Logan escaping the full might of the law. The Landlord knew most of those now seated around the ancient stone table and he also knew, without doubt, that Logan was in deep trouble.

"What's wrong?" Morgan had noticed the grim look on his friend's face.

"Logan has few here who will argue for clemency; only Rosalind will do so for certain."

"How can you be sure?" Morgan hissed.

"The witch over there,"—he pointed to an ancient old crone with deep lined features and wizened hands—"I don't know her. Nor the wizard sitting opposite. But the rest..." He shrugged. "Some will be hostile and the others will not go against the leader's will."

"You think Portia is intent on condemning Logan?"

"Don't be naïve, Morgan. She is the leader; she has no choice!"

There was silence as Morgan scrutinized the council. "What about him?" He nodded to a tall, gray-haired figure with sharp and angular features. He appeared to distance himself from the group and took no part in their whispered conversations. *Perhaps he's just a loner?* he thought. *Or one who doesn't much like the company of others?*

"He is the real threat here," the Landlord warned. "He will attempt to sway the others, those who are as yet undecided. As a boy, he was the only one of the council who scared me a little. Apart from Anarkus himself, of course."

"That's not good."

"Don't worry, my friend,"—the Landlord smiled—"all is not lost." His smile faded. "And he doesn't frighten me now."

Morgan looked at the grim set of the Landlord's mouth and, not for the first time, thought how he would not like to have him as an enemy.

"But," the Landlord continued, "he and Anarkus were once great friends. That is the type of wizard we are dealing with. This will not be easy."

As if he knew he was being discussed, the gray-haired wizard fixed a cold gaze upon them and his forehead creased into a heavy frown. Nothing about him displayed even a hint of warmth.

The monobrow didn't help much, either.

"Tell me," the Landlord asked, "why are you so anxious that Logan doesn't receive the... you know?"

"The death penalty, Cornelius. You can say it."

"Well, yes, the death penalty. I know he's your brother and all that, but he *hates* you!"

"Because there is good in him somewhere; I'm convinced of it. I remember when we were boys. There was a time when we were close."

The Landlord bit back a sarcastic comment already forming on his lips and looked sympathetically at his friend. But he was saved from finding a suitable reply by a clattering noise, then the sound of footsteps. The room brightened and the Dark Wizard was led in, chains rattling. He stood before the council, erect and proud, determined not to reveal how frightened he was.

Despite himself, Morgan felt a flicker of pride at his brother's refusal to be cowed. He aimed a nod of approval towards him but it was ignored.

"Logan," Portia began without preamble. "You have allowed

jealousy of your brother to corrupt your soul."

"So?" he sneered. "We can't all be *perfect,* can we?" Now he looked at his brother and, although it was filled with contempt, Morgan couldn't help seeing something else there. A look of appeal perhaps?

"This is the indictment," she continued, picking up a long roll of parchment and starting to read. "First of all, there are your associations with Kanzser, the Demon King. Then the killing of your father; and of course, Morgan's."

Was there a trace of guilt in his expression at that? Morgan wondered. Of all Logan's crimes, the murder of their father was the one he found hardest to forgive. But Portia was speaking again.

"Even then there was time for you to turn to the right path. When the Demon King abandoned you, *that* was your chance, Logan. But no! Instead you sought out the Necromancer!" She stopped, recognizing her anger was getting the better of her. "Oh for goodness' sake." She threw the indictment onto the table. "The list is long. Let us consider your latest, and to my mind, your *greatest* crime. Because of you the mortal world is aware of the existence of our kind. What gave you the right!"

She paused again, remembering she should at least show a pretense of impartiality. She turned to the council, who sat grimly watching, already making up their minds, although most had done so long before the trial had started.

"Are there any who would speak in his defense?" she asked, knowing there was only one.

Rosalind stood and cleared her throat, nervously. And then she attempted to justify the unjustifiable. She spoke for ten minutes, acutely aware of the sniggers and barely disguised whispered comments, the looks of disdain and open hostility as she tried to explain her views on the sanctity of life. She acknowledged the many wrongs Logan had done and begged for him to have the chance to atone. But eventually, as the sniggers and mutters grew louder, her voice lapsed into silence. Afterward, Morgan and the Landlord agreed her attempt had been courageous.

"Your comments are noted, Rosalind," announced Portia. "This council thanks you for your words. Now, have you all reached your verdict?"

There were nods from each of them and then silence as they communed, their minds melding as they each gave their decision. It didn't take long.

"The council has decided." She looked at Logan without the slightest trace of sympathy. "We have each voted on this and there are only two dissenters. You know of one." She nodded at Rosalind. "The other I will not reveal. Therefore..."

"I killed the Demon King for you!" Logan blurted before the sentence of death could pass Portia's lips; the ancient laws forbade it from being revoked, once spoken.

"For me?" Portia asked, feigning surprise, annoyed at the interruption. She'd never become accustomed to these death trials, though she'd conducted many, and wished it to be finished quickly. "Or perhaps you mean for *us?*" She gestured to her companions. "Are you suggesting we are indebted to you, wizard?" Her eyes glinted dangerously.

"N... no, of course not," stammered Logan, who was quite literally pleading for his life, "but surely it counts for something?"

"And anyway," Portia cut in, having no intention of allowing him to plead, "the moment of Kanzser's death was pre-ordained the instant the wizard Cornelius created the blood moon!" She paused and glanced toward the two wizards who were, as yet, forbidden to speak. "Isn't that correct, erm... Landlord?"

Now her eyes were filled with amusement, some of her natural good humor restored now that the difficult part was over and Logan knew his fate, even if it had not been formally pronounced yet. The Landlord, probably wisely, elected to remain silent. Portia composed a look of cold sternness onto her face before turning to the Dark Wizard again.

"The fact that you were the instrument of the Demon King's death is irrelevant and makes no difference to these proceedings."

But despite the direness of his situation, Logan barely heard and was staring instead at the Landlord. *What does he have to do with the blood moon?* he wondered and, not for the first time, *Who is he?*

"And this council has made its decision. You have been judged guilty of your crimes, Logan, self-styled *Dark Wizard*. Your other crimes might have been forgiven, but you are responsible for the current situation in the mortal world, and for that there can be only one penalty!"

Logan's attention was firmly back on the ancient wizard, his eyes fixed with a sick fascination on her lips. Any words of defense had lodged securely in his throat, and anyway, he knew they would be futile, that his fate was sealed.

"And that penalty is—"

"Wait!"

Portia turned furiously. "Morgan! You dare to interrupt this council?" Some of her carefully controlled power escaped and fury sparked from her eyes. Her voice reverberated around the room, causing it to shake, but Morgan was undaunted as he stepped from shadow into the light.

"Yes, I dare to interrupt, Portia. Because this council, which means *you,* bear at least some blame for the *current situation.*"

The gray-haired wizard was on his feet in an instant. "You will allow this disrespect?" he shouted, but Portia stilled him.

"Wait, Suluhura. I think our friend here is trying to make some sort of point?" She looked at Morgan, her eyes like ice. "Just what *is* your point, Morgan?"

"My *point* is that you did not have to let it come to this! But you sit there on your thrones, all of you, sat in your omnipotent judgment. Yet who judges you?"

Outraged, Portia opened her mouth to speak but he glared at her with such ferocity that the words died on her lips.

"Many times over the millennia you could have intervened to help the mortal world. You could have educated them; shown them the benefit of our greater technological advances and prevented some of their greater excesses! Why do you not *weep* with grief at the countless millions who have died and suffered in their wars!"

The room was silent now and everyone stared at Morgan in rapt attention. Even the Landlord, who'd long criticized the council's policy of non-intervention, couldn't have expressed these ideas more eloquently.

Quieter now, his voice almost soothing, Morgan continued his damnation of the witch and wizard council. "You came to this solar system and, like some all-conquering God, you had the nerve to *steal* its planets. And then, if that wasn't bad enough, you invaded their own by placing dimensions there, thus exposing them to horrific peril. The demons! They came within a hair's breadth of defeating the Sanctuary!"

He was shouting now, unable to contain the emotion that permeated his very soul, so deeply did he abhor what the council had done. "If not for Aeryn and if not for Cornelius's blood moon, the mortal world would now be overrun with that filth!"

Logan, who had been temporarily forgotten, watched with everyone else, and stared in amazement at his brother. He'd always known, deep within himself, that Morgan was the more powerful of the twins, but this was different. His brother was expressing ideas that he, Logan, could never have imagined; uncomfortable ideas to be sure, but ones that could not be ignored. For the first time in centuries, perhaps ever, Logan looked at him with something akin to respect.

But Suluhura had had enough and he tried to rise. If Portia wouldn't silence this upstart, *he* would. "I think we've heard more than is necessary," he said smoothly, smiling at the council. "Are we really going to let this—"

"Sit *down!*" Morgan thundered. "I haven't *finished!*" Blue lines of static flashed from his eyes. "Not even the most diseased societies of the mortal world are as corrupt as you!" He raked them all with a look that oozed contempt. "All of you, you make me want to *vomit!*"

"Stop!" Portia leaped angrily to her feet, but Morgan, with a flick of his mind, flung her back into her seat and pointed at Logan. He knew it was a dangerous move but he was beyond caring.

"You could have helped him! He's a *wizard;* one of our kind. Flawed, certainly, but still one of us! You are the council. You had a *responsibility!*" All at once he was exhausted and he staggered backward, totally spent.

Portia sat in stunned silence, overawed at the power Morgan had just displayed.

The arguments could have ended there but then Suluhura laughed, an ugly sound, and turned to Portia. "You will allow him to speak to you thus?" He sneered at Morgan. "Perhaps *he* should stand trial also!"

A gasp escaped the Landlord's lips and even Portia looked surprised. *You fool!* she thought, *do you wish to provoke him again, just as his temper has cooled?* As for Rosalind, she looked as if she wished herself anywhere but in that place; this whole thing was far worse then she had ever imagined.

"Oh, you do not answer?" Suluhura held both arms wide in mock surprise. "But it is curious, is it not, how he so stoutly defends his brother, despite all his crimes? And think! Do you really believe this pathetic excuse for a *wizard,*"—he pointed at Logan—"would have anywhere *near* the power needed to defeat the Demon King, without the help of his brother? I say they are traitors together!"

Morgan was too exhausted from his tirade and too dumbfounded at Suluhura's words to do anything but stare in disbelief. But, for the Landlord, this was too much and he marched to the dais where the council sat. Instead of addressing Suluhura directly, he turned to Portia.

"And why does your esteemed companion think it would be so wrong if Morgan *had* helped kill Kanzser? After all, he was content enough to stand by and watch while the Sanctuary came under threat from the demons. And all, Morgan included, almost paid with their lives!" It was a non-too subtle admonishment that the *entire* council had failed to intervene, and it was not lost on Portia but, despite his accusations, she realized she didn't mind so much. After all, Cornelius had been making them for centuries.

"It *is* the Sanctuary's mission to protect the mortal world after all," the Landlord said, his tone deliberately mild. "Could it be he is tripping over his own argument?" He gave her a withering glance. "I must say, I'm surprised, Portia, that you allow someone who is so clearly *confused* to sit on your council!"

"Watch your words, Cornelius," Portia warned. "I allow you *some* latitude, but there are limits, even for you." She sighed, still unable to believe how this farce of a trial was turning out. She was acutely aware that the sentencing still hadn't happened. *Goodness knows how that's going to work out,* she thought. "But you do have a point. Now we will hear no more."

"Yes, but I was just using that as an example! Obviously!" Suluhura broke in, his expression conveying scorn and disbelief that nobody realized it. "I'm talking about all the *other* crimes; there are dozens of documented examples!" He picked up the sheaf of papers before him and slammed them back down to emphasize the point. "It doesn't take much intelligence to realize that it is not Logan but his *brother* who holds *a little* power, at least." His attempt to disparage Morgan impressed no one. "He *must* be in league with the prisoner." He turned to Portia. "How can you not see it? I say again, they are traitors; let them be executed together!"

"Enough!" barked Portia, who was now so frightened of Morgan's power she dared not even censure him for his actions. "You go much too far, Suluhura. You will apologize to Morgan for your insulting words and you would be wise to hope he accepts!" *No,* she thought, *you should pray that Morgan accepts it. If he and Cornelius turn on us and seek to take control...*

But Suluhura was given no chance to apologize as the Landlord leaned over the table until his face was close to his. "And what would you seek to gain from their execution?" None were fooled by the deceptive softness of his voice, and all present, even Morgan, were chilled by its low, dangerous tone. "You are a fool. I have never liked you and for sure, I've never trusted you." Suluhura opened his mouth to reply but the Landlord waved him to silence. "You would rid us of a wizard with more integrity than all of us here combined?" Suddenly his wand was in his hand and some council members reached instinctively for theirs, but Portia raised a placating hand to prevent them.

"How did he get that past the guards?" whispered one, a little too loudly.

"No idea! Shhh, let's see what happens."

But Portia was not surprised at *anything* the Landlord did; nor was she worried, for she knew the wizard had no intention of using his wand.

And indeed, the Landlord proceeded to point and gesticulate with it, as if admonishing Suluhura as one might a small child. This was not lost on the wizard, who felt increasingly uncertain about how this was turning out.

"You don't impress me, Cornelius," he blustered. "You might have been important once but now you're just an old fool who sits in his railway station waiting for a train that never comes!"

The Landlord smiled, unperturbed. "A fool I may be, but smart enough to get a wand past your guards, eh? But let's talk about you. I question *your* motives, Suluhura, and if I were to presume to offer advice to this council,"—none present were under any illusion that this was *precisely* what he was doing—"it would be that they should question them too!"

Portia opened her mouth but then closed it again, deciding to let the argument run its course. It was rather fascinating to watch and though she trusted Suluhura implicitly, sometimes he did need taking down a peg or two, and Cornelius would certainly do that.

"How dare you?" Suluhura found his voice again. "What gives you the right—"

"I haven't finished." It was not a shout, not even a slight raising of the voice and yet, such was the authority and power it held, Suluhura was stunned into silence. "Morgan's leadership of the Sanctuary has protected the mortal world for nigh on four hundred years and he is one in a long line of custodians who have done so for millennia. Yet you dare to question, to threaten?"

Allowing no reply, he turned to the other members of the council. "I would respectfully point out that many times over the centuries, I have been asked, invited, even *begged* on occasion, to become a member of this council. And that each time I have declined the... *honor* regretfully."

In the background, Morgan smirked, knowing his friend despised officialdom of any kind.

"But had I not declined, I would most probably be sitting where you fine people are now, perhaps even in *your* seat, Portia."

"Yes, but you are not, Cornelius," Portia pointed out, but without heat, "are you?"

The Landlord inclined his head in agreement. "As you say, Portia, I am not. Yet you and I have not lived these thousands of years without amassing some kind of wisdom." He paused, belatedly realizing he needed to convince the others too. "And you also." He turned to one of the older witches and gave her his most charming smile, which she was not entirely immune to. "Were you the one who argued *against* execution?"

She looked at him, her face revealing nothing. "I was still a young witch, present on the day you took Mitra," she told him severely. "I have no love for you, wizard. Don't think you can deceive me with your good looks and your silver tongue."

"You were? I thought you looked familiar!" He grinned. "That was quite a day, wasn't it?" He turned to move away, then stopped and turned back. "Agnes? Is it really you?" He smiled delightedly.

"Yes, it is I, Cornelius." She did not return the smile. "And I well remember the day you escaped from my prison, taking Mitra with you."

"But it was you who..." He stopped as comprehension dawned.

"I still have no idea how you managed to escape, Cornelius,"— Agnes let an eyelid lower in an infinitesimal wink—"but perhaps you will enlighten me some time."

Before he could respond, the old witch he'd first noticed when they'd arrived chose to speak. "The rights or wrongs of our actions are of no concern to you, wizard. We are the council! You sow blame as easily as a farmer sows corn." She pointed a bony finger. "Seeing as how you enjoy casting blame, how about this? The beloved witch Mitra is no longer here. But for *your* actions, she would be alive still!"

Oh, be quiet, you old crone, what do you know? But the accusation stung, for he couldn't deny the truth of it. "You are biased and know nothing!" he shot back and turned furiously to Portia. "Is this how you manage your council? I remember when the witch and wizard council name was a byword for integrity!"

"Enough!"

"Oh no, Portia. I haven't even *started* yet!" The Landlord's hand tightened around his wand as he fought to control himself, and the movement was not lost on anyone. Even Morgan laid a warning hand on his arm, only to have it shrugged away, impatiently. "You say that only two voted for Logan? How do we know that?" Suddenly he found himself arguing for Logan without understanding when, or even *if* he'd made the decision.

"We commune silently." Portia recognized a note of defensiveness in her voice. "Do not think you can influence this council!"

"Oh, how very *convenient!*" the Landlord mocked. "And what about *your* influence? What threats did you make to ensure your desired verdict?"

"I threatened no one! How dare you suggest I manipulated the verdict!" Portia was incandescent with rage. "I said earlier I allow you latitude, Cornelius! Well that latitude is long gone! I am not the one on trial here!"

"No?" He forced his heart to stop pounding and lowered his voice. "Perhaps not, but I'm telling you now, *this* trial is over."

"What?" At once, the entirety of the council was on its feet, except for Rosalind who had watched the turn of events with dismay. She *knew* that Portia had manipulated the vote and that not all had agreed Logan's crimes warranted the taking of his life. All had been threatened with dire consequences if they dared to go against the majority but only she and Agnes had still refused to find Logan guilty. This was Portia's dirty little secret and it was in danger of being exposed.

"I will give you a choice, both of you. Leave now or I will call the guards. You have spoken treason here!"

"Treason?" Morgan interjected mildly, coming to the Landlord's side. "We have merely voiced our opinions. Are you now saying this is a crime also?"

"Just leave," Portia replied coldly. "And do not return."

"They should be imprisoned!" shouted Suluhura. "Never have I witnessed such disrespect!"

"Be quiet, you fool!" Portia quailed at the thought of trying to contain Cornelius in one of her jails.

"Oh yes, we are leaving," the Landlord agreed. But Portia's sigh of relief was short-lived. "Morgan, get your brother." Instinctively she raised her wand, as did all the others, except Rosalind and Agnes. "Don't," he warned. "Tell your guards to move."

Portia had never doubted Cornelius before but now, seeing his cold, implacable look, she knew he would use his wand if he had to. She also knew she was not nearly quick enough to prevent him, and she nodded at the two wizards who guarded the portal. Reluctantly they obeyed.

Logan shrank back in fear as Morgan approached, then gaped stupidly as his chains fell to the floor around him.

He really means to rescue me! he thought. *Why?*

"Come on," Morgan snapped, "before they gather their wits and try to stop us." He took Logan by the arm and pulled him toward the portal.

The Landlord muttered the incantation and gave a lightning fast flick of his wand before levelling it again at Portia, and the blinding white doorway of light appeared once more. "Quickly, inside," urged the Landlord as he backed carefully towards it.

"You should go with them," murmured Agnes in Rosalind's ear.

"What?" Rosalind looked at her, startled. "I can't do that; the council would never forgive it!"

"We voted *against* the council. Do you really think they're going to just ignore that?" But Rosalind's mind was whirling with the events of the last hour and this new development was too much to process. "Quickly!" Agnes forgot to speak quietly and a few heads turned towards them.

"Come with me then. You are in danger too!"

"No," Agnes muttered, "don't worry about me, I can look after myself. They will not harm me, but you should go."

"Please, Agnes."

"No!" she hissed, far too loudly. More heads turned toward them, suspicious now, and the Landlord had almost reached the portal. "Go!"

Rosalind had only an instant to make her decision. "Wait! I'm coming with you!" She dived toward the portal just as it closed at the Landlord's command.

He grabbed her clothing and dragged her in just in time, then shouted the incantation that would send them hurtling toward safety. He flung a bright stream of wand fire upwards and, as if they were pulled by some celestial string, they were propelled at even greater speed.

Chapter 54

Portia wasn't about to let them escape so easily. She thrust aside her shock and outrage and shouted the incantation that would once more open the portal. Within seconds, she and Suluhura, who had followed close behind, were hurtling up the portal in pursuit.

"Can't you make this thing go any quicker?" Morgan shouted above the noise.

"This *thing?*" The Landlord grinned. "It isn't a racing car, Morgan."

"I know! But they're gaining on us!" Sure enough, Portia already had halved the distance between them and was gaining rapidly.

"Oops," deadpanned the Landlord, "so they are." He jabbed his wand downwards and sparks of fire danced along the edges of the portal, forcing their pursuers to slow down.

It seemed to Morgan that it was going on interminably. "How you doing?" he asked Rosalind. "We'll be okay, you know."

"We'd better be." She rolled her eyes. "A swift death awaits me if we don't escape this."

"Oh, nobody's going to die just yet," said the Landlord. "Look." And sure enough, far above them, they could just discern the outline of a doorway.

"Good thing I left it open," the Landlord said to no one in particular. Morgan had no time to comment on what was, to him, a rather casual approach to the danger they were in as, in an undignified manner, they tumbled in a heap into the passage-between-the-worlds.

Instantly the Landlord was on his feet and calling the incantation that would close the door. He was only just in time as, with the words pouring from his mouth and fire from his wand, he held the door closed and tried to lock it. He felt a pressure of resistance and knew that on the other side, Portia was trying to prevent him. This would be a battle of wills and of strength, but he doubted that Suluhura would have the skill to aid her, whereas *he* had Morgan and Rosalind...

Logan, who had remained silent throughout the journey, made his first contribution; his first foray into the difficult task of thanking his brother and the Landlord for his deliverance. Even *he* realized it had been close. *So dreadfully close!* He shivered.

Striving to hide his dislike of his brother, because now he didn't know if *he* still did dislike him, he said, "I hope he knows what he's doing. Or else we're all buggered."

Morgan smiled; this was something Logan might have said when they were young, and he felt the first stirrings of hope. "Don't worry, he does. He's the Landlord."

"Yeah, and if you two would stop chatting and, oh I don't know, *help?*" But then he remembered. "Sorry, you don't have a wand, do you, Logan?" He couldn't help smirking. "You two, hold the door closed while I figure out how to lock the damned thing."

The battle of wills went on for some time and Logan found himself wishing he *could* help. Not for the sake of survival, just *because.*

And, all at once, it was done. The door locked and on the other side and, unheard by the three wizards, Portia gave a howl of frustration and anger.

"Excellent!" The Landlord clapped his hands in delight.

"They'll get through that," Rosalind said. "It's only a locked door."

"Not after I've finished with it." He touched his wand to the wall and a large section cracked, then crumbled at their feet, leaving a big pile of rubble.

"Did you *have* to do that?" Morgan groaned; he hated mess almost as much as the Landlord. "You *do* realize I'm going to have to mend that?"

"Get Luke to do it. He has far too much time on his hands. Probably. Now for the next part. You do know we can't just let you go, Logan." His demeanor changed and he fixed him with a steely glare. "Don't you?"

"What's to stop me running down this passage and escaping?"

"Oh, I don't know, this?" He held up his wand. "Anyway, you'd still need a wand to get out of the circular room, *and,*"—he took great delight in repeating it—"you don't have one. Come on then," and he led them up the Corridor of Dimensions.

Logan should have been annoyed at the very least, but he found himself smiling. Not since he and Morgan had been children had he engaged in any kind of banter and he found he quite liked it. "It seems I've swapped one jailer for another." He held out his wrists. "No chains?"

"You won't need any where you're going," Cornelius said.

"Which is?" Morgan asked. "We've passed all the doors."

"All the doors but,"—he came to a halt—"this one."

"There isn't..." Morgan stopped and looked in amazement at the door, which was exactly like the others. "Except there is! How?"

"You can't see it unless you know it's there. The perfect camouflage."

"And it leads...?"

"To the Chasm of Nothingness."

"So there *is* a door which leads there! For goodness' sake, Cornelius, do you ever tell me *anything?*"

"Sorry." The Landlord grinned. "Must have slipped my mind. I'm awfully forgetful, you know." He touched his wand to the door and it swung open. They stepped through and were met by a desolate landscape almost entirely clothed in swirling mist.

"I've often wondered why this place exists at all," said Morgan, feeling a pang of sympathy for Logan. "It doesn't seem to fit, somehow."

"It was one of the council's prisons. A secret one. It was used for those whom they wanted out of the way. Undesirables, put here whether they'd committed a crime or not."

"But that's impossible!" Rosalind exclaimed. "I would have known about it!"

The Landlord turned to her impatiently. "Haven't you worked out yet that the witch and wizard council isn't quite so *whiter than white* as they'd have everyone think? By which I mean that for millennia they've fooled everyone into thinking they are morally honest and beyond reproach!"

"What's to stop the council just using that door to come and get me?" Logan asked.

"Good question. You're cleverer than you look." It was a petty revenge but the Landlord still hadn't forgotten his ill treatment as Logan's prisoner. The irony of their current situation wasn't lost on him. "Because I moved the door."

"Moved it?"

"Yes. It used to be at the bottom of this corridor. And on the opposite wall. So now they have no idea where it is. See? Camouflage."

"I will starve! It is still a death sentence!"

"You have the wand the goblins gave you. We'll toss it in some time."

"That poor thing?"

"It is adequate enough for you to grow food and summon water. You have no need for, nor will you be allowed, anything else. Now stop prevaricating." He gave Logan a shove. "We'll check in on you in, oh, I don't know, about five years. See ya!" And before Morgan could protest, he was pulled back into the Corridor of Dimensions, Rosalind following close behind, and the door slammed shut.

"So we rescued him just so he can spend the rest of his life in there?"

"I haven't thought that far ahead yet. Anyway, do you have an alternative? He still can't be trusted, you know."

"I know, but..."

"There is no *but,* Morgan," the Landlord said gently. "Not yet, anyway."

"So, what now?" Morgan turned to his friend.

"Now?" The Landlord put an arm around his shoulders and they all walked down the Corridor of Dimensions and into the passage-between-the-worlds. "Now, we wait."

When they reached the entrance to the Sanctuary, Morgan said the incantation and they stepped inside to be met by Molly, who was waiting, arms folded, foot tapping impatiently.

"And where the bleedin' hell have you two been?" she demanded, her forehead furrowing into a deep frown. "Oh, hi, Rosalind, I didn't see you there for a minute." She grinned widely before her face lapsed once more into disgruntlement. Then she took a deep breath and prepared herself to complain. Loudly.

Epilogue

It took Anarkus many hours and a supreme effort of will to reach the one place that might offer refuge – the Dark Wizard's mansion. Once inside, exhausted and disoriented as he was, he realized the Sanctuary would come searching and he looked around in desperation for a place to hide.

There was nowhere, not a single place they wouldn't look. As panic set in he thought of the dungeons. *Perhaps I can create a glamour down there,* he told himself, *maybe they won't discover me.* He knew the thought was hopeless, but he staggered to the top of the dungeon steps and peered down into the darkness. Delirious now, his foot searched tentatively for the first step but he misjudged it and tripped, unable to prevent himself from tumbling down.

As he lay there on his back, dazed and confused, his eyes gradually adjusted to the gloom and they roved around, frantically searching. Then he spotted a small hole in the brickwork, high up at one end of the short corridor. Unknown to him, nor would he have cared, it had been created when the Landlord had been a prisoner here and his dog, Oscar, had forced his way inside to rescue him. For Anarkus, it offered salvation and he felt hope surge within.

He got slowly to his feet and stood, the room swimming before his eyes. The hole seemed impossibly high and his heart sank. *Courage,* he told himself sternly, *you can do this.* He reached deep inside and summoned the last dregs of his power. Instantly, he felt a little of his strength returning, but he knew it wouldn't last long and he hastened to the wall and began to climb.

It was difficult, for there were few footholds and he was still weak, but at last his fingertips touched the edge of the hole. As his strength drained away, he managed to pull himself in, his shoulders squeezing with difficulty into the narrow aperture, and he lay, gasping for breath, his tortured muscles burning.

A great weariness overcame him and he couldn't have moved even if he'd wanted to. As his vision dimmed, his final thoughts were of the Sanctuary and how he'd been thwarted. A wave of anger consumed him as he lost consciousness. *I will be avenged,* he promised, *I will make them pay...*

Soon, all was quiet in the Dark Wizard's mansion as Anarkus began his long sleep, and gradually images appeared within his mind. As he dreamed, he knew deep within his subconscious that the dream was reality.

Anarkus had never set foot within the Sanctuary yet he saw the girl and her surroundings clearly; many times he saw her. Sometimes she stared from a window, as if longing to be free, other times she raged at her captors, vile vitriol spewing from her mouth.

His dream shifted to a dark, desolate place, devoid of all life. Devoid except for one solitary figure who wandered aimlessly, his entire body insinuating defeat.

Ah, Logan, Anarkus said from inside his dream, *stupid enough to get yourself captured, I see.* Perhaps if he'd been awake, Anarkus would have seen the irony in his words, given his current situation. Sometimes it seemed as if Logan heard him, for his head would snap upwards, his shoulders straightening and his gaze sweeping keenly around as if he suspected someone was there. But then, knowing it was impossible, he would return to his purposeless meandering.

It was early in his dream when, unknown to him, his body tensed and his senses screamed danger! It seemed he heard noises close by, the sounds of someone searching. Then footsteps approached the dungeon, *so close!* And a voice; *it's no bleedin' good, Luke, we've searched everywhere. He's not bleedin' here.* And his body tensed even more, for he recognized who it was. *The witch!* Then the footsteps receded and gradually the house was still. His body relaxed and his mind stilled as the dream abated for now.

When it returned, he saw his enemies abroad in the mortal world; the witch, Morgan and even the traitor, Cornelius. It was he whom Anarkus hated most, for long ago Cornelius had made a vow never again to aid the Sanctuary in their quest, and to never again wield his wand for the sake of mortals. And then there were his more recent crimes; *he should show loyalty to the council, yet he works against them!* Again, his subconscious mind knew nothing of irony. Hadn't he, Anarkus, foresworn that loyalty too?

Thoughts of the witch and wizard council turned his dream in their direction. Portia was raging, swearing vengeance on Morgan and Cornelius and on the Sanctuary itself. Long its advocate, she had transformed into its enemy, for there were murmurings she should be replaced as leader as punishment for her failure, an action unprecedented in the long history of the council.

None yet spoke openly of revolt, but its members were already splitting into two factions; no, three, for Rosalind and Agnes had their own agenda. The realization entered Anarkus's mind that he would need to find out; these two would definitely need watching...

But when, in his slumber, he returned to those of the Sanctuary, he was filled not with tension this time, but spasms of anger. Now he called out in his sleep, though his instincts warned him to do so softly. Curse upon curse was sent their way but, of course, they could do no harm, for he did not yet have his power.

As those at the Sanctuary entered all the portals they knew of, which was most of them, they traveled the world undoing the harm he had wrought. They cast glamour's and spells, removed bad memories and replaced them with good ones. Gradually they removed all knowledge of the secret world which had lain there, protecting the mortals for thousands of years.

Of course, there was the internet, and photos and videos; these the Sanctuary could not alter, for there were too many to find. But Luke knew that photographs could be manipulated, images deep-faked, the internet made to deceive. He was confident the mortals could be convinced this was what had happened, and with that, the others had to be content. And, as time passed, Luke was proved right; memories of witches and wizards faded and those few who insisted they existed were dismissed as *not quite right in the head*. Gradually, the mortal world returned to normal.

Subconsciously, Anarkus watched it all and as the years passed he began to see someone else, a young girl, and felt puzzlement, for he did not know who she was. Then suddenly it came to him, *the girl in the red coat!*

He remembered how he'd watched with amusement as Logan had destroyed the girl's mind. Now here she was again, a little older but still damaged and vulnerable. Even in his dream he sensed power in her, just as he sensed she could be manipulated into using it for evil. He stored the thought, ready to be resurrected when the time came.

More than a decade passed and sometimes he dreamed, sometimes he did not, but his desire for vengeance against the Sanctuary remained strong. Infinitesimally, the depth of his slumber lessened until one day his eyes opened wide and he drew a long, shuddering breath.

Instinctively he reached for his wand and felt it thrumming with magic, and as he stretched his cramped limbs, he felt power surging through him. He shuffled backward until he reached the edge of the hole, then jumped nimbly down into the passage. His clothes were caked with dust, his hair matted with cobwebs, but he didn't care.

Already, his thoughts were turning toward the Sanctuary.

The End

Acknowledgements

I'm often asked where my ideas come from, how do I conjure up new characters and develop the ones I already have. And how do I know what direction the story is going to take next.

Well, on the last point at least, the answer is that quite often I don't know until I start to write – then the ideas seem to flow. It is a constant quest to keep the story fresh and, this being a story about good versus evil, not descend into a never-ending series of battles – the swords and wands, blood and guts kind – which would quickly become boring for all to read.

My idea to focus on Mitra in book two came to me quite early on. She appears only briefly at the start of *The Sanctuary,* and I wanted to develop her relationship with the Landlord more fully. And by doing so I was able to explore the depths of the Landlord's insecurities and in particular his tortuous battle with guilt over Mitra's death. He has so many of the human emotions that we all experience in our lives and he provides a fabulous opportunity to delve more deeply into these.

Plus by retreating into the past I was able to include the Demon

King in the story again. He's such a thoroughly nasty, horrible, depraved - feel free to insert your own adjective – creature that I can unleash my imagination, making him an incredibly fun character to write.

I hope you've enjoyed reading *The Desolation of Mitra* as much as I did writing it. You'll notice I have purposely left a lot of unanswered questions - be prepared for book three!

Now to what is, in many ways, the most difficult part of all to write – the acknowledgements. Difficult, because there are so many people I want to thank that I could fill several more pages. So, working on the theory that I've thanked so many people in person anyway, I will name only a few of the others here.

First my dear friend Fiona who has been a rock during some of the darker days. She is, absolutely, the best friend a person could hope to have. To her I send my special gratitude.

Paula Telizyn who has again done such a marvelous job of the interior book design and is always an unending source of advice and encouragement.

My editor, Jess Lawrence who reigns me in, sorts out some of the more waffly scenes and never criticizes my unfailing misuse of commas.

Jacqueline Abromeit for her fabulously imaginative cover designs. She only needs to read my manuscript to know exactly the kind of design I want. I suspect she may be a witch herself.

The quote, spoken by the Landlord in chapter 48, "*if wishes were fishes, we'd all cast nets,*" was taken from *Dune* written by Frank Herbert.

Finally, to you, my readers, thank you for continuing to enjoy the '*passage-between-the-worlds*' series and for your kind comments and support on social media and in person. See you in book three!

Michael